UNCOMMON THIEF

UNCOMMON THIEF

A NOVEL

by

WILLIAM MANCHEE

UNCOMMON THIEF

© COPYRIGHT
William L. Manchee
2016
adapted from the novel Twice Tempted

Top Publications, Ltd.
Plano, Texas

ISBN # 978-1929976744

Chapter 1

Love at First Sight

Summer, 1965

When Fred Fuller was young, morality—like sex—wasn't often discussed with his parents or teachers. There were plenty of rules laid down that had to be followed, but little discussion as to the rationale behind them. At the time Fred didn't think much about morality. Good behavior was just expected, so he did what he was told simply to avoid having angry parents or teachers. Deep down inside, he believed he was of the highest moral character. He assumed his parents and friends felt the same way about him; no one ever told him differently. But he had never explored the depth of his morality and was not prepared for the challenges that befell him in the fall of 1965.

Fred Fuller's greatest regret was the embarrassment and humiliation he brought to his family and friends. He could endure the consequences of his own behavior, but he knew they didn't deserve what he had brought down on them. It grieved him greatly to see their expectations shattered, particularly since it happened before the national media. Despite his contemptible behavior, though, his friends and family had stood beside him and helped him through those most difficult times.

It all started when Fred spotted a very attractive brunette, Maria Shepard, at the UCLA orientation program at the beginning of the summer. Fortuitously for Fred, he found himself seated next to her at one of the programs. She had olive skin and large, incredibly beautiful brown eyes that took his breath away. Unfortunately, being somewhat shy, he failed to ask for her telephone number—a stupid mistake he kicked himself for time and again thereafter. Eventually, he decided to track her down and ask her out, no matter what.

After diligently searching all of the Ventura County telephone books and calling over thirty-seven of the Shepards listed, Fred located her and asked her out for the following Saturday night. Much to his surprise and delight, she accepted with alacrity. He was to pick her up at six at her place. It was about a twenty-minute drive east from Ventura to the small town of Ojai, and he was very nervous. Everything so far had been too easy, and Fred was expecting something to go wrong.

As he approached Maria's house, he was impressed. It was located in a quiet, upper-class neighborhood of large Spanish-style homes. Each one had a white stucco exterior and a red tile roof. Magnificent eucalyptus trees towered high above the homes, providing not only shade but also privacy from the rest of the city. The lawns and bushes were neatly manicured, and many of the homes had private tennis courts and swimming pools.

This setting was a little uncomfortable for Fred, as he was not accustomed to an affluent lifestyle. His father was a clerk for a local insurance company, and his mother was a checker at Von's Grocery Store. They made a decent living but had always lived in a modest neighborhood and had just recently moved to a trailer park since his father's retirement was near.

It was five 5:45 p.m. when Fred got to 4436 Sunswept Terrace. Since he was early, he cruised around the neighborhood a while to kill time. At precisely six, he knocked on the door and waited eagerly.

The door opened, and a dark-haired little girl stood looking up at him.

"Hi. Is Maria in?" he asked.

She gave him a hard look and then replied, "You must be Fred."

"Yes, I am."

"Ma . . . ri . . . a!" she yelled in a voice so loud he figured Maria must be in the back yard under a mattress.

In a few minutes, Maria appeared and stood before him with a broad smile. She was wearing a Ventura College t-shirt and white shorts. She was even more beautiful than he had remembered. He took a deep breath in an effort to maintain his composure.

"Fred! Come in," she said, taking his arm and escorting him inside.

"Thanks."

"I guess you met my little sister, Jessica?"

Jessica gave him a little curtsy and a big smile.

Fred nodded. "Briefly," he replied. "She's got quite a voice."

"That's for sure," Maria agreed.

"How old is she?"

"Ten, but you wouldn't know it from the way she acts sometimes," Maria said, giving Jessica a disapproving look. Jessica narrowed her eyes and feigned great emotional injury. Maria sighed, stifling a laugh. "I guess I can't complain though . . . she's pretty good most of the time. Come in the kitchen. I want you to meet my parents."

Maria took Fred's hand and pulled him into the kitchen, where her mom and dad were seated at the kitchen table. They looked up and gave him a once-over.

"Mom and Dad, this is Fred Fuller. Fred, this is my mom, Mary, and my dad, John."

Fred smiled and nodded, wondering what they were thinking. Do they like me? I hate meeting a girl's parents. It's so awkward. "Nice to meet you."

"Hello," Mr. Shepard replied with little enthusiasm.

"Hi," Mrs. Shepard said smiling. "Maria told us about meeting you at orientation, and she was so happy when you called her."

Maria frowned. "Mom, you're not supposed to repeat everything I tell you."

"Oh, I am sorry, honey. I didn't—"

"That's right, Mary. What were you thinking?" Mr. Shepard said. "God forbid a woman should tell a man how she actually feels about him right off the bat. No, she's got to keep him off balance and in the dark for a while. It's standard female torture."

Maria laughed and shook her head as she took Fred by the arm. "Fred, I think we should leave. I don't like where this conversation is heading."

"What do you mean?" Mr. Shepard replied playfully. "You just can't stand to hear the truth, can you?"

She gave him a sardonic smile. "You're a real hoot, Dad." Then she turned to Fred and shook her head. "Don't pay attention to him, Fred. He gets jealous whenever I go out on a date. Bye, Mom. Bye, Dad."

"Okay, honey, drive carefully. Don't be too late," Mrs. Shepard said. "Nice to meet you, Fred."

"Thank you. It was a pleasure meeting both of you."

As they left the house, Fred felt like they'd just gone 'round and 'round in a revolving door. Things were developing faster than he had expected. They got in the car and drove twenty minutes back to Ventura to a Polynesian restaurant called the Kon Tiki. Maria was very open and candid, as if they had been dating for a long time. She asked Fred some very penetrating questions and shocked him by sharing some of her innermost secrets. He was somewhat disarmed by all of this and began spilling his guts to her as well, which was very uncharacteristic of him. Most people considered Fred very quiet and introverted, but Maria opened him up like a can of tuna. After dinner, they continued to talk.

"So, what have you been doing this summer?" she asked.

"Well, I've been working for Bank USA."

"Oh really? What do you do for them?"

"I'm a messenger. I deliver and pick up data processing from half a dozen or so branches between Ventura and Fillmore."

"Do you like it?"

"Oh yeah, it's a sweet job, and it pays well. Luckily, I'm going to be able to transfer down to LA when school starts."

"That's great. I hope I can find a good job like that."

"You probably will. UCLA has a great placement office."

The waiter brought their check and placed it next to Fred's plate.

"Well, . . . are you ready to go to the movies?" he asked.

"Not really. It's been so much fun talking. I'd rather just go somewhere quiet and continue our conversation."

"Okay. I know a really pretty place where we can sit and look at the lights of the city."

"That's perfect."

Fred didn't mention it to her, but the place he had in mind was the most popular teenage parking spot in Ventura County. He wondered what she'd think when she realized it. When they got to downtown Ventura, they went up a very steep hill to the beginning of the road that led to 'the Cross', as it was called by the locals. It was the burial site of several missionaries who had lived and worked at Mission San Buenaventura.

Fred always worried that his car wouldn't make it up the hill since it was so steep, but somehow it always did. They slowly made their way up the switchbacks until they were high over the city. From the Cross, you could see the spectacular California coastline by day and the dazzling lights of the city and ocean traffic by night. Surprisingly, the parking lot was deserted, so they parked in the spot with the best view. Fred turned off the engine and slid over to be next to Maria.

"This is magnificent," Maria exclaimed.

"Isn't it?"

"Yes. The lights are so pretty. I didn't know this place even existed."

"Yeah, I love it up here."

"How many innocent girls have you brought up here before me?"

"I don't know . . . I don't ask them if they're innocent."

"Well, I'm innocent," she said.

"That's good to hear."

At that moment, their eyes met and they began inching toward each other. Soon they were in each other's arms kissing passionately. Maria's soft, sweet lips felt wonderful to Fred. He hadn't dated much, so he'd never felt such pleasure. They'd been going at it about ten minutes when they heard a pounding noise on the window. Startled, Fred pulled away and looked up only to be blinded by two glaring lights.

"Shit! It's the cops," Fred whispered.

"You kids can't park here!" the officer yelled.

Rolling down his window, Fred said irritably, "Okay, Officer, we're moving on."

The stern-faced officer stood there and watched Fred as he fumbled with the keys. Fred had never been so humiliated in his life. *My first date with Maria and I get hassled by the police. Damn it!* Quickly, Fred started the car, and drove off. They descended down the steep winding road from the Cross and headed back toward Ojai.

Maria was silent for quite a while, and Fred felt sure she'd never go out with him again. After a few minutes, though, she turned toward him and shook her head. "Well you'd think the cops would have something better to do than harass innocent kids minding their own business."

Feeling much relieved, he smiled back at her. "God, I know. They ought to be spending their time catching thieves and dope dealers rather than bullying teenagers."

"Really. Listen, I know a place not too far from my house

where we can go and, you know, finish our conversation without fear of arrest."

Fred smiled broadly. "That would be nice."

As they got to her neighborhood, Maria pointed to an alley and indicated Fred should go down it. They drove several blocks before she pointed to some servants' quarters. "Park here," she said. "No one ever comes back here after dark."

Fred wondered how she knew this, but he was afraid to say anything that might jeopardize the rest of the evening. They began kissing again, gently at first and then more passionately until the windows started to fog up. While their lips were locked together, Fred's hand wandered down to Maria's soft, smooth leg. It felt so good he was afraid to breathe for fear Maria would stop him. After a while he wondered how it would feel if he went even farther. Maria seemed to be enjoying it too, so he inched his fingers farther and farther up her thigh until she grabbed his hand and broke away.

"Remember. . . . I told you I'm innocent," she said, "and I'm going to stay that way until my wedding night. Do you have a problem with that?"

"No. Absolutely not," Fred said worriedly. He'd never felt such excitement with a woman and feared he'd upset her. "I am sorry. I just got a little carried away. Can you forgive me?"

Maria sighed. "It's okay. I'll forgive you this time."

Fred was glad he had been forgiven but didn't want to push his luck, so he took Maria home. By the time they got to her door, he had an intense urge to use the toilet, so he asked her if her parents would mind if he came in and used her bathroom. She said they wouldn't, so he followed her in the house. She pointed down a hallway. "It's the second door on the right," she said.

Just as he was approaching the bathroom door, Jessica tore by him, went inside and locked the door. Really needing go badly, Fred figured there would probably be another bathroom somewhere in the house, so he walked back toward the kitchen to ask Maria. As he approached the kitchen, he couldn't help but overhear Maria talking to her mother. Not wanting to interrupt them, he hesitated before entering.

"Hi, Mom."

"Hi, honey. How was your evening?

"Great. I had a wonderful time."

"That's good. Fred seems like a nice young man."

"I think so."

"So, are you going to go out with him again?"

"Oh yes, without a doubt. He's the one I've been waiting for."

Mary frowned. "Huh? What do you mean, honey?"

"I mean, he's the man I'm going to marry."

"But you just met him," Mary protested.

"So, what's that got to do with anything."

Mary knew when her daughter made up her mind about something, there was no dissuading her, so she decided to tread lightly.

"But how can you be so sure? This was only your first date."

"I've seen him before in my dreams."

"In your dreams? But—"

"Goodnight, Mom." With that, Maria left her stunned mother in the kitchen and came back into the living room. When she saw Fred standing there, she said, "You're done already?"

"Well. . . . yeah, I guess I am."

"Okay. You better go. My parents won't like us alone here in the living room."

"Sure. Thanks for letting me use your bathroom."

"No problem."

"I had a great time tonight. I'll call you, okay."

"Okay."

Fred felt a little guilty about overhearing Maria's private conversation with her mother, but he was glad he had since he was very much attracted to her and flattered by her comment. Knowing Maria had strong feelings for him would make him much more comfortable and confident around her. Driving home that night, he felt like the luckiest man in the world.

Chapter 2

Cover-up

Congressman Charles Bartlett had been in a Republican Congressman for nearly twenty-two years. Born and raised in Ojai, California, he had been a star football player for Ventura High School and later went on to USC on a full scholarship. He did well in college but a knee injury prevented him from being drafted into the NFL.

Even though his football career was over when he got back home to Ventura County he was still popular and in high demand as a guest or speaker at schools, clubs and business venues around the county. He got many offers of employment too when he returned home after graduation, but wasn't sure what he wanted to do. He eventually took a job selling commercial real estate as his notoriety got him lots of listings, yet the job wasn't so demanding that he couldn't play golf at least two or three times a week.

Much to his delight, the local country club offered him complimentary membership with the unwritten stipulation that he would play with the club owner's friends and family from time to time. Bartlett had no problem with this as he was quite gregarious and enjoyed meeting new people, particularly if they were likely to send some listings his way.

Ventura County had long been a Republican stronghold so; it was inevitable that eventually Bartlett would be courted by the party to become a candidate for public office. The inevitable came to fruition in December 1955 when the district's eleven-term congressman Burt Smallwood died. This meant a new candidate for congress had to be found quickly as the primary election was only six months away.

When the offer came, Bartlett jumped at the opportunity as he didn't particularly like the commercial real estate business and saw a much more promising future for himself in politics. Once he got the nomination that first time, reelection had pretty much been a sure thing. He could be a congressman the rest of his life, if he wanted, or move on to higher office. He knew the only things that could derail him would be poor health, public scandal or disgrace. Since he was happily married, watched his drinking and exercised regularly he wasn't worried about any of those things, but perhaps he should have been.

It was the fall of 1965 and his reelection campaign was just gearing up for another run. Bartlett had gotten an ominous phone call from his finance chairman, Tom Barnes, demanding an immediate meeting to discuss a very serious matter. Bartlett didn't like the tone of the phone call and the fact that he'd had to cancel a tee time in order to accommodate the meeting.

The one aspect of running for Congress that had bothered Bartlett was campaign finance. Bartlett knew nothing about bookkeeping or accounting and even had trouble balancing his checkbook. So, when Barnes and Brewer, one of the most prestigious accounting firms in the county, offered him help in raising contributions and agreed to manage his campaign fund, he was greatly relieved and accepted the offer with alacrity.

Bartlett wasn't in a good mood when he entered the firm's reception area and walked up to the receptionist Margie Small. "Hi, Marge. I'm here to see Tom. He's expecting me."

"Yes, Congressman. I'll buzz him right away and let him know you are here."

"Thank you," Bartlett said and took a seat in an overstuffed chair. Just as he was about to pick up the latest edition of Life Magazine Tom burst out of his office.

"Congressman. Come on in. Sorry to keep you waiting."

Bartlett got up and followed Tom into his spacious office overlooking downtown Ventura. Tom went directly to his chair and opened a ledger. Bartlett took a seat across from him and waited expectantly.

"I've got some bad news, really bad news," Tom said anxiously. "I should have seen this sooner, but you just don't expect something like this to happen."

"What is it?" Bartlett said irritably. "Spit it out for godsakes!"

"It's your campaign manager."

Bartlett squinted. "Joel Roberts? What about him?"

"He's been embezzling money from you."

"What! No. You must be mistaken. That couldn't be true."

Tom shrugged. "I think so. It's the only explanation for the mission cash."

"Missing cash?"

"Right. Five million dollars."

"Five million dollars! What are you talking about? How could five million dollars be missing?"

"Well, actually $4.7 million."

"What? Haven't you been paying attention to your job! How do I know you didn't steal it?"

"I don't write checks. I'm a bookkeeper. He's been hiding it very well. I just noticed it today. He's been writing checks to bogus companies and depositing money into an off-the-books account."

Bartlett stood up and began to pace back and forth angrily. "You're absolutely sure about this?"

Tom nodded meekly. "Yes, there is no doubt."

"Have you told anyone?"

"No. You're the first to know. We should contact the FBI."

"No. We can't do that. There would be an investigation. I'd be disgraced and a dozen people would run against me for reelection. We have to keep a lid on this."

"But, how? We're missing $4.7 million. What happens when we need to pay bills with that money?"

"I don't know. Maybe, Joel will have some ideas for us. He's a lawyer and I'm sure he doesn't want to go to prison for the rest of his life."

"Okay, I'll set up a meeting. Sorry to be the bearer of bad news."

"Yeah, you should be. If you'd have been doing your job you could have prevented this or at least caught it before it was a nuclear disaster. God damn it! I can't believe this."

Tom swallowed hard but didn't say anything. Bartlett shook his head and stormed out angry and confused. Feeling tears welling in his eyes, he couldn't look at Marge when he rushed by. When he got into the elevator, was alone and the door closed behind him, he pushed the stop button so he'd have a moment to compose himself.

That morning when he woke up he'd been looking forward to a little golf, some sunshine and a pleasant day at the club, he thought, taking a long deep breath. Now he was facing scandal, ridicule and ruin and he hadn't done a goddamn thing wrong. "How could this have happened?" he moaned to himself. He closed his eyes. He had to fix this, he thought. There had to be a way out of this. If he lost his seat over this bullshit, somebody was going to fucking die!

Chapter 3

Bank USA

Steve Robins and Randy Hanson were Fred's best friends. They had all met and become friends in elementary school. Steve and Randy were both tall and slender, but Steve had a slightly heavier build. That was the extent of any similarity. Steve was quiet and shy, whereas Randy rarely closed his mouth and always wanted to party. Politically they encompassed the entire political spectrum—Steve the conservative, Randy the liberal, and Fred the moderate. They had grown very close over the years since they had spent so much time together and none of them had a brother.

Randy had just gone off to college at the University of Pittsburgh, where his father and grandfather had gone before him. Steve and Fred, both a year older than Randy, decided to go to UCLA and rent an apartment together. They had gone to Santa Monica in June to select the apartment. They had looked at the campus dorms, but they'd both lived in dorms their freshman year and wanted more freedom and privacy. The new off-campus coed dorms, where male and female students lived together on the same floor, were intriguing but far too expensive. Both Steve and Fred were basically on their own financially. Their parents would have liked to have helped out, but really couldn't afford it. They finally settled on a two-bedroom apartment about fifteen minutes from campus called the Westgate Apartments. The apartment had a typical two-story rectangular design with one end opened to provide access to the pool and common area. It was probably ten or fifteen years old and fairly well maintained. The tenants were mostly students with a few retired couples and blue-collar workers.

Steve and Fred arrived in separate cars, both bursting with all the necessities of domestic life. Steve had a black 1957 Chrysler that used to belong to his father. It was a big car and had lots of room to haul junk back and forth to school. The only problem was that it was a gas guzzler and kept poor Steve financially drained.

"Let's go to the manager's office and check in," Fred said.

Steve looked around. "Where is it?"

"Around the corner. Apartment 101."

Steve nodded, and they walked around the corner looking for the number. When they found it, they went inside. The manager—'Mrs. Walker', according to her name tag—was sitting behind a desk in the corner of the small room. She looked up at the two of them and smiled.

"Ah, Mr. Fuller."

"Yes, that's right. You remembered. You've got a good memory. This is Steve Robins. He's going to be my roommate."

"Nice to meet you, Steve. Your apartment is ready. Come with me, and I'll take you to it," she said as she got up and walked outside. They followed close behind her, anxious to see where they'd be living for the next several years. She went across a courtyard and down a long walkway to Apartment 118, opened the door, and held it for them.

"You have a pleasant inside view of the pool area. The apartment has been recently painted, and the carpets have been shampooed."

"Thank you," Fred said. "It looks great."

"Well, if you need anything, just give me a holler."

"Thanks."

After Mrs. Walker left, they carefully checked out each room and imagined how it would look once they'd moved all of their stuff in.

"It looks pretty clean," Steve observed.

"Hey, did you notice the chicks working on their tans near the pool?" Fred asked.

"Yeah. I think we may need to take a swim here pretty soon," Steve suggested with a sly grin.

"Definitely," Fred agreed.

Since the apartment was furnished, getting settled in didn't take long. After a couple of hours, they'd moved in most of their stuff and had everything in its place. When they were done, they sat down to relax.

It was a warm day in southern California. The temperature was about eighty-five degrees and, of course, there was no air conditioning since Santa Monica always had a cool breeze coming in from the Pacific Ocean. To take advantage of the breeze, most everyone had their windows opened, which made it quite pleasant.

Steve was about to turn on the television when they heard a loud moaning sound from the next apartment.

"Ahhh . . . Ahhh . . . Ahhh . . . Oh. Oh . . . Ahhh," a female voice moaned. "Ahhh . . . Ahhh . . . Oh. Oh . . . Yes! . . . Yes!" she continued.

Steve looked at Fred with a puzzled look on his face. Neither one of them had ever heard such a noise from a human being. Fred frowned, not quite sure what to make of it.

"Ahhh! Ahhh! Ahhh! Yes! Yes! . . .Oh! Yes!" she screamed.

Just then, they heard a male voice say, "Honey, if you're going to make love with the windows open, you've got to keep your voice down."

Steve looked at Fred and began to laugh. "I think I'm going to like this place," he said.

Fred nodded enthusiastically. "I think so too."

That night, they went swimming and met some of the girls around the pool area. They were all pleasant and friendly, but as Fred talked to them, he kept thinking of Maria and felt guilty and uneasy. Later, he tried to call Maria, but the switchboard operator didn't know her room number yet.

On Tuesday, Fred reported to the data processing center for Bank USA in downtown Los Angeles. His transfer had gone through, and he was to report to Henry Sinclair, the Transportation Supervisor, for assignment. Bank USA was headquartered in Pasadena, California. The Transportation Division was divided into seven regions: LA, San Diego, Ventura, San Francisco, Eureka, Sacramento, and Bakersfield, each servicing its own data processing center. Every night, all banking transactions were processed on large mainframe computers. Each morning, bank messengers delivered the night's work to each of 545 branch banks throughout the state. In the evenings, the messengers delivered each branch's work to the data processing center.

Each messenger covered seven to ten branches, which were an average of eight miles apart. This meant the average messenger's route was fifty to sixty miles and took three to five hours to complete. Most of the routes in the LA Division were short ones between the myriad of cities that made up the Los Angeles metro area. A few routes were longer, however, stretching out north and south 100 miles or more from downtown LA.

Fred was not totally a newcomer to LA. His father had taken him to a few Dodgers games at Chavez Ravine, and they had been to Pasadena many times to visit his aunt and uncle. Nevertheless, downtown LA was a pretty unique experience for him, having come from a small town like Ventura. As he drove past the tall buildings and hordes of people walking the streets, he felt out of place and a little scared. Then he remembered he was being paid $7.50 per hour for simply driving around. This thought quickly overshadowed all his fear and discomfort.

All of his life, Fred had been very ambitious. He was the kid who walked the streets selling all-occasion cards, candy, and even a magazine called Grit. He was the newspaper boy, the one who cut your lawn, and the one that waxed your car. If there was any way he could earn money, he would be out there doing it. But all these jobs involved hard manual labor, and he dreaded every minute of them. Not only was the work grueling, but it was also tedious.

Driving, on the other hand, was a pleasure. He loved to drive anytime, anywhere—a passion he had inherited from his father. Almost every weekend, his father would pack up the family in the old Nash Rambler and take them out on the road. They must have visited every state and national park, museum, monument, fort, lake, river, and dam that had been built—from the depths of Death Valley to the summit of Mt. Shasta and from the magnificent Redwoods to the Mojave Desert.

Fred often wondered why his father loved to travel so much. As he got older, he realized it was an escape from the boredom of his job. Every morning, he'd go to work at seven and shuffle papers until four. It had to be incredibly tedious. After he got home, he'd eat dinner, watch four hours of network TV, and then end the day listening to George Putnam and the Channel Eleven News. Day after day, he followed the same routine with little variation.

Although Fred's father was home every night and always did his best to make life as comfortable as he could for Fred, there was very little communication between them. He was forty years of age when Fred was born, and Fred guessed this age difference made it difficult for them to be close.

But on the weekends, his father became a different man. From a dull office worker, he was transformed into a great adventurer, full of anticipation for what he might find over the next hill or around the next turn. Every Friday at four, Fred's father was set free to live his dreams, and Fred knew he was fortunate to be able to go along for the ride. So, the thought of getting paid just to drive around was like a gift from God, and Fred was certainly going to enjoy every minute of it.

The LA division headquarters took up one square block of downtown LA. It was a large, beige, single-story, windowless, brick building that could easily be mistaken for an underground parking garage. A fourth of the area was a parking lot, and the balance the motor pool. Fred was told to report to the motor pool.

Fred parked his car around the corner and walked into the motor pool area. A tall, lean man about forty years old was pumping gas into a white Impala. He looked up, smiled, and greeted Fred in an Australian accent. "Hi, mate. I am Jim Wells. You must be Fuller."

"Yes, I am Fred Fuller. Glad to meet you," Fred said, extending his hand. Jim took it and gave Fred a bone-crushing shake. Fred struggled not to scream.

Jim laughed at Fred's discomfort. "Mr. Sinclair is waiting for you in the office," he said with a grin. He pointed toward a loading dock adjacent to the building and then began filling up another gas tank.

Fred thanked him, walked over to the office and went in. A short, grey-haired man was busily writing at a desk. "Mr. Sinclair?" Fred asked.

He looked up without smiling. "Yes?"

"Hi. I'm Fred Fuller from Ventura. I was told to report to you."

Sinclair nodded. "Oh yes, Mr. Fuller. Come in. Give me a minute, and I will show you around and introduce you to some of the guys."

"Thank you," Fred said, giving the place a cursory glance.

Sinclair finished his paperwork and then led Fred around the facility, explaining everything that was going on. Pointing to the parking lot next to the motor pool, he said, "As you can see, the cars you will be driving are over in that lot. Each day, you'll be assigned a car. The keys will be on a board in my office. If you have any problems with your car, report them to Jim, whom I think you met when you came in."

"Yes, sir."

"The cars will be full of gas. When you come in at night, take your car to Jim and get it re-fueled. As you know, it's critical that each messenger stays on schedule, so don't forget to gas up before you leave. I don't want anyone getting a late start or running out of gas because you forgot to fill up your car."

"No, sir."

"Do you know the LA area at all?" he inquired.

"Pretty much. My dad brought me here a lot, and I've got a good sense of direction," Fred said.

"Good. I don't want any of my messengers getting lost. Now, go report to Jim, and he'll send you out with Jake to learn your route."

"Yes, sir. Thank you."

Three cars were parked at the gas pumps, and the messengers were standing around talking to Jim. Fred walked over and stood near them, waiting for Jim to get finished so he could talk to him. Jim was telling the other messengers a story, and they were listening intently.

"Well, I was in the Alley Cat last night, and I saw this wench that would knock your bloody socks off. Every guy in the joint was staring at her, wondering what line he could use to get into her pants, but everyone that tried got a chilly rebuff. So, my buddy bets me ten bucks I can't get to first base with the pretty lady. I told him it wasn't a problem and took the bet. I promised him I'd have her in the sack inside an hour."

"So, what happened?" someone asked.

"Well, I go over to where she's nursing a drink, sit down beside her, stare straight ahead, of course—not wanting to look her directly in the eye, you see—and then casually mention 'You probably haven't had decent sex in months'."

Everyone laughed. "What did she say to that?" someone asked.

"She turns and looks at me, trying to act offended, but I knew I'd got her interest. So, I casually observed that the young bucks in this establishment didn't know how to please a lady. The moment they got inside a woman it was slam, bam, thank you, ma'am, and it'd be all over in a jiffy. Of course, they'd all be happy as a hog in garbage heap, but the lady'd be left so bloody frustrated she could scream."

Everyone laughed again.

"By this time, the wench had drawn herself up indignantly, but I kept on talking. I informed her I just wanted her to know that I, myself, was not like the young boys she was used to and that I knew how to please a woman."

"How do you please a woman, Jim?" someone asked.

"Well, I don't like to brag, but when I get inside a lady, I roll and thrust like ocean waves pounding on the beach—not just once or twice, but all night long, from dawn to dusk, bestowing on the lucky recipient of my relentless passions an incredible sexual experience."

They all laughed.

Jim continued. "She just stared at me, a bit overwhelmed and incredulous, so I tipped my hat, pointed to my drinking buddy, and told her I'd be with my friend over there if she needed me. Then I turned around and went back to my seat.

"She stared at me for several long seconds and then turned away. My buddy laughed in delight and suggested I pay on the bet, but I told him he was a bit premature in claiming victory."

"She surely didn't fall for that line?" someone asked.

Jim shrugged. "Well, we sat there maybe five more minutes drinking our beers. All the time, the lady keeps looking over at me nervously. Then, suddenly, she jumps up and marches straight to me. My buddy's mouth falls open as she gets right up next to me, looks me in the eye, and says I better not be shittin' her! Then she drags me out of the bar to go to her place."

The men roared with laughter, and Jim stood before them, glowing with masculine pride.

"Hey, Jim, were you bull shittin' her?" one of the drivers asked.

"Not at all. She's at my place right now, too sore to walk."

The drivers again roared with laughter, this time so loudly that Sinclair heard them and came outside to see what was going on. "Hey, come on! You've got routes to run!" he yelled. "Get your gas and get out of here."

Jim saw Fred finally and said, "Hey, Fuller, you're going out with Jake Johnson." He pointed to a dark-haired, stocky man of about twenty-eight. "Hey, Jake, this here's your shotgun. Sinclair wants you to take him with you to learn the route."

Jake turned around expressionless and motioned for Fred to join him. Fred walked over and introduced himself. Jake shook his hand with little enthusiasm and told him to get in the car. Fred was a little taken aback by Jake's demeanor. What's eating at this guy?

"Where are we headed?" Fred asked cautiously.

"This is the North Beach route," he replied stiffly, "Palos Verdes, Redondo Beach, Hermosa Beach, Venice Beach, El

Segundo, and Santa Monica."

"Is this your usual route?"

"Yeah, at least it was until yesterday."

"What happened?" Fred asked, hoping for an explanation for his rude behavior.

"Nothing you need to concern yourself about."

"Oh. Okay. Never mind then if it's a sore subject," Fred said reeling a bit from his rebuff.

Jake didn't respond and it was obvious to Fred that he resented having to teach him the route.

Then Jake let out a long sigh. "Okay. If you must know. I've been with the bank seven years now. You'd think they'd let one little misstep slide, but no, I lose my route and then they rub it in my face by making me train my replacement."

"What misstep?" Jake asked.

"I was way ahead of schedule so I stopped at a bar and had a beer. Big fucking deal!"

Drinking was one of two things that weren't tolerated by the bank; the other one was picking up hitchhikers. Jake had been lucky he hadn't been fired right there on the spot. Instead, as his punishment, Sinclair assigned him to thirty days of sorting bags and distributing them to drivers, the worst job in the motor pool and usually reserved for rookies. Fred knew even though he had nothing to do with what had happened or the reprimand that every time Jake saw Fred it would remind him of his humiliation and he'd get angry. Fred wasn't used to having someone hate him, and he didn't like it much. Worse, he feared Jake would try to make his life miserable and, as it turned out, he was right.

Chapter 4

Venice Beach

After arriving home that night from his first day on the job, Fred immediately called Maria. He hadn't seen her since he'd arrived at school, and he missed her terribly. He rang the dorm and the operator answered. This time, the operator was able to find her room number and put Fred through immediately.

"Hello?" Maria said.

"Maria, this is Fred."

"Well, it's about time you called me."

"I know. I'm sorry. I tried last night but couldn't get through. The operator didn't know what room you were in."

"That doesn't surprise me. This place is so unorganized it's ridiculous."

"Hey, can I come see you?"

"Well, I'm not finished with my homework, but I guess I can do it later."

"Good, I'll pick you up in front of your dorm in twenty minutes."

"Okay, see you soon."

Fred rushed to his car and within twenty minutes was driving up to Maria's dorm. She was standing just inside the double glass doors when he drove up. He got out of his maroon 1960 Ford Falcon and came around to open the car door for her. When she spotted him she smiled and pushed through the dorm door and briskly walked over and kissed him lightly. He savored the kiss then grinned thinking she looked great in her burnt orange sweater and brown skirt; fall colors suited her. She jumped in, and Fred gently shut the door.

As they drove off, Maria cuddled up next to him and took a deep breath. "I've missed you these last few days, you lousy bum. I was worried when you didn't call."

"I'm sorry, babe. I should have come over yesterday when I

couldn't get through to you on the phone, I guess. It's just . . . you know . . . the first few days of school are always so crazy."

"That's for sure."

"Where shall we go tonight?" Fred asked as they drove down the hill from the dorm.

"I don't know. What do you feel like?"

"I don't care. You decide."

"Well, let's see. A hot fudge sundae would be good," Maria suggested.

"Okay. The Carnation place?"

"That'll do," Maria agreed.

Fred turned the car onto Wilshire Boulevard and proceeded south through Beverly Hills. This was one of the ritziest streets in the world, and he wanted Maria to see it. It turned out she'd been there before; in fact, she bragged that one time she'd seen Dean Martin with a cute blond coming out of a restaurant. Fred was impressed.

"So, how did the job go?" Maria asked.

"Not bad. My boss is pretty cool. He's all business, but he seems to be fair. There's a really interesting guy named Jim who runs the motor pool. He's very friendly and apparently a real lady killer."

"Really? Did you find out where your route will be?"

"Yeah. . . .They sent me out on it with a guy named Jake. I guess he got caught drinking on the job, and they busted him down to a bag sorter. He was really pissed about it and took it out on me."

"Oh, great. Aren't you so lucky? So, where does your route take you?"

"Right along Route 1—along the beach from Palos Verdes to Santa Monica."

"You're kidding! That means you'll be down at the beach every afternoon around all those bikini-clad surfer girls."

Fred hadn't thought of that, but the idea of it did seem pleasant. "I suppose so, but somebody's got to do it, right?"

Maria frowned disapprovingly. "Yeah, right. Such a sacrifice."

The Carnation store was busy, but they managed to find a seat in the corner. Maria ordered her usual hot fudge sundae, and Fred a banana split. She told him all about her day as he gazed, in rapture, into her big brown eyes. When they'd lingered about as long as the management would allow, he reluctantly paid the tab and took Maria back to her dorm. Instead of dropping her off in front, he pulled into the parking lot where it was dark and he could get reacquainted with her luscious lips. It was always this way with them, neither wanting their evenings together to end. Finally, Maria got out of the car and ran into the dorm. Fred watched her disappear, then started the engine and reluctantly drove off.

That night, Fred was tormented by a dream—a recurring dream that he had endured for years. In the dream, he is sitting on a huge rock beside a pool of crystal clear water. There are cottonwood trees and thick bunch grass around the pond. It's hot, and a variety of birds can be heard chirping and cawing above. A few seconds into the dream, his attention is drawn to the sound of water splashing. Turning in the direction of the sound, he sees a naked woman walking slowly through the water toward him. She has long blond, silky hair and lustful breasts. By the time she reaches him he is greatly aroused and takes her willingly into his arms. They begin kissing and caressing each other frantically. In his exuberance, he squeezes her so hard she whimpers in painful delight.

At this point in the dream, the setting changes. The naked woman is now standing by the pond, drying herself. Fred is watching her with great satisfactions when, much to his shock and dismay, she suddenly becomes frantic and starts screaming. Fred is alarmed and frantically searches for the source of her terror but his dream ends abruptly before he can figure it out.

Fred looked over at the clock radio and saw that it was 3:25 a.m. For a moment, he just sat there, mulling over the details of the dream. After a while he rolled over and tried to go back to sleep, but the vision of the naked women haunted him. Who was this woman? For the rest of the night, Fred tossed and turned, unable to shake the dream from his thoughts until he finally heard the Beep! Beep! Beep! of his pesky alarm clock.

Rolling over quickly, Fred adroitly shut it off. He'd set it for eight, as his classes usually started at nine. That didn't allow much room for error given the thirty-minute drive to school but he was a night person and hated to get up in the morning. As soon as he was up, he peeked outside to see what the weather looked like. It was foggy and drizzling outside, so he decided to skip breakfast since traffic would be moving slow. The dream was still on his mind as he drove through bumper-to-bumper traffic. Unfortunately, his dream of the desert goddess wasn't his only recurring dream. His chain gang dream was even more unsettling.

In this dream, Fred would find himself walking down a red

line painted on a concrete floor. Suddenly, he would hear the sound of steel crashing against steel behind him. Turning quickly, he'd see a massive steel gate looming over his head. Cringing in terror and disbelief, he'd begin to sweat. Then there was the sound of chains beneath him. Looking down warily, he'd be horrified to see that he was in ankle irons. At that point, the realization of his predicament would be driven home: He was convict in a prison! Horrified and panic-stricken, he'd try to run, only to fall flat on his face and hear the angry insults of his prison mates. Then he'd be rudely yanked back to his feet and punched by the guard for his clumsiness. Finally, after a long march through the cold, damp corridors of the prison, he would be separated from the chain gang and thrown into a cell. There, he'd huddle in a corner, lonely and afraid.

Fred had always had a vivid imagination so it was only natural for him to have a lot of dreams, but he struggled with the meaning of these two that often haunted him. He thought their origin was an incident that occurred when he was thirteen. While exploring an old ghost town in the Mojave Desert called Devil's Canyon Mining Camp, he had been bitten by a rattlesnake and nearly died. While he was unconscious and near death he had the desert goddess dream for the first time. The setting for the dream was Crystal Springs, a desert oasis where he had been bitten by the snake. The other recurring dreams began shortly thereafter. Fred had grown to fear that these dreams were not just dreams, but glimpses into the future. Something happened to him the day he was bitten by the rattlesnake. Perhaps he had died and crossed into the afterlife, only to be yanked back to this world, or maybe the venom from the snake unleashed some psychic power within him. He'd had other visions since then too.

The first dream that proved to be a vision concerned his Aunt Virginia. She lived close by, and he used to go visit her often. They'd usually go play tennis or just sit in her kitchen and play Hearts. One night, he had a dream that she was living in his parents' house. He had walked into her room, and she began yelling at him, accusing him of talking behind her back. He was scared. He didn't understand why she was saying those things. He loved her and would never do or say anything to hurt her. Then suddenly, he was in a room with a lot of adults, listening to a man in a suit reading aloud. Fred wasn't paying attention to what the man was saying until suddenly everyone turned around and stared at him coldly.

For about six months, this dream had haunted Fred relentlessly. He'd often wake up from it in a cold sweat. He was sure his parents would have taken him to a shrink had they not been Christian Scientists.

About a year later, his aunt became ill and could not take care of herself. The family couldn't afford a nursing home, so she came to live at Fred's house. Fred's sister Mary gave up her room to Aunt Virginia, and Mrs. Fuller bought bunk beds so Mary could sleep with Fred in his room. Fred's aunt's condition worsened rapidly, and she suffered from dementia and became extremely paranoid. She would often accuse Fred or Mary of talking about her behind her back, and one day when Fred walked into her room, she screamed at them and accused them of wanting her dead.

After that, his mom and dad had her admitted to a state mental hospital, where she died several months later. Several weeks after her death, the family was summoned by her attorney for the reading of her last will and testament. Nobody suspected she had any money since she had simply been a secretary all her life, but she had lived a meager existence and somehow had managed to save over $50,000. Fred hadn't been paying attention to the attorney reading the will, so he was surprised when he noticed everyone staring at him. He later found out Aunt Virginia had left everything to him. His dream had become reality!

After that, he had more dreams that came true—some good but others quite disturbing. Although excited to be able to see into the future at first, he soon grew weary of it. Often the dreams were incomprehensible leading to hours and hours of worry and stress. Soon he wished the dreams would stop. The recurring nightmare of the chain gang had him particularly worried. *What if it comes true? Am I destined to go to prison?*

On Wednesday, Fred had three morning classes: political science at nine, chemistry at ten, and English at one. He was a political science major with a minor in economics. His objective, ever since his twelfth birthday, had been to be a lawyer. Most of his friends didn't know what they wanted to do with their lives and had a really hard time choosing a major, but Fred was different. He knew exactly what he wanted to do and had no second thoughts about it.

It wasn't that he wanted to practice law, per se, because he really didn't know anything about the law. What he wanted was to be a politician, and it didn't take him long to figure out that most politicians were lawyers. In high school, he had always done very well in history and government and was active in local politics, so he was confident he wouldn't have any trouble as a political science major. He wasn't entirely correct in that regard, however.

Fred walked into his first political science class at five minutes to nine and sat down. It was a good size class of about fifty to seventy-five students. Everyone was excited, and the room was quite noisy.

The professor walked in with a stern look on his face. He rapped the podium with a pointer, and the room suddenly became still. "My name is Dr. Oliver T. Smith. This is Political Science 101. I want to go over a few rules with you from the very outset so there is no confusion. For those of you who are used to getting A's and B's you're in for a rude awakening. I rarely ever give an A, and you will have to work harder than you have ever worked before to get a B. Most of you will be lucky to get a C, and far more of you than you ever imagined will fail."

Fred's excitement was suddenly turned to fear as he realized this class wasn't going to be pleasant. Dr. Smith gave them their homework assignment and dismissed the class early, since "There is nothing yet to talk about," he said, "until we have done some reading."

After class, Fred met Maria for lunch, and somehow, they got into a discussion about religion. Maria was Catholic, and Fred had been raised a Christian Scientist. Maria was concerned about that becoming a problem if they got married.

"My mom says Christian Scientists hate Catholics. Is that true?" Maria asked.

"Yeah, pretty much. My parents weren't too fond of them," Fred responded.

"Why?"

"Beats me. I never understood it myself."

"Well, what are we going to do if we have children?"

"I don't know. What do you think we should do?"

"Well, I want to raise them as Catholics," Maria said.

"I believe a family should all go to the same church," I replied. "It's stupid for me to go one place and you and the kids to another, don't you think?"

"Of course," Maria agreed, "but that's not always possible."

"I'll make a deal with you."

"What's that?"

"I'll become a Catholic if you become a Republican."

She frowned. "What? You want me to become a Republican? Are you crazy?"

Fred laughed. "No. It's only fair that we both have to make a sacrifice."

They discussed the matter for some time until Maria finally agreed it was the best solution. "Okay, but you're not putting any damn Nixon bumper sticker on my car!"

Fred laughed again, feeling much relief that he'd dodged that bullet. "Good. That's settled then. We'll become a good Catholic-Republican family."

Maria rolled her eyes.

"No one can accuse us of being conformists, right?" Fred noted.

"I guess not."

After lunch, Fred went straight to work. It was his first day on his new route, and he was a little unsure of himself. The route was pretty complicated, and even though he had paid pretty close attention, he was a little worried about getting lost. When he walked up to the loading dock, Jim greeted him.

"Afternoon, mate."

"Hi, Jim."

"Well, are you ready to do the beach route on your own, Fred? Or should I get Jake to go with you one more time?"

"No, I can handle it, I think," Fred assured him.

"Well, just in case, here's a map with the route marked on it for you."

"Thank you! That will help a lot," he said.

Jim grabbed a set of keys from the big key board and handed them to Fred. "Here, take Number Thirty-Two. She's gassed up and ready to roll."

"Thanks," Fred said, accepting the keys with a smile. "I'll see you in a few hours."

After driving off, he hopped onto the Harbor Freeway and headed south. When he got to the Pacific Coast Highway fifteen minutes later, he went north. Fred's first stop was Torrance, followed by Palos Verdes, Redondo Beach, Hermosa Beach, Lawndale, Manhattan Beach, Playa del Rey, El Segundo, and, finally, Venice. An hour into the route, he noticed a quaint little street that led from the Pacific Coast Highway down to the beach. It was lined with an assortment of retail shops, restaurants, and street vendors. On the corner, he noticed a convenience store.

The street was quite busy with tourists, skaters, hippies, and surfers enjoying the warm weather. He was a little ahead of schedule, so he stopped at the convenience store to buy a Coke and a candy bar. Leaving the store, he was drawn down the street toward the beach. There were a lot of young people his age, but they were very different from his friends back in Ventura. Suddenly, Fred felt a tap on his shoulder. He swung around and was delighted to see a pretty young girl. She was wearing a violet bikini that left little to the imagination.

"Hello," Fred said.

"Can I have a sip of your Coke?"

"Huh?" he said, bewildered by her request.

"Just a sip, please," she asked meekly.

Fred shrugged. "Yeah, I guess."

He handed her the Coke, and she took a long swallow. When she was done she sighed deeply and handed it back to him. "Thanks. I was really thirsty. It's been a long time since I've had a Coke," she said, eying Fred's candy bar. "You going to eat that?"

Feeling badly for her, Fred said, "No, here, you take it."

She took the candy bar and devoured it in short order. Then, taking Fred's hand like they were on a date, she led him to the end of the pier. Fred didn't resist, feeling as if he were in a trance and quite helpless. "Don't you love the beach?" she asked, as if they'd known each other for years.

"Sure. It's wonderful," he said, still in a daze.

"You got any money?"

"Money?" Fred said. "Why do you ask?"

"I got a little place up the beach. You could buy some beer, and we could have a party."

A sudden rush of excitement came over him. The thought of going to her place sounded awfully good. She was beautiful, sexy and so easy going. He imagined them frolicking naked in her bed. The image aroused and excited him beyond belief, but then a wave of guilt washed over him. Deep down, he knew he couldn't accept her invitation for more reasons than he had time to count. So, Fred reluctantly gathered his willpower and forced a smile.

He sighed. "Oh, God, I'd love to but—well, unfortunately, I'm working right now. I've got to get going or I'll get in lot of trouble. I'm really sorry."

"It's okay. Some other time?" she suggested.

"Sure," he said, relieved that she had left her invitation open.

"Before you go, can you loan me a few bucks? I'll make it up to you when I see you again."

Fred shrugged. How could he turn down such a beautiful creature? He pulled out his wallet and handed her a five-dollar bill.

She smiled, grabbed it, and turned to leave. Then she looked back and said, "Just ask for Ginger. Everyone around here knows me. Bring some friends if you want, and don't forget the beer."

The delightful spell this Ginger had cast over him suddenly began to dissipate as he realized he'd lost fifteen minutes. He rushed to his car and took off toward Venice Beach. As he drove down the highway, he couldn't help but wonder what he had missed out on. Fred knew he had done the right thing in leaving, but he still felt sick.

"Damn it!" Fred said to himself, suddenly realizing how little he knew about life in the big city. He had lived a sheltered life in the suburbs and wasn't prepared for the real world. He felt so stupid and naive it made him sick. He had so much to learn, but learning he realized could be dangerous, very dangerous. He felt confused. He wanted to do the right thing, but he also wanted to fully experience what life had to offer.

When Fred got to the Venice branch, several bank employees were still working. He went inside but didn't see any bags ready for him to pick up. A man approached him and introduced himself. "Hi. I'm Harold Clifford, and you must be our new messenger."

"That's right. I'm Fred Fuller."

"Glad to meet you," he said with a big smile. "Listen, I am really sorry, but we're running a little late tonight. One of my tellers is out of balance, and we can't load up the bag until she gets it straightened out."

"Okay. I'll wait," Fred said, thankful that now he could blame his tardiness on Clifford rather than admit a cute hippie had lured him momentarily away from his duties.

It wasn't really unusual for the tellers to be late, as balancing cash could be tricky business, so he didn't think much about it. While Fred was waiting, he went into the bank break room and began to read a magazine. After about ten minutes, he began to wonder what was taking so long. Walking out into the bank lobby, he saw Mr. Clifford arguing with a teller. When they saw him, Clifford gave him his big smile and said, "Just another minute or two."

Fred went back into the break room and impatiently resumed reading the magazine. After a few more minutes, Mr. Clifford finally appeared and advised him the bag was ready. Finally. Jumping to his feet, he rushed to the teller's window and took the bag. Now that he had lost another twenty minutes, he felt hurried. He couldn't afford to make a bad impression on his first day of work. As Fred went out the door, he turned and forced a smile. "Nice meeting you."

Clifford raised his hand and replied, "Likewise. See you tomorrow."

The rest of the route went quickly, and Fred managed to make up some of his lost time, rolling into the motor pool only ten minutes late. No one seemed to notice his tardiness, so Fred was relieved that he didn't have to make any excuses. After he took the car over to Jim to be filled with gas, he left for home. He wanted to go straight to Maria's dorm, but they had mutually agreed the night before not to meet, since they both had tons of homework.

When Fred finally arrived home around nine, Steve was watching TV and doing his homework on the kitchen table. Fred sat across from him and told him about his new job, Sinclair, Jim Wells, his encounter with Jake, and most importantly, Jim's wager at the Alley Cat. Eventually, the incident at the beach came up.

"She wanted you to have a private party with her?"

"Yes. Can you believe it?"

"Oh my God! I don't know if I could have turned her down."

"You don't have a girlfriend. Besides, I was on the job."

"True, and she might have had a friend at her house waiting to beat you up and rob you."

"I don't think so. She seemed very nice."

"Well then, maybe when Randy gets in town at Thanksgiving, we should all go to Venice Beach and have a party with—what's her name?"

"Ginger."

"Right, with Ginger and her friends. It sounds like fun."

Fred thought about it a moment. It was tempting but fraught with risk. "Maybe," he finally agreed and left it at that.

Chapter 5

Summoned by the FBI

On Thursday, when Fred arrived at work, several men were in Mr. Sinclair's office. When he went to pick up his keys, Jim motioned that he wanted to talk to him. That startled Fred, as he feared Jim was going to chew him out for coming in late the night before. Reluctantly, he went over to him and asked, "What's up?"

"Mr. Sinclair wants to see you."

"Why?" Fred asked worriedly.

"I don't know. There's some kind of investigation going on, and he wants to talk to you. I think the FBI is here."

Looking over at the men in Sinclair's office, Fred swallowed hard. "The FBI? Why would they want to talk to me?"

"It beats me, lad. Just go find out."

Fred walked to the end of the motor pool, climbed up onto the loading dock, and entered Sinclair's office. Two men dressed identically in dark gray suits, blue ties, and spit-shined shoes were sitting on Sinclair's desk. Mr. Sinclair was standing in the corner. "Jim said you wanted to talk to me?" Fred said.

Sinclair took a step forward and nodded. "Yes. These are Special Agents Joe Harper and Jim Walters from the Federal Bureau of Investigation. They'd like to have a word with you, Mr. Fuller."

Harper was a short, middle-aged man, fit and trim with thinning grey hair. Walters was tall, looked to be in his thirties with thick black hair and was a bit overweight. They both stood up, and they all shook hands.

"Pleased to meet you," Fred said. "So, what can I do for you?"

"We just need to ask you few questions."

"About what?"

"Not here. Why don't you go with them downstairs to the conference room?"

Fred's curiosity was aroused by all of the mystery and suspense. Feeling confident that he hadn't done anything to warrant the FBI's attention, he followed Harper and Walters into the elevator. It creaked and moaned as they descended deep below ground into the bank's data processing center. Ordinarily, this area was off limits to drivers, so Fred was feeling pretty good about being able to see it for the first time. He figured it would give him something to brag about to the other drives the next time they were all huddled together by the gas pumps listening to Jim's tall tales about his bedroom conquests.

As they stepped out of the elevator, Fred noticed several large conveyor belts. They were used to carry the bags the drivers brought in each night to tables where the items were sorted. He could see several large mainframe computers in the distance. Dozens of employees were hard at work sorting checks, entering data, and operating the big IBM computers. Harper motioned to Fred to enter a small room with a round walnut table and four chairs.

"Please have a seat," Harper said. "If you don't mind, Mr. Fuller, we are going to tape this interview."

Fred shrugged. "Okay."

"Mr. Sinclair tells us you run the North Beach route."

"That's right. I just started last night, as a matter of fact."

"That's what we're interest in."

"Okay."

"Did you stop at the Venice Beach branch last night?" Harper asked.

"Well, yeah, that's my last stop."

"Did you see anything unusual?"

"No. They were running late though."

"Who was there when you arrived?"

"Clifford. . . . Harold Clifford. I believe that's what he said his name was. I think he said he was the cashier."

"What did he look like?"

"He was maybe six feet, 220 pounds, black hair, brown eyes, and he had a mustache."

"What did he say to you?"

"He told me to have a seat and that it would be a few minutes."

"What did you do while you waited?"

"I went into the break room and had a Coke and read a magazine."

"What happened next?"

"Well, I got tired of waiting and went into the lobby to see if the bags were ready yet. As I walked toward the teller's window, I overheard Mr. Clifford arguing with the teller about something. I couldn't hear what it was all about."

"What did the teller look like?"

"She was short, a little plump with red hair. I didn't get a good look at her. I wasn't paying all that much attention."

"What happened then?" Harper asked.

"The bags were ready a few minutes later, so I took them and left. . . . Oh yeah, one kind of strange thing did happen. Clifford walked me out to the door, let me out, and then locked the door behind me."

"Is that unusual?" Harper asked.

"It has never happened before. I have my own key, and I always let myself in and out. I've never been escorted out of the bank before. Usually nobody pays much attention to me. It was almost like he wanted to get me out of his hair."

"Did you report his strange behavior to anyone?"

"No. It wasn't that strange, and it was my first night at this bank, so I didn't know if Mr. Clifford always did that or what."

"Do you know a messenger named Jake?"

"Jake? Yeah. He used to have my route. I rode with him the first day."

"Did anything unusual happen the day you rode with him?"

"No, other than he wasn't very friendly."

"How do you mean?" Agent Harper asked.

"Well, the reprimand and everything left him pretty bitter, I guess. He didn't seem too happy about having to train his replacement."

"Right. I guess that makes sense. Okay, that's all we have for now unless Agent Walters has something."

Walters shook his head. "If you think of anything later on, give me a call," Walters said as he handed Fred a card.

"Thank you for your help, Mr. Fuller," Harper said.

"You're welcome, but just out of curiosity's sake, why all the questions?"

"We are conducting an investigation of some irregularities at the Venice branch. That's all I can tell you at this time."

Fred nodded. "Okay, well, nice meeting both of you."

"Oh, one more thing, Fred," Harper advised. "Sinclair is going to assign you to another route."

"Another route? Why?"

"It's possible you might be needed as a witness, so we don't want you to have any contact with Mr. Clifford for a while."

Fred gave Agent Harper a hard look. He'd liked the beach route and was sorely disappointed to hear he'd already lost it. He sighed. "Okay, whatever."

When Fred got back upstairs, he took off on his route, wondering why the FBI was interested in Harold Clifford. He figured there had to be some money missing. Nobody was at the Venice branch went he got there, so he went in and out without incident. While he was there, he tried to reconstruct in his mind every minute of the previous night's encounter to see if there was anything he had forgotten or overlooked. Nothing popped into his mind from that exercise, however, so he pushed the matter out of his mind.

When he got back to the motor pool, however, the place was buzzing with excitement. A rumor was out that the cashier at the Venice branch had been embezzling money from the bank. The word was that one of the tellers had discovered it the night before. He figured the heated discussion he'd heard from the break room was the cashier trying to convince the teller to keep her mouth shut.

That night, Fred called Maria and told her about the excitement of the day and that he might be called as a witness. She was concerned about him getting involved and said she wished he hadn't seen anything.

When Fred went to bed that night, he was so keyed up he couldn't get to sleep. Eventually, he dozed off and drifted into a familiar dream. He was walking down a red line painted on a concrete floor. Suddenly, he heard the sound of steel crashing against steel behind him. When he woke up, he wondered how long it would be before his nightmare would become reality. He was pretty sure it would happen eventually, but he wondered how long it would be before he had to face it. The thought of going to prison terrified him. He'd heard such horrible stories about what went on in prisons and wondered if there was anything he could do to avoid such a horrible fate or if it was his certain destiny.

Chapter 6

Santa Claus

The next day when Fred reported to work, Jim told him he had been assigned to a new route. Of course, he was expecting this to happen, so he wasn't surprised. Jake, however, still angry and a bit vindictive, was shocked and excited by what he perceived as a demotion. "Hey, Fuller, I heard you got bumped off the north beach route already," he said gleefully. "What happened? Couldn't follow Jim's cute little map?"

Fred looked at Jake coldly, not knowing exactly how to respond. "No, I can read a map fine, but they may need me as a witness on that Venice Beach heist, so they didn't want me having any contact with Mr. Clifford. . . . But you know what was interesting? When the FBI questioned me they were sure interested in you and what you've been up to."

"They were?" Jake asked suspiciously.

"Yeah, you wouldn't know why, would you?" Fred asked, enjoying Jake's discomfort.

Jake gave him a thoughtful stare for a moment and then said, "No. You're lying to me Fuller, aren't you?"

"No. I swear to God. They were very interested in you, Jake, for some reason. I don't know why."

"Well, I don't believe you. You're full of shit!"

Fred shrugged. "Fine, I don't care if you believe me or not. It's your hide, not mine. Catch you later," he said as he walked off.

Fred's new route took him all the way to Palm Springs with eight stops in between. It was the longest route of them all and covered some 200 miles.

Palm Springs was not a strange town to Fred, as he'd traveled there many times with his family as a child and teenager. It was the gateway to the wonderful desert. In school and the movies, the desert is often portrayed as a vast wasteland, but Fred's experiences in the desert were quite to the contrary. Fred figured it was because they'd always had plenty of food and water and survival was never in question.

Up ahead, Fred saw a single-story, glass-faced building with a large sign that read, 'Bank USA'. The design of the building was similar to dozens he'd seen before. Fred conjectured that Bank USA management didn't want to make any architects rich, as all of the branches were nearly identical.

Fred walked in at 5:20 p.m. A pretty blond teller was closing the bag. She looked up at him and smiled. "All ready," she said cheerfully.

"Good timing," Fred replied, noticing her incredibly hot body. He swallowed hard and thought immediately of Marilyn Monroe.

"My name is Candy."

Of course it is, Fred thought. "Hi, Candy. It's nice to meet you," Fred replied eagerly.

"Are you going to be our permanent messenger?"

"I certainly hope so," Fred replied with a big smile.

"We've had so many different messengers lately," she complained evenly. "I can't keep track of them anymore."

"Well, I hope they keep me on this route," Fred said as he gazed into her sexy blue eyes. "I mean; I really prefer to drive on the open road rather than in the city."

She smiled at his awkwardness, then asked, "Do you work for the bank full-time?"

"No. I am student at UCLA."

"Oh. A college boy. I'm impressed. What's your major?"

"Political science. I'm going to go to law school."

"Oh wow! You're going to be a rich lawyer, huh?"

"Well, actually, what I really want to do is go into politics."

She gave Fred a hard look. "Hmm. I could see you as a congressman or senator, perhaps."

Fred raised his eyebrows, astonished that she would make such a bold statement when they hardly knew each other. Fred wasn't used to girls flirting with him. Dating in high school had been sparse for him, and Maria was only his second serious relationship. Candy had certainly gotten his attention and made him forget about everything else in the world, if only for a few moments. He was enjoying his flirtations with Candy so much, he lingered as if he had no place to go. Candy seemed to be enjoying herself as well.

"Are you planning a career in banking?" he asked, fumbling

for things to say.

Candy let out a snicker and replied, "Are you kidding? No way!"

"Oh, okay, then what are your plans?"

"To be an actress," she said as she gave him a glowing smile.

Fred returned the smile and added, "I could see you as an actress. . . . Definitely."

"Well, it's all yours," she said as she handed him the bag.

"Oh. Okay," he said disappointed that she was dismissing him. He took the bag from her and turned to leave.

"Nice talking to you," she said. "See you tomorrow."

Fred nodded without looking back and left the bank in somewhat of a daze. *What a cool girl and so friendly. I wonder if she really likes me or does she treat everyone like that?* He felt a tinge of excited just thinking about Candy. *Oh, I'm really going to love this route!*

As his encounter with Candy began to fade in his mind, he turned his attention to his next stop, Banning. To get to Banning, he had to traverse a small mountain pass of about 5,000 feet. This was great because it was such a nice change from the boredom of the freeway. The scenery was enchanting, too, with tall pine trees, grassy hillsides, and rushing streams. He picked up the bags at Banning, right on time at 6:15 p.m. From Banning, he went to San Bernardino, where he had to meet the driver from Big Bear and Lake Arrowhead and get their bags to add to his load.

Fred arrived at San Bernardino at 7:10 p.m. Jim had warned him about the driver from Big Bear. His name was Sam Stewart. Sam was in his mid-fifties and had apparently served time many years prior for some unknown offence. He lived up in the mountains and was pretty much a hermit, according to Jim, and his large stomach, long white hair, and white beard made him the spitting image of Santa Claus. Jim warned Fred not to bring that up, however, if he valued his teeth.

They were to meet at the San Bernardino branch at 7:15 p.m. The bank was in a strip shopping center on the outskirts of the city. When Fred pulled up to the bank, it was closed and the lights were out. He went inside, retrieved the bag, and came back out and waited. A few people were wandering in and out of the Savon Drug Store that was situated next to the bank. After two or three minutes, a red Volkswagen Beetle drove up quickly and stopped with a screech. The door opened, and out popped Sam. He wasn't wearing a red suit (which would have suited him) but instead was outfitted in a plaid shirt and blue jeans.

"Hi, I am Fred Fuller," he advised.

"Pleased to make your acquaintance, Fred. I'm Sam Stewart."

Sam went to the trunk of his car and stuck his key into the lock. It popped open.

"That's a good-looking VW," Fred observed. "I've got a friend whose got one just like it."

Fred's best friend Randy swore by his bug.

"Oh really? Does he like it?"

"He loves it."

"Me too. You know, this little rascal is the best car on the road."

"How does it do up in the mountains?"

"Great, especially in the snow. When everyone else is stuck, my VW and I are moving right along."

"Huh. That's great."

"Yeah, it's a pretty slick piece of machinery," he said, handing Fred the bags. "Well, here you go, Fred. Nice to meet ya."

"Likewise. Thanks. . . . See ya tomorrow."

Fred went to his car and was just about to get in when a little girl and her mother came out of Savon Drugs. The little girl took one look at Sam, and her face lit up. She pulled on her mother's dress and said, "Mama! Mama! Look, it's Santa Claus!"

"No, I don't think so, dear," her mama said.

The little girl broke free of her mother and ran over to Sam and asked excitedly, "Are you Santa Claus?"

Sam gave the little girl a dirty look and growled, "No! Leave me alone." The girl's face fell, and tears began to well in her eyes. Sam shook his head and then got in his bug and tore off toward the mountains. Fred chuckled as Sam drove away. The mother looked disapprovingly at Fred and he shook his head apologetically.

When Fred got back to LA, he unloaded the bags and then went straight to Maria's dorm. They had plans to go to Griffith Park Observatory, as they often did, to look at the nighttime skyline and make out in the moonlight. It was quite peaceful, and he felt so happy with Maria in his arms. "I couldn't imagine ever being separated from you," he said as he looked into her big brown eyes.

"Don't worry. We'll always be together," she promised.

Fred slipped his arm around her shoulder and pulled her lips gently to his. They kissed with great passion, and then Fred slid his hand gently under her sweater across her flat stomach and inched upward farther than he had ever dared go before. She offered only nominal resistance as he felt her warm, supple breasts for the very first time. Thank you, God, for bringing Maria into my life. Is tonight the night we consummate our love? Having felt her breasts, he thought for a moment that she was ready for more. He retreated momentarily from her breasts and started to slide his hand down into her pants, but she reacted quickly, grabbing his hand and sitting up abruptly.

"I told you I wouldn't make love until my wedding night," she said angrily.

Feeling very guilty, Fred said, "Right. I'm sorry. For a moment there, I just. . . . well . . . I just got carried away. You know what you do to me, don't you? You are so beautiful and incredibly sexy, and it feels so good to touch you. I lose all self-control when I am alone with you."

"Oh sure, I've heard that line before."

Maria folded her arms and stared out stone-faced at the city lights. After a minute, she abruptly turned to Fred and sighed. "Okay, I'll take care of your problem. I know men have needs."

"Huh?" Fred said, wondering what she meant.

She scooted over to Fred's side of the car and snuggled up close to him. Then, much to his shock, she slid her hand slowly down into his pants. Her touch felt so amazing he could barely stand it.

"Is this what you want?" she said as she began rubbing him into a frenzy.

"Yeah. . . . Oh yeah! That'll work."

Chapter 7

The Right Man

After leaving the bank, Candy raced across town to the community center where she had acting classes. It was operated by Lawrence Barr, a flash-in-the-pan actor who had starred in one major motion picture during a short career, but hadn't been offered a contract since. She didn't like Larry much, but he was a decent acting teacher and gave her special attention because he wanted her to be more than a student. He also knew everyone in Hollywood and promised to help her find a good agent as soon as he felt her skills were marketable. She hadn't succumbed to his advances yet, but she knew it was just a matter of time before he'd end up in her bed.

Candy was exhausted when she got home after class. It was after nine and she hadn't eaten since lunch, so she picked up the phone and ordered a pizza. Then she made another phone call and invited her friend, Jenny, over to share the pizza with her. Jenny was like a sister. In fact, they had lived together in a foster home for a while. When the doorbell rang Candy let her in.

"So, another long day, huh?" Jenny asked.

"Yes. Larry likes to hear himself talk and he has a captive audience, so we get a boring new story every class."

"Really? How annoying."

"Yes. He says there is something important to learn from each one, but I haven't learned a damn thing other than the fact that he's an egomaniac and a womanizer."

"Well, you better get used to it. I'm afraid that's going to be the norm with Hollywood agents and producers."

"True, and I'll play their game if I have to, but wouldn't be nice if there was another way."

"There is another way, but only for those lucky enough to have a mother or father who is already a famous actor, producer or director. They can get work without having to sleep with anybody."

"Yeah," Candy said. "But you and I didn't even get regular parents, let alone celebrity parents."

There was a knocking on the door.

"Ah, our pizza is here," Candy said as she strolled to the front door and opened it. A handsome young man smiled at her and held out their pizza. She returned the smile, paid him and gave him a tip. He nodded, turned and left. Candy closed the door and took the pizza to the kitchen table. "Now, there's a cute kid. I'd take him to bed in a heartbeat."

"Yeah, he'd be a good in bed but he's not going to be a provider. If you fell in love with him, it would be a disaster in the long run."

"You're right. Actually, I met the perfect guy today. He's our new messenger. He's cute as hell and ambitious. He's going to UCLA and plans to go to law school."

"Wow! What's his name?"

"Fred Fuller. He wants to go into politics. He's already had a job with Congressman Bartlett up in Ventura."

"Sounds wonderful, but he won't even have a job for another four or five years. Does his family have money?"

"No," Candy said sorrowfully. "He's as poor as us."

"Too bad," I guess Larry's still your best bet.

"Yeah, I suppose, but Fred's got an apartment and a good job with the bank. They pay messenger's very well, I'm told. I think they belong to the Teamsters Union, or something. He gets way more than I do."

"Really?"

"Yes, so we could live together and maybe I wouldn't need to work."

"You've just met the guy and you're already moving in?"

She smiled. "Hypothetically. I really like him and he's so young and naive. After a few romps in the sack, he'd do anything for me."

"You are evil, girl," Jenny said, partially joking.

"No, I'm not. I will make him very happy," Candy promised. "I will be the best thing that ever happened to him."

"Well, you have to seduce him first. It may not be as easy as you think. If he's smart enough to be a lawyer, then he might see right through you."

"No. He's already in love with me. I could see it in his eyes. All I need to do is get him alone."

"Well, I can't wait to meet this poor guy. I feel sorry for him already."

Candy laughed then picked up a piece of pizza and took a bite, thoughtfully.

Chapter 8

The Solution

Joel Roberts ran his hands through his long black hair nervously. He had gotten a frantic call from his best friend Charles Bartlett who he'd help get elected to Congress. There was money missing, a lot of money. Joel hadn't stolen the money, so he'd immediately launched an investigation to find out who did it and the Congressman wasn't going to like what he'd discovered.

They had been team mates in high school and roommates in college. But when Bartlett came home to Ventura, Roberts went on to law school. When Roberts graduated and had passed the bar, he came back home and hung up his shingle. Bartlett, of course, was his first client and referred him a lot of business. In fact, Roberts got so much referral business from the Congressman he scarcely had the time for other clients.

Henry Sinclair was another fellow high school football star and the mutual friend of Bartlett and Roberts. Sinclair had been Roberts' roommate at Stanford where Roberts got his law degree and Sinclair got his MBA. With school behind them they all settled down in Ventura County and remained good friends. In fact, they usually played golf together at least twice a month.

When the Congressman arrived, he was immediately shown into Roberts' office. Henry Sinclair was already there sitting on a brown leather love seat with papers scattered around next to him. Roberts stood up and forced a smile.

"Chuck. Thanks for coming by. I thought it would be better to have this meeting here rather than at your office."

"Okay," the Congressman spat. "I'm here. Now tell me you have found the missing money."

Roberts took a deep breath. "I wish I could, but after doing an audit of our funds, the money is definitely missing."

"Did you take it?" the Congressman asked accusingly.

"No! No. Of course not. I would never do something like that. You know me."

"I thought I did. I thought I could trust you."

"No. I'm not a money guy. I delegated campaign finance to Henry. You know that."

Bartlett turned his gaze to Sinclair expectantly.

"Don't look at me that way," Sinclair said. "I didn't steal the money either. It was a bank officer at one of our branches who did it."

"Oh, my God! How could you let that happen?" the Congressman said irritably. "Don't you watch your employees?"

"We do, of course, but he was very clever in the way he embezzled the money."

"Spare me the excuses. Will the bank make good on the loss? They have insurance, don't they?"

"Sure, but if the press gets wind of this there will be a scandal. You'll lose your seat in Congress, Joel's law career will crater and I will lose my job with Bank USA."

"Aren't you over reacting a bit?" the Congressman said, "Why would I lose my seat? I didn't do anything wrong."

"You're the candidate," Sinclair reminded him. You're ultimately responsible for the campaign contributions. If you can't even manage your own staff, how can you be an effective Congressman. That will the argument."

The Congressman frowned then took up the offensive. "Then what are you going to do to make this right without it costing me my seat in Congress."

"Yes, well that will be tricky," Sinclair admitted.

"But, Henry's got some ideas," Roberts added.

"Exactly how much was stolen?" the Congressman asked.

"4.8 million and some change."

"Jesus! How did he spend that much money?" the Congressman asked.

"A divorce with the usual legal fees, alimony, child support, college expenses and prostitutes."

"Okay, but that couldn't have cost $4.8 million."

"No, it was his drinking and gambling that I think really got him in serious financial trouble."

"So, should I call the FBI and let them sort this out?"

"As your attorney," Roberts replied, "that's what I would

advise, but as a friend and someone who knows how much being in Congress means to you, I would say you might want to wait a while and let us see if we can find another $4.8 million to replace what was stolen."

"Where could you raise that kind of money? Is one of you a magician now?"

"No," Sinclair said, "but I think there is a way the embezzler can raise the money. It's risky for him, but if it works it will keep him out of jail and make the campaign fund whole again."

"What's this asshole's name?" The Congressman asked.

"It's best I keep that to myself. The less you two know the better."

The Congressman shook his head. "So, tell me how this magic trick is going to work?"

"Well, like I said, you don't want to know," Roberts replied. "In fact, we never had this meeting."

"Right, but what do I tell Tom? He was all ready to go to the FBI."

"Don't worry about Tom," Roberts replied. "He's a client and a friend of mine. I'll deal with him."

"Okay, I'll leave you two to your magic then," the Congressman said warily. "See you on Saturday at the club?"

"Yeah," Roberts replied. "Business as usual."

The Congressman left the meeting feeling much relief. He trusted his two best friends and had confidence in them. Even so he was curious as to what they had up their sleeve. He almost wished they would have told him, but he knew Joel was right about keeping him in the dark. He didn't want to do anything that might jeopardize his seat in Congress.

Chapter 9

The Mistress

It was a cool autumn day, and Fred was on his way to Palm Springs again, just as he had been every night for several weeks. The route had become very familiar, and he was getting to know the branch personnel pretty well. When he arrived at the Palm Springs branch, one of the tellers was out of balance, so the bags weren't ready. While he was waiting, Candy invited him into the break room to wait. The tight red sweater and short plaid skirt she was wearing immediately had Fred mesmerized.

Candy's flirting with Fred had continued nonstop since the first day they'd met. This pleased Fred enormously, as she was the hottest woman he'd ever known. They talked at length each time they met, and being a very open person, Candy often shocked Fred with intimate revelations about her personal life. On this particular day, she seemed even more excited to see him. It was obvious she had something on her mind.

"You know, I've been doing a lot of thinking about us," Candy said thoughtfully.

"You have?" Fred asked, surprised that she'd had thoughts of them as a couple.

"Yes. Hey, you know, we could help each other out."

"How's that?" Fred asked warily.

"Well, I could be your mistress."

He frowned, not following her logic. "My mistress?"

"Right. Every big shot lawyer has a mistress."

"They do? Really? I didn't know that."

"Of course, they do."

"Okay, go on," he said, wondering what other revelations about the legal profession he was about to hear.

"You know how hard it is to become an actress? You've got to go to acting school, audition all the time, go to all the Hollywood parties, and even sleep with the right people."

Fred raised his eyebrows. She smiled at his obvious shock.

"You'd go that far to get what you wanted?" he asked evenly.

"If I had to."

"Well, my dad always told me that if you want something badly enough, you can always get it. It is just a matter of setting your mind on your goal and doing whatever it takes to achieve it."

"Exactly. That's why I should be your mistress. If you set me up in an apartment and took care of me, I would be there for you whenever you needed me. But in the meantime, I could work on becoming an actress without having to waste eight hours a day working in this stupid bank to survive."

It was an intriguing thought, but Fred immediately thought of Maria and began to feel guilty even talking about a mistress. "I guess I didn't tell you I have a girlfriend and am seriously considering asking her to marry me."

"Congratulations. That is so cool!" she replied genuinely.

"And I don't plan to have a mistress, no offense."

She gave him a wounded look that made him feel terrible.

Before he knew it, he found himself recanting. "If I were going to have one, though, I couldn't think of anyone I'd rather have as a mistress than you."

"Give me a break! You're not telling me you're going to be faithful to one woman, are you?"

"Well, that's kind of what I had planned," Fred admitted.

"What are you, some kind of Boy Scout?"

He laughed. "Well, actually I was a Boy Scout—an Eagle Scout, in fact."

"Oh God, I should have known."

"You don't like Boy Scouts?"

"I like Boy Scouts okay. My little brother was one. It's just that all that trustworthy, loyal, helpful, friendly stuff is garbage."

"I don't think it's garbage exactly. It's an ideal, a goal you try to achieve."

"You are really idealistic, aren't you?" Candy complained.

"I don't know. I've never really thought that much about it."

"Well, think about it. It would be a fantastic arrangement. I like you a lot, and I can see in the way you look at me that the feeling is mutual. We could have a lot of fun together without fear of any kind of permanent relationship getting in the way of our dreams. We could trust each other implicitly because our relationship would be strictly a business arrangement, each washing the other's back, so to speak."

Luckily, the bags were ready, and Fred was summoned back into the bank lobby. He turned to leave, but Candy grabbed his arm and pulled him up close. She smiled wryly, wrapped her arms around him, and said, "Maybe you need to sample the merchandise before you make a hasty decision." She gave him a long kiss and then let him go. Fred stood there a moment in total shock. Candy smiled, then turned and walked away. After a minute, he regained his composure, grabbed the bag and left. On the way to his next stop, his mind replayed the conversation over and over again. He was so shaken by the encounter, that he went right past the Beaumont branch without stopping and didn't realize it for several miles.

Never in his life had he been confronted with such a temptation. Candy represented every evil he'd ever been warned about, yet as hard as he tried to despise her, he couldn't feel anything but delight. She was so alluring and her plan so intriguing that, for a moment, he thought it might even be possible.

But as the evening progressed, he began to think of Maria and the complete trust she had in him. How could he betray that trust? The answer was clear: He couldn't. One woman is all a man needs, he told himself. Promiscuity will lead to nothing but grief.

When he pulled into the motor pool, Jim was leaning against the gas pump, looking pretty restless. He was the last driver in at night, so when he was late, it meant Jim had to work overtime.

Fred pulled in, got out of his car, and immediately began to apologize. "Sorry I am late, Jim. Palm Springs wasn't ready when I got there, so I got way behind from the start."

"I forgive you, but I don't know if my lady friend who's waiting for me will."

Fred smiled at that and then wondered if Jim might know something about Candy. "Hey, have you ever heard of a teller named Candy at Palm Springs?"

"No, can't say that I have. Why? You got an eye for her?"

"No, she's got an eye for me. In fact, she's offered to be my mistress."

"What? Your mistress? As I recall, you're not married, Fuller, so if you took up with her, she wouldn't be classified as a mistress, now would she?"

"She wants to be my mistress after I am married and become a lawyer."

"Well, lad, I have heard of planning ahead, but this takes the bloody cake."

"Well, I just wondered if she came on to all of the messengers like that."

"I've certainly never heard any tales about her. What do you plan to do about it?"

"Nothing. The whole idea is crazy. Besides, I am in love with Maria."

"Then why did you ask me about it?"

"I know you've been around and experienced a lot," Fred said.

"Well, a professor I knew one time told me that whenever one is considering a course of action, he should ask himself, 'What would be the worst thing that could happen if I embark down this path?' After you have answered that question, the decision becomes easy. If you can live with the worst thing that could happen, then you should do it. So, what's the worst thing that would happen if Candy became your mistress?"

"Well, the worst thing would be if Maria caught us."

"Of course. What do you think Maria would do if she caught you two doing nasty things?"

"Well, I'm pretty sure she would stick me with a sharp knife and twist it slowly."

Jim laughed. "Good, lad. Just keep that thought in your mind whenever temptation confronts you. Too much candy isn't good for you, my friend, no matter how sweet it tastes. No pun intended."

Chapter 10

The Accident

The next day, Fred drove to work as usual and parked a few blocks away from the motor pool on Canal Street. It was a narrow street, and with cars parked on both sides, there was only room for one car to pass at a time. After finding an empty spot, Fred carefully backed into it and shut off his engine. As he was opening the front door, he heard tires shrieking behind him, so he looked in the rearview mirror just in time to see a black 1963 Chevy barreling toward him. Glancing to his left, he saw that his door was extended too far out into the street to allow the Chevy to pass. He reached for the handle to close it quickly, but it was too late. The Chevy hit the door head-on, severing it from his car.

Upset but somewhat relieved that he had only lost a car door and not an arm, Fred jumped out of his car and swore at the fleeing driver. After watching the black Chevy disappear around the corner, he looked over at his mangled door in the middle of the street. Unfortunately, there were no witnesses to his misfortune, as the street was deserted. A sinking feeling quickly overcame him as he realized he had no insurance and would have to pay for this repair himself. "Shit!" he yelled, as if someone was there to commiserate with him.

Disgusted, he threw the door into the back seat and walked over to the motor pool. Jim was busy as usual, helping drivers get on the road. As Fred approached, Jim looked up at him and immediately knew something was wrong.

"What's up, lad? You look like your mama just died."

"Some asshole just took off my car door!"

"You're shittin' me!"

"No. I was just getting out of my car, and this black Chevy comes sailing around the corner and clips off my front door."

"Oh, tough luck, but I guess that's why you have insurance."

"The jerk didn't bother stopping and giving me insurance information. I only have liability coverage . . . couldn't afford comprehensive and collision."

Jim frowned. "Oh, that's a shame. Well, you can't be driving around without a door, now can you?"

"No, but I can't afford a new one either."

"I know where you can get a used door cheap. The owner of the place will even help you put it on."

"Oh really? Where?"

"Loma Linda Auto Salvage," Jim replied. "The owner's an old drinking buddy of mine. When you get in tonight, I'll give you his name and address and directions how to get there."

"Great. I really appreciate that, Jim."

That night, Jim gave Fred directions to Loma Linda Auto Salvage, and the next day, he skipped classes and went there. The salvage yard was surrounded by an eight-foot chain-link fence and guarded by a dog named Prince. As Fred entered the yard, Prince came running at him, barking wildly. Fred was a little scared, but he knelt down anyway and cautiously extended his hand so Prince could smell him. He knew most dogs were friendly by nature and would warm up to strangers as soon as they knew no one meant them any harm. Prince approached cautiously and sniffed Fred's finger.

"Here, boy. I won't hurt you. Come here."

Prince slowly moved closer and closer until Fred was able to gently pat the top of his head. After a few minutes, Prince and he were friends.

While Fred was petting Prince, the owner showed up, a man named Elmer. He did a double-take when he saw Fred petting Prince. "You're the first person I can remember Prince allowing to pet him. How did you manage that?"

"I love dogs. I guess they can sense I'm a friend."

He nodded. "Hmm. So, what can I do for you?"

"I need a front door for a '59 Ford Falcon. Some jerk ripped mine off yesterday."

"Oh my. I hope you weren't hurt."

"No. Miraculously, I escaped injury."

"Well, let me see. I think I've seen a '59 Ford Falcon around her somewhere. Follow me, and we'll see if we can locate it."

After searching for thirty minutes or so, Elmer found a 1959

Ford Falcon. He said the left front door was Fred's for thirty bucks. Fred told him Jim had mentioned that he might help him put it on, which he offered to do for an additional ten bucks. Since Fred was not mechanically inclined, he jumped at the offer.

Elmer told him to pull his car into his shop, which Fred did immediately. He pushed an old wheel barrow out to the wrecked car, removed the door, and placed it on the wheel barrow. Then he pushed the wheel barrow back to the shop and installed it on Fred's car.

Other than the contrast of a blue door on a maroon body, it was as good as new. Fred took the car by the motor pool later that evening and showed it to Jim. He concurred that it looked good and said he even liked the two-tone paint job. Fred thanked him again and went home feeling much better.

Chapter 11

The First Temptation

Several weeks later, Maria and Fred were sitting under a tree in front of the UCLA library having a late lunch. It was a pleasant October day, as the morning fog had finally given way to the warm rays of the sun. Fred was relaxing with his head in Maria's lap. The sweet aroma of her body was intoxicating to him, and he could have lingered there all day.

Maria was running her fingers through his hair as they discussed what to do on the weekend. "I've got to study a lot this weekend," Maria warned.

"You can take time out to go to the football game, can't you?"

"Maybe. When is it?"

"Seven o'clock, but we'll have to leave at five to make it there on time."

"Okay, but that's about all I will be able to do this weekend. I've got a biology test on Monday."

"You've got to eat, don't you?"

"Not necessarily, but it would be nice."

"And I can't imagine you missing mass."

"No. I wouldn't dare miss mass. God might punish me by letting me flunk my biology test."

"Okay then. I'll take you to mass at ten thirty, and then I'll buy you lunch. That way, you won't starve, God will help you pass your biology test, and I won't have to go a whole day without seeing you."

"Do you always get what you want?"

"Of course. I am going to be a lawyer."

"I hate to mention this, but it's three o'clock. You'd better get moving or you're going to be late for work."

"No, don't make me go. I'd rather stay here with you."

She laughed and tried to pry him up. "Come on, you lazy bum. Get out of here. I don't want you to get in trouble."

Fred sighed. "Okay, I am gone." After he gave her a long kiss, he took off. It was twenty-five minutes to downtown, so he had to hustle.

When Fred arrived, Jim threw him the keys and said, "Better get rolling, Fred. You're five minutes late already, and I don't want to be waiting around all night for you again."

"What, your lady friend's complaining again?"

"Not yet, but I don't want to get her started."

"Okay, you can count on me. I'll have you out of here on time, don't worry."

"Quit your bloody jabbering and get a move-on."

"Okay, au revoir."

Fred hit the San Bernardino Freeway, and, even though he was only five or ten minutes late, traffic was already getting pretty heavy. He wasn't able to make up any time until he got out of San Bernardino, and even then only a few minutes. When he arrived at the Palm Springs branch, he walked in the bank lobby and saw Candy at the end of the counter. She wasn't smiling, which made him feel uneasy.

Fred felt he needed to apologize to her for running off the way he had the last time he'd seen her. He approached her cautiously. "Hi, Candy."

She forced a smile. "Hi, Fred."

"Hey, about the other day. I'm sorry I was short with you. It's not that your idea wasn't enticing, because it was, believe me. Actually, I've given it serious consideration, but I just don't know if I could pull it off. It's just not me."

"I understand. You're just too much of a Boy Scout."

"Well, I don't know about that, but anyway, I hope we can still be friends."

"Sure. Your Maria is a lucky woman to have someone so faithful."

"Well, you certainly put my fidelity to the test."

"But you are turning me down, right?"

Fred paused a moment for reflection, although it was a simple question with an obvious answer. Then Fred heard himself say, "Well, yeah, for now."

"You mean there's still hope?" Candy asked cheerily.

"There's always hope."

Candy gave him a calculating look, and Fred knew immediately he was in trouble. What had he done? Why hadn't he just told her there was no chance in hell of her mistress idea ever happening? Why had he left the door open? He should have been upset with himself for how ineptly he had handled the situation, but somehow, he didn't feel bad at all. She was the most desirable woman he'd ever known, and she had invited him to be her lover, for godsakes! What else did he want, an engraved invitation? How could he close the door to such an exciting relationship? The fact was, he couldn't.

Up to that evening, he'd been able to analyze the situation with Candy somewhat objectively. It was obvious from his moral and religious training that any relationship with her was out of the question. Besides, he wasn't entirely sure Candy's proposal was genuine, as it had occurred to him she might just be teasing. After all, she was planning to be an actress. But that night, Candy seemed genuinely hurt and disappointed that he had rejected her proposal. For the first time, he was convinced she wasn't teasing; she was absolutely serious. If I pass up this opportunity now, I might regret it for the rest of my life. And what if what Candy said was right? What if it is possible for us to have this relationship and always keep it a secret? How could I pass that up?

Luckily, by the time Fred got to the Redding branch, he was starting to regain his senses and realized the idea was ludicrous. Then and there, he decided to go to confession and get some spiritual guidance before he found himself giving his soul to the Devil.

But, if Fred thought his moral scrutiny was over for the evening, he was woefully mistaken. As he drove into the San Bernardino Branch parking lot, he saw Sam Stewart leaning against his VW, waiting for him. He looked at his watch and was horrified to see he was ten minutes late.

"How's it going?" Fred asked. He wanted to add 'Santa' to his greeting but restrained himself.

"Can't complain. You're running late again, I see."

"Yeah. I've been trying to catch up all night but haven't had any luck."

"Well, I reckon I should warn you. In a few weeks, you'll be waiting for me every night."

"Really? Why's that?"

"Come November, there's gonna be lots of snow up there in them mountains around Arrowhead and Big Bear. Driving will be mean, and it will take a lot longer than usual to get down off the mountain."

"Well, I guess I'll bring a good book."

"You just might hit some of that there snow yourself between Palm Springs and Banning. Yeah, I used to have your route years ago, and several times I got caught in some near blizzards."

"That should be fun." As sarcastic as it sounded, Fred was serious. Snow fascinated him. He guessed this was due to the fact that he saw so little of it living in California. "Speaking of snow and the approach of winter, have you ever thought of playing Santa Claus during the holiday season? You'd be a natural. I am sure you could make a mint."

"Let me just ask you one question," Sam said icily. "Have you ever had 200 snotty-nosed kids coughing and sneezing all over you?"

"No, but it sounds like you may have."

"You're damn right I have, and it's no fun—believe me."

"Okay. Just curious. I guess I better go. Jim's got some hot woman he's meeting tonight, and he already warned me not to be late."

"Jim has hot women after him every night. Don't rush on account of him and his libido."

"That's true. Okay, see ya later."

As Sam got in his car and drove off, Fred turned toward the bank and walked to the front door. He unlocked it, stepped inside and locked the door behind him, just as he always did. Then he started walking to the place where the bags were usually left for him. It was dark, and he couldn't see too well, but there was a nightlight that illuminated the bank enough so he could get around without running into furniture. He spotted the bags and walked toward them, but as he scanned the bank lobby, he noticed something odd. The bank vault appeared to be open. Fred wandered over to it to get a closer look, and sure enough, the massive steel door was wide open!

A million thoughts began to run through Fred's head. How much money is in there? Is there any kind of alarm inside the vault? If someone were to walk in when it was open, would anything happen? Who would be so stupid to leave a bank vault open? I wonder if they'd miss $1,000 or even $10,000?

After staring in the vault for several minutes, Fred knew the right thing to do was to call the motor pool and report to them that the bank vault was open. He picked up one of the bank phones and dialed the number. It rang several times.

"Hello. This is Sinclair."

"Mr. Sinclair, this is Fred Fuller."

"Fuller? What's wrong?"

"Well, I am over here at San Bernardino, and I noticed that someone left the bank vault open."

"Oh shit! Okay. Stay right there, and I'll have someone get over to the bank in just a few minutes."

"Okay."

"Thanks for calling, Fred."

After about fifteen minutes, a dark blue Cadillac drove up. A short, stocky man got out of his car and approached Fred. He seemed a little wobbly as he walked, his speech was slurred, and he smelled of liquor. "You Fuller?" he asked.

"Yes," Fred replied.

"I'm Harvey Hamlin, the cashier here. I understand we have a little sit-uration."

"Yeah. I noticed the bank vault was left open, so I reported it to my supervisor."

"Well, aren't you (burp) Mr. Honest Abe?"

"I thought if someone happened to look in and see the vault open, it might be somewhat of a temptation."

"What? You mean someone might want the six million bucks that's in there right now?" He started laughing like Fred had told him a hysterical joke.

"Is that really how much is in there?" Fred asked incredulously.

"You're most certainly damn right. (burp) Counted it myself this afternoon."

"Damn! Isn't that a lot of money to be in a small branch like this?"

Hamlin shook his head and wobbled. Fred grabbed his arm to steady him. "Not when you got three major defense plants (burp) less than (burp) two miles away with 12,000 employees. On payday, we can shell out two or three million easy."

"Six million is a lot of money," Fred said. "With the vault open like that, could someone really just walk in there and take it?"

Hamlin laughed. "I don't know why not. The alarm isn't

activated until I close the vault."

"Really?"

"Yeah, you missed your opportunity, (burp) Fred. You could have just walked in there and taken six million dollars. Instead, you called Sinclair. What a dumb ass!"

He started to laugh again and then went inside the bank, staggered around a bit, and headed for the vault. He went inside the vault, Fred guessed to check and see if all the money was still there, then tried to swing the heavy steel door around but staggered and nearly fell over. "How about a little help here, Fred?" he asked.

Fred rushed over and helped him push the vault closed. Then Hamlin turned the wheel on the front of the vault, which Fred figured activated the locking system and the alarm.

"You can go now, Fuller. The bank's money is safe, or the insurance company's money is safe actually. The bank wouldn't have lost a dime even if someone had cleaned them out entirely."

"Really? Not a dime?"

"Nah. Some insurance company's profit would dip half a percent—no big deal."

"I know it's none of my business, but I am curious about what happened. Why was the vault left open?"

He stiffened. "You're right. It's none of your damn business!" Hamlin replied irritably.

"Okay, okay. Just curious. Like you said, no big deal."

He sighed. "If you must know, my wife, she left me." Fred could see tears welling in his eyes and he began to choke up. "She took the kids, and she didn't even leave a note." He took a deep breath, like he was trying to calm himself, then exhaled slowly. "I don't know how it happened. Everyone had gone. I was about to close the vault when my mother-in-law called. She told me her daughter had finally taken her advice and dumped me. It was so upsetting I just dropped everything and left."

"Why do you think she left you?"

"I guess she finally got tired of being married to a drunk."

"Hmm. I'm so sorry, Mr. Hamlin. I hope you find your family," Fred said sympathetically.

"Thank you. I'm sorry I messed up your evening."

"You didn't mess anything up. I only lost about an hour. It's no big deal."

"Well, you'd better get out of here. Sinclair is going to be looking for you."

"Okay. Can you make it home alright? I could drive you home and you could pick up your car in the morning."

"No, that's okay. I am starting to sober up now. I'll make a cup of coffee and take a nap on the sofa before I try to drive."

"Good. I'll see you later then."

It was already nine, and Fred had nearly an hour's drive ahead of him. He knew Jim was going to be furious, so he raced home as fast he could, keeping a lookout for the California Highway Patrol. As it turned out, his race back was unnecessary, as Jim had been sent home and Sinclair was waiting for him at the motor pool.

"Did Hamlin show up?" he asked.

"Yes, sir. He came about fifteen minutes after I called."

"Did you see him close the vault?"

"Yes, sir. He went inside, checked it out, and then I helped him close it."

"Good. Nice work, Fuller. It's good to know we have an honest employee."

"No problem, sir."

It was too late to go see Maria, so Fred went straight home. When he walked in, Steve was watching TV. He went to the refrigerator, got a Coke, and then plopped himself down on the sofa.

"How was Maria tonight?" Steve asked.

"I don't know. I just got off work."

"How come you're so late?"

"You won't believe what happened."

"What?"

"The cashier over at the San Bernardino branch left the vault open with over six million dollars in it."

"You've got to be joking!"

"I had to wait around for him to get his drunk ass over to the bank to close the vault."

"He was really drunk?"

"Yeah, downright plastered."

"I bet he was relieved that you discovered it before someone robbed the bank."

"Not really. He said I was a dumb ass for not taking the money."

Steve laughed. "You'd be their first suspect!"

"Not necessarily. What if I took the money and then closed

the vault?"

"What about the alarm?"

"Mr. Hamlin says the alarm doesn't activate until the vault is closed."

"Too bad you didn't know all that before you discovered it open."

"You mean; you think I should have taken the money?"

"Not really, but six million dollars is a lot of temptation," Steve said, "even for a Boy Scout."

"Yeah, with that kind of money, you could go just about anywhere in the world and live like a king for the rest of your life," Fred mused.

"But you would have to leave all your friends and family, and you could never come back to the United States," Steve noted.

"Unless they didn't know you took the money."

"But Hamlin would have remembered he left the vault open and told the FBI, don't you think?"

"That would be the big gamble, but I am pretty sure he would lie to save his ass. He wouldn't want anyone to know he did something as stupid as leaving the bank vault open. Besides, he was so drunk he might not have known whether he left the vault open or not."

For a moment, they both sat silently, pondering the situation and what they could have done with six million bucks.

After several minutes, Steve smiled and then broke the silence. "Well, it's a moot point now since the vault is closed and the money is safe. It's probably a good thing you didn't know then what you know now or you might have taken the money and ended up ruining your life, not to mention Maria's."

"Yeah, I guess you're right." Fred looked at his watch. "Speaking of Maria, I'd better call her before it gets any later." Fred went into his bedroom, dialed Maria's number and told the desk clerk he wanted Maria's room. He immediately rang her number. The phone rang several times.

"Hello?"

"Hi, babe."

"Hi, Fred. Where have you been? It's almost ten thirty."

"I got slightly delayed at San Bernardino."

"What? They didn't have the bags ready again?"

"No, it wasn't that. This time, some idiot forgot to close the vault."

"How could someone forget something like that?"

"He had some domestic problems. His wife left him."

"So, what did you do?"

"I called my supervisor and then had to wait for Mr. Hamlin to come and close the vault."

"Damn. I missed seeing you tonight."

Fred's curiosity was aroused as to how Maria would have reacted if he'd decided to steal the money. What would she do if she had to choose between me and her family and friends? He knew it was a cruel thing to ask her, but he couldn't help it. He wanted to know. "Maria, what would you have done if I had called you and said I had six million dollars and we needed to leave the country tonight?"

"I would have said you are crazy."

"I'm serious. That vault had over six million dollars in it, and all I would have had to do was walk in and take the money."

"Come on! You couldn't have just taken the money."

"Yes, I could have. The alarm is not activated until the vault is closed. Hamlin said I could have walked right in and taken the money."

"But they would have known you took it."

"That wasn't my question. What if I called you and said I've got six million dollars and we need to leave the country tonight? What would you have done?"

"I would have said goodbye."

He sighed. "That's what I figured."

"Well, I am not going to leave my family and friends to go off to some third world country and hide the rest of my life."

"Don't you love me?"

"Of course I do, but the man I love is a decent, honest man, Fred—not a thief."

"Doesn't the thought of having six million dollars tempt you just a little?"

"No. I know you will be making lots of money when you become a lawyer, and I can wait. Anyway, I've always been told a law license was a license to steal, so be patient. Wait until you get a license before you start stealing other people's money."

"You're a real comedian."

"I know. You're lucky to have me."

"Yeah, well I guess I better go do some studying or I'll never get that law license you're depending on so much."

"That's right. Get to work, Fred."

"Okay. Goodnight. Love ya."

"Love ya too. Bye."

By Monday, Fred had managed to purge the six-million-dollar question out of his mind; however, when he got to Palm Springs, another temptation was waiting impatiently for him.

"Well, if it isn't the Boy Scout," Candy spat.

"What's that supposed to mean?"

"I heard about the open bank vault."

"Oh, that. Who told you about that?"

"Joe, the morning messenger. It's the talk of the motor pool."

"Hmm. Wonderful."

She shook her head. "You just walked away from six million dollars, just like that?"

"First of all, I didn't know there was six million dollars in the vault, nor did I know that the alarm wouldn't go off if I took the money."

She sighed. "I know. I'm sorry. It would have been just so fabulous had you been able to take the money."

He looked at her in disbelief. "So, if I had called you Friday night and said 'I've got six million dollars. Pack your bags, we're leaving the country', you'd have said—?"

"What time are you picking me up?"

Fred laughed. "That's what I figured. What about your family and friends?"

"Money attracts friends. I'll have all the friends I'll ever need with that much money."

"What if you could never come back to the United States again?"

"With six million dollars, we wouldn't need the United States."

"What about your career?"

"Career? With that kind of money, we'd have enough to make our own movies, and I could star in them."

"What if we got caught and you went to jail as an accomplice?"

"You're too smart to get caught. Anyway, life isn't any fun if you don't take a little risk once in a while."

"One last question. How would I know I could trust you?"

"Like you say, I'd be an accomplice. My neck would be on the line too. So, if you got caught, I would get caught. And who knows? I might just fall in love with you."

"Wouldn't that mess up our business relationship?"

She shrugged. "Maybe, or maybe I wouldn't care."

About that time, the bank manager walked in and saw them talking. He looked at his watch and said, "Shouldn't you be halfway to Beaumont by now?"

"Yeah. I am out of here. Bye, Candy."

"See ya, Fred."

Again, Fred had been ambushed by Candy. She had a way of totally immobilizing him. She was so gorgeous and sexy that he couldn't think rationally when he was around her. But when she told him she might fall in love with him, that was a major jolt—at least a 6.7 on the Richter Scale. If Candy really loved me, that would change everything.

Fred couldn't take his mind off of Candy all evening. She was so different from Maria, like they were from different planets. How could he choose between them? Deep inside, he didn't want to choose; he wanted both of them. It was selfish and stupid, but it was how he felt. Candy wouldn't care if he married Maria as long as he took care of her, but unfortunately, Maria would not share him with anyone. What a perilous existence it would be to try to have them both!

That night, Fred had trouble sleeping again. Life had become too complicated. He knew he should steer clear of Candy, but she excited him, and he didn't know how long he could resist her if she didn't stop ambushing him.

Chapter 12

The Plan

Harvey Hamlin sat stiffly at his big oak desk wondering why Henry Sinclair was coming to visit him. Nothing had changed since their last meeting weeks ago when Sinclair had confronted him about the missing five million dollars from Congressman Bartlett's campaign fund. He wondered if he was bringing the FBI with him to arrest him for the embezzlement. It was surprising to Hamlin that it hadn't already happened, but Sinclair had kept a lid on it for some reason.

As usual, Hamlin had turned to the bottle when adversity struck. He hadn't been sober a single day since the confrontation and his drunkenness had gotten him into more trouble. Not only had he yelled and cursed at a bank auditor, but he'd forgotten to close the vault when he went home the night after the verbal altercation. This had gotten him an official reprimand which put his job in jeopardy.

Sinclair showed up alone five minutes before the scheduled 11:00 a.m meeting. When his secretary announced he had arrived, Hamlin pulled out a bottle of mouthwash, took a swig, and swallowed it, grimacing from the harsh taste. Then he stood up, straightened his tie and went out to greet Sinclair.

"Henry," he said as he extended his hand.

Sinclair shook Harvey's hand and replied, "Thanks for meeting with me on short notice."

"It's no problem. Come on back."

Sinclair followed him in the office and Hamlin shut the door. Hamlin took his seat at his desk and motioned for Harvey to sit across from him in a brown leather chair.

"So, are you going to have me arrested?" Hamlin asked.

"Well, that is an option I have discussed at length with the Congressman and his legal counsel, but your arrest will have serious ramifications not only for you, but the Congressman as well."

"I know, Henry. I feel terrible about it. With enough time, I'm sure I can figure out a way to replenish the fund."

"Come on, Harvey. You know that will never happen. What do think you're going to do—win the lottery?"

"No, but—"

"Oh, I got it. You're going to call your bookie and place the perfect bet, right. You got a tip on the Super Bowl or the Kentucky Derby maybe?"

Hamlin took a deep breath. "Okay, okay. You're right. I'm sorry. The money's gone. So, why are you here? If you are not going to turn me in, what do you want from me? What could I possibly do to make it up to the Congressman?"

Sinclair gave Hamlin a hard look. "There is one thing you could do."

"What's that?"

"You could steal the money from the bank's vault and put it in the campaign fund."

Hamlin chuckled. "Yeah. Like that would work."

"Actually, I think it will. You have a propensity for leaving the vault open at night, right. Fred Fuller told me all about your little lapse last week."

"So, big deal. The money wasn't at risk. Nobody would have known about it had Fred not discovered it."

"I don't know about that, but if you were to do it again and the money in the vault disappeared, it wouldn't be hard to make it look like Fuller took the money."

"What? That's crazy."

"Is it? You don't think you could pull it off to stay out of prison. I think 5to10 years is what you'd get for embezzlement, isn't that what your lawyer has told you? You have consulted a lawyer, I hope."

Hamlin ignored the question. The fact was he hadn't talked to an attorney. He hated attorneys and hadn't even hired one for his divorce. "What about Fuller? You'd be willing to sacrifice an innocent kid like that?"

"I'm not sacrificing anybody. If anybody asks me, we never had this conversation. You're the one who made this mess. You need to decide what you're willing to do to make this nightmare go away."

Hamlin ran his fingers through his coal black hair nervously. Then he stroked his chin thoughtfully. Finally, a glimmer of a smile came over his face. "Okay, hypothetically, if I made this happen. What about the two million or so after the 4.8 million is repaid to the fund?"

Sinclair shrugged. "Just make sure Fred Fuller gets caught with at least a million so people will think he acted alone and stashed the rest of the money somewhere. All we want is the money you embezzled returned and Fred to take the fall for the bank robbery. You can keep the other million or give it to the Salvation Army, whatever."

Harvey nodded. "Okay. Let me think about this scenario. It might have possibilities."

Sinclair stood up. "Good. This problem needs to go away. If it doesn't and the Congressman has to cover this loss himself, don't think that will be the end of it. He's not going to let you walk away unscathed. Think about what is going to happen to you. You have an MBA, do the math."

Sinclair turned and stormed out of Harvey's office. Harvey stood up and began pacing. Do the math? What the hell does that mean? They want me to rob my own bank. Are they crazy? Do the math? What the—? Then it hit him. Oh my God! They're gonna kill me if I don't pull this off!

Chapter 13

The Second Temptation

Two weeks later

Between Maria, the upcoming elections and his heavy involvement with the Young Republicans, Fred was able to keep his mind off Candy. Although he would see her briefly every week day, he tried to avoid any lengthy encounters that might lead to trouble. They had become good friends and engaged in many interesting conversations, but Fred knew better than to even suggest seeing her outside of the bank. He simply didn't trust himself around her. On this particular night in mid-October, he was anxious to get home to study. When he pulled into the bank parking lot at 6:30 p.m., it surprised him slightly that Sam wasn't there. The weather had been good, and he expected Sam to be on time. When he wasn't there, Fred surmised that either Sam had experienced car trouble or one of his banks was late. He wondered if he should go in and get the bags now or just wait for Sam. Then he noticed a note taped to the front door of the bank. Intrigued by the note he got out of the car.

As he walked toward the bank's front door, he noticed a policeman driving by in his squad car giving him a hard look. He assumed the police knew messengers went in and out of the bank all the time and didn't pay much attention to them. Nevertheless, a chill darted down his spine as he watched the cop disappear over the hilltop.

Turning back to the note, he removed it from the window, unfolded it and read the message. "Sam called. Will be 20 minutes late. Harvey."

Fred considered what he should do. Since he had time to kill he decided to go inside and wait where it was warm. After pulling out his ring of keys, he fumbled around to find the right one. Successfully identifying it, he slid it in the key hole and opened the glass door. Not being in a great hurry he wandered around the lobby for a minute and sat down on a large beige sofa. It was dark with but one small light dimly illuminating the entire lobby area. Scanning the room, he noticed the bags on the floor near the tellers' windows. He glanced outside to make sure Sam hadn't arrived, then looked over at the plush office of the bank President and decided to sit in his chair. The President's office was quite lavish, and as Fred leaned back and relaxed, he wondered what it would be like to be in such a position of power and prestige. Not so bad, but how many bank Presidents could you name?

Startled by a scuffling noise, Fred vaulted out of the chair, walked warily into the lobby, and looked around. He didn't see the source of the noise, but he knew somebody must be in the bank. He glanced outside again to be sure Sam's car wasn't there yet and then scanned the bank lobby once more. Everything seemed normal to him until, to his shock and dismay, he noticed the bank vault. It was open again!

For several moments, he stood there staring at the open vault in a state of disbelief. An eerie feeling overcame him as his mind contemplated the opportunity the open vault offered him.

If I took the money I could close the vault, and I'd have until Monday to get away. Maria won't leave the country with me, but Candy might. Six million dollars is a lot of money, but being a fugitive for the rest of my life would suck. Where would I go? Mexico? Canada? They both could extradite me if they found me. I'd eventually have to go to Argentina or one of the other safe havens for American fugitives.

A heavy dose of guilt washed over Fred just thinking about stealing the six million dollars he suspected was in the vault. He turned away from the vault a moment and looked outside anxiously for any sign of Sam. The parking lot was quiet.

Fred sighed and gave his head a quick shake, trying to break himself out of the greedy, foolish trance he'd fallen into. He took another deep breath and gathered his strength. As much as he'd like to have the money, he knew it wasn't an option. It would be foolish and doomed to failure. It was time to call Sinclair.

He walked over to the phone and picked it up, but he couldn't dial the number. He realized if he reported the vault open again, Hamlin would get fired. Fred felt sorry for Hamlin since the poor guy had already lost his family. It would be very easy for Fred to just go over and close the vault for him. Then nobody would ever know it had been left open again. If anyone needed a break, it was Harvey Hamlin, Fred figured.

Fred tried to think if there was any danger to him in closing the vault. Hamlin had shown him how to do it. He couldn't think of anything rational, so he decided to go ahead and do it. It would be the honorable thing to do. After checking the front door again to be sure Sam hadn't arrived, he made his way slowly over to the vault and peered inside. Unfortunately, it was dark, so he couldn't see a thing inside. Being unfamiliar with the vault, he didn't want to make a mistake and set off some kind of alarm.

He went into the kitchen and searched all the drawers for a flashlight or a match. Finding none, he remembered a flashlight was standard equipment for bank messengers and there would be one in his glove compartment. He walked quickly to the front door, opened it, and headed for his car. Suddenly, two headlights blinded him. Instinctively, Fred lifted his arm to shield his eyes from the glare. Startled by the light, he immediately panicked, fearing the cop who'd been cruising the neighborhood had come over to see why he was loitering around the bank. What am I going to tell him? The door opened slowly as Fred stood paralyzed with fear.

Then a voice said, "Fred, what in the devil are you doing running across the parking lot? I nearly ran you down."

Fred let out his breath. "Sam? It's you. You startled me."

"Who did you think it was going to be, Bigfoot?" Sam laughed.

"No, I was expecting you. I just didn't see you coming."

"Hey, I didn't see you lock the door when you came out."

"I didn't. I came to get a flashlight. Something's wrong with the night lamp, so it's really dark in there."

Fred knew he couldn't tell Sam that Harvey had left the vault open again. He wouldn't be at all sympathetic and would likely call Sinclair himself. Plus, Fred would have had to explain why he hadn't already called him.

"Hmm. I thought maybe they left that there vault open again and you were loadin' up on some cash."

"Yeah, I wish," Fred laughed shakily. "Hey, how come you're so late?"

"Them rascals up at Big Bear don't know how to count. Two

of them tellers were out of balance for nearly thirty minutes, if you can believe that." Sam walked around to the trunk of his car and opened it.

"Yeah, I don't think they hire tellers for brain power," Fred noted.

"No, them bankers are pretty smart. They get them good-looking chicks to sit there behind the counter and smile pretty at all them young executives who control all them corporate dollars."

"You think so?"

Sam reached into the trunk of his car, pulled out the Arrowhead and Big Bear bags, and handed them to Fred. "Sure thing. Haven't you ever noticed that the nicest little building in every town you'll ever travel to is a bank? And if you step inside, you'll find the prettiest women in the entire town sittin' there, ready to serve. Sure enough, women like to be around money, I gaur—an—tee."

"I guess you're right," Fred said. "That hadn't ever occurred to me before."

"Well, you best be getting out of here. Ol' Jim's going to be pretty damn anxious for you to finish your run with all them hot women waitin' for him."

"You're right. I better get my flashlight and retrieve those bags."

"Be careful. Don't trip over anything."

"I will. . . . be careful, I mean. See ya later."

"Adios." Sam jumped in his car and drove off.

After opening the trunk, Fred threw in the two bags without paying any attention to the bags that were already in his trunk and then went to the glove compartment to get the flashlight. Walking quickly back into the bank he locked the door behind him, then turned to peer into the darkness. Breathing heavily, he walked over to the vault and shone the light on it. It seemed like a pretty simple task to push the vault closed and then turn the big wheel. He'd seen Hamlin do it when he was drunk for godsakes, but he was still a little afraid he might do something wrong and an alarm would go off. Finally, he gathered his courage and pushed the heavy door closed. He held his breath as he spun the big wheel and heard the mechanism engage. Fortunately, nothing happened. He took a deep breath and exhaled slowly.

Fred looked at his watch and saw it was nine fifteen. He was thirty minutes late, so he had to get out of there immediately. He grabbed the bags and moved them near the front door, unlocked it, and then put the bags outside. After locking the front door again, he carried the bags to the car and put them in the trunk. As he was closing the trunk, he noticed something was wrong. He had an extra bag. It looked like one of the bank's bags, but it was much bulkier than usual, and it wasn't locked. He counted the bags in the trunk, and sure enough, he had one extra. Slowly, he untied the stray bag, opened it, and gasped. It was full of stacks of hundred-dollar bills!

A wave of fear washed over him as he tried to figure out what was happening. As he was reeling from the shock of finding a bagful of money, he noticed the police car he'd seen earlier drive by. The officer gave him another hard look. Fear gripped him like a vice. He quickly closed the trunk, got in the Impala, and cautiously drove toward the parking lot exit. When he got to the street, he looked back, relieved to see the cop was driving away. After he'd driven a few blocks, he pulled into a Jack-in-the-Box and parked between two cars where he could be inconspicuous. He needed time to think, and there was nothing suspicious about going out for a burger after dark.

How did a bag of money get in my car? Somebody is obviously trying to set me up! Whoever it is, they must have already robbed the bank. That's why the bank vault was open. If I hadn't already closed it, I could have gone back and put the bag of money back. Damn it! They left me some of the money, so the FBI would think I was the bank robber! Shit! What do I do now? If I call Sinclair and tell him the truth, what are the chances he'd believe me?

Fred began to shake. His stomach was twisting into knots, and he felt like throwing up. Think! Don't panic! There has to be a way out of this. Maybe I should just hide the money and act like nothing happened. The FBI won't have any evidence against me if they can't find the money.

Fred started the car and drove back to the freeway. He was now a full hour late. As he drove back to LA, he wondered how he'd explain his tardiness. The logical thing would be to fake some kind of car trouble. Let's see. . . . I could pull out a spark plug wire and then call AAA, but what if they sent someone from the motor pool out to get me? How would I get rid of the money? What if I ran out of gas? No. . . . they wouldn't buy that since the car was filled up before I left. Then, the perfect solution came to him.

Fred looked in his rearview mirror and saw that the road was clear behind him. He pulled over on the shoulder of the freeway, walked behind the Impala, and pulled out his pocket knife. Kneeling down, he opened the hole punch and then stuck it firmly into the tread of the tire. Instantaneously, one corner of the car began to sink as air rapidly escaped from the tire.

Immediately, he pulled out the spare tire and began to change it. Luckily, he had changed his own tires many times and was pretty good at it. When the task was complete, he threw the deflated tire in the trunk and sped off. At the next gas station, he stopped to call Jim.

"Hello, motor pool," Jim said.

"Jim, this is Fuller."

"Where the Dickens are you, Fred?"

"I got a flat tire."

"Oh, what bloody rotten luck. Have you fixed it?"

"I had a bitch of a time, but it's fixed now."

"Where are you?"

"Just outside of Pomona. I should be back there about nine forty-five or so."

"Okay. I'll tell Sinclair. He's been asking about you."

"Okay. See you in a few minutes."

Jim seemed to have bought his story pretty much, so now all Fred figured he had to do was get rid of the money before he checked into the motor pool. As he drove into downtown LA, he wondered who had actually robbed the bank. He thought it had to be Hamlin, but he had no way of confirming that suspicion.

Fred couldn't believe he'd been dragged into the robber's scheme, whoever he was. There had to be a way out of it, but he couldn't think of what it could possibly be. No matter what he said or did, everyone would presume he'd been in on the heist because he'd been at the bank and now was in possession a bagful of money.

I'm screwed! If I get rid of the money and deny I ever had it, someone might see me ditch it and call the police when they discover what it is. That would be my luck. What's going to happen Monday when they open the vault? Will I be a suspect? Ha! The number one suspect, surely. Maybe I should make a run for it during the night? I could be in Mexico or Canada long before Monday morning, but what about Maria? She said she wouldn't leave the country, even to be with me.

Suddenly, Fred looked up and saw he was almost past his exit. He made a hard right, his tires screeching, and he narrowly missed the yellow protective barrels in front of the dividing wall. "Don't be stupid," he mumbled to himself. "All I need now is to get into an accident with a bagful of stolen money in my trunk!"

As he neared the motor pool, he took a detour to where his car was parked. It was two blocks away, and he was sure no one would be there at this hour. He pulled up next to the maroon Falcon, jumped out, and took a look around. A car was driving by, so he waited until it passed before transferring the bag. When the street was clear, he made the switch. The bag of money seemed very heavy. He wondered how much money was in it as he closed both trunks. Then he drove over to the motor pool.

As he pulled in the driveway, he noticed Jake had just pulled up to the gas pump too. He was surprised to see him in the motor pool at this late hour, so he decided to ask him what had happened.

"Sinclair put you back on a route, I see?" Fred noted.

"It looks that way, doesn't it?" Jake replied coldly.

"I didn't know there were any routes that came in as late as mine."

"Well, you don't know a lot of things, Fuller."

"I guess there's no chance you'll ever get that chip off your shoulder so we can be friends."

"There isn't a chip on my shoulder, Fuller. I just don't like you."

"Well, if you ever figure out why, let me know. I'd be interested."

Before Jake could launch another verbal grenade, Jim walked out from Sinclair's office and said, "Hey, you made it?"

"Yeah, finally."

"Unload your cargo and bring me your car."

"Okay."

Fred proceeded to unload the bags on the loading dock and then drove back over to the gas pumps. Jim took his keys and opened the trunk. As he examined the tire, Fred held his breath.

"Looks like you ran over a nail. I'll send it to the garage in the morning to be fixed."

"Okay. Sorry I kept you so late. See you Monday."

"Oh, before you go, Sinclair wants to see you."

"Sinclair?" Fred said soberly.

"Yeah. He said to come by and see him before you left."

"Oh, okay."

After Fred picked his heart up out of his shoes, he reluctantly wandered over to Sinclair's office. Sinclair was sitting at his desk filling out a report when Fred walked in. "Sir, you wanted to see me?"

"Yes, Fuller. You had a rough night, I see."

"Yes, sir. I kinda did."

"Well, I am glad you know how to change a tire. Some of these drivers don't, you know."

"Really? Well, I've had to change my own tires plenty of times, so this was no big deal."

"Oh, thanks for calling us and telling us you were going to be late. We were worried about you, and it was good to hear from you. You've got a lot of common sense for a kid your age."

"Thank you, sir."

"Okay. Have a good weekend."

"Yes, sir. See you Monday."

Feeling relieved, Fred turned to leave when Sinclair started speaking again. "Oh, Fuller, you didn't happen to see Harvey Hamlin at the bank, did you?"

Fred hesitated a second, trying to retain his composure. Then, he turned around slowly and gave Sinclair a blank look. "Hamlin? The cashier at San Bernardino?" he asked innocently.

"Yes, you've met him."

"Right. No, sir. The bank was deserted when I got there. As a matter of fact, it was pitch black. I had to use my flashlight to find the bags."

"Oh really?"

"Yeah. The night lamp was out."

Sinclair gave him a pensive look. "Gee, that's strange. You'd think somebody over there would notice something like that and take the time to change a light bulb."

Fred shrugged. "You'd think. . . . So, why did you ask if I saw Hamlin?"

"Oh, his ex-wife called looking for him. Apparently, he didn't come home from work. He was probably out at some bar somewhere."

Fred shrugged. "Did you say ex-wife?"

"Uh huh."

"Huh. He told me his family just left him."

"No. The divorce was over a year ago."

"Really? Well, I must have misunderstood him."

Sinclair gave Fred a hard look that made him feel uneasy. Fred wondered what he was thinking. Then abruptly Sinclair said, "Okay, that's all, Fuller. Goodnight."

"Thank you, sir. Goodnight."

Fred walked quickly to his car, opened the door, and fell into his seat. Now what? He looked at his watch and saw it was 10:00 p.m. Where should I stash this money? My apartment is out of the question, and I obviously can't leave it in my car. What about Ventura at my parents' house? No, if the FBI came after me, they might search all of those places. Where can I put the money so no one could ever find it, yet it would be kept safe for later retrieval? What about a safety deposit box? Wouldn't that be ironic, the bank's money in the bank? No, that wouldn't work because there would be a record of me depositing the money into the safety deposit box the day after the robbery. That wouldn't be too cleaver.

There has to be a better place. What about if I bury it somewhere. I could get a trunk, line it with plastic, and bury it deep beneath the earth in some secluded place. Where is a good secluded place? Perhaps up in the mountains? Hmm. . . . no, better yet, the desert. There would be less chance the money would decay in a dry environment. But where in the desert?

Suddenly, he remembered Devil's Canyon where he'd been bitten by the snake. That's the place! Fred hadn't been there for six or seven years, but he knew it would be the perfect hiding place. No one will ever find the money at the Devil's Canyon Mining Camp, if I can just remember how to get there.

He knew Devil's Canyon was about four hours from LA, so he had to get going. Suddenly a car turned onto the street about a block away. It traveled slowly like it was searching for something. Fred wondered if it was the police. Of course, the assholes who set me up probably called the cops and told them I'd robbed the bank. He started the engine and took off like a bat out of hell toward the on-ramp to the freeway. The car sped up and gave chase.

Traffic was light at this time of night, so he made good time. He looked in his rear-view mirror and saw the car was still following him. In fact, he was only a few car links behind. If it was a cop he would have already pulled me over. It must be one of the people who set me up. They just want to keep tabs on me, I guess.

Fred has seen many chase scenes on TV so he knew exactly how to lose the asshole who was following him. There was an exit ahead that he knew well because he'd gotten off there many times to get snacks. He moved over to the left lane and floored it until he was going about 80 mph. The car behind changed lanes and accelerated to keep pace. Fred stayed in the left lane and just as he was almost parallel to the exit ramp her swerved violently across three lanes and onto the exit ramp.

Angry motorists honked their horns, tires screeched and Fred was jolted up and down violently. He feared he was going to crash but somehow, he managed to keep all four wheels on the pavement. The car that had been following him tried the same maneuver but failed miserably as cars to his right blocked his path to the exit ramp. When the car finally made it to the shoulder a fence prevented it from exiting the freeway.

Fred parked behind the convenience store and waited to make sure the car following him didn't find a way off the freeway. He knew the next off ramp was two miles down the road and there was no direct way back to where he was, so he felt fairly safe. As he was sitting there, it occurred to him that Maria would be worried about him, so he decided he had better call her. He got out of his car and went inside to a pay phone.

"Hello?" Maria answered.

"Baby doll, how are you?"

"Fred, what happened to you?"

"Nothing. I got a flat tire and didn't get back to the bank until late."

"Oh no! Are you alright?"

"Of course, I'm alright. I know how to change a tire."

"I was so worried about you."

"Nothing to worry about, but I am kind of tired."

"Maybe you should go home and go to bed."

"Yeah, you're probably right."

"Okay. Go home and go to bed and sleep late. I won't call you before eleven."

"Okay," Fred said, yawning.

"Goodbye. I love you."

"I love you too."

Luckily, Steve was on a road trip with the UCLA Band, so Fred didn't have to worry about checking in with him. After he got back into the car, he opened the glove compartment and took out a map of California. He mapped out the route to Devil's Canyon in his mind and started the car. He didn't dare get back on the freeway right away, so he took several surface streets that paralleled the freeway for a long time until he felt it was safe to get back on it and continue his journey.

For the first time that evening, he began to relax as he got out onto the open road. Maybe everything will work out. After a while it occurred to him that he hadn't eaten anything since lunch. Maybe I should call Candy and see if she's hungry since I'll be going right by her place. Wouldn't she be surprised? Maybe she'd like to go to Argentina for a bite to eat.

He laughed. The idea of seeing Candy excited him. He knew he should be feeling guilty about it, but he wasn't. If he was destined to be a bank robber, maybe Candy would be a more appropriate companion, he rationalized. He certainly didn't want to drag Maria into the quicksand he had fallen into. He couldn't do that to her.

When he got to Palm Springs, he stopped at a gas station and looked up Candy's phone number. He dialed and waited.

"Hello?" Candy said.

"Candy, this is Fred."

"Fred?"

"Yeah, Fred Fuller."

"Oh, Fred, what's going on?"

"I am in town and thought maybe you would like to get something to eat. I haven't eaten since lunch, and I hate to eat alone."

"Well, I already had dinner, but I would certainly be happy to keep you company."

"Would you? That's great. Where do you live?"

"Why don't I meet you somewhere?"

"Okay. There's a Denny's right off the freeway. Would that be okay?"

"Sure. I'll be there in ten minutes."

"Okay. Bye."

"Bye."

Now that they were actually going to meet outside the bank, Fred began to wonder what he was going to say to her. What will my excuse be for wanting to see her? Where will I tell her I was going? I could tell her I was on my way to bury a bag of money in a mining camp in the middle of the Mojave Desert. That would certainly get her attention, but that would be a little risky at this stage of the game.

Without resolving his dilemma, Fred jumped into his car and headed for Denny's. When he arrived, he got a booth and waited.

After about fifteen minutes, Candy arrived. She was wearing a white halter top, red shorts, and white tennis shoes. When she spotted him, she smiled brightly and walked briskly to his table.

"Hi, Fred."

"Hi, Candy."

"Gee, it was sure a surprise to get a call from you tonight."

"I'm sorry I called you so late, but I was passing through town and thought of you."

"Well, it's about time you thought of me. I was beginning to think you didn't like me."

"No way! I think you're great. You just blew my mind with that incredible proposition you made."

"Well, perhaps I was a little premature in hitting you with such a radical idea."

"I was very flattered that you would consider such a relationship with me, but I didn't know how to deal with the gravity of the proposal."

"I'm sorry. It must have really been a shock to you since we hardly knew each other."

"How could you know whether I could deliver my end of the bargain anyway? Getting into law school isn't easy. I may not even be accepted to law school. If I am, I still have to graduate and pass the bar. Then I have to find a job and I am not necessarily going to get rich overnight."

"That didn't concern me. You have an aura of success about you. Besides, even if you didn't get rich, I kind of like you, so our time together wouldn't have been a total loss."

"Why is it that the women in my life are so sure of themselves?"

"What do you mean?"

"Maria told her mother she was going to marry me after our first date."

Candy smiled. "You see what an effect you have on women."

The waitress came over and asked them what they would like. Fred ordered a cheeseburger and fries, and Candy ordered a banana split.

"So, what are you doing in Palm Springs tonight?"

"Well, I'm going to play golf with a friend in the morning," he lied.

"I didn't know you were a golfer."

"I'm not very good at it, but it's fun to play."

"So, does your stopping tonight mean you're considering my proposal?"

"Perhaps," Fred said cautiously. "If you are really serious about it. I wasn't sure if you were just teasing me or not. I'm not really good at reading women."

She laughed. "I'm not teasing you. I'm dead serious. I'm a pragmatist. It would be a good way for both of us to get what we want."

Fred gave her a hard look. "Then I guess we need to start getting to know each other better."

Candy smiled at Fred and began to laugh. "You little devil. I knew you'd come around."

"You knew I would?" Fred questioned. "How is that?"

"I just did."

Fred shook his head. "You're amazing. I'd sure like to know what makes you tick."

"Shall we go to my place so you can examine me more closely?"

Glancing at his watch, he saw it was ten minutes to twelve. "Actually, it's pretty late now. I've got an early tee time. Can I get a rain check for Sunday night?"

"I suppose so," Candy said, "but you sure you don't want to spend the night with me now? You could leave early in the morning and still make your tee time."

"That is very tempting, but I probably would have trouble getting up in the morning after a night with you."

She smiled wryly. "Well, that's true. So, what time on Sunday can I expect you?"

"How about four or five o'clock? We can spend the evening together. I'll take you to any restaurant you want."

"Any restaurant? It's dangerous to give a woman carte blanc, Freddy boy."

"I like to live dangerously. As a matter of fact, my life is becoming more perilous each day."

"It's fun, though, isn't it?" she said giggling.

"I don't know. I haven't made up my mind yet."

She winked at him. "Don't worry. You're going to love it."

"I'm sure I will. . . . But, I should go now."

They both got up and walked outside to Candy's car. Before she got in, Fred put his arms around her, and they kissed for the first time. It was a pleasant kiss, long and sensual. When it was over, Candy sighed and said, "Not bad for a Boy Scout."

Candy drove off and Fred got back in the Falcon to finish his journey. He headed east out of town into the Mojave Desert. He had pinpointed pretty much where he thought Devil's Canyon was located, but he was not sure exactly. It was going to take a little searching to find it.

At 3:00 a.m. he got to Hackberry State Park. Then he remembered the road was just three miles ahead. It was a dirt road, and the night was very dark. He put his headlights on high beam and proceeded down the road. After about thirty minutes, he began to wonder if he was on the right road. To him, all the little dirt roads out in the desert looked alike. Fortunately, he had inherited his father's sense of direction. It was amazing, but once he had traveled to any particular place, he could almost always find his way back, even years later.

After a while, he began to recognize the distinct landscape of Devil's Canyon. It was a desolate place, fifty miles from the nearest civilization, the perfect hiding place for his newly acquired stash. Finally, he passed the broken sign welcoming visitors to Devil's Canyon Mining Camp.

He drove through town toward the assayer's office, parked near the front door, and got out. After retrieving his flashlight from the glove compartment, he walked over to the door and tried the handle. It wouldn't budge. He remembered from his first visit, however, that a swift kick would open the door. Sure enough, it did.

Once inside, he shone his light all around. The laboratory looked like it hadn't been touched since he'd been there many years earlier. Now, where would be the best place to leave the money? I could put it in one of the barrels, but if someone visited the lab, they might take the barrel as a souvenir. No, the best place would be under the floor.

He went to his car and got a large screwdriver and a hammer out of the tool box. After prying up three or four slats, he placed the bag in the crawl space under the floor. The bag was made of a tough plastic material, so he was confident the money would be well preserved. As he started to put the bag in its place, he realized he didn't even know how much money it contained, so he pulled it back out and dumped it on the floor. He counted it quickly: eighty-five stacks of hundreds, each containing $10,000; twenty-one stacks of fifties, each containing $5,000; and thirty stacks of twenties, each containing $2,000—for a grand total of $1,115,000. He stared at the money for several minutes and then shook his head. He'd always thought someday he'd be a millionaire, but he never dreamed this would be the way it would happen.

He deposited all of the money back in the bag except for one stack of twenties and a stack of fifties, which he took for expense money. From watching Perry Mason mysteries on TV he knew he couldn't be spending money on luxury items or it would arouse suspicion. He would have to wait until he got out of law school, and then he could spend the money more readily. *Assuming I make it to law school and don't end up rotting in prison.*

Looking at his watch he saw that it was 5:00 a.m. He needed to get out of there immediately, so he secured the bag under the floor and nailed the slats back securely. Before leaving, he marked one of the slats with three notches to make it easy for him to find the money when he returned later to retrieve it.

After burying the money, he drove straight home to Santa Monica. At 9:11 a.m. he walked in the door of his apartment, went directly to his bedroom, and crashed.

At precisely 11:00 a.m. Maria called. "Hi, honey. How did you sleep?"

"Like a log," he replied sleepily.

"How do you feel?"

"I am still pretty tired. I think I'll sleep a few more hours."

"Okay, but don't forget we've got tickets for the football game this evening."

Suddenly, he became alert. He loved college football. "Oh, that's right! The game's tonight. We're playing USC. I'll pick you up at five, okay?"

"Alright. Go back to bed."

"Thanks. Goodnight."

Maria didn't care much about football, but she tolerated it for Fred's benefit. In talking to Maria, he had momentarily forgotten the events of the previous day. Although it had only been a few hours since he'd returned home from the desert, it all seemed a bit fuzzy to him. Was stashing a million dollars in the desert just a dream? He hoped it had just been a dream. Then he remembered the expense money. He climbed out of bed and walked over to the chair where he had thrown his coat. Slowly, he stuck his hand in one of the pockets. It was empty. He felt a glimmer of hope as he gently stuck his hand in the other pocket. The hope faded quickly, though, when he felt two neatly wrapped packets of cash. He pulled them out and stared at them, still having trouble getting his head around the reality that he was a now an unwitting bank robber—and a millionaire.

Chapter 14

Taking the Plunge

By four o'clock, Fred was awake and fully recovered from the fatigue of the previous day. As he started to move around, he tried to forget that yesterday had ever happened. He had taken a class in psychology and learned that the mind was very good at repressing unpleasant thoughts. If he could put the whole affair totally out of his mind, then he wouldn't be likely to do anything unusual that might attract attention. He knew it was a pretty sure bet that the FBI would consider him a suspect and would be watching him, and he needed to try to act normal.

His first concern was what to do with the $7,000 he had taken as petty cash to spend on expenses. If he were found with it, he could be linked to the robbery. In retrospect, he wished he hadn't taken it, as it seemed it was going to be difficult to hide. He couldn't leave it in his apartment or his car for fear that they might be searched. It didn't seem like all that much money, so he thought about just putting it in his bank account, but then he might have to explain where he got it. After pondering different ideas, the solution finally came to him. He would rent a private mailbox, buy money orders with the $7,000, and then mail them to the box. When he needed money, he would just go pick up what money orders he needed and cash them. Since the box had a combination lock, he had no key and thus nothing to connect him to the box full of money orders.

With that problem worked out, when it came time to pick up Maria for the game, he was feeling pretty good. First, however, since he was now a millionaire and feeling really guilty about his conversation with Candy the previous evening, he stopped at a jewelry store and bought Maria a present.

When he got to her dorm, she wasn't anywhere to be found, so he went inside and used the house phone to call her room. She answered and told him she'd be right down.

The dorm was laid out like a resort hotel. There was a front desk, a large lobby area, recreation room, cafeteria, and elevators to all of the rooms. The dorm had two wings: one for the women and one for the men. There was no mingling of the sexes allowed, and curfew on weekdays was midnight and 2:00 a.m. on weekends.

Fred sat down on one of the sofas in the lobby and began reading a magazine. There was a clear view to the elevators from where he was sitting, so he wasn't worried about missing her. After a few minutes, one of elevators opened, and Maria hurriedly walked out. She was wearing yellow shorts, sneakers, and a blue UCLA t-shirt. "Hi, Fred. Sorry I'm late, but I couldn't get my hair to cooperate."

Maria had shoulder-length, dark brown hair which she wore in a variety of styles. Today, it was in a ponytail, which was Fred's favorite. "Your hair looks great," he informed her.

"Thank you. You're a good liar."

"I'm not lying. You know I love it this way."

Maria smiled as they grabbed each other's hand and starting walking toward the front door.

"Where do you want to go eat?" Fred asked.

"I don't know. What do you feel like?"

"It doesn't matter. You pick."

"Okay. I feel like pizza."

"Okay. How about Shakeys?"

"Let's go."

They jumped in his car and got on Santa Monica Boulevard until they reached Shakeys and went in. The waitress took them to a large red booth, and they slid in close to each other as they always did. They ordered a large sausage pizza and drinks. Fred was anxious to see Maria's reaction to his little gift, so he pulled out a black velvet box and handed it to her.

"What is this?"

"Well, open it and you'll find out."

She opened the box, and her eyes lit up as she gazed at it. "Oh, a necklace! It's so beautiful." She smiled at him and then frowned. "You must have paid a fortune for this!"

"Do you like it?"

"I love it. Thank you," she said as she studied the necklace more closely. "Are those real diamonds?"

"Well, they're diamond chips."

"Gee, Fred, how could you afford this? It's not even my

birthday."

"Well, you deserve it. You've been so good to me."

Maria looked at him with a sexy smile, put her hand on his leg, and then leaned over and gave him a tender kiss.

"You're so sweet, Fred. I love you."

With those words, Fred suddenly felt sick. What had he done? How could he ever leave Maria if he had to escape to Argentina? Tears began to well in his eyes, and he fought to hide the emotions he was feeling.

Maria must have sensed his anguish. "What's wrong, Fred?"

"Nothing. I'm just so glad you liked your present. Just remember, no matter what happens to us, I love you."

Maria frowned again. "What's that supposed to mean? Is something going to happen to us?"

"Nothing, nothing . . . but you know, either one of us could get run over by a bus tomorrow. Life is unpredictable."

She gave him a skeptical look. "You've never been a pessimist, Fred. What's got into you?"

"Nothing. Forget it," he said, wishing he'd never brought up the subject. She shrugged and looked away.

When they'd finished eating their pizza, he paid the bill and they left. On the way to the football game the following day's agenda came up.

"What are we going to do tomorrow, Fred?" Maria asked.

"Oh, tomorrow? Well, I suppose I better work on my government paper since it's due next week. We can go to church in the morning, but then I've got to hit the typewriter."

It was a lie, but he couldn't think of anything better to excuse his absence while he was visiting Candy. He felt very guilty lying to Maria, but he had convinced himself it didn't make much difference anymore since he was now a felon. It was only a matter of time before Maria would find out he'd been involved in a bank robbery, and then it would be over between them.

"This is the first gift you've given me just because you love me," Maria said. "I'm so happy, Fred."

Fred's heart sank again as he was wrenched by another dose of guilt. "I'm glad," he said meekly. How could this have happened?

The next morning, they went to mass at St. Monica's Cathedral on Wilshire Boulevard. They had driven by it several times and were awed by its magnificence. They decided to go to mass there so they could see the interior. They imagined it must be something to behold, and they were not disappointed. When they went inside, Fred suddenly felt uncomfortable sitting in the house of God, knowing that he had just violated one of the Ten Commandments and committed a mortal sin.

A million thoughts crossed his mind. Why didn't I just call Sinclair when I found the vault open? Why did I have to be Mr. Nice Guy and close it? Will Sinclair and the FBI believe what really happened? They might have until they searched my car and found a million dollars in the trunk. Maybe I've seen too many movies where innocent men were bullied into phony confessions by the police. I could just see myself in the interrogation room with a couple of special agents in my face. I would be no match for them.

Feeling very depressed, Fred thought of going to confession and getting advice from a priest, but he had never had much faith in the priest-penitent confidence. With most priests, he would probably be safe, but not all priests were true to their vows, and he wasn't about to take any chances. It was best if he kept the whole thing to himself. He knew, of course, that Steve and Randy would never betray him, but they couldn't be protected from the law, and he didn't want them getting hurt.

After mass, Maria and he had lunch at McDonalds on Western Avenue, and then he took her back to her dorm. He told her he was going to spend the rest of the day in the library working on his term paper. She said she had homework, too, and asked him to call her later. It felt horrible lying to her. He knew he was going to have to end their relationship very soon for Maria's sake, but he dreaded the thought.

Once he got on the open road, his thoughts turned to Candy. Where is our relationship going? Will she really wait around for six years for me to finish my education? That's kind of hard to believe. Could it be that she really does love me and the whole mistress routine is just a way to get my attention? Is there an ordinary woman under that cool, calculating façade? Maybe I should call her bluff and find out.

At about 3:00 p.m., Fred entered the city limits of Palm Springs, California. He called Candy from the same phone booth that he had called her from before. She gave him directions to her apartment, and he was at her front door within ten minutes. He knocked at the door with great anticipation, and she opened it with no less enthusiasm.

She smiled brightly. "So, you came. I wasn't sure you would."

He smiled back at her eagerly. "I told you I would."

They embraced and kissed briefly. Then she led him to a white leather sofa, where they sat down. The apartment was small but nicely furnished. A gray cat strolled by and gave Fred a hard look.

Candy noticed the cat's look and said, "She's jealous. That's why I usually don't bring men to my apartment."

"Really? She wants you all to herself, huh?"

"Of course."

"Well, I can't say I blame her."

Candy smiled approvingly, then gave him a once-over. "Well, you look much better than you did Friday night."

"What do you mean?" He asked, a little offended.

"You seemed kind of nervous and very tired. You must have had a really bad day."

"Was it that obvious?"

"It was pretty noticeable."

"Well, I'm sorry. I've gotten a lot of sleep since then, so I'm feeling a much better."

"Good. So, what do you want to do the rest of the day?"

"Just hang out. It occurred to me on the way over here that I don't really know much about you—like what kind of things you like to do for fun."

She shrugged. "I don't know."

"Well, do you like going to the movies?

"Yes."

"That's good. I am movie freak myself. How about football? Do you like football?"

Her eyes lit up. "Who doesn't?"

"Then you're a UCLA fan?"

"Of course!"

"So, what did you think about the game last night?"

"Totally awesome. I wish I'd have been there."

"I was, actually," he bragged, careful not to mention that Maria had accompanied him.

"Wow! We're going to get along great."

"Now it's my turn," Candy stated. "Do you like to read?"

"Not particularly. It reminds me too much of school."

"Well, I love to read, but that's okay."

"Do you play tennis?"

"Sure do. I was on my high school tennis team," he advised her proudly.

"I'm on the junior college team," she replied.

"Hmm. Maybe we shouldn't play tennis then."

Candy laughed. "I think we should. It will be a distinct pleasure to beat you."

"You may not want to beat me. I am a sore loser."

"I don't believe that."

"What about golf?" he asked.

"Never played it."

"Well, I'll teach you sometime. I'm not very good at it, but it's nice to be outdoors, and there are a lot of beautiful golf courses around the country."

"What about eating?" she asked jokingly.

"Yeah, I kind of like to eat.

"Good, because I am hungry. Oh, and I did pick out an excellent restaurant as you requested—very expensive."

"Excellent. I'm a rich man. Let's go. You can give me directions on the way."

She agreed and locked up the apartment while he went for the car. They drove about fifteen minutes before arriving downtown. Candy pointed to a red building with a green roof. Its exterior was ornately trimmed in black and gold. "There it is, the Golden Dragon Restaurant," she said. "It has the best Chinese food in town."

Fred pulled the car into the parking lot, and they went inside. The interior of the restaurant was very ornate and quite beautiful. The restaurant was not crowded, as it was still early. A young Chinese girl in her native garb greeted them and seated them in a quiet little table in a secluded part of the restaurant.

"There's another thing we have in common. We both like Chinese food," Fred observed.

"I knew from the very first time I saw you that we would be perfect together," Candy admitted.

"How could you know that?"

"Women's intuition."

"Well, since you've got this whole thing worked out, I've got a couple of questions for you."

"Okay, I'm listening," she said with curiosity in her eyes.

"Let's say I took you up on your proposition. What do you plan to do for the next six years while I'm getting my law license?"

"I still have to finish college and get some acting experience. You just can't become a credible actress overnight. It would be nice if I didn't have to work, but I guess that's not in the cards."

"Why don't you find someone who already has money so you can quit work right away and get on with your life's ambition?"

"I don't want just any man to take care of me. I want someone special. I've been searching for just the right person for a long time. When you walked into the bank that first time and told me you were going to be a lawyer, I knew that person was you."

"Come on! How could you possibly know that from just seeing me for the first time?"

"I don't know, and I can't explain it. I just knew."

"Do you believe in fate?" he asked.

"Yes."

"I never did until Friday."

"What happened Friday?"

"Friday, I realized you and I were meant to be together."

"See, I'm much more perceptive than you. It took you six weeks to figure out what I knew the first day."

"You are definitely amazing," Fred agreed.

She gave him a seductive smile. "You haven't seen anything yet."

"Is that a promise?"

"Definitely," she said with a wry smile.

The waitress finally showed up with some appetizers and hot tea. While Candy was digging into the pu pu platter, Fred was pondering whether to take the plunge with her or not. It really seemed inevitable, and it certainly appeared they were brought together by fate. Why resist?

He gathered all his courage, pushed his trepidation aside, and finally dove in. "Well, I've got some good news for you."

She looked up at him curiously. "What's that?"

"About five or six years ago, my Aunt Virginia came to live with us. She was estranged from her husband for some twenty years and had worked as a secretary for all that time. She and I got along really well. We played tennis and cards together and were good friends. Unfortunately, all those lonely nights got to her, and she began to have mental problems. My mom didn't want her to have to go to the funny farm, so she came to live with us."

"Really? That's sad," Candy said.

"So, last year she died, and we found out, much to everyone's shock, that she had been stockpiling her money all those years and had accumulated over $50,000. When her lawyer read her will, guess who she left the money to?"

"Who?"

"Moi."

"You're kidding!"

"Nope. Now no one is supposed to know about this, so don't you dare ever tell anyone."

"I wouldn't tell a soul," Candy promised.

"So, I figure with $50,000 we could just about make it through college and law school without you working—assuming you'd be happy with a modest lifestyle."

Candy looked stunned. Tears began to well in her eyes. "I don't know what to say."

"Now, tell me dreams don't come true," Fred said.

"I wouldn't dare," she replied softly.

"Of course, we could do it a little differently."

"What do you mean?"

"I've given it a lot of thought. I know you have your plan to be a big actress and everything, and obviously you don't want anything to get in your way, but what if I were to ask you to marry me?"

"What about Maria?"

"I love Maria too much to betray her. I know you wouldn't care if I married Maria, but Maria would care a lot if she found I had a mistress."

Candy nodded.

"It would be much more comfortable for me with just one woman, and I am willing to make a choice."

"You'd choose me over Maria?"

"Yes, if I believed you loved me and you could make a commitment to me."

Candy sat silently and stared into Fred's eyes. After a few moments, she responded, "I do love you, but I can't make a commitment. All of my life I've had this dream. Someday, that dream is going to come true unless I do something to screw it up. No matter what it takes, I am going to be a great actress. I would like you to be there with me, but I can't promise that I will be faithful to you, if being faithful will jeopardize my career."

Fred sighed, disappointment showing on his face. "Hmm. I was afraid that would be your answer."

"It's important to me that our relationship is honest. I don't want to play the jealousy game. You can do what you want, and I can do what I want, and we can tell each other everything without feeling any guilt."

"You really think that would work?"

"I know it will," Candy said fervently.

"Okay," Fred said and then reached into his pocket, pulled out an envelope, and handed it to her.

"What's this?"

"The beginning of the fulfillment of your dreams."

Candy opened the envelope curiously. She smiled when she saw four blank money orders, each in the amount of $500. "Is this for me?"

"Yeah. Did I ever tell you I am a man of action? I don't pussyfoot around."

"You didn't have to tell me. I knew that."

"So quit your job and start concentrating on becoming an actress. I figure $1,000 a month ought to pay your rent and keep a little bread on the table."

"Yeah, it's as much as I make at the bank."

"Now, what was it you were telling me about sampling the merchandise?"

Candy smiled. "Okay. After dinner, I'll take you home for some dessert."

"Fine. I'm done. Are you finished?"

She laughed. "Not yet. I haven't read my fortune cookie." Candy picked up her fortune cookie and snapped it apart. "Wisdom is rare in youth and beauty." She frowned. "Do you think that's true?"

Fred thought about it a moment and replied, "Probably."

She laughed. "Honesty, I like that. What does yours say?" she asked.

He cracked his open and read it aloud. "It is the fate of the fish to swim and the thief to run." Fred's stomach twisted on the word thief. He would have never dreamed in a million years that he'd become one. He shuddered at the thought and wondered if the message of the fortune cookie was just a coincidence.

"Very interesting," Candy said, not noticing his anxiety.

"Okay, let's get the hell out of here."

Fred hailed the waitress and asked her for their check. She obliged, he paid it, and they left. By the time they got to Candy's apartment, they were both ready to explode from the sexual energy that had been slowly building all evening. Before they got to the front door of her apartment, they began to attack each other furiously. She fumbled for her keys and tried to unlock the door while kissing him passionately. A neighbor looked on with great amusement.

Finally, they got inside. Fred kicked the door shut, and they ripped off each other's clothes. Candy was more than Fred could have ever dreamed—passionate, sensual, and voluptuous beyond belief. He felt like the luckiest man on the planet as he felt her body next to his. Sure, he knew she was going to cost him plenty, but at that moment, he believed she was going to be worth every penny—and with a million dollars to play with, he could certainly afford it.

After their passions finally succumbed to exhaustion, they cuddled up in each other's arms and fell asleep. A few hours later, they reluctantly got up and Candy made them some coffee. Fred was feeling relaxed and content. Their first sexual encounter had been incredible. At least that's what Fred had thought. He didn't know what was going through Candy's mind, but she seemed happy and hadn't kicked him out yet. They may have commenced a rather bizarre relationship, but at that particular moment, it seemed right and was apparently their destiny. Unfortunately, Fred couldn't stay the night since he had an 8:00 a.m. class the next morning. With much regret, he finally went to the door, kissed Candy goodbye, and left.

Chapter 15

A Friendly Ear

When Fred got back to his apartment, he was so worked up he couldn't go to sleep. He had to talk to someone, but he didn't want to talk to Steve because he was very religious and morally rigid. He would just chew Fred out for being stupid. Randy, on the other hand, would be more understanding and sympathetic. After searching a minute through his address book, he found his number and called him. After a minute, he answered.

"Fred? Is that you?"

"Yeah, I'm afraid so."

"Huh. Didn't expect to hear from until Christmas break."

"I know. I just wanted to talk to you."

"Okay," Randy said cautiously. "So, how are you?"

"Not so good, I'm afraid."

"What's wrong?" he chuckled. "You still a virgin?"

"No. Actually, I'm not."

"You're not? Maria finally came through, huh?"

"No."

"No! Who then?" he asked excitedly. "Tell me everything."

Fred told him about Candy, how they'd met, her outrageous proposition, and their most recent encounter.

"Wow! I'm in shock. I can't believe it. I thought you were hopelessly in love with Maria."

"Well, I still love her, but circumstances are such that it won't be possible for me and Maria to continue our relationship."

"What circumstances?" Randy asked, bewildered.

"Someone is trying to set me up for a crime I didn't commit. They stashed some money in my car hoping I'd be caught with it and take the fall for their heist. Come tomorrow morning, I'm going to be in very serious trouble, and I didn't want to drag Maria into it."

Randy sighed. "I can't believe this."

"I'm going to need your help figuring out what to do next."

"Of course. I can catch a flight out and be at LAX in five or six hours."

"Good, but not today. I'll call you when the time is right."

"Okay. I'll be on standby."

"I'll pay for your flight. I've got money."

"Glad to hear it. Mine is in short supply these days."

"You need me to send some now?"

"No. I got it covered."

"What about your classes? Will missing a few days' mess you up?"

"Not a problem brother. It sounds like you really need my expert guidance."

"I do. Thank you."

Fred felt better after he hung up the phone. It was good to have someone he could talk to candidly; someone he could trust. He knew tomorrow was the day of reckoning, the day when the vault would be opened. He'd have to either show up for work and act dumb or make a run for it.

If he was going to show up, he'd have to appear surprised and shocked by what had happened. He couldn't act scared or nervous. Although he'd been able, so far, to put the matter out of his mind, it would be nearly impossible once the media got wind of the robbery and the FBI started to investigate.

He needed his sleep too. If he were tired, he might lose his focus and make a mistake. Normally, he had no trouble sleeping, as he'd developed an effective technique to combat insomnia. If he couldn't sleep, he would concentrate on something very pleasant. He had learned this from a motivational speaker he had listened to one time on the radio. Usually, he would focus his thoughts on a beautiful place, a beautiful woman, or a happy event from the past and imagine he was there. Tonight, nothing worked until he thought about Candy and ran their encounter over and over in his mind. Soon, he was asleep and began to dream.

He was alone, sitting on the shore of a pond. The sound of splashing water startled him. As he turned toward the sound, he saw a beautiful woman emerging from a pond of water surrounded by dense tropical vegetation. He could see her pretty face, her wet blond hair, her mysterious eyes, and those voluptuous breasts. She came toward him, smiling and laughing. She splashed water at him and giggled in delight. They embraced and kissed, and then she walked out of the pool with her back toward him. She walked a few steps, turned her head around at him, smiled, and winked. As he gazed delightfully at her naked body, his knees buckled, and he became overwhelmed with joy. He struggled to keep his composure. Surely, he was in heaven. But then he heard her screaming. She turned toward him once again, and this time, there was terror in her eyes.

Fred woke up in a cold sweat, contemplated the dream for a while, then fell back asleep. When he opened his eyes again, the display on the clock radio read 6:45 a.m. Still feeling exhausted, he turned over and considered hitting the snooze button. Then he remembered it was Monday and all hell would be breaking loose at the bank. He groaned, wanting to call in sick, but he knew that would look bad. The only thing he could do was go to work and act like nothing had happened. He was confident his mind could repress all recollection of Friday night. It was possible; he knew it was possible. He'd keep his mind focused on Candy and all the fun they were going to have together.

Chapter 16

Career Maker

Samuel P. Whitehead had always wanted to go into politics. It was his dream to be governor someday, and if that went well, to run for President. Unfortunately, fate had sent him in other directions. He didn't quite rank high enough in his law school class at USC to get offers from the most prestigious law firms in LA, so he reluctantly went to work at the Los Angeles County District Attorney's office. He did well there, as he was a ruthless litigator and would do anything to get a conviction. His prosecutorial talents, coupled with the political connections he'd forged in the local Democratic Party, soon got him national notice. This led to an appointment as an assistant U.S. Attorney. Once he had his foot in the door, it wasn't long before he was the number one federal prosecutor in LA.

It was fall in LA, which is usually fairly pleasant as the

temperature rarely got above 75° or below 50°. Whitehead had just

gotten to his office when he received a telephone call from Jim Walters, a special agent with the FBI that he frequently worked with. "Did you hear about the bank robbery in San Bernardino?" Walters asked.

"No. What bank?"

"Bank USA. I just got here. The cashier didn't show up for work, so they called in a supervisor from their main office to help get the vault open."

"Yeah?"

"When they got the vault open, they found the cashier inside, bound, gagged, and dead as a stump."

"How much did they get?"

"$6.7 million and some change."

"Jesus! That's quite a heist. Any suspects?"

"Two. A couple of bank messengers had access to the bank about the time the robbery took place. It had to be an inside job—not a shred of evidence showing a break in."

"Who are the messengers?"

"A Sam Stewart, an ex-con living up in the mountains. I'd say he'd be our most likely suspect, except it's hard to see how he could have done it without the other messenger, Fred Fuller, being in on it."

"How do you figure?"

"Well, Fuller is the main messenger at San Bernardino, and he would have been there about the time the heist went down."

"Have you found out anything on Fuller?"

"He's a college student at UCLA, no record, a political activist but not anti-war, a Republican, chairman of the Young Republicans, and with some past ties to Congressman Bartlett up in Ventura."

"Really? The press will be all over this one when Bartlett's name pops up."

"Probably so."

"What was the cause of death?" Whitehead asked.

"Don't know yet, but there's no external injuries, which is odd."

"Have you located Fuller and Stewart?"

"Fuller's not at home, but he's due for work this afternoon. We'll see if he shows up."

"If he does, talk to him, but don't spook him. If we keep an eye on him, he might lead us to the money. What about Stewart?"

"It seems Friday was his last day. He gave notice two weeks ago. The local sheriff says he left Saturday for Vegas. We've got agents there looking for him now."

"Alright, I'm on my way. Should be there in about an hour."

"Okay. See you soon."

Whitehead hung up the phone, feeling almost giddy. Was he finally getting the break he needed to launch his political career? The case that was unfolding in front of him seemed too good to be true. He grabbed his briefcase and almost ran to his car.

An hour later, at the crime scene, he met up with Jim Walters and his partner Joe Harper in the lobby of the bank. The place was a bustle of activity between the crime scene investigators, bank examiners, local police, Bank USA executives, and insurance company reps.

"Anything new?" Whitehead asked.

"The coroner thinks the cause of death was a heart attack," Walters replied.

Whitehead frowned. "A heart attack?"

"Yeah, induced by the stress of the robbery, he thinks. He may have been drinking. There was an empty flask of bourbon in his office, an open bottle in his desk drawer, and he'd been reprimanded for drinking in the past."

"I can't believe they'd trust over six million dollars to a drunk," Harper said, shaking his head.

Whitehead shrugged. "You gotta wonder."

They moved to the vault and went inside. The body had been removed, but there was a chalk outline where Hamlin had been found. There were eleven teller carts with their empty drawers extended.

"What about prints?" Whitehead asked.

"Fuller's are all over the bank—even in the President's office."

"Anything inside the vault?"

"No, but they found them on the door of the vault. He must have closed it when he left."

"What about Sam Stewart? Any of his prints inside the bank?"

"No."

"So, what do you think happened here?" Whitehead asked.

"I can't see Fuller pulling it off himself. Hamlin would have had to help him," Harper said. "There was an incident about six weeks ago when Hamlin left the vault open and Fuller found it. Fuller reported it, and Hamlin got reprimanded. When this happened, they were alone together for about a half hour. Perhaps that's when the idea was hatched."

Whitehead frowned. "Hmm. That's a stretch. Something like that would more likely make them enemies, not co-conspirators."

"Yeah, except Hamlin was pretty easygoing and smart enough to know Fuller wasn't the reason he got in trouble," Harper added. "The incident might have gotten him to thinking it might be possible to rob the bank and not get caught if he had some help. You've got to admit, stealing over six million dollars from a bank with a state-of-the-art alarm system is quite a feat."

"Or," Walters suggested, "Hamlin got drunk and left the vault open again, and this time Fuller decided to take the money. Maybe Hamlin was drunk in his office and caught Fuller taking the money. That could have led to the confrontation that caused his heart attack."

"I like that idea," Whitehead said. "That's the most plausible explanation I've heard so far. We need to find the money, though, so let's give Fuller some rope so he can lead us to it—and then we'll hang him with it."

Chapter 17

Felony Murder

All morning, Fred managed to focus his attention on his classes, homework, Maria, and Candy with little thought of anything else. But before he knew it, the hour had come to go to work. He parked his car in the usual place and walked over to the motor pool. Jim was standing at the pumps filling one of the bank vehicles with gas.

"Hi, Jim," he said, trying to act natural.

"Hello, Fred," Jim replied, somewhat subdued.

"Did you have a good weekend?"

"Yeah, not so bad. How was yours, mate?" he asked.

"Fabulous."

"Fabulous? Well then, you must have done something quite extraordinary. Let me guess. . . . One of your women came through or you went to that football game everyone's been talking about?"

"Right on both counts."

"Both counts? You did have a fabulous weekend."

"You're not a football fan, are you, Jim?"

"Well, not American football for sure. But I like what you Yanks call soccer."

"Did you go to the game?"

"No, but I had it playing on the radio alright. Of course, I can't say I heard much of it since my young lass was keeping me pretty busy."

"Maria wasn't too interested in the game either."

"So, you went to ball game with Maria and got lucky with—what's her bloody name?"

"Candy."

"Candy, the girl who wants to be your mistress, right?"

"Right."

"Tell me, Fred, when you and Maria get married, are you going to invite Candy to the wedding?"

Fred smiled and laughed at Jim's sarcasm. He had decided he couldn't hide the situation with Candy, and it might actually help in making his life appear ordinary. "Probably not. Although she would probably like to come."

"You better be careful, lad. As I remember, Maria was unforgiving and good with a knife."

"Well, you're the master at juggling women, so how about some pointers?"

"My only advice is not to fall in love with either one of them. If you do, the other one will feel it in the way you treat her, and she'll know there is another."

"It may be too late then," Fred said. "I actually do love them both already."

Just then, their conversation was interrupted by Sinclair's shouting. "Fuller! Get up here. I need to talk to you."

Sinclair's voice sent shivers up and down Fred's spine. He knew the dreaded moment had arrived. He took a deep breath, looked at Jim, raised his eyebrows and said, "I wonder what he wants."

"I've got some idea," Jim replied.

"What?"

"You better go ahead and see Sinclair, but stop by here before you leave. I need to tell you a few things."

"Okay."

As he walked toward Sinclair, Fred felt his heart pounding rapidly. Calm down. Relax. He took a few deep breaths and exhaled slowly. When he got to Sinclair's office, Fred gave him a puzzled look.

"Fuller, there is going to be a change in your route today."

"Really?"

"Yes. There won't be a bag at San Bernardino."

"How come?"

"Didn't you hear the news today?"

"No. I've been at school all day."

"San Bernardino got robbed."

"What? You're kidding!" he said, feigning surprise.

"And Harvey Hamlin is dead."

"Huh?" Fred gasped. "What happened?"

"They found him dead inside the vault."

Fred thought back. He hadn't looked in the vault because it

had been so dark.

"Consequently, the bank's closed today."

"Did Harvey get shot?"

"No, but he might as well have."

"What do you mean?"

"He died of a heart attack during the robbery. When they catch the robbers, they'll be charged with felony murder since Harvey died while a felony was in progress."

Sinclair's words stunned Fred. It was one thing to be dragged into a bank robbery, but murder was an entirely different story. For a moment, he couldn't breathe, but he couldn't afford to let Sinclair see his reaction, so he turned away. After a long moment, he finally took a breath and managed to say, "Damn! That's horrible."

"Oh, Sam quit, too, so you'll have to pick up Arrowhead and Big Bear in addition to your regular route."

"Jesus! I won't be back here until midnight."

"Well, we don't have any other choice just now."

"Okay. Well, I better get going then."

"Oh. . . . before you go, those guys you talked to before from the FBI want to talk to you again for a minute."

Fred's stomach twisted. He'd known he'd eventually have to face the FBI, but he wasn't prepared for it quite yet. He felt nauseous and struggled to keep from throwing up.

"You okay?" Sinclair asked.

"Sure, but if I've got to do two routes, I need to get going now."

"It will just take a minute," Sinclair replied in a voice that indicated Fred had no choice in the matter.

"Okay. So, where are they?"

"Take the elevator down to where you met them before."

"Okay, thanks."

As the elevator descended, Fred felt like he was sinking into the pits of hell. He didn't think they knew anything about the bag of money he'd hidden, or else Sinclair wouldn't be sending him out on a run. Nevertheless, he couldn't stop his hands from shaking. As he entered the conference room, he put them in his pocket so they wouldn't give him away.

"Mr. Fuller," Agent Harper said as he entered the room. "Thank you for coming down."

"No problem."

"Do you remember Agent Walters?" Harper asked.

"Yes, sir. Nice to see you again," he replied, not wanting to take his hands out of his pockets to shake theirs. They gave him a hard look but made no comment.

"I guess you've heard about San Bernardino," Harper continued.

"Yes. Mr. Sinclair just told me about it. I can't believe it. Poor Mr. Hamlin." Fred shook his head and looked down at the floor.

"Did you see anything unusual Friday night?"

"No. Nothing in particular comes to mind."

"We need you to tell us everything that happened. We need a minute-by-minute account, and don't leave out any details, even if you don't think they're important."

"Why?"

"You may have seen something and didn't realize it."

"Okay. Well. . . . uh. . . . when I drove up I was pretty much on schedule, but Sam wasn't there yet. I guess you know I have the longest route, so I'm the last driver to get in at night. Sam is supposed to be there when I arrive so that I'm not delayed, but there was a note on the door from Hamlin that said Sam was going to be twenty minutes late."

"What did you do after you read the note?"

"I went inside to get the bags."

"Did you do anything inside the bank other than bring out the bags?"

Fred gave Harper a calculating stare, wondering if he was trying to set a trap. Reluctantly, he responded, "Well, when I got inside, I noticed it was pitch black. The night lamp was apparently out, so I went back outside to get a flashlight. Just as soon as I got out the door, I was blinded by headlights. It scared the shit. . . uh, excuse me, the crap out of me. Luckily, it just turned out to be Sam."

"Did Sam say why he was late?" Walters asked.

"Yeah. He said one of the tellers was out of balance, I think."

"How long did Sam hang around?" Harper prodded.

"Just a couple minutes."

"Then what did you do?"

"Well, I put Sam's bags in the car and went inside to get the bags that were still inside."

"Did you see anything unusual inside?"

"Well, other than it being really dark . . . wait. . . actually, I did see something kind of unusual, now that I think about it."

Walters leaned forward and asked, "What?"

"In the darkness, there was a light from down the hall. I thought maybe someone was still in the bank, so I went down to talk to them and tell them the night lamp was out."

"Go on," Walters said.

"It was Harvey Hamlin's office. His light was still on. I knew it was his office because he had taken me in there one time for something."

"What did you see?" Walters asked.

"Nothing really. It was empty. Nobody was there, so I just turned off the light and left."

"Did you do anything else, anything at all?"

Harper's question bothered him. If he had left a fingerprint somewhere else in the bank, they would find it sooner or later. Should I tell them I went into the President's office? It would be better for me to tell them than for them to discover it later. "No, I just dropped by the kitchen and bought a Coke from the vending machine."

"I thought it was dark. How could you see to buy a Coke?"

"I turned on the kitchen light. It's quite a ride from San Bernardino to LA, so I usually buy a Coke to drink on the way back."

"Okay. Is there anything else you want to tell us?"

Fred frowned and shook his head. "No, nothing I can think of."

"That will do then, except we'll need to take your fingerprints."

"My fingerprints? What for?"

"Fingerprints can be most helpful in determining what happened at a crime scene. We need to know the identity of every print in that bank. Since you were there, admittedly, it's protocol. Walters will take your prints right now."

"The bank already has them. They took them when they first hired me."

"We need our own set."

"Okay. . . . I guess I better tell you one more thing," Fred said with a sigh. Walters' eyes narrowed as Fred continued, "I know I shouldn't have done it, but, well, you know, I've always kind of wondered what it would be like to be a bank president. Since I was killing time Friday night, waiting for Sam, I went into the president's office and sat in his chair just to see what it felt like, you know? I didn't touch anything though. . . . at least I don't remember touching anything."

"How long were you in his office?" Walters asked.

"Just a minute or two."

"Anything else?" Walters said.

"No. That's it, I think."

"Oh, by the way," Harper added, "I understand you found the vault open at San Bernardino a few weeks ago?"

"Yeah. Can you believe that?"

"Well, Mr. Sinclair was pretty impressed with your honesty in that situation."

"I am sure any other messenger would have done the same thing," Fred replied.

"Not necessarily," Walters noted.

Fred shrugged and turned to leave.

"Uh, your fingerprints?" Harper reminded him.

"Right," Fred said nervously. He reluctantly took his hands out of his pocket and extended them to Walters.

"Okay, right over here," Walters said as he pointed to a pad and some fingerprint charts at the end of the table. Walters took each of his fingers and pressed them onto the ink pad. Then he pressed them onto the chart in the appropriate spot. Fred tried to let his hand go limp so his fingers wouldn't shake, but apparently Walters felt the tension.

"Don't worry. It's just routine."

After Walters was done, Fred left, then went to talk to Jim, curious as to what he had to tell him. There were several drivers at the pumps as he walked up, so Fred waited for them to leave before he began talking to Jim.

"What did Sinclair want?" Jim said.

"Agents Walters and Harper are downstairs, and they wanted to talk to me."

"I figured as much. I saw them come back with Sinclair."

"Come back from where?"

"FBI Headquarters. Sinclair had a meeting there today with Walters and Harper, some new agents, and a couple bank officials. He told me all about it."

"Really? What happened at this meeting?"

"They read the coroner's preliminary report. They know Hamlin died of a heart attack, but they don't know what caused it. Being robbed might have done it, but being involved in the robbery could have caused it too. Hamlin had a history of pretty serious heart disease and an alcohol problem to boot, so it's anyone's guess."

"He told me his wife had just left him too and he was pretty broken up about it," Fred added.

"That's interesting. There was more to Hamlin than meets the eye then. Sinclair is bloody sure Hamlin was in on the heist, but they can't figure out who was working with him. Everyone knew he had a serious drinking problem, so some professionals might have approached him knowing he was vulnerable. It could have been a double-cross, or else Hamlin might have just succumbed from all the stress he was under, they just don't know."

"Couldn't someone have just surprised Hamlin and overtaken him?" Fred asked.

"They don't think that's likely since the perpetrator had to have had inside information."

"Why is that?"

"There was no sign of a forced entry. They apparently waltzed in and out of the bank unnoticed. Nothing unusual on the bank's surveillance cameras."

"Hmm."

"The assistant cashier has been cleared. She had half the combination to the vault and should have stayed there to make sure Hamlin closed it, but she says Hamlin made her go home before the vault was closed. She claims to have protested, but says Hamlin insisted she leave. I guess her alibi checked out."

"So, do they have any other suspects?" Fred asked timidly.

"That's why I wanted to talk to you, Fred. You're their number one suspect, and they have you under surveillance."

A chill darted down Fred's spine. "What? I can't believe this. What about Sam Stewart?" he asked angrily. "Isn't he a suspect?"

"They said Sam quit his job on Wednesday and hasn't been seen since. The problem is, they knew he was quitting. He gave them notice two weeks ago."

"So, he obviously had the heist well planned out. Why else would he conveniently quit his job and disappear right after the robbery?"

"That's what I told Sinclair, but apparently Sam stopped to buy some ammo at an army surplus store on his way in from Big Bear. The owner is quite sure about the time, so it would have been nearly impossible for him to have been at the bank any earlier than you."

"So, they think the robbery took place before I got there?"

"It must have happened just before you got there, according to the time-line they've worked out."

"It's pretty convenient that Sam quit on the day of the robbery," Fred argued.

"I don't think Sam has been ruled out entirely. They've got agents looking for him, but you definitely have number one billing at this stage of the game, lad."

"What do you think I should do, Jim?"

"Keep your mouth shut, for one thing. They've got a tail on you and probably a lot of bugs. You might warn your family and friends, too, since they're sending agents up to Ventura."

"Oh my God! You've got to be kidding! They took my prints down there but told me it was just protocol, just routine."

"I'm afraid you're in deep trouble, Fred, whether you deserve it or not."

"Listen, Jim, if you hear anything else, will you tell me?"

"I damn bloody will. I don't want to see an innocent man take a tumble."

"You really believe I am innocent?"

"No, I didn't say that, but even if you took the loot, I wouldn't blame you. If they leave money laying around, it's their own fault if someone takes it. I'd have done the same given the chance."

"You're a good man, Jim. Can I get your phone number in case I need to call you?"

"Sure," Jim said. He reached in his pocket for a scrap of paper and wrote his number on it. "Don't be alarmed if a young lass answers."

"Oh, believe me, I wouldn't be."

"If by chance you're not here tomorrow, take care."

"Thanks, Jim."

After talking to Jim, Fred got the hell out of there as fast as he could without attracting attention. Once on the road, he took a deep breath and tried to relax. After fifteen or twenty minutes, he had calmed down and was looking forward to seeing Candy at the Palm Springs Branch. Then it occurred to him she might be gone since he was running late. He prayed she'd still be there. A little panicked at the thought of missing her, he increased his speed to try to make up time. Tonight—of all nights—he needed to see her. By the time he got to Palm Springs, he had made up ten minutes.

When he approached the bank, there were no cars, and the bank was dark except for the night lamp. His heart sank as he realized he wasn't going to see Candy. Depression overcame him quickly as he walked to the door of the bank and slowly unlocked it. Tonight, he really needed Candy. "Damn it!" he blurted out to the empty lobby. As he walked toward the bags, he looked around hopefully but saw nothing. He picked them up and started to leave when he heard a whisper.

"Fred, where have you been?"

He looked toward the voice and saw someone standing in the dark behind the tellers' windows.

"Candy? Is that you?"

"Who else do you think would be waiting around for you?"

His heart began to pound with excitement. He dropped the bags and quickly ran over to her.

"Oh, I am so glad to see you. I thought for sure I would miss you."

"Actually, this worked out pretty well because everyone is gone and we're alone."

They put their arms around each other and began to kiss. Then Candy broke away. "Boy, you sure are tense," she said.

"It's been a tough day. You won't believe it, but I've still got to go to Banning, Arrowhead and Big Bear tonight."

"You're joking?"

"No, unfortunately, I'm not. Sam quit."

"Well, good. No one will notice if you're an extra fifteen or twenty minutes late."

"No, probably not? What did you have in mind?"

"Come with me, and I'll show you."

Candy grabbed his hand and led him down the hall into the ladies' room. Just inside the door was a sofa. Candy sat down and laid back, her eyes beckoning him to follow her. He knelt down and began kissing her thighs. She closed her eyes and moaned gently.

A half hour later, Fred remembered he had a route to finish and sat up. He looked down at Candy's naked body and wished he could stay longer. Words could not describe what had happened between them. He didn't want to go, God knew he didn't, but he had no choice. He started to get up to leave, but Candy yanked him back.

"You can't go yet," she said softly. "You can't leave a woman in this condition."

He sat up and looked at her. "But I am almost forty-five minutes late already."

She put her hand on his arm. "Just hold me a minute longer. Please? Just another minute. . ."

"Okay," he said, rolling her over on top of him and holding her tightly. "Did you enjoy that?" he asked looking up at her.

"Mmm, I sure did. Did you?"

He nodded. "God, did I ever."

She smiled, put her head on his shoulder, and took a deep breath. He closed his eyes, enjoying the heat of her body. After a few minutes, she pushed herself up and gave him a serious look. Her breasts were so beautiful he just stared at them, mesmerized.

"Fred, can we talk for a few minutes before you go?"

"Huh?"

"Can we talk?"

"Sure. I'd love to talk to you, honey, but I am really late. I've got to get out of here right now, but we can talk tomorrow."

"But it's important."

"I'm sure it is, but wouldn't you rather talk about it when I'm not rushed?"

She sighed. "Okay, okay. Go on. . . . get out of here."

They got dressed and made their way to the door. Candy peered outside to make sure no one was around. The coast seemed clear, so they walked outside. Fred locked the door behind them, and then they kissed and said their goodbyes.

The road from Palm Springs to Banning was mountainous and full of dangerous curves. He knew it wouldn't be possible to make up too much time, but he tried anyway. The wheels of the white Impala shrieked as he sailed around each bend. Suddenly, he realized he was rapidly approaching a slow-moving car ahead. The road seemed clear beyond the car, so he passed it quickly. He looked at his speedometer and noticed he was traveling 75 MPH.

As Fred approached the summit, he observed a car parked in a lookout adjacent to the road and some people admiring the view. Suddenly, out from behind the car came a little girl. There was no time to stop, so Fred swerved sharply to the left, barely missing the child. His heart nearly stopped as he narrowly averted plunging over the cliff on the other side of the summit. He looked in his rearview mirror and saw the child's mother lift her up. *She's okay. Thank God!*

The near accident brought him back to his senses. *They are expecting you to be late. Just relax.*

When he'd resigned himself to the fact that he was going to be late and couldn't do anything about it, he began enjoying the drive again and particularly the memory of his latest encounter with Candy. Before he knew it, he was in San Bernardino, passing by Bank USA on his way to Arrowhead and Big Bear. As he drove past, he scrutinized the bank carefully. It was dark, and the parking lot was empty. To a stranger, it would seem as if nothing had happened. Then he noticed a dark blue car parked near the drug store. A man sat inside, sipping a cup of coffee. He surmised that it was an FBI agent watching to see if the bank robber would return to the scene of the crime, as they often did. Sorry, friend—not this unwitting thief.

As he headed into the mountains, he thought of Sam, and he wondered what had happened to make him quit his route so suddenly. He certainly had not mentioned quitting to Fred. The memory of the little girl calling Sam Santa Claus amused him. It seemed to Fred that he could have made so much money if he had been willing to play the role, filling December malls with the laughter of children. It couldn't be that hard, and the financial rewards would be worth the drudgery of having hundreds of naïve youngsters sit on his lap.

When he got into Arrowhead, Fred noticed he was getting low on gas. He saw a Union 76 station, so he pulled in and drove up to the pumps. A burly man with a beard came out and walked over to his window. "Fill it up," Fred ordered.

The man nodded and then set the hose on automatic while he washed Fred's windshield.

While watching the attendant do the windows, Fred observed a small grocery store across the street. In front of the store, a red Volkswagen Beetle was parked, and it looked just like Sam's. As the attendant finished the front window and proceeded to the rear, Fred thought he saw Sam coming out of the store with a load of groceries and getting into the VW. By this time, the attendant had come around. Fred handed him a credit card and asked, "Do you know Sam Stewart?"

"Yeah. Everybody knows Sam."

"Isn't that him getting in the car over there?"

"Sure looks like it."

"Hmm. I'd like to go talk to him for a minute."

"Well, it looks like you're too late. He's leavin'. Maybe you can drop by his house."

"You know where he lives?"

"Sure. I'll give ya his address."

Seeing Sam got Fred curious. If he was in town, why haven't the FBI agents been able to talk to him? They must not be looking very hard. When the attendant came back, he gave Fred directions to Sam's house, but it was way out of his way, so Fred blew it off.

After picking up the bags at the Arrowhead branch, he proceeded toward Big Bear. It was a beautiful trip through the tall pine trees during the daylight. After dark, however, there wasn't much to see—just miles and miles of winding road. It was still peaceful, though, and he thoroughly enjoyed the ride.

He finally arrived back in LA after midnight. The motor pool was deserted when he pulled in. As he unloaded his bags, a security guard came over and said he would take his bags downstairs. Fred thanked him and left. It had been a very long, trying, somewhat terrifying day, but he had survived it. In retrospect, he realized he couldn't have planned it any better than it had actually turned out.

When he got home, the daily newspaper was lying in front of his apartment door. He took it inside, turned on the light, and opened it up. The headline jumped out at him: 'BANK ROBBERS GET $6.7 MILLION FROM BANK USA, Cashier Found Dead in Vault'. Fred gasped as he realized whoever had masterminded the bank robbery had given him a million and escaped with 5.7 million dollars. He wondered why they'd been so generous. He was sick as he read the article over and over, memorizing every detail. The story said the police and FBI were baffled by the crime. They thought it might be an inside job, but they really had no clues. There was no sign of forced entry, no evidence of a struggle, and no one saw anything unusual. As he was pondering the article the phone rang. He picked it up.

"Hello?"

"Fred, where have you been?" Maria asked.

"Maria, hi. I just got in from work." He suddenly felt very guilty.

"It's after one, and I was worried sick about you."

"Sam quit, and I had to take his route and mine."

"You're kidding!"

"No. I wish I was, but it was a very long night."

"Did you hear about the robbery?"

"Yeah. I was just reading about it when you called."

"Isn't that one of the banks on your route?"

"Uh huh. It's usually my last stop."

"You didn't see anything Friday night, did you?"

Fred hesitated.

"Ah. . . . Not really. The FBI asked me the same thing."

"The FBI has already talked to you?"

"About a half hour before I left today."

"Do they know who did it?"

"Apparently not—according to the newspaper anyway. Of course, they won't tell anyone anything until they have something solid."

"Did you know the guy who got killed?"

"Harvey Hamlin? Yeah, I knew Harvey. He was a pretty nice guy when he was sober."

"You're so lucky you didn't get to the bank during the robbery, or you might have been killed too."

"Hmm. I suppose you're right, but I hadn't given that much thought."

"Now I am going to worry about you every time you go to work."

"You needn't worry, babe. The odds of this happening again are very remote."

"I hope so."

"Listen, babe, I am really beat, and I need to hit the hay."

"Okay. Well, I'm glad you made it home safely."

"Thanks. Sweet dreams."

"I love you."

"Me too. Goodnight."

It's not a lie, Fred thought to himself—he did love her. It was possible to love two women—not too smart, but certainly possible. He didn't want to break up with Maria, but he knew it was the only decent thing to do. She'd get over him and find someone who would be true to her. In a few days, he would tell her, but right at that moment, he needed sleep.

Chapter 18

Saying Goodbye

Fred was looking forward to the weekend to relax and do some serious thinking. Since he hadn't got up the nerve yet to tell Maria their relationship was over, he was planning to juggle the weekend between her and Candy. On Saturday morning, he slept late, as he planned to meet Maria at noon for lunch. When he went outside to get the paper, he noticed a man in a suit sitting by the pool, reading a magazine. He figured the man was the FBI agent assigned to keep an eye on him.

Maria and Fred went to Denny's for lunch, and then they had planned to go to the Los Angeles Museum of Modern Art. As they were leaving the restaurant, he noticed two men in dark suits standing outside the restaurant reading their newspapers. He recognized both of them. One of them had been outside his apartment earlier in the day, and the other agent was the man he had seen the previous week staking out the San Bernardino branch of Bank USA. Having two agents assigned to him was a major concern. Why have they assigned a second agent to me? Are they getting ready to arrest me? Did they discover some incriminating evidence in the bank? He looked back and saw them walking fifty yards behind them.

"Oh, shit," he said under his breath.

Maria gave him a funny look and said, "What's wrong with you? You look like you saw a ghost."

"Nothing. . . . Nothing's wrong," he assured her. "Let's get to the museum before it gets crowded."

"Okay, honey. You sure you're alright?"

"Yeah, let's go."

They found their car and took off down Wilshire Boulevard. He kept an eye on the rearview mirror and immediately observed a dark blue sedan following them, the same car he'd seen in San

Bernardino.

"Damn," he inadvertently blurted out.

"What's wrong?" Maria asked again.

He rubbed his forehead, as if he were in pain, "I have a headache."

Maria gave him a concerned look. "Do you want to go home?"

"No, I'll be okay. It will go away in a minute."

"Are you sure? I'm worried about you."

He looked over at her and sighed. "Maria, I love you."

"I love you too. But what's wrong?"

Tears began to well up in his eyes, and he struggled to keep from crying. "Maria, something has happened. I'm in terrible trouble."

"Huh? What it is it?" Maria asked, on the verge of tears herself.

"I can't tell you. If I did, it would be dangerous for both of us. I may have to leave town soon."

"Leave town? What are you talking about?" Maria asked, beginning to sob.

"I'm going to take you home now. I don't know when I will see you again. I wish I could explain everything to you, but I can't."

"I'll go with you."

"I can't let you quit school and give up everything just because my life is screwed up. Besides, you may not want to be with me after you find out what I've done."

"Is this about the bank robbery, Fred?"

"Don't ask. The less you know, the better. It's for your own good."

"I can't bear to think you'll be gone and I won't even know where you are."

"I'll call you from time to time to let you know I am alright. I can't call you at the dorm, though, because the phone will probably be tapped."

"Damn it, Fred, how could you let this happen? Our life was so perfect!"

"This isn't something I planned, honey. I know it will sound like a lame excuse, but I really was just at the wrong place at the wrong time."

"So, what am I supposed to do without you?" Maria sobbed.

"I don't know how long I will be gone. I may never be able to come back. You need to forget you ever met me."

"You can't forget someone you love."

"I know, but you've got to try."

When they arrived at Maria's dorm, Fred parked the car. They sat silently for a while, not wanting to leave each other. "You've got to be strong," Fred said. "You'll get through it."

"No! This can't be happening! You can't do this to me—to us!"

"I am sorry, babe. I am really sorry, but it's out of my control."

After a minute, he got out of the car, walked around to Maria's door, and opened it. "Come on. I'll walk you inside." Taking Maria's hand, he escorted her inside the dorm. They embraced, he told her he loved her, and left. As he looked back, she turned and slowly walked away. He wondered if he'd ever see her again.

As he drove home, he questioned if he had done the right thing. He hadn't planned to say goodbye right then to Maria, but he just couldn't lie to her anymore. It was better for her to be rid of him and all his troubles, even if it hurt for a while. There was no telling what the future held for him, but the most important thing was to protect her from whatever it might be.

He looked in the rearview mirror and saw that the dark blue sedan was still following him. Why are they following me? Are they worried I'll flee the country, or do they think I'll lead them to the stolen money? They must not have enough on me to arrest me, or they would have done it by now. But how will I know when they do have enough? Can I afford to wait around for them to nab me? Fred's mind was racing, trying to analyze every aspect of his desperate situation. By the time he'd gotten back to his apartment, he had worked himself into a frenzy. He needed to talk to someone, so he decided it was time to call Randy back. As he was about to pick up the phone, he remembered it was probably bugged.

He remained in the apartment for a few minutes, just for the appearance of normalcy and then he got back into his car to go call Randy. After driving around for ten minutes he stopped at a convenience store and used the pay phone.

"Hey, Fred. What's up?"

"Remember our last conversation?"

How could I forget?"

"The time has come, I'm afraid. The situation is getting desperate. I need your advice."

"Well, my suitcase is packed. I can be on a plane within an hour or two."

"Good. So you'll be home late tonight?"

"Right. My mom will pick me up. Do you want to meet tonight at the airport?"

"No. That won't work. Meet me at Meyer Beach tomorrow morning at nine. You know. . . . where we used to camp out."

"Yeah, okay."

"See you then."

The next morning Fred was up bright and early. He was eager to tell Randy everything. Keeping it all bottled up inside him was killing him. It would have been a pleasant ride for him along the coast had it not been for the FBI tail. He found it rather unsettling to have someone following him. When he arrived at Meyer Beach, Randy wasn't there yet, so he found an empty picnic table and sat down to wait. It was a warm day, but a cool ocean breeze made it quite pleasant. There were quite a few sunbathers lying out soaking up the sunshine. He could see a group of surfers gathered on a point where the waves were the biggest. The setting brought back pleasant memories of past experiences on that very same beach, and Fred recalled them with a smile. After a few minutes, he spotted Randy's Volkswagen pulling into the parking lot, so he got up and went to meet him. They shook hands and gave each other a short embrace.

"Thanks for coming," Fred said. "Sorry to drag you away from school."

"Nonsense. That's what friends are for, right?"

"Let's take a walk. I've got the FBI following me."

"Really?" Randy said as he looked around nervously.

"I am afraid so."

"Is this about the bank robbery I read about?"

Fred nodded. "Before I say more, I need to warn you that what I am about to tell you could be dangerous for both of us."

"You know I would die before I'd betray your confidence."

"I know. That's why I am here. I've got to talk to someone, and you are the only one I can trust, but if you didn't want to get involved, I would completely understand. It's totally unreal stuff."

"I am already involved. You're my friend, Fuller, so just tell me what in the hell's going on."

"You read about the bank robbery in San Bernardino, right?"

"Yeah. It was in all the papers."

"You remember when I told you someone was trying to set me up?"

"Uh huh."

"Well, whoever it was stashed a million dollars in my car, hoping I'd get caught with it and take the fall for the bank robbery."

"Oh my God! A million bucks?"

"Right. A little more than that actually."

"But someone was killed in that robbery, weren't they?" Randy asked in a deadly serious tone.

"Yeah, Harvey Hamlin. So now, if they tie me to the robbery, I'll be charged with murder too."

"What did you do with the money?"

"Remember I told you about that old abandoned mining camp called Devil's Canyon?"

"Oh yeah."

"It's there."

"Damn. . . . and I thought I was the wild one."

"Upstaged you on this one, didn't I?"

"What in the hell are you going to do now?"

"That's what I want you to tell me."

"Yeah, right. That's what I was afraid you'd say."

"So far, they've just been tailing me, so I guess they don't have enough to arrest me. The question is, do I sit tight and hope they never get enough or lose the tail and get the hell out of the country?"

"It's too dangerous to hang around, I'm afraid. If they discover that you have the money, they're not likely to believe you were set up."

"I know. That's why I buried it."

"Without the money, what evidence do they have against you?"

"I don't know what evidence they could have. I'm just afraid the robbers might have planted some evidence to lead them to me."

"Yeah, and if they did, you're sunk."

"Where should I go?"

"They would probably expect you to go to Mexico since it's close by. They are probably watching the border pretty closely."

"The airports are obviously out of the question," Fred said.

"Canada. If it were me, I'd go to Canada," Randy said.

"Why Canada?"

"They'll just think you're another draft dodger if you go up there. You wouldn't be so conspicuous. . . . plus, they speak English in Canada."

"The U.S. has extradition treaties with Canada," Fred pointed out.

"Well, with all that money, you should be able to buy a new identity without much trouble."

"I'm going to take Candy with me, if she'll come."

"That's probably a good idea. Aside from the fact that you'll have some pleasant company, a man and a woman traveling together are less conspicuous than a man alone. The only question is; can you really trust her?"

"Yeah, I think so. She'll love the adventure, particularly when she finds out we're millionaires."

"Keep a close eye on her, buddy. You may not know her as well as you think."

"I will."

"Listen, I need to lose the Feds. Got any ideas?"

"Yeah. Take a walk down the beach, and I will disable their car while you're gone. When you come back, they won't be able to follow you."

"You sure? If you get caught, they'll arrest you."

"Don't worry. They won't see me."

"Alright. Thanks a lot."

"Good Luck."

They gave each other a hug, and Randy pretended to drive off but actually only drove out of sight and then parked and waited. Fred took off his shoes and started to walk down the beach with the agents following closely behind. Two girls were walking along the beach ahead of him, so he hurried to catch up with them. "Hi. Mind if I walk with you a minute?" he asked. "I'm Fred."

"Hi, Fred," one of the girls responded with a smile.

"Beautiful day, isn't it?"

"Yeah, it is."

"You girls go to school around here?"

"No. We go to USC."

"Oh no, the enemy. I go to UCLA."

"Well, I guess we won't hold that against you."

"You're so kind."

"So, what can we do for you, Fred?"

"I was just feeling a little lonely when I spotted you two gorgeous women walking down the beach. Just seeing you picked up my spirits so much. I just wanted to thank you."

The girls giggled, and the vocal one responded, "That's a pretty good line, but we're on our way to meet our boyfriends."

"Oh no. Now you've ruined my day."

"Sorry."

"Well, can I just walk with you a minute? I want to meet these lucky guys."

"I guess so. . . . if you really want to."

Fred looked back. The Feds were about 100 yards behind him, and he could see in the distance that Randy was working on their car. When he saw that Randy was finished and had left, he thanked the girls, turned around, and walked back toward his car. As he walked past the Feds, he nodded, smiled, and casually said, "Good afternoon."

"Afternoon," one of them responded with a nod.

When Fred got back, he jumped in his car and took off. A moment later he looked back in his rearview mirror and saw that the road was clear. "Free at last," he said. "Thank God!"

Chapter 19

The Getaway

Fred knew trying to outsmart the FBI would not be easy since they were experts and he was just an amateur. Success would depend on meticulous planning, unpredictable behavior, and a lot of luck. The first problem was his car. Every law enforcement agency in southern California would be looking for his little maroon Ford Falcon. He could have rented another car, but rental cars were easy to trace, not to mention expensive. Stealing a car wasn't a viable option either, as Fred still considered himself to be a relatively honest person, presumed bank robber or not. He knew others might not see it that way, but it was important to him. The only solution he could come up with was to disguise the Ford Falcon or buy another car. The $5,000 he had available wasn't enough for a new car, so he'd have to buy a used one, and that scared him. The last thing he needed was an unreliable vehicle. He remembered seeing Kwik Paint commercials on TV advertising $99 paint jobs. That would probably be his best option, he thought.

Remembering he had seen a Kwik Paint location off of Hollywood Boulevard, he altered his route and headed for the Hollywood Freeway. Spotting the big Kwik Paint sign from the freeway, he exited and drove in. The paint job was supposed to take four hours: one hour to get the car ready, an hour to paint, and two hours to dry. That meant he could be on his way to San Bernardino by six. While his car was being painted, he did some shopping since he obviously couldn't go back to his apartment. He bought a suitcase, some clothes, and shoes. When he was done, there was still another hour to kill, so he stopped in a restaurant to eat dinner. Before he ate, he decided to make a few phone calls. He needed to check with Jim to see if he had heard anything new, and he wanted to call Candy to alert her that he was coming to see her. He found a phone booth, got some change, and proceeded to dial Candy's number. She answered on the first ring.

"Where have you been all day?" Candy asked irritably. "I've been trying to call you."

"It's a long story that I would like to tell you in person if you are game."

"Right now?"

"That was my plan."

"Good. I've been missing you."

"You have anything going on tomorrow?"

"No, nothing particular."

"Pack your bags then. We're going to take a little trip."

"Oh cool! Where are we going?"

"That's a surprise."

"Oh? A surprise? Hmm. I like surprises, but how will I know what to pack?"

"You'll need warm clothes."

"Okay. I'll be packed and ready to go when you get here. Are you leaving right now?"

"Yes, ma'am. See you soon."

He hung up the phone and proceeded to call Jim. A woman answered and when he asked to speak to Jim, she gave him the phone.

"Hey, I just wanted to call to see if you'd heard anything new . . . you know, about what we talked about yesterday."

"Actually, I did hear something from Sinclair just before I left work."

"What?"

"He said the FBI lost you, something about sabotage to their car. They're really pissed off at whoever helped you shake them."

"Oh God. Do they know who it was?"

"I don't think so, but they definitely think you're the thief now, especially since you went to all that trouble to ditch them."

"Shit!"

"Oh, and they're watching your two lady friends too. They're hoping one of them will turn on you."

"Well, I guess that makes sense. I was just on my way to see Candy. They haven't talked to her yet. I hope they don't try to make contact with her before I get there. She has no idea what's going on."

"Be careful. She may be cooperating with them."

"I don't think she would, but then, who knows? Thanks for the warning anyway."

"My pleasure. Now, don't disappoint me and let them bloody bastards catch you."

"I won't, Jim."

Fred's newly painted dark blue Ford Falcon was parked outside the office of Kwik Paint. He walked around the vehicle, inspecting it carefully. It was a pretty good job, which surprised him. When he went inside to pay for the work and compliment them, a long-haired kid in a t-shirt was manning the cash register.

"I guess my car is ready—the Ford Falcon?"

"Yeah, here's the ticket. It comes to $103.95 with tax."

"You guys did a great job," Fred said appreciatively.

"It'll look good for about six months, and then you'll wish you went somewhere else."

Fred laughed. "Really? Why didn't you tell me that before I had it done?"

"Hey, I am not a salesman. I am just the cashier."

"Obviously," Fred agreed. "Well, if it lasts six months, I guess I'll be happy. It's still a bargain. Thanks for your help."

It was past six, so Fred took off toward San Bernardino. There was just one more thing he had to do to further disguise his vehicle—the license plate. By now, it had been broadcast to every law enforcement officer in southern California. He had to change his plates, and he knew exactly where he could change them. He would need a big steak bone, however, so he stopped in at the first grocery store he saw and headed for the meat department to bum a steak bone from the butcher.

With a steak bone neatly wrapped up in butcher paper, he continued his journey. After about an hour, he pulled up about a block away from Loma Linda Auto Salvage. It was starting to get dark, and the yard looked deserted except for Prince. He hoped Prince would remember him, but he had brought the bone just in case.

With a screwdriver in his back pocket, he strolled slowly up to the fence that encircled the yard. Prince immediately charged the fence and jumped up, barking fiercely.

"Prince! Hey, hey now. Calm down. Remember me?"

Prince continued to bark, so Fred sat down in front of the fence and waited. After a while, he quit barking and paced back and forth behind the fence.

"Now Prince, I am going to climb the fence. Don't have a fit now. If you're a good dog, I've got a surprise for you."

By this time, Prince seemed to remember him, so Fred slowly climbed the chain-link fence and descended down the other side. Prince continued to bark and pace but was not threatening. Fred unwrapped the butcher paper and fed Prince the bone. Prince wagged his tail happily and ran off to savor his snack.

With Prince occupied, Fred searched for the '59 Ford Falcon from which he had procured a new door. It hadn't been moved since he'd seen it last. There were a few other parts missing, and the weeds had grown since he'd last seen it, but otherwise, it was fully intact. Checking out the front and back, he was relieved to find that the license plates were still there. With his screwdriver in hand, he removed the plates and replaced them with his. Not wanting Elmer to notice that the plates had been switched, he smeared them with mud to camouflage the numbers.

With his mission accomplished, he cautiously walked back to the fence and noticed that Prince was still munching happily on his bone. Fred walked over to the dog, stroked his thick fur a few times, and then climbed back over the fence.

"Goodbye, Prince. Good dog."

After putting on the new plates, he got back on the San Bernardino Freeway and continued to Candy's apartment. After about an hour, he saw the Palm Springs exit and got off the freeway. When he got to the street leading to Candy's apartment, a strange uneasiness overcame him. As he approached the apartment complex, he saw a car similar to the one that had been following him earlier. Not wanting to be recognized, he continued past the apartment complex and parked several blocks away.

Candy's apartment had a parking area in the rear that provided sufficient cover for him to make his way to the rear of her apartment without being seen. Once in the complex, he scanned the area for any sign of FBI agents, but it seemed quiet. He walked up to Candy's door and knocked gently. The door swung open, and Candy appeared with a big smile. He stepped inside, closed the door, and they kissed.

"Hmm. . . I missed your sweet lips," Fred said.

"You did, huh?"

"Uh huh."

"I'm all ready to go," she said.

"Good. Where are your bags?"

"Right by the door."

"Okay. Get whatever else you need, and let's go."

Candy grabbed a large paper bag and a jacket, and they left.

"My car is in the back."

"In the back? How come?"

"Um, I couldn't find a parking spot out front."

"Gee. . . . I've never had that problem. Maybe's someone's having a party."

They slipped around back and walked down the alley until they finally arrived at Fred's car.

"This isn't your car," Candy complained.

"Yes, it is. I got a paint job."

"You did? Why?"

"Don't you remember my door was blue and the rest of the car was maroon?"

"Oh, that's right. I had forgotten about that."

"Get in. Let's go."

Before long, they were on the open road, and Fred felt much better. He looked into his rearview mirror and was relieved to see that no one was behind them. He took a deep breath and smiled at Candy.

"Isn't this great?" he said. "There is nothing better than to hit the open road and embark on a new adventure, particularly with a beautiful woman to keep you company."

"When are you going to tell me where we're going?" Candy asked expectantly.

"I guess now is as good a time as ever."

"Good. So where are we headed?"

"We're going to a place my parents took me to years ago called Devil's Canyon. We weren't intending to go there, actually . . . well, I better start from the beginning. It's a kind of long story."

"That's alright. I want to hear it."

Chapter 20

Panic

Joel Roberts threw down the afternoon edition of the LA Times in disgust. He couldn't believe Harvey Hamlin had been found dead in the vault at Bank USA. He knew exactly what that meant. Their worst-case scenario just catapulted from bank robbery to murder. He couldn't imagine what had gone wrong. He picked up the phone and called Sinclair. "I just saw the paper. What the hell happened?"

"Ah. I don't know, but don't worry. Everything is fine. The campaign fund is whole again."

"Well, that's good news, but what about Fred?"

"Don't worry about him. If he's smart he'll take his million bucks and disappear. It's perfect, if you think about it. If they think Fred is responsible for the robbery they won't be looking for anyone else."

"The Congressman is going to be pissed, though. He likes Fred and wouldn't have agreed to let him take the fall for murder."

"I know, but Fred was the perfect patsy, young, naive and honest to a fault. It's unfortunate about Harvey, but that's just one less thread that might come unraveled."

"So, did Harvey's really die of a heart attack?"

"That's what my guy tells me, but you'll have to wait and see what the coroner says."

"What does that mean?"

"It means Harvey had to die and the deed is done," Sinclair said irritably. "Did you really think I'd trust a drunken asshole like Harvey Hamlin to keep his mouth shut."

Joel took a deep breath. "No. I suppose not."

"Don't worry. Everything is falling into place. Just keep your cool and don't let the Congressman give you any shit about Fred Fuller. Sometimes there is collateral damage you don't like, but there's nothing you can do about it. It's just fate."

Joel hung up the phone. He was relieved the campaign fund was whole again, but Fred Fuller worried him. If he got caught and pled innocent, a good defense attorney would do a thorough investigation and their whole plan might get unraveled. Then he had a thought. If Fred got caught, he could volunteer to be his attorney. A smile crept across his face.

Chapter 21

Devil's Canyon

Fred stared out at the open road ahead as he thought back to the summer of 1961. "I was thirteen years old and had gone to bed early one Friday night since we were leaving the first thing in the morning for the Mojave Desert. My dad had an old college friend who was working in an iron ore mine in the desert, and we were going to visit him and then do some exploring. During the night, there was an earthquake that rattled the house pretty bad and woke everybody up.

"Fortunately, there wasn't any damage to the house so Dad didn't cancel the trip. We traveled in our sky-blue Nash Rambler station wagon, which was a roomy car but prone to having mechanical problems, especially overheating.

"Ventura is about sixty miles north of LA, so by ten, we were passing through Palm Springs and heading east into the desert. My dad had an excellent sense of direction and he could travel anyplace on the Earth as long as he had a map. In fact, our glove compartment was the depository of every map you would ever need in North America.

"After a couple more hours, we arrived at Whispering Ridge Construction Camp where Walt was living. We visited with he and his wife for a while, had lunch and then Walt showed us around the camp. They invited us to stay for the afternoon, but Dad wanted to find a place to camp for the night and thought we should get going.

"Walt suggested we camp at an old abandoned mining camp about forty-five miles away in the Hackberry Mountains called Devil's Canyon. He said it was a beautiful spot that very few people knew about. That intrigued my father so we got directions on how to get there and were on our way. It wasn't easy to find the place but four hours later we pulled into this cool little ghost town.

"As we drove through the town we saw a couple of hotels,

some shops, a saloon, a café, and a telegraph office. Most of the buildings were made of adobe since there was no wood in the desert. There were a few frame buildings apparently made from wood hauled in many miles from the Sierra Nevada Mountains to the north. Just past the downtown area, someone had built some picnic tables, so Dad pulled in next to them.

"While my Mom and Dad were setting up camp Mary, my dog Sheila and I went into town and explored the hotel and all the other buildings there. The town must have been abandoned in a hurry because most of the furnishings were still in place. We were really quite amazed by what we had found and after lunch we all went exploring again. It was then that I discovered the assayer's office.

"It was a frame building on the outskirts of town that housed a sweet little laboratory. There were three large tables with test tubes, Bunsen burners, flasks, and bottles of chemicals. Five or six big barrels were set up against the wall. I tried the window to see if it would open, but it wouldn't. I tried the front door, but it was securely latched so, in frustration, I kicked the door and, much to my surprise, it swung open.

"My dad was angry with me for breaking in until we discovered a calendar and realized nobody had been in the lab since August 23, 1921. That made him realize nobody would care that we broke in. So, we all took a few souvenirs, locked up the laboratory as best we could and went back to the camp.

"My parents slept that night in the car and Mary, Sheila and I slept under the stars. Sheila and I got up early the next morning and hiked up the toward Crystal Springs. It was the mining camp's only water supply that had dried up in 1921 and was the main reason the camp had been closed. Surprisingly, the earthquake the day before had reopened the springs and water was flowing again. As I got to the base of the dam I noticed trickling water coming out from beneath a large manmade pile of boulders that acted as a dam. So, I climbed to the top of the dam and, sat on a huge boulder and looked out over Crystal Springs.

"As I sat quietly enjoying the silence of the desert, I wondered what life in a mining camp must have been like forty years earlier. Unexpectedly, my meditation was interrupted by a terrifying hissing sound. Sheila began to bark and growl incessantly.

"My pulse quickened as I observed in my peripheral vision a rattlesnake to my right. I knew from my Boy Scout training not to move or make any noise, but my instincts told me to run. I suddenly darted toward the water. Unfortunately, I tripped on a rock and fell down. The snake attacked swiftly with one vicious bite to my calf and then slithered off into the brush. Sheila took off after the snake. I yelled at her to come back, but she was too preoccupied with her hunt and her quest for vengeance on my serpentine assailant to pay any attention to me. She chased the snake as it escaped toward the mountains. Suddenly, the snake stopped, coiled, and struck Sheila in the abdomen. Sheila reacted by pouncing on the snake, sinking her teeth into its head, and violently shaking it back and forth until it was dead. After killing the snake, Sheila came over to me and began licking my face.

"Panic overcame me as I realized my worst nightmare had suddenly become reality. Snakes had always terrified me. Quickly, I began to feel an intense pain around the area of the bite. I began to cry and moan as the pain intensified and began to spread. I knew then exactly what I had to do. Snakebite procedures had been covered many times in Scout meetings. Two small incisions across the bite would be required, and then I would have to suck out the venom. This had always seemed like a kind of obscure and theoretical task. Never in a million years would I have thought I might actually have to do it.

"I could feel the venom spreading and knew time was of the essence. Reaching into my jeans, I pulled out my knife and opened the longest blade. I swallowed hard, staring at the bite, which was quickly swelling. I knew I had to make the cuts, but I couldn't force myself to do it. The knife quivered in my hand as I slowly forced myself to make the incisions. As it turned out, I hardly felt the sharp steel blade because the pain from the snake venom was so excruciating. I leaned down to suck out the blood, but I wasn't flexible enough to reach my calf. Again and again I tried, but I couldn't do it. I decided the best thing I could do would be to squeeze as much blood out of my leg as I could. After a few minutes, I grew weak and passed out from blood loss and pain—and probably a little bit of terror and shock.

"While I was unconscious, I had a dream. In my dream, I was sitting on a rock, just as I had been right before the snake attack. Before me was Crystal Springs, except it had swollen from a pool to a pond that now encompassed the entire basin. There were cottonwood trees and thick bunch-grass around it, and birds could be heard chirping. My attention was then attracted to the sound of splashing water. I looked toward the noise and saw a naked woman walking slowly through the water toward me. She had long, blond, silky hair and lustful breasts. When she reached me, we began kissing and embracing one another.

"I passed out again and didn't wake up until the next day. When I opened my eyes, Mom was asleep in a chair beside me and Dad was at the window, just staring outside. When they told me Sheila had died saving my life I was crushed."

Chapter 22

Vision of Death

"Wow, that was some story," Candy said, shaking her head. "I'm sorry about your dog."

"Thanks. She was a great dog. . . But anyway, the funny thing is, the earthquake opened up the spring, and there was water once again."

"Does anyone else know about this place?" Candy asked.

"No, I don't think so. Nothing seems to be disturbed from the last time I was here. I doubt anyone has discovered it."

"Oooh. . . this is going to be fun."

Candy cuddled up next to Fred and laid her head on his shoulder. It was very dark and peaceful. "You know, I really didn't expect you to accept my proposal," Candy confessed.

"You didn't?"

"No. I thought you were hopelessly in love with Maria and I had no chance."

"You are very different from Maria."

"In what way?"

"Maria is great. She'd make a wonderful wife and a great mother, but she'd never be able to excite me the way you do. Every time I see you, I get so aroused it's difficult for me to control my passions."

"Who says you have to?"

"I can't make love to you every minute, babe."

"Why not?" Candy said as she put her arms around him and began kissing him passionately. The car swerved over the center lane toward an oncoming car. Fred pushed Candy aside and narrowly missed a head-on collision. "Hey, watch it! You're going to get us killed! Save that for later—when we're safely inside a motel."

She laughed. "I'm sorry. I am just so excited. This the

happiest day of my life."

"Mine too. I think we better find a motel soon so we can bring the day to a proper conclusion."

"Too bad we don't have some champagne."

"Well, if I were old enough, I would stop and get some."

"I just turned twenty-one."

"You did? Hmm. I wondered how old you were. When's your birthday?"

"June 17."

When they got to the next town, they found a liquor store and a motel and settled in for the night—and what a night it turned out to be. Candy got exactly what she wanted, and she was a happy woman. The night was so great, in fact, that Fred almost forgot he was running for his life.

The next morning, the couple ate breakfast at a little café across the street from the motel. Candy called her friend Jenny and asked her to feed her cat, and then they continued their journey to Devil's Canyon. It was a beautiful day, and they were thoroughly enjoying each other's company. Fred hadn't decided exactly how he was going to break the news about the bank robbery to Candy, but he knew he had to do it soon, as it would not be long before they got to Devil's Canyon and his stash. Having procrastinated as long as he could, he finally addressed the issue. "Candy, have you ever been to Canada?"

"Canada? No, why?"

"How would you like to head on up to Canada for a while after we go to Devil's Canyon?"

Candy turned her head and gave Fred a funny little grin. "What are you talking about?"

Fred looked over at her briefly, returned the grin, and then continued his questioning. "If I had to go to Canada to avoid the draft, would you go with me?"

Candy frowned and hesitated before responding. "Gee, I don't know. How would we live?"

"Let's assume money is not a problem."

"Money's not a problem? Hmm. Well, in that case, maybe for a while, I could study acting in Canada, but after a few years I would need to get back to Hollywood or go to New York. Why? Have you been drafted?"

"No, but I can't go back to LA."

Candy shifted her body around toward Fred and gave him a puzzled look. "What?"

"I can't go back to LA."

"LA? You mean Los Angeles. Like home?"

"Yes."

"Whoa! You're full of surprises today. What's happened?"

"If I go back to LA, I'll be arrested."

"Arrested? For what?"

"Bank robbery."

Her eyes lit up like someone flipped a switch. "The San Bernardino heist?" she gasped.

He nodded. "I wasn't in on the job," he hastened to add, "but someone is trying to set me up. The thief left a bag of money in my car, hoping I'd get caught with it, I guess, so the Feds would blame the robbery on me and stop looking for them."

"Holy shit, Fred! How much money are we talkin' about here?"

"A million bucks and some change!"

Candy just looked at Fred incredulously. "Oh, my God! I can't believe this. I'm speechless."

"You've never been speechless in your life. Isn't this what you wanted? If I am a millionaire, you're a millionaire. Money will never, ever be a problem again—for either of us."

Candy's contemplated the thought of being a millionaire for a moment not knowing what to say. She was obviously stunned, but Fred was convinced she'd soon regain her composure. "But what if they find out you have the money?" she asked.

"They already think I have the money—all the money—all six, nearly seven million dollars. That's why we're going to Canada. I figure we can just change our identities, and I could pose as a draft dodger."

"Aren't you worried I'll turn you in?"

"A little, but you must care about me some, or you wouldn't have handpicked me to be your, uh. . . . business partner. Besides, this is your dream come true, isn't it? Why would you do anything to spoil it?"

"Okay, I'm game, but I don't want to go to jail as an accessory if something goes wrong. I never planned to do anything illegal—immoral, unethical, sure, but not illegal. I value my freedom more than anything."

"You won't be an accessory. As far as you know, we're going to Canada because I am a draft dodger, alright?"

"Alright. You sure there was a million dollars in the bag?"

"Yep. I counted it myself."

"Wow! This is so exciting. I feel like I've just won the lottery."

"Wait until you see the money."

"Oh, so you stashed the money in Devil's Canyon?"

"Yeah. After I saw you Friday night, I went straight there."

Candy just kept grinning at Fred, barely able to contain her joy. "Oh my God! I can't wait to see it. Step on it!"

"We can't speed. We can't afford to get stopped by the Highway Patrol."

"Oh, yeah, you're right. We've got to be careful, law-abiding citizens—at least until we get to Canada."

"Now you've got the picture."

They finally arrived at Devil's Canyon at about 2:00 p.m. It was fairly warm, probably near 80°. Fred scanned the road into town and the hills around it for any sign they were being watched, but he saw nothing suspicious. They drove slowly through downtown and stopped the car at the picnic tables on the north side and turned off the engine. After they got out of the car, Fred looked at Candy in the light of the bright desert sun and froze. It suddenly dawned on him that Candy was the woman in his vision! "Oh my God!" he exclaimed.

Candy twisted around and looked at Fred anxiously. "What? What's wrong?"

He laughed. "I'm sorry. I didn't mean to scare you. I just realized something quite amazing."

"What?"

"Do you believe a person can see into the future?"

"Well, I don't know. I haven't really thought about it that much."

"I've told you about my recurring dreams, right?"

"Uh huh."

"I didn't realize it until just now, but I've seen you in my dreams—before we ever met."

"You have?"

"Yes. Remember I told you I was bitten by a rattlesnake here and went into a coma?"

"Right."

"While I was unconscious, I had a vision in which a beautiful woman and I were swimming in a spring not too far from here. I've had that same vision many times since then. It wasn't until just now that I realized you are the woman of my dreams—literally."

Candy raised her eyebrows. "That's bizarre."

"I know, but it's true. We were destined to be together."

At that, a naughty little smile came over Candy's face. "Well then, I guess we better fulfill our destiny," she said with a provocative smile.

Fred frowned. "What do you mean?"

"I mean, as I recall, your vision involved skinny dipping. It's so hot, I feel like a swim, but I forgot to pack my bathing suit."

"Ah, yes, you're right," Fred agreed. "We must embrace our destiny!"

Taking Candy by the hand, he led her up toward the dam with joyful anticipation. After about a thirty-minute hike, they reached its base. The dam was overflowing, creating a small creek that wound its way toward the camp. They carefully negotiated their way up to the top of the dam and peered down at Crystal Springs. The landscape had changed dramatically in the last seven years since Fred had been there. The barren wasteland had given way to a tropical paradise. Cottonwood trees, monkey flowers, and ivy were abundant around the springs, and birds chirped endlessly. Mother Nature had created a wonderful oasis in the desert, just for them.

Candy stopped and gave Fred an appreciative look. "This is the most beautiful place I have ever seen. I can't believe we have it all to ourselves."

"I know. Isn't this incredible?"

Candy sat on a big boulder and began taking off her clothes as Fred watched with great interest and excitement. As she waded into the pool, she looked over at him, smiled, and asked, "What are you waiting for?"

At that, he ripped off his clothes and dived into the water. When he surfaced in front of Candy, she splashed water in his face and taunted him. He swam after her, caught her by the arm, and pulled her close to him. By this time, he had become so aroused that he must have squeezed her too hard, for she whimpered in painful joy. They kissed passionately as he stroked her sweet bottom and tender breasts beneath the sparkling water. Finally, she put her arms around his neck, wrapped her legs around his waist, and they made love to the rhythm of the desert wind blowing through the cottonwoods.

After their sexual cravings had been momentarily fulfilled, Candy strolled out of the water, looked around, and giggled. "We don't have any towels."

"I'm sorry. I hadn't planned on going swimming today."

"Well, aren't you glad we did?"

"Oh, most definitely," he sighed. "I guess you'll have to just lay out a little while and let the sun dry you naturally."

"Yeah, right. You just want to gawk at my naked body. I know you."

"You can't blame me, can you? I'm only human."

"Hmm. I guess I'll go over and sit on that rock. This place better be uninhabited."

"It is, don't worry."

After about fifteen minutes, they were dry and began putting on their clothes. When Fred was fully dressed, he walked over to the top of the dam to look out over Devil's Canyon. A familiar rustling sound in the bushes sent a shudder through him. He spun around and immediately spotted a large rattlesnake directly behind Candy. His heart skipped a beat. "Candy, don't move!" he whispered urgently.

She looked up. "What's wrong?"

"Whatever you do, don't move. There's a snake behind you."

"A snake!" she screamed and instinctively twisted around to look for it.

The snake, provoked by her sudden movement, viciously attacked her, biting her several times on the leg and ankles. She screamed and fell hard to the ground, holding her leg in agony.

"Oh my God!" Fred said as he ran toward her. When he reached her, he picked up a large rock and threw it at the snake. The rock stunned the slender beast, and it slithered away into the brush.

Fred's mind was suddenly flooded with memories of his previous encounter with a rattlesnake at that very spot. "No! Please God! No! This can't be happening—not again!" he wailed.

Candy began to scream in pain as the venom began to spread up her leg. Knowing exactly what he had to do, he pulled out his knife and cut two small incisions across each of the bites. Then he sucked out the poison and spit in onto the ground. Candy squirmed and cried until the pain was so intense she passed out.

Once he had sucked out as much of the poison as he could,

he picked her up and carried her two miles back to the car. He knew she needed to get to a hospital as fast as she could to get some anti-venom. He laid her on the back seat and put a pillow under her head. As he gazed at her pale face, he wondered where his parents had found medical help when he had been bitten.

In the glove compartment, he found a map and pulled it out. According to the map, the closest civilization was a town called Kelso, about fifty miles away. He couldn't go too fast on the dusty, bumpy road, as he knew that any jarring or movement of Candy's body would cause the poison to spread. Finally, he got to the main road and pushed the pedal to the floorboard.

It seemed like forever, but eventually he arrived in Kelso, California. The sign going into town said 'Population: 1,337'. Still, he didn't know where in the hell they all were because the town seemed deserted. The only buildings of any consequence were a bank and the post office. Opting for the post office, he parked in front and ran inside. An elderly man was seating behind the counter. "Sir, my girlfriend has been bitten by a snake! Where can I get her some medical attention?"

"There are no doctors around here. I'll have to call in for a Medivac helicopter," the man advised.

"Please call them right now! She may be dying."

"Okay. I'll call right now."

As soon as the call had been placed, Fred went back out to the car to attend to Candy. She was still unconscious. Her body was cold and clammy, and her breathing was strained. They waited and waited for what seemed like an hour until the helicopter finally arrived.

Once on the ground, the paramedics emerged with a stretcher. "Where's the victim?" the first paramedic asked.

"In the car," Fred replied.

"How long has it been since she was bitten?"

"About two and a half hours. I came for help as quick as I could."

"Where is the bite?"

"There are actually three bites, sir. There are two on her leg and one on her abdomen."

The paramedic examined the two bites on her leg. "It looks like someone rendered first aid."

"Yes, I made an incision on each bite and sucked out as

much of the poison as I could."

"It's a good thing. She'd probably be dead if you hadn't."

"Oh, God, I hope she's going to be alright."

"We won't know until we get her to the hospital. Okay, let's lift her on the stretcher," he said. "You can come with us. They might need to talk to you."

"Thanks. Where are we going?"

"Memorial Hospital in Barstow. They have some good doctors there, and they have lots of experience in treating snake bites."

"Good."

The helicopter lifted off, and twenty minutes later, they arrived at the hospital heliport. The moment they landed, the paramedics rushed Candy into the emergency room, and Fred took a seat in the waiting room. How ironic for Candy to get bitten by a rattlesnake just as I did seven years earlier, Fred thought. Was this another act of fate?

Then, Fred recalled the dream and the terror he had seen in Candy's eyes. He hadn't understood it until now. Why didn't I figure it out sooner? I should have known something bad was going to happen, damn it! I had been warned but didn't heed the warning.

As he sat in the waiting room, he realized he'd have to alter his strategy. He couldn't flee to Canada with Candy critically ill in the hospital.

Maybe Canada would have been a mistake anyway. Perhaps I was jumping the gun in running. What if the FBI doesn't have anything on me? They certainly had ample opportunity to arrest me yesterday if that had been their objective. He didn't know what to do. His instincts told him to run, but logic told him that running would make it clear that he was guilty.

If I go back to work on Monday and act like I'm totally innocent, maybe I can beat this thing. It's risky, but if I don't show up for work on Monday, everyone will assume I am the bank robber, and I'll spend the rest of my life as a fugitive.

The nurse walked in and advised him that Candy had been moved to intensive care. Her condition was stable, but she was still unconscious. Since he hadn't eaten all day, he went down to the cafeteria to see what kind of food was available. Two police officers were sitting at a table drinking a cup of coffee. Their presence made him nervous, so he grabbed a sandwich and a Coke and went straight back to the ICU waiting room. In the corner of the room, a small television set was turned on. It was nearly ten, so he turned on the evening news.

Midway through the broadcast, Fred's attention was averted to a story on the Bank USA robbery. The correspondent was about to interview Agent Joe Harper of the FBI. "Agent Harper, does the FBI have any suspects yet in the recent bank robbery of Bank USA in San Bernardino?"

"We have a couple of suspects but nothing conclusive yet."

"Does the FBI think it was an inside job?"

"We don't know for sure, but it certainly looks that way. There was no forced entry, and the alarm system had not been activated. Unfortunately, the only person who could tell us for sure is dead."

"You're referring to Harvey Hamlin?" suggested the correspondent.

"Yes. Mr. Hamlin was found bound and gagged in the vault."

"Did he suffocate in there?"

"No. There is a ventilation system in the vault. It appears he had a heart attack from the stress of being tied up and gagged and left inside the vault for over two days."

"What are your plans now for continuing this investigation?"

"The FBI is working very hard to solve this mystery. Sooner or later, the perpetrator of the crime will make a mistake, and his or her identity will become clear."

"Thank you, Agent Harper."

Harper's interview convinced Fred he should go back to work. He didn't want to make the mistake Harper had eluded to in his statement. After the news, Fred's fatigue finally overcame him, so he collapsed on the stiff waiting room sofa and closed his eyes. Within a minute or two he was snoring softly.

Chapter 23

Barstow Memorial

The next day, Candy's condition had not changed. She was still in a coma, and the doctors didn't have any idea when or if she would come out of it. Fred wanted to stay with her at the hospital, but he knew if he didn't go to work, it would look suspicious. He assumed Harper wasn't lying on the television when he said the FBI didn't have enough evidence to pin the robbery on anyone yet.

As Fred was leaving the hospital, he suddenly realized his car was still in Kelso, so he took a cab to the Greyhound station and got on the bus to Las Vegas. When the bus went through Baker, California, he got off and hitched a ride to Kelso. It was well after midnight when he finally got back to his apartment in Santa Monica.

The next day, he slept through all of his classes and went straight to work. As he walked into the motor pool, he felt everyone's eyes on him, although he knew it was probably his imagination. Jim had a clipboard in his hand and was writing intently.

"Afternoon, Jim," Fred said.

Jim looked up and replied, "Afternoon, mate. What in the hell are you doing here?"

"What do you mean? Shouldn't I be here? I'm scheduled to work, right?"

"I don't know. I thought maybe you'd be, uh, vacationing by now."

"Right. Well, maybe I like to live on the edge."

"I hope you don't slip off, mate."

"Me too. So, what's going on?"

"You tell me. The FBI has been snooping around here all morning asking about you."

"What did they want to know?"

"If anyone knows you very well, where you hang out, if any of us know where you were this weekend—that kind of stuff."

"Well, I don't know why they're so interested in me. I've already talked to them and told them I don't know anything."

"They are so bloody frustrated over this robbery. They don't have any clue as how it could have happened or who was responsible. The fancy bank security system was a bloody failure, and now the brass at Bank USA are worried about their other branches."

"There must be other suspects besides me," Fred complained.

"Sam Stewart is a suspect, but they don't really think he did it."

"I don't understand that," Fred protested. "He quit right after the heist and he's not a suspect? What do they want, an engraved confession?"

"I'm just reporting what I hear, Fred. I can't say I understand their logic."

Fred shook his head. "I know. It's just frustrating that I've got to take all the heat."

"So, where did you go this weekend after you lost your escort? You're looking kind of tired."

"Candy and I went on a camping trip in the desert. What a mistake. She was bitten by a rattlesnake."

"No! Don't be kiddin' me, lad."

"I wish I were. We went swimming in this secluded pond that I discovered many years ago. As we were leaving, a rattlesnake slithered up behind Candy. When I saw it, I told her not to move, but she panicked, and the snake attacked her."

"Oh, Jesus, Mary, and Joseph! What a cruel twist of fate. I'm so sorry, Fred."

"Yeah, so I've been at the hospital all night with her."

"How is she?"

"Not good. She's still in a coma and was in intensive care when I left. I pray to God she pulls through."

"I am surprised you're not taking today off, considering her condition."

"Well, I knew the FBI was pissed off that I lost their tail. I figured if didn't show up today, they would be sure I was their bank robber. As you said, they're desperate to solve this case. Besides, I am going right back to the hospital right after my route, so Candy won't even know I was gone."

"Well, I hope she gets better."

"Thanks. I better get going."

As Fred turned to go pick up his keys, he spotted Agent Harper walking out of Sinclair's office. He hesitated momentarily and then walked straight at him, poker faced. As he approached, he smiled and said, "Agent Harper, I saw you last night on the ten o'clock news."

"Oh. The interview, right?"

"Yeah. How's the investigation going?"

"Oh, we've got a few leads," he said as he looked at Fred suspiciously. "Did you have a nice weekend?"

"Not really. I spent last night in the hospital, if you can believe that. My girlfriend was bitten by a rattlesnake."

"A rattlesnake? My God! Is she going to be okay?"

"We don't know yet. She's still in a coma."

"Well, I hope she recovers. What a horrible thing to happen."

"I know. I still can't believe it."

"So, what hospital is she at? I'd like to send flowers."

"I'm sure she would love that, but she's in intensive care and can't receive flowers yet," Fred answered, wisely avoiding the agent's prying question.

"Oh, is that right?"

"Yes, I am afraid so. Listen, it was nice seeing you, but I've got to get on the road. Good luck with your investigation."

Fred knew Agent Harper would alert his team that he had showed up for work and the FBI would resume following him as he left the motor pool. So, after he checked in he wasn't planning on doing anything out of the ordinary. While he was at the Palm Springs branch, he advised the branch cashier of Candy's hospitalization and asked him if he had her mother's or father's address. According to her personnel file, her mother and father were dead, and the only person listed as an emergency contact was a friend named Jenny Madeira. The cashier gave Fred Jenny's address and telephone number, and he left. Immediately after completing his route, Fred returned to Barstow and arrived there about midnight.

The hospital was quiet at that deserted hour. Fred went to the intensive care unit and asked the charge nurse how Candy was doing. She said he needed to talk to Dr. Winston, who was in the emergency room at the moment treating an accident victim. She offered to go find him, so Fred took a seat and waited.

About thirty minutes later, Dr. Winston strolled into the waiting room and went up to him. "You came in with Candy Clisby, right?" he asked.

"Yes, sir," Fred replied.

"Were you related to her?"

"She's my girlfriend."

"I am sorry to have to tell you this, but . . . well, she didn't make it."

His words hit Fred like a sledgehammer. "What!" he gasped.

"She died a few hours ago. I'm very sorry."

Fred shook his head in disbelief. "No! No, that's not possible. She was breathing fine when I left her."

"She could have probably survived one bite, but the toxin from three bites was too much."

Fred rubbed his forehead and tried to breathe. "She can't be dead. Don't tell me she's dead. Please! Didn't you give her anti-venom?"

"We did, but it was too late. Again, we did all we could, and I'm very sorry."

Tears began streaming down Fred's cheeks. "But I sucked the poison out of her immediately after she got bitten. I didn't wait a second."

"You may have sucked a lot of it out, but enough managed to spread throughout her system to kill her."

Fred shook his head. "She can't be dead. . . . she just can't be!" he moaned. "She was a strong girl. Not Candy. No way! She can't be dead."

"Are you going to be alright, sir? Would you like me to prescribe something to help you sleep tonight?" Dr. Winston asked.

"I can't believe she's dead. It's just not possible," Fred moaned.

"I'll prescribe something to help you sleep."

Fred shook his head angrily. "No. . . I'll be alright. Just leave me alone!"

As Dr. Winston was leaving the room, Fred tried to pull himself together, but he just couldn't manage it. "She can't be dead!" he bellowed. "We were on our way to Canada to start a new life. Oh God, this can't be happening. What am I going to do without her? Couldn't you do anything to keep her alive? Damn you! Why did you let her die?"

Fred collapsed on the sofa and began crying uncontrollably. Dr. Winston called one of the nurses and told her to watch him and make sure he was okay before he left the hospital. He reiterated how sorry he was and then excused himself. The nurse was very sympathetic and concerned about Fred. She came by the waiting room every few minutes to make sure he was okay. She confided in him that she'd lost her mother several months earlier and knew how he felt. Finally, Fred regained his composure, thanked the nurse, and left the hospital. As he was leaving he looked at his watch and saw it was after 2:03 a.m.

He drove around aimlessly for a while, wanting to talk to someone—someone who knew Candy. The only person he could think of was Candy's friend, Jenny Madeira. It was the middle of the night, but he figured she would want to know her friend was dead. He found a pay phone and gave her call.

"Hello?" a sleepy voice whispered.

"Hi. Is this Jenny Madeira?"

"Yes. Who is this?"

"Jenny, this is Fred Fuller. I am sorry to call you at this hour, but—"

"Oh, Fred, that's okay. What's wrong?"

"I don't know how to tell you this, but . . . but—"

"What's wrong?"

"Candy is dead."

"Huh?"

"Candy died a few hours ago."

"Oh my God! What happened?"

"She was bitten by a rattlesnake."

"What? A rattlesnake?"

"I tried to save her, but we were so far from the hospital by the time I got her there, it was too late."

"Oh no," Jenny said, choking up.

"I'm so sorry this happened," Fred said. "It's all my fault. I shouldn't have taken her out there."

"Where are you?"

"I am in Barstow at a pay phone."

"What are you going to do tonight?"

"I don't know. I'll go back to LA, I guess."

"Why don't you come to my place? I don't want to be alone tonight, and you shouldn't be either."

"Where do you live?"

"Just a few doors away from where Candy lived, Apartment 131."

"Okay. I am on my way. It will probably be a few hours before I get there."

"I'll have a pot of coffee on."

About 4:00 a.m. on Tuesday morning, Fred arrived at Jenny's apartment. She invited him in and poured him a cup of coffee. "I was dying to meet you after Candy talked about you. . . . but not under these circumstances, of course," Jenny said.

"This whole thing was a total shock to me. Yesterday, Candy and I were so happy, and we had made so many plans. It's just not fair."

"I know. I'm so sorry."

"So, how did you and Candy meet anyway?" Fred asked.

"We lived for several years in the same foster home together. Candy was like my sister, and we were very close."

"So, you and Candy have no relatives?"

"No known relatives."

"That must have been very lonely for you."

"That's why we were such good friends. We both felt alone without a real family. We needed each other."

"What do you do for living?"

"I am a secretary by day and student by night."

"What are you studying?"

"I want to be a paralegal."

"Oh really? I am going to be lawyer."

"So I heard."

"I guess you know about the mistress thing too?"

She rolled her eyes. "Yes. Candy is. . . . er, was a piece of work sometimes. She told me about it the night you paid her the $2,000."

"I thought she was just teasing me at first, but she persisted, so I decided to call her bluff."

"You know, I think she really loved you, but she was so obsessed with becoming an actress that she convinced herself she didn't have time for love. You could only be in her life if there were no strings attached and you would help her attain her dream."

"Well, I was prepared to live with that. I believe women are entitled to the fulfillment of their dreams just as much as men are."

"That's what I thought when she described you to me. She told me the other day—when she called and asked me to feed her cat—that you told her you would give up Maria for her."

"Oh, she told you that?"

"Yes. That made her realize how much you did love her and, for the first time, how much she loved you. I don't think she knew what love was before you came along."

"I did love her. I would have done anything just to be with her."

Up until then, Fred had maintained his composure, but at that point, he broke down and began to sob. "God, why did this happen to Candy—to us? It's not fair."

Jenny put her arms around him and held him tightly. Before long, his tears had become contagious, and Jenny was likewise weeping.

"I still can't believe she's dead," Fred said. "I'm going to miss her so much."

After a time, they both succumbed to their exhaustion and fell asleep. At sunrise, Fred woke up and discovered Jenny in his arms. He carefully untangled himself from her embrace and laid her down gently on the sofa. Then he went into the kitchen to make some fresh coffee.

After a few minutes, Jenny woke up and wandered into the kitchen. "I am hungry," she said. "Let's go get some breakfast. I don't feel like cooking."

"Yeah, that sounds good," Fred replied. "It's been a long time since I've eaten."

"Let me take a quick shower, and then we can go."

"Okay. I think I heard your newspaper arrive, so if you don't mind, I'd like to read it."

"Help yourself."

Opening the front door, Fred was startled to see an FBI agent standing at the end of the walkway. He had momentarily forgotten that he was now living in a fish bowl with God-only-knew how many people watching every move he made. He gave the agent a disgusted look and slammed the door.

At breakfast, Fred told Jenny about the FBI following him, but he didn't go into the details of the situation. He just explained that he was an innocent suspect that had to put up with the FBI investigation until the real criminal was apprehended. Jenny offered to arrange to have the body picked up. They agreed to an inexpensive funeral for Candy since there was virtually no family. To help defray the expenses, Fred gave Jenny the remainder of the $2,000, and they agreed to stay in touch.

Chapter 24

Investigation

After Fred had ditched his FBI tail, Agent Walters was angry and decided it was time to talk to Fred's family and friends to see if they knew anything about the bank robbery or had any idea where Fred might have stashed the money. The first names on his list were Fred's mother and father, who lived up the coast in Ventura. He took the Ventura Freeway from downtown LA and made it to the Victoria Trailer Park, where the Fullers lived, about ninety minutes later. It was an upscale trailer park geared for the retired more than the working class. He walked up to the door and rang the doorbell.

A big woman in her early fifties answered the door. "Hello. Can I help you?" she asked warily.

"Are you Mrs. Fuller?" he replied.

"Yes, I am."

Walters flipped out his FBI credentials and said, "I am Jim Walters of the Federal Bureau of Investigation, and I would like to ask you a few questions."

"The FBI?" she gasped. "Why? Did we make a mistake on our tax return or something?"

"No, no, ma'am, this isn't about you. It's about your son."

"Fred?"

"That's right."

Mrs. Fuller opened the door and let him in. They took chairs across from each other at the kitchen table. He smiled at her, trying to put her at ease. It didn't work. She stared at him with a worried look on her face.

"So, have you seen your son lately?"

"Well, it's been several weeks. He's in school at UCLA."

"Has he telephoned you in the past ten days?"

"No, sir. Is he okay?" Kristina asked fearfully.

"Yes, as far as we know," Walters replied.

"What's this all about?"

"I am not at liberty to discuss the details of an ongoing investigation. Have you been home the past two weeks?"

"Yes."

"Is it possible your son could have come home without your knowledge?"

"No. I would have seen him."

"Does your son have any friends in Ventura?"

"Yes. Steve and Randy are his best friends."

"What are their full names?"

"Steve Robins and Randy Hanson."

"Do you have their addresses?"

"Yes, of course."

"Can you get them for me."

She sighed. "Sure. I'll write them down for you," she said and then went a few steps to a small desk. She rumbled around in a drawer, found an address book and a blank piece of paper, and wrote down the information. When she was done, she walked back and handed it to him.

"Thank you. I just have a few more questions, if you don't mind."

"Well, I would really like to know what this is all about. Is Fred in some kind of trouble?"

"I can't comment on that now, Mrs. Fuller. Like I said, we are just conducting an investigation, and nothing has been determined yet. If I could just ask you a few more questions, I'll be out of your way."

"Okay. Go ahead," she said irritably.

"Has your son ever been in any trouble?"

"Absolutely not," she said indignantly. "My son was an A student and salutatorian of his high school class. He's a fine boy who has never been in trouble. He's even an Eagle Scout. If you think my son did anything wrong, you're mistaken. Fred wouldn't ever do anything dishonest."

"Well, I hope you're right, ma'am."

"Did anyone ever tell you the story about when he was a Congressional Intern?"

"He was a Congressional Intern?" Walters asked, a little surprised by the revelation.

"Yes, he was. He's going to go into politics someday. His

father and I think he may be become President. Well, anyway, he was working for Congressman Bartlett during the summer, and one day he opened up his paycheck and saw that they had given him $500 too much."

"Really?"

"Yes, and do you know what he did?"

"No, I guess I wouldn't."

"Well, he marched right over to his supervisor and reported it to her."

"Is that right?"

"And you know what she told him?"

"No, how would I?"

"She said, 'Fred Fuller, you are a stupid fool. Why didn't you just keep the money? The federal government wouldn't have missed it. Now I am going to have to do all kinds of paperwork to get this straightened out. You're just too honest for your own good'."

Walters laughed. "That sounds like a bureaucratic response."

"Why, do you know that last month Fred walked into a bank with the vault wide open and six million dollars staring him in his face and he didn't even flinch? He went straight to the telephone and reported to his supervisor that the vault was open. Now, you tell me, is there a more honest person on this Earth?"

"Well, you've convinced me, Mrs. Fuller," Walters lied. "I've got to be going now."

"I could tell you dozens of other stories," Kristina offered.

"No, that's okay Mrs. Fuller. Maybe another time. Thanks for your help."

Agent Walters left, shaking his head, and returned to his car. Kristina glared at him as he walked away. Walters closed the car door and picked up his Mapsco to locate Randy Hanson's residence from the address Mrs. Fuller had given him. After he'd worked out the route, he drove to Randy's house and knocked on the door.

Walters suspected Randy had been the one at the beach who had helped Fred lose his FBI surveillance team, but he had no proof. He was hoping to get Randy to admit it, so he'd have some leverage.

Randy was on the sofa eating a bowl of cereal when he heard the knock. He got up, walked to the door, and peered out the peep hole at the tall man dressed in a gray suit with a scowl on his face. Walters flashed Randy his FBI badge. Randy opened the door warily, wondering if they'd discovered it was he who'd so aptly disabled their car.

"My name is Jim Walters of the Federal Bureau of Investigation. Are you Randy Hanson?"

"Yes. What can I do for you?"

"I would like to ask you a few questions."

Randy stepped back from the door. "Come on in and have a seat," he said, trying not to appear nervous.

He showed Agent Walters into the living room and directed him to sit on the sofa. Walters began the interrogation without wasting time on pleasantries.

"I understand you are friends with Fred Fuller?"

"He's my best friend."

"Have you seen him lately?"

"Yes. I saw him the other day."

"When was that?"

"Let me see . . . it must have been Saturday."

"Where?"

"At the beach. We go girl-scouting from time to time there."

"Girl-scouting?"

"Yeah, you know. . . . some pretty good-looking chicks hang out at that beach. We've managed to land some pretty hot dates there."

"What did you talk about?"

"Nothing in particular. We just planned our strategy in meeting some girls."

"Why would Fred be out looking for more girls? He's already juggling two girlfriends, right?"

"Yeah, well, you never know when a woman will dump you."

"You know it's a criminal offense to lie to an FBI agent."

"I'm not lying; I have been dumped many times."

"You should take this interview seriously, Mr. Hanson."

"I am."

"When you met Fred at the beach, weren't you really there to help him get clear of his surveillance detail?"

"What? No way. He just wanted to talk."

"Do you know it's a felony to tamper with federal property?"

Walters' words cut like a knife through Randy's gut. He struggled to maintain his composure. "Is that right?" he replied shakily.

"Yes, and if you don't cooperate with us, you might find yourself indicted for that offence."

"I have no idea what you're talking about," Randy said, poker faced.

"You know goddamned well what I am talking about! You sabotaged the automobile our agents were driving so that your friend could escape our surveillance."

"You've got a vivid imagination," Randy replied angrily.

"Now, what did you and Fuller talk about?" Walters persisted.

"How often seagulls shit on dark blue cars," Randy spat.

Walters' face turned red. He took a deep breath. "You know, I can haul you down to FBI Headquarters and resume questioning you there if you'd like!"

Randy stood up. "Be my guest," he challenged, "but I promise you, it will be a waste of your time. I have told you all I know."

Walters stood up. "Okay. Have it your way. We'll continue this conversation at another time, but let me tell you one thing, this isn't over, my friend. Believe me, this isn't over. Have you ever heard the word accessory? You'll wish you'd been more cooperative when we throw your lying ass in jail!"

Randy pointed to the door. "Get out of my house! You don't have a damn thing on me, and you know it."

Walters glared at Randy. "Don't get too cozy. I'll be back. You can bet on it," he said and stormed out the door.

Randy followed Walters out the door, determined to get the last word. "Don't bother coming back unless you have a warrant!" he spat.

Chapter 25

Friends and Family

After Walters left, Kristina went straight to the telephone to call her son. Fred had just gotten in when the phone rang. He picked it up and heard his mother's frantic voice. After she'd finished filling him in on her encounter with Agent Walters, he tried to reassure her that everything was alright.

"Don't worry, Mom. The FBI has to investigate everyone connected with the bank. Since I am the bank messenger who stops there every day, they have to investigate me too."

"I am so scared, Fred. Are you sure you're not in any trouble?"

"They'll figure out eventually that I'm not the bank robber and leave me alone. Don't worry about it."

It upset Fred that Walters had dragged his parents into the investigation. Getting them involved was totally unnecessary from his viewpoint, and now Walters had probably talked to Steve and Randy too. Fred told his mother he'd call her later, hung up, and called Steve to see if he had also heard from Agent Walters. Steve told him that indeed Walters had stopped by, but that the interview had been very short since he knew nothing. Relieved, Fred then dialed Randy's number and waited.

"I am so pissed," Randy said as soon as he knew it was Fred on the line.

"Not at me, I hope."

"No. Some FBI agent named Walters came by. He's a real asshole."

"What happened?"

Randy filled Fred in on the visit and the shouting match it had quickly become. The way Randy had handled himself delighted Fred, and he complimented him on it.

"I am glad you didn't take any shit from that bastard, but I don't want you to get in any trouble."

"Don't worry. They can't prove a damn thing."

"So, what about me?" Fred asked. "Am I in deep shit or what?"

"No, they must have completed their analysis of the crime scene by now, so if they had found enough to arrest you, they would have already done it."

"It doesn't matter much anymore. I might just as well give myself up and tell them the truth."

"What are you talking about?"

"Candy died yesterday."

"What?"

"She was killed by a rattlesnake."

"Oh God! What a horrible way to die."

"Now I've lost both of the women I love."

"What happened to Maria?"

"I dumped her a few days ago for Candy, if you recall."

"Oh, that's right."

"She'll probably never talk to me again."

"That's probably true," Randy agreed. "I'm really sorry, Fred. What are you going to do now?"

"I don't know. I can't go to jail though. I know that much. I'd just as soon put a bullet in my head."

"Don't talk like that. This will all work out somehow."

"I don't see how. Anyway, I'm sorry the FBI hassled you. I better go. I am really tired and I feel like shit."

"Sure. I'm really sorry about Candy. If there is anything I can do, let me know."

The idea of suicide had crept into Fred's head more than once since his nightmare began, but he had dismissed it each time as rash and cowardly. Now, however, things were a lot worse. He wondered what he had to live for with Candy and Maria no longer in his life. If he was convicted, best case he'd get five years in federal prison but it would be a lot worse if the felony murder charge stuck. When, or if he ever he got out of prison, he'd be lucky if he could get a job at a gas station. Even worse would be the humiliation. How could he even look at his friends and family after being convicted of bank robbery and murder? A handful of sleeping pills seemed to Fred more and more like an option to consider.

The next day when Fred arrived at work, Jim took him aside to give him the latest news from Sinclair. He had overheard a conversation between Agent Harper and Sinclair about a meeting between the FBI and the United States Attorney, Samuel P. Whitehead, who had been assigned to the Bank USA case. "This Whitehead character has plans to go to Sacramento, you know," Jim said.

"Really?" Fred replied.

"He thinks you're his ticket there, from what I hear."

"Oh, that's great news," Fred moaned.

"They were talking about some witness from the hospital where Candy was treated."

"What witness?"

"Some doctor who overheard something you said."

"What? I don't remember saying anything to anyone."

"I don't know, but the FBI is pretty excited about it."

"Well, I sure as hell don't know what it could be."

"One other thing," Jim said.

"What?" Fred asked.

"They're definitely going to make a move on Maria. Since you dumped her, they figure she may testify against you."

"No way. Maria wouldn't betray me. Besides, she doesn't know anything."

"I guess they don't know that."

"Hmm. Well, thanks for the information, Jim. I am going to owe you one when this is all over."

"Ah, don't worry about it. It's been kind of fun snooping around here the last few days. I've really enjoyed it."

"Good. I'm glad someone's having fun," Fred said. "Well, I better get going. It's getting late. See you in a few hours."

"Drive carefully," Jim replied, "and watch your ass."

"Thanks. I'll do that."

Chapter 26

Painful Reunion

After all that had happened, Fred was too ashamed and embarrassed to call Maria. He knew she must be very confused and hurt after the way he'd abruptly broke up with her. He thought about calling and telling her he'd made a mistake and wanted her back, but it would have been a lie, and he couldn't lie to her. He knew it would only be a matter of time before he ran into her, and he feared that inevitable encounter, as he had no clue what he'd say. Much to his chagrin, that very day, when he walked out of his poli-sci class, there she was. She stopped in her tracks, obviously shocked to see him.

Fred hesitated a moment and then smiled. "Maria! I was hoping to run into you today."

Her eyes narrowed. "What are you doing here? I thought you had to leave the country?"

"Something came up, and I couldn't leave."

"Is this just a game you're playing? If you wanted to break up, you should have just said so. I don't need this kind of bullshit. I've been worried sick about you, and now you show up acting like nothing happened."

"I know. You must really hate me. The last few weeks have just been a nightmare."

"I thought we had a good relationship of trust and confidence, but you obviously don't trust me enough to tell me what in the hell is really going on."

"It's not that. I just don't want to get you involved."

"Involved in what?"

Before Fred could respond, two men in blue blazers and tan pants came up from behind, and one of them tapped him on the shoulder. "Are you Fred Fuller?"

Fred gave Maria a long look, turned around, and responded, "Yes."

"I am Don Harris with the Federal Bureau of Investigation. You are under arrest for the robbery of the San Bernardino branch of Bank USA and the murder of Harvey Hamlin. Please raise both of your hands and place them flat against the building."

Maria gasped in shock. "What are they talking about?" She demanded.

"I don't know. It must be some kind of a mistake. I didn't do anything."

Reluctantly, Fred complied with the agent's instructions while the other agent frisked and then cuffed him. Fred wasn't surprised by the arrest. He had half expected it all along, and he had resigned himself to his fate, but he hadn't wanted Maria to see it. The FBI's timing couldn't have been worse.

The agents escorted him to one of their familiar dark blue Buicks and put him in the back seat. They then drove off toward downtown LA, and after thirty minutes or so, they arrived at the Federal Building. Harris drove the car into the basement garage, where they were met by two deputy U.S. Marshals. They escorted Fred up to their sixteenth-floor offices. After they took him inside, they emptied his pockets, inventoried the contents, and completed an intake sheet. Finally, they led him into a small, windowless room with a table and two chairs.

After another thirty minutes, Agent Harper joined Fred in his holding cell. "Mr. Fuller, we meet again."

"What is this all about?"

"I think you know, Mr. Fuller."

"Well, your agents said I am being charged with bank robbery and murder, but I already told you I don't know anything about either of them."

"Well, unfortunately your story just doesn't hold water. Your prints are all over the bank."

"I explained that to you."

"I know, and that was very clever, but why did you pick this particular day to fantasize about being a bank president? Did you think you were coming into some money?"

Fred shook his head in disgust. "I would never kill anyone. The thought of taking another person's life is repugnant to me."

"You know, I believe you, but I think what happened is Harvey Hamlin died unexpectedly. He was helping you rob the bank, wasn't he? Did the stress get to him? Is that why he had a heart attack? Is that what happened, Fred?"

"Since you don't believe what I have already told you and obviously there is nothing I can say to convince you that I am innocent, I am not going to talk to you anymore without first consulting an attorney."

"We might be able to work this out if you will just be candid with me. You've never been in trouble before. The judge would probably be lenient given your young age."

Fred glanced around. "I don't see my attorney here."

"Whose idea was it, yours or Hamlin's? If it was Hamlin's idea, that would even be more reason for leniency."

"I know what you're trying to do. I'm a Perry Mason fan. You're not going to trick me into making a confession. You've got the wrong man, and I don't have anything else to say."

"Maybe there is a way you could convince us that you are innocent. Don't you think we should explore that possibility? If you clam up, we have to assume you're guilty and act accordingly."

"I can tell you've already made up your mind, so there's no point to any further discussion. Please let me make a phone call so I can obtain legal counsel."

"Alright, have it your way. I'll arrange for you to have a phone call, but you're making a big mistake."

They let Fred sweat for several hours and then one of the U.S. Marshals came in and escorted Fred to a pay telephone. He gave him a dime and said he had ten minutes. Fred asked him for a telephone book, and when it was delivered to him, he looked up the telephone number of his old boss, Congressman Bartlett.

"Hello. Congressman Bartlett's office."

"Is Mrs. Thompson there?" Fred asked. Mrs. Margaret Thompson was the staff supervisor at the Congressman's district office. Since Fred had worked there the previous two summers, he knew her pretty well.

"Hello. This is Mrs. Thompson."

"Hi, Mrs. Thompson. This is Fred Fuller."

"Fred! How are you?"

"Not so good actually. I need your help."

"What's wrong?"

"I've been arrested, and I need a lawyer."

"Arrested!" she exclaimed. "For what?"

"Bank robbery and murder."

"Oh my God! You've got to be kidding."

"I wish I were, but I am at the U.S. Marshal's office in LA, and I need a lawyer desperately. Could the Congressman recommend one for me?"

"Of course, Fred. I'll call him immediately. He's going to be really upset about this."

"Thanks a lot. I really appreciate your help."

For over six years, Fred had put in countless hours helping Congressman Bartlett with his re-election campaigns. Now, Fred figured all that effort might pay off. Surely, he'd be able to help him out of this mess just like he had helped countless numbers of other constituents with a myriad of legal problems. It was an aspect of a Congressman's job that Fred had never understood or appreciated prior to working for him. He was expecting to work on new legislation and campaign strategy, but instead, he spent most of his time listening to constituents' problems with welfare, Social Security, immigration, and many other problems with the federal government. All of these people were in trouble and turned to their Congressman for help, and Fred knew Congressman Bartlett did an extraordinarily good job of solving their problems.

But he couldn't help worrying that Congressman Bartlett may not want to get involved and would try to distance himself from Fred. That would probably be best for him. Bartlett had an election every two years, so he couldn't afford to associate himself with anyone who might taint his political reputation. What am I going to do if he won't help me? I don't have anyone else to turn to! Fred knew the court would appoint him an attorney, but that wouldn't be an ideal situation. Court-appointed attorneys were notorious for insisting their clients plead out, and Fred didn't want an overworked and underpaid attorney whose main objective was closing the file and moving on to the next case. He prayed the Congressman would help.

Chapter 27

Legal Counsel

Joel Roberts perked up when his secretary advised him that Congressman Bartlett was on the phone.

"Well it's your lucky day?" Congressman Bartlett advised.

"Really? How's that?"

"I just got a call from Margaret. Fred Fuller has been arrested for the San Bernardino Bank USA robbery and murder and he wants me to recommend a good criminal defense lawyer."

"Oh, really? That is good news."

"I don't like this one bit. Fred is a decent kid and he doesn't deserve this?"

"Yeah, that's true, but the important thing is we can control the fallout now. We can make sure none of this blows back on you."

"You're right, I know, but it still stinks all the way to Fresno."

"Maybe I can get him to plead out for a reduced sentence. He's young, if I can arrange for him to get out in five or ten years it wouldn't be so bad. We could make it up to him."

"Yeah, perhaps," the Congressman conceded. "Anyway, you should go volunteer to represent him before another firm comes along looking for a high-profile murder case to take on pro bono."

"Right. I'll get right on it. Where's he being held?"

"The U.S. Marshal's office in LA."

"Alright. I'm on my way."

A strong, cold wind was blowing off the ocean as Joel left the office. He looked up at the fog laden sky and could see a dim outline of the sun, but there was no warmth filtering through. He was cold through and through and he felt like crap. But he knew it wasn't the weather that had him feeling this way. He was about to violate at least a dozen rules of professional conduct, not to mention committing the crime of obstruction of justice. But he kept telling himself it was for good reason. Congressman Bartlett was a great man and his political career should not be derailed by a drunken campaign staffer.

By the time he made it to LA a few hours later, he had convinced himself he was doing the right thing and was feeling much better. He walked into the U.S. Marshal's office and told the woman sitting at the reception window that he wanted to see Fred Fuller.

"You his lawyer?" she asked.

"Not yet, but I probably will be before the day is out."

"Good luck with that."

"What do you mean?"

"He's guilty obviously, got a witness who says he was already talking about running. Only guilty men run."

"Who told you this?"

"I don't remember. Forget I mentioned it. Take a seat. I'll get someone to take you to see him."

Suddenly Roberts felt nervous and sick to his stomach. He took deep breaths trying to calm himself. A few minutes later he was escorted into a small room split in two by a transparent partition. Fred and Roberts sat across from each other and talked through small holes in the glass.

"Fred, I can't believe you're in here," Roberts said stiffly. "What in the hell is going on?"

"I don't know. They think I robbed Bank USA and murdered a guy named Harvey Hamlin."

"Did you know this guy, this Harvey Hamlin?"

"He was the branch cashier."

"Do you know anything about any of this?"

Fred hesitated, not knowing whether to level with him or not. He decided to be cautious for now. "No, not much. When I got to the bank that night, everything seemed normal, other than it was darker inside the bank than usual."

He explained to him about the nightlight, Sam being late, finding the vault open, and closing it. He didn't mention the million dollars he later found in his trunk.

"Well, if what you say is true," Roberts said, "we should be able to successfully defend you. It won't be pleasant though. This looks to be a high-profile case, and the media will be all over it."

"Wonderful," Fred moaned.

"Should I contact your parents about financing your legal defense?" Roberts asked.

"No. They don't have any money, but I've got $5,000 in savings I can give you."

"That will be fine for now," he said even though that was a tenth of his usual retainer. "Let me go see if I can get you bailed out of here. It won't be easy because of the murder charge and some talk about you trying to flee the country."

"What?" Fred gasped. "What are they talking about?"

"Someone at the front desk just told me a bizarre story about you and some bank teller being on your way to Canada when she got bitten by a rattlesnake and died. What's all that about?"

"My girlfriend and I went camping out in the Mojave Desert, but we weren't going to Canada," Fred lied. "If we were going to Canada, why would we be camping out in the Hackberry Mountains?"

"It didn't make much sense to me either," Roberts admitted.

"They just don't have any idea who robbed the bank, so they decided to pin it on me."

"Well, everyone knows Whitehead wants to be Governor someday, so the publicity of a trial like this would be very attractive to him. But don't worry. We'll figure out a way to get you out of this mess."

"I hope so. . . . I can't spend the rest of my life behind bars," Fred said desperately. "I'd rather die."

Chapter 28

The Bond Hearing

Around three o'clock, Fred was escorted before a magistrate for a bond hearing. As he entered the courtroom, Joel Roberts was standing at one counsel table, and a tall, dark-haired man—who Fred soon learned was Samuel P. Whitehead—was at the other. The bailiff escorted Fred in and told him to sit beside Joel. A pretty young woman joined Mr. Whitehead at the prosecution's table. Fred assumed she was his assistant. The room was packed with newspaper reporters and photographers.

Fred was quite surprised at the crowded courtroom and looked around to see if there was another defendant being arraigned. As far as he could tell, there wasn't anyone there but him.

After several minutes, the bailiff stood up and said, "Please rise for the Honorable Harold T. Washington, Magistrate for the Southern District of California."

Judge Washington walked in and asked everyone to be seated. The bailiff handed him a file, and for several minutes he reviewed it, then he called the case, "United States versus Fred Fuller."

Mr. Whitehead immediately stood up and approached the podium with Joel closely behind.

"Sam Whitehead for the United States, Your Honor."

"Joel Roberts for the defendant, Fred Fuller, Your Honor."

Mr. Whitehead continued, "Your Honor, the government considers Mr. Fuller to be a flight risk and would ask that bail be denied. As the Court is aware, Mr. Fuller is charged with the murder of one Harvey Hamlin and the robbery of the San Bernardino Branch of Bank USA. The government has not yet recovered the 6.7 million dollars that was stolen. If Mr. Fuller is let out on bail, there would be a strong likelihood that he would try to collect that money and flee the country."

"Your Honor," Joel said, "Fred Fuller was born and raised in Ventura, California. His mother and father live there, and he's currently a student at UCLA and plans to go to law school. Over the years, he has been an outstanding citizen, a school leader, an Eagle Scout and even worked two summers as a Congressional Intern for Congressman Bartlett. There is absolutely no flight risk here, Your Honor, and we request bail be set at $10,000."

"Your Honor, the government has a witness who will testify that Mr. Fuller told him less than one week ago that he and a lady friend were planning to leave the country and go to Canada."

"Bring on your witness, Counsel," Judge Washington ordered.

"The government calls Dr. Dennis Winston," Whitehead replied.

From the crowd of reporters came Dr. Winston, wearing a light gray suit and red tie. He was directed to the witness booth by the bailiff. The judge then asked, "Do you swear to tell the whole truth and nothing but the truth, so help you God?"

"I do," Dr. Winston replied.

The judge nodded at Whitehead. "Your witness."

"Please state your name for the Court," Whitehead asked.

"Dr. Dennis Winston."

"How are you employed, sir?"

"I am a resident at Barstow Memorial Hospital."

"Did you have an occasion to meet Fred Fuller last

week?"

"Yes, I did."

"And can you identify Mr. Fuller?"

"Yes. That's Mr. Fuller over there at the table."

"Let the record show that Dr. Winston is pointing to Fred Fuller, the defendant. Now, Dr. Winston, under what circumstances did you meet Fred Fuller last week?"

"His girlfriend, Candy Clisby, was in the ICU of our hospital. When she died as the result of toxins from multiple snake bites, I had to break the news to him."

"How did he take that news, Doctor?"

"Not very well. He got very upset and started rambling about how unfair it was that she died. He said they had plans to go to Canada and start a new life."

"You are quite sure he said he and Miss Clisby were planning to go to Canada?"

"Yes, that's what he said."

"Very well," Whitehead said. "Pass the witness."

Joel stood and began, "Mr. Winston, did Fred Fuller say when he was going to Canada?"

"No."

"Did he say to what part of Canada he was going?

"No."

"I believe you testified that Mr. Fuller was grieving the loss of someone he loved and that he was not totally coherent—'very upset and rambling'—correct?"

"That's true."

"So, you could have misunderstood what he said or meant, isn't that right?"

"Not what he said, but perhaps what he meant by it."

"Or, Doctor, Mr. Fuller may not have even realized what he was saying, isn't that possible?"

"That is true. He was upset and confused. A lot of what he said didn't make much sense."

"Isn't it true that Miss Clisby and Mr. Fuller were camping in the Hackberry Mountains in the middle of the

Mojave Desert when this snake attack occurred?"

"Yes, I believe that is true."

"If you were heading for Canada, would you go via the Mojave Desert?"

There was laughter in the gallery, and the judge immediately slammed down his gavel, "I'll have order please!"

"No, it would be quite a bit out of the way actually."

"Do you think Fred Fuller and his girlfriend were really heading for Canada?"

"No, not when this mishap occurred."

"Pass the witness, Your Honor," Joel concluded.

"No further questions," Whitehead advised.

"Call your next witness."

"No further witnesses, Your Honor."

"Mr. Roberts, do you have any witnesses?" the Judge asked.

"Yes, Your Honor. The defense calls Margaret Thompson."

A heavyset, well-dressed woman of about fifty-five years of age stood up and approached the witness box.

"Please state your name for the record," Joel began.

"Margaret Thompson."

"Mrs. Thompson, how are you employed?"

"I'm on the staff of Congressman Bartlett from Ventura, California."

"And what are your duties for the Congressman?"

"I run his local office."

"Do you know the defendant, Fred Fuller?"

"Yes, I certainly do."

"How do you know him?"

"For two summers, he was a Congressional Intern for the Congressman and worked in our office. Besides that, he's been helping Congressman Bartlett in his campaigns ever since he was twelve years old."

"What is your opinion of Mr. Fuller?"

"He is an outstanding young man, and I am quite

confident he had nothing to do with these heinous crimes."

"Do you think that if bail were granted, he might flee the country?"

"Absolutely not. His mother and dad live in Ventura. He's going to school at UCLA, and, besides, we're coming up on an election year, and he would never abandon the Congressman's campaign."

Once again, there was laughter in the gallery, and the Judge banged his gavel and demanded order.

"Thank you, Mrs. Thompson. No further questions. Pass the witness."

"No questions, Your Honor," Whitehead said.

"Alright then. Since Mr. Fuller apparently has an untarnished record as a young man and has strong family roots in the community, I am going to allow bail. However, due to the severity of the charges against him, I am going to set bail at $100,000.00. Accordingly, Mr. Fuller is remanded into the custody of the Federal Marshal until such time as he posts bond in the amount prescribed."

Whitehead was visibly upset by the Court's decision, and when the judge left the bench he walked over to where Joel and Fred were standing and began ranting, "I just want you to know that just because your client got bail doesn't mean you have a ghost of a chance of winning at trial. So, why don't you save the taxpayers a lot of money and plead guilty."

"Oh, you're certain you're going to win?" Joel questioned.

"Yes. We've got enough evidence to put him away for the rest of his life—and maybe then some."

"Well, since Fred here tells me he's innocent, I think we'll go ahead and have a trial, if that's okay with you."

"Suit yourself, but it's just a matter of time until we put him permanently behind bars where he belongs, Eagle Scout or not."

"I wouldn't make any campaign promises on that score, because if the jury finds Fred innocent, your political career will be in the dumpster."

"Okay," Whitehead snorted. "I'm trying to do you a favor, but I can see talking to you is like talking to a bowling ball."

Joel shrugged smugly, and Whitehead stormed out of the courtroom with a dozen or so reporters scrambling to keep up with him. Joel turned to Fred and said, "What an asshole, huh?"

"What does he have against me?" Fred asked.

"It's not personal. You're his ticket to the Governor's mansion. He's been waiting for a high-profile case to propel his political career. But forget Whitehead. Now the hard part. . . . where are we going to find $100,000 to bail you out of jail?"

"That's a good question," Fred replied. He knew he could get $100,000 quite easily if he went to Devil's Canyon and retrieved it, but that wasn't an option. If he suddenly showed up with $100,000, it would just prove he was the bank robber. "My parents don't have that kind of money," he added.

"Well, you don't really need $100,000. You just need a good bail bondsman who is willing to put up the bond. Do you think your parents might have some real estate or something they could pledge as collateral?"

"No. They don't have anything like that."

"Well, I am afraid you'll have to spend the night at the county jail. Hopefully tomorrow, we'll be able to post bond."

"I have to go all the way to the county jail?" Fred questioned. "Why can't I just stay here in the Federal Building?"

"Where they have you now is just a holding cell. They don't keep prisoners there overnight. I am sorry."

"It's not your fault. I'll survive, I guess."

"It won't be so bad. Just hang in there," Joel said.

Joel left, and the bailiff escorted Fred back to the Marshal's office. After a few minutes, he was taken downstairs and loaded onto a bus to be taken to the LA County Jail. On the way, he thought back to that moment of decision when he found the vault open. What were the odds that he'd find the same vault opened twice, he wondered? A million to one? He wished to hell he'd called Sinclair just like he had the first time. Then he began to think, why was Harvey Hamlin still at the bank so late, and why hadn't Hamlin closed the vault? It was almost like Hamlin wanted him to find the vault open. Fred knew he'd been set up, but by whom he didn't know. Harvey Hamlin and one or more accomplices had planned to rob the bank and blame the heist on him! He knew that because somebody other than Harvey had put the bag of money in is car. He figured it had to be Sam. It would have been a pretty cleaver plan had Hamlin not gotten stressed out and had a heart attack. But with Harvey dead and Sam nowhere to be found, how could he ever prove he'd been set up?

Chapter 29

LA County Jail

So much had happened since morning that Fred hadn't had time to dwell on his predicament. The situation changed abruptly, however, when he arrived at the LA County Jail. Gradually, he became more and more depressed as he realized he might never be free again. All the little things he had taken for granted all of his life suddenly flashed through his mind. Would he ever jump in his car again and hit the open road as he so loved to do or hike in the mountains and smell the clear, cool mountain air? Would he ever hold Maria's hand again and feel her sweet, succulent lips?

After they booked him, he was escorted with four or five other prisoners down a long hallway. Three solid lines—red, green, and blue—had been painted on the floor. A sign along the way advised that the solid red line led to the main cell block. Two jailers led them along the red line until they came to a solid steel gate. One of the jailers rang a bell and then talked to someone inside though an intercom. After a few moments, the steel gate began to retract, clearing the way for the prisoners to enter. After they had entered the cell block, the gate began to close, and the sound of the steel doors slamming shut sent shivers down Fred's spine.

They continued along the red line until they finally arrived at a door next to a glass window reinforced with steel mesh. Behind the glass sat another jailer in front of a control panel. As he saw them approach, he pushed a button that set off a buzzer that indicated the door was unlocked. They escorted them through the door, and one by one, assigned each of them to a cell. Each cell was designed to accommodate two inmates, but Fred was placed in a cell all alone. This was a great relief to him, as he was afraid of many of the inmates he'd seen and didn't relish being locked up with one of them.

That night, Fred couldn't sleep. His mind raced through the events of the last six months. Where did I go wrong? What could I have done differently to avoid the mess I'm in now? He pondered this for some time but finally decided there wasn't an answer. Anything he might have done could just as easily have landed him in jail. It all came down to fate, he decided.

Never in his worst melancholic state would Fred have ever thought he'd wind up in a jail cell facing life-imprisonment or the gas chamber. The worst part of his plight was the fact that he couldn't tell anyone what really happened, not even his attorney. He had been taught all his life to be honest and truthful, but if he told the truth now, nobody would believe him, and he'd surely end up on death row. *Oh God! What will become of me?*

Fred guessed anyone could eventually adjust to prison life, and he was starting to resign himself to the fact that he might be compelled to make that adjustment. After staring in the dark for quite a while, he finally fell into a shallow sleep and found himself in Devil's Canyon looking at a pond and hearing water splashing.

He saw himself making love with Candy. They were both so full of life and happiness. Then, suddenly, she was sitting on a rock. He yelled at her frantically, "Watch out! There's a snake!" but she couldn't hear him, as he was in another dimension. Suddenly, he saw the snake attack her and heard her screams of pain. Then he was holding her limp body in his arms. The sight was unbearable, and he began to moan and tremble in terror until he was jolted back into consciousness. As he looked around, there was only the cold steel and the stark furnishings of his cell. The only sound that could be heard was a distant snoring from an inmate who had apparently made peace with his environment. He couldn't imagine himself doing that, being at peace in this junkyard of human misery.

After what seemed like an eternity, the night did finally come to an end. At 6:00 a.m. sharp, the guards awakened them and took them by chain gang to the cafeteria for breakfast. The food was tolerable, but Fred had no appetite. His body was so exhausted and his depression so deep that food had no appeal to him. After thirty minutes of staring at his plate, they returned him to his cell. After the door had been slammed shut, he laid down on his bunk, finally succumbing to exhaustion, and fell asleep.

A short time later, he was rudely awakened by a jailer calling his name. "Fuller! Get your ass up. You've made bail."

Fred opened his eyes and looked up. "What?"

"Somebody must love you," the guard said. "They came up with a hundred grand to bail your ass out of here."

"Who was it?" Fred asked, incredulous.

"How the hell do I know? Just get your ass up and go find out before I lose this paperwork."

"Okay." Fred jumped up and followed the jailer out of his cell. He led him back to the control room. Outside the window, he could see Joel Roberts pacing back and forth. After a minute, the buzzer sounded, and Fred was a free man. He eagerly pushed open the door and greeted Joel with a big smile. His depression had vanished, and he looked around and breathed a deep sigh of relief. "Man, am I glad to see you!" he said.

"I bet. I hate this place. It gives me the creeps."

"It gives you the creeps? You ought to spend the night here."

"No thanks. Come on, let's get out of here."

"You don't have to ask me twice."

"Are you alright?"

"Now I am."

"Tough night?"

"Horrible. I didn't think it would ever end. How did you raise $100,000 for my bail?"

"You'll see in a minute. There is someone waiting for you in the lobby."

Fred was very anxious and curious to find out the identity of his mysterious benefactor. As he came to the end of the solid red line and turned the corner he was shocked to see Maria.

Considering the way he'd treated her, Maria was the last person he expected to see. Tears began pouring from his eyes as he embraced her. "I never thought I'd see you again."

Maria also began to cry at seeing Fred. "You underestimated me. I wouldn't let them keep you locked up."

"But how did you get $100,000?"

"I didn't. I just convinced my parents to guarantee your bond with our home."

Fred's heart sank. "What! Oh my God!"

"You better not skip town."

"How did you convince them to do that?"

"I told them if they wanted to keep their daughter out of the lunatic asylum, they would have to put up your bond."

Fred swallowed hard. "Maria, you must have heard about—"

"Yes, I did, and we'll definitely talk about that later. For now, let's just get out of this depressing place."

Fred looked back at Joel, and he waved him on. "Go with Maria, but be in my office tomorrow at 9:00 a.m. to start on your defense. We've got work to do if we're going to get you off."

"Okay. Thanks."

As they walked through the revolving doors in front of the jail, a mob of reporters surprised them.

"Mr. Fuller, how were you able to post bond?" a short, dark-haired reporter yelled.

"No comment. Thank you," Fred said, quickening their pace.

"What is your reaction to the U.S. Attorney's announcement that they found your fingerprints inside the vault?" a second reporter asked.

Fred cringed. "That's not possible. . . . Let us through please."

"Ms. Shepard, how do feel about Mr. Fuller's affair with Candy Clisby?" a lady reporter asked.

Fred glared angrily at the reporter and shouted, "She has no comment. Now leave us alone!"

The crowd squeezed around them, blocking their exit. Fred slowly pushed a path toward the parking garage. TV cameras ran as reporters continued demanding answers to their questions. Finally, two uniformed policemen noticed their plight and intervened to help them extricate themselves from the mob. In a few moments, they were driving Maria's car out of the parking garage and into downtown LA. They headed immediately for the on ramp to the Ventura Freeway and headed north.

"Oh, man, it feels so great to be driving down the freeway. I was afraid I would never be able to do that again."

"It must have been horrible last night," Maria said.

"It was unbearable. I can't go back there."

"Hopefully you won't have to."

"I sure hope not."

"Now that I got you out of jail, are you going to tell me what in the hell is going on?"

"I suppose I should, but if I tell you the truth, you may not be able to forgive me, and I'm afraid I will lose you again—this time forever. If I lie to you, you will know it and surely abandon me. I can't win either way."

"Just tell me the truth. Otherwise, we're finished, Fred."

"Okay, you're right. I owe you the truth."

As Fred started to spill his guts, a cold chill surged down his spine. He was about to confess his sins to Maria when it suddenly occurred to him that her car may be bugged. He almost blurted out a confession that may well have sent him to federal prison and put Sam Whitehead in the Governor's mansion.

As they continued to drive down the freeway, Fred turned on the car stereo louder than any normal person could stand. Maria looked at him curiously.

"The bugs are sure thick tonight," he advised.

She frowned at him, trying to figure out what in the hell he was talking about, and then suddenly she got the message. "Oh. I guess it's all the rain we got this spring. Shall we go up to Griffith Park to look at the city lights?"

"Yeah, that's a good idea."

Griffith Park Observatory was one of their favorite places to go and just talk, among other things. When they arrived, they got out of Maria's car and strolled around the grounds.

"Do you really think my car is bugged?" Maria questioned.

"Yeah, it probably is. The government wants my ass pretty bad."

"I can't believe they would do that," Maria said.

"Oh, from what I understand, Whitehead would do just about anything to get elected Governor."

"Hmm, you're probably right," Maria agreed.

Fred looked intensely at Maria. "Thank you so much for getting me out of jail. I can't believe you made your parents pledge their house. I didn't expect to ever see you again after you heard about Candy."

"Well, you don't know how much that hurt me. For a while, I wanted to break your neck. It was such a shock that you could betray me the way you did, but then I began to think, we aren't married, and you haven't actually asked me to marry you. Technically, you were free to date other women and even screw them, I guess."

"You told me you wouldn't leave the country with me, so I figured it was over between us. Candy jumped at the chance to go with me."

Tears welled in Maria's eyes. "I didn't think you were serious. Had you told me what was going on, I might have gone with you."

"Well, I didn't press you on the issue because I didn't want to ruin your life. I love you too much for that."

"What about Candy? You didn't mind ruining her life?"

Fred shrugged. "She was a willing accomplice. I don't know how much I loved her or if she loved me. We didn't honestly know each other that well. She was older, worldlier and seemed to know what she wanted, so I didn't feel as protective of her."

"Well, she is dead now, so I won't have to worry about her stealing you away from me again."

"If we somehow get through this, I promise I'll be the

most righteous person on the planet."

"I hope so. If you do any screwing around after we're married, I'll hire the best divorce lawyer in California, and you'll be sending me a fat monthly alimony check until the Dodgers move back to Brooklyn!"

Fred laughed. "Okay, okay. I get the picture."

"Now, are you going to tell me what in the hell is going on or what?"

"Yeah, I was working up to it."

"No more lies, Fred Fuller."

"Okay. Hamlin and Sam Stewart and maybe some other people tried to set me up. I found the vault open again, but I didn't go inside. I closed it so Hamlin wouldn't get in trouble. On my way home, I discovered there was a bag of money in the trunk of my car. The robber apparently had planted it there to make the FBI think I was in on the bank robbery. Luckily, I discovered the bag and hid the money before I got back to the motor pool."

"So, you had nothing to do with the robbery?"

"No, but I do have a million of the 6.7 million that was stolen."

"Give it back! Tell them what happened."

"Do you think for a minute anybody would believe me? I don't want the money. I'd love to give it back, but if I do, I'll end up in prison for something I didn't do."

Maria thought a minute. "You should have called Sinclair immediately when you found the vault open. Then they'd have believed you when you told them you found the money in your trunk."

"You're probably right, but Hamlin had given me this sad story about his wife leaving him, so I felt sorry for him and didn't want to get him in trouble and lose his job. But he lied to me. He said his wife had just left him, but it was actually over a year ago. Hamlin must have been part of the heist and not the victim they are making him out to be. Since he's dead, though, there must be an accomplice out there—Sam Stewart would be my guess. He had to be the one who put the bag of money in my car. There was nobody else around."

"How could this have happened?" Maria said, tears streaming down her cheeks.

"I know. I wish I could turn the clock back, believe me. It almost seems like it was my fate to have the money. You know, two of my visions have come true this week."

"What do you mean?"

"Candy turned out to be the woman in the pond who always ends up screaming in agony. I swear when Candy was bitten by the snake, it was like déjà vu."

"That's bizarre."

"And last night, I lived my prison dream—walking in the chain gang, through the big steel gate, along a thick red line."

Maria shook her head in disbelief. "So, what are we going to do now?"

"I wish I knew."

Maria pondered the situation a moment and then said, "I guess we could leave the country."

"Seriously? You'd leave the country with me now?"

"Of course. I love you."

"I wish I would have known that."

"I didn't want to give you any encouragement. Leaving the country is the last thing I'd ever want to do, but when you left me and I thought I might not ever see you again, I realized I couldn't live without you. So yes, I'll go anywhere with you."

Fred pulled Maria's lips to his to express his gratitude for her staunch loyalty and devotion. He knew he didn't deserve her, but somehow God had blessed him with her love.

"There's no way we can get out the country now," Fred

said. "The FBI is going to be watching us like a hawk, and I won't risk your family's home like that."

"What are we going to do then?"

"I don't know about tomorrow, but I definitely know what I want to do now."

"What's that?"

"I want to feel your lips on mine, smell the sweet scent of your body next to me, and hold you and never let you go."

Maria put her arms around Fred and pulled him close. "You promise?"

"Yes. I promise."

"Good," she whispered and then kissed him like he'd never been kissed before.

Chapter 30

Secret Betrayal

Joel Roberts and Congressman Bartlett sat in their golf cart on the 3rd hole waiting for the golfers ahead of them to get out of their way so they could tee off. It was a cool December day but cool in southern California meant low 60's, nothing that would deter an avid golfer. Bartlett turned to Roberts and frowned. "So, how did Fred manage to get out on bond? I didn't expect that."

"No. I didn't either. Maria's parents put up their house as collateral, if you can believe that."

"I can't. Don't they know he cheated on their daughter?"

"They must," Joel replied. "It's been in all the papers. I guess Maria must really love him."

"And be one forgiving woman, that's for sure," the Congressman said shaking his head.

"Yeah. Unless Fred's told her about the million dollars he's got stashed away somewhere."

"You think that's it?"

"He may have now, but he didn't have an opportunity to tell her before the bond was put up."

"It's too dangerous for him to be out on bond," the Congressman warned. "Can't you do something about that?"

"Well, I'm hoping he'll try to get some of the cash. The FBI's is keeping a close watch on him, so he'll probably get caught and with the cash in his possession it will be all over."

"Good. We need to put a lid on this whole affair."

Roberts smiled. "What about Fuller? I thought you didn't want him to get hurt. If they catch him with the money he'll go to prison for a long, long time."

"Better him than you and I, right?" the Congressman said bitterly.

Roberts sighed. "True."

"But, Fuller's no dummy. He may not go for the money."

"I'll put some heat on him to get cash for his defense. I can threaten to withdraw from the case if he doesn't come up with more money. He'll have to go for it then."

"Okay, but if he's not caught trying to access the money, you better come up with some other way to have his bond revoked."

"Right," Roberts said thoughtfully. "Don't worry I'll come up with something."

The golfers ahead of them moved on, so Roberts got a ball and his driver and prepared to tee off.

"Watch out for that trap on the right," the Congressman said. "I always manage to fall into it."

"No problem. I'm slicing today for some reason. I won't get close to it."

"Yeah. You're nervous. . . . Relax. We'll get through this. I have a lot of confidence in you."

"Right. But, I can't help feeling guilty about leading Fred straight to prison. It's against every instinct I have as a defense attorney."

"Don't worry," the Congressman replied. "When he gets out of prison he'll have a million dollars."

"If he doesn't screw up and lead the feds to the money."

"Either way, you and I are clear. We can always help him out down the road and make sure Maria is taken care of, if he goes in for a long stretch."

Roberts swallowed hard and the Congressman forced a smile. Roberts took a practice swing and then drove the ball down the fairway. As expected, he sliced the ball past the trap and it came to a stop on the edge of the fairway.

The Congressman got his driver and prepared to tee off. His ball went straight down the fairway then suddenly hooked into the trap. "Damn it!" he cursed.

Chapter 31

Return to Devil's Canyon

The next morning, Maria and Fred went home to Ventura to see their parents, as they knew they were all very worried about them. Since they were paranoid about their conversations being monitored, they played the radio as loud as they could stand it and didn't talk about anything sensitive. There were some things they needed to discuss, so on the way to Ventura, they stopped at Meyer Beach so they could talk privately.

It was a cool day but, without the usual sea breeze, it was pleasant enough. Seagulls squawked overhead, and the sound of the tide rolling in soothed their battered nerves.

"How are you going to pay Joel for your defense?" Maria asked.

"Well, I've got $5,000 I'm going to give him."

"Don't trials like this cost a lot more than that?"

"Yeah. Joel doesn't seem to be worried about it."

"He isn't now, but down the road, he's going to expect you to raise some money for your defense."

"I guess you're right. I don't know what I am going to do."

"We're going to have to go get some of that money. Where did you stash it?"

"Are you serious?"

"Yes. What choice do we have? You're going to have

to hire private investigators, expert witnesses, and pay court reporters for depositions. If you want Roberts to defend you well, it's going to get costly. Where do you have it stashed?"

"It's at a place called Devil's Canyon."

"Devil's Canyon? I've never heard of it."

"That's why I buried it there. It's not on any tourist map. It's out in the middle of the Mojave Desert."

"Then I guess we'll have to go to Devil's Canyon."

"But the FBI is all over us." Fred turned around and looked back down the beach. "Look there, . . . they're not even 100 yards behind us. We wouldn't stand a chance getting away from them."

"It would be easy to sneak away during the night and be back before they noticed us."

"How do you mean?"

"Well, I'll drive my car over near your apartment tomorrow afternoon. Then I'll get a taxi or take the bus back to the dorm. When you come to pick me up, we'll go out just like we always do, except I will come home with you to your apartment. The FBI will just think you got lucky. During the night, we'll sneak out and run to my car."

"Hmm. It might work," Fred agreed.

They finally ended their stroll on the beach and continued their journey to Ojai to see Maria's parents. Fred didn't know what he was going to say to them. He still couldn't believe they put their house up for collateral on his bond.

When they drove up in front of the house, Maria's sister Jessica was sitting on the front porch. She ran over to Maria as she stepped out of the car. "Maria! Maria! You're finally home."

"Yes, I am, you little squirt."

"You've been gone for so long. I've missed you," she said and then gave Fred a hard look. "Oh, hi, Fred. You're in big trouble. I've seen you on TV. They say you're going to prison for the rest of your life."

Fred's heart sank from the jolt of her blunt remark. Kids are so brutally honest, he thought. He knew she was right, though, because his future did look pretty bleak. He walked past her as if he hadn't heard what she said.

"Jess! That is very rude. Don't you dare talk to Fred like that," Maria admonished. "Fred is innocent, and he won't go to prison."

"But they said so on TV."

"Jess! No more talk about that."

By this time, Mary and John Shepard had appeared on the front porch. Maria approached them anxiously and gave them both a big hug. Fred followed right behind, treading cautiously.

"Hi, Fred," Mrs. Shepard said.

"Hello. It's so good to see both of you."

"You've had a tough week, I guess, son," Mr. Shepard said.

"It's been pretty rough. I want to thank both of you for what you did for me. I'm just overwhelmed by your generosity and the trust you have shown in me."

"Well, you can thank Maria. She convinced us you were worth the risk," Mrs. Shepard said.

"I'm sure she did a little arm twisting, but nevertheless, you didn't have to agree to it."

"A little arm breaking is more like it," Mr. Shepard noted.

Fred laughed. "I bet, but I want you to know I will be forever grateful for what you did."

"You're welcome. Just don't skip the country now," Mr. Shepard said with a little hint of anxiety.

"Don't worry. I wouldn't do anything to jeopardize your

home."

"When is your trial?" Mrs. Shepard asked.

"I don't know yet. I don't think it's been set."

"Do you have a good lawyer?"

"Oh yes, the best. His name is Joel Roberts. He used to work for the DA's office, so he knows what he is doing. I knew him from Congressman Bartlett's campaign. He just recently went into private practice."

"He sounds expensive."

"I don't know. We haven't talked much about money so far."

"Are your parents going to help you out?"

"No. My dad is retired, and they barely have enough to live on."

"Maybe Mr. Roberts will do the case just for the publicity."

"I hope so."

"Alright, enough trial talk," Maria said. "Give Fred a break. Let's change the subject."

That night, Fred slept on the sofa, and Maria slept in her old room. Despite all they had been through, Maria was still dead set on being a virgin on their wedding night—if they ever had a wedding night. The next morning, they got up early and headed back to Santa Monica, as it was time to carry out Maria's plan. Before they left, they searched the car thoroughly for bugs but found nothing.

"You know, if we get caught, they'll think we were trying to escape and revoke my bond. Your parents could lose their house."

"I know. We've got to be careful—very careful."

"Maybe we should forget it. I've caused everyone enough grief already. God, if your parents lost their house, I think I'd kill myself."

"Fred, this is your life and our future we're talking about here. Without money, you're going to get a half-ass defense and end up in prison. We don't have any choice."

"You're right, but I'm just scared something will go wrong."

"Listen, I don't like this one bit either. You don't think I'm scared? If we get caught, I'll go to jail, too, you know."

"So why help me?"

"Because I had the misfortune of falling in love with you."

"Your luck is almost as bad as mine."

"Tell me about it."

Fred dropped Maria off at her dorm and went back to his apartment. Maria used the back entrance, moved undetected to her car, and drove away toward Santa Monica. She parked her car three blocks from Fred's apartment and then called a cab to take her back to the dorm. She had the cab driver drop her off in front of the Student Union so she could sneak in the back door of her dorm without anyone knowing she had been gone.

At five that evening, Fred drove over to Maria's dorm and picked her up to go out for dinner. They stopped at an Italian restaurant in Westwood and then went back to the apartment. Wherever they went, the dark blue FBI car followed them. When they were in the apartment, an agent was stationed in the adjacent courtyard. They walked into the apartment and closed the door.

Fred turned on the TV so they could whisper without risk of being overheard. "Okay," he said, "are you ready?"

"I guess so."

"We'll need a distraction. Fortunately, we usually get one each night about now. Our neighbors like to make love after dinner. They do it every night like clockwork. The woman is very noisy, and they never shut their windows."

"Are you serious?" Maria giggled.

"Yes. Get ready."

A few moments later, the neighbors began their naughty nightly performance. The shameless woman began to moan and pant and carry on such that the entire apartment complex could hear her. Two minutes later, Fred and Maria opened up their back-bedroom window and made their escape. Before long, they were driving away with no dark blue car in tow. Their plan had worked, and they were alone at last! Fred looked at his watch and saw it was nearly eight, which meant they had twelve hours to make it to Devil's Canyon and back to avoid detection.

"That was quite a performance. You say that happens every night?"

"Pretty much."

"That's so funny," she said, closing her eyes and settling back in her seat. "How long until we get to this Devil's Canyon place?"

"About four hours."

"I am going to sleep. Wake me when we get there."

"Okay."

It was a beautiful night. The traffic was light, and the humming of the tires rolling down the road had Fred almost in a trance. For some reason, time flew when he was driving. Before he knew it, they were in Palm Springs, halfway there. Fred decided to get gas since stations beyond Palm Springs were few and far between.

Maria woke up when they stopped. "I've got to pee," she informed him.

"There's a bathroom around the side. You'll have to get the key from the desk."

When Maria returned, she still looked half asleep. "I'm

hungry," she complained.

"Well, what do you feel like?"

"I don't care. Just feed me something."

"How about a hamburger at Foster Freeze?"

"Okay, and a large order of fries, a Coke, and a dipped cone for dessert."

Fred laughed. "I guess you are hungry."

"I've been so sick since you took off on me that I haven't felt like eating. Now that I've got you back, I'm famished."

They drove down the street to Foster Freeze. Once inside, they placed their order and found a booth in the corner.

"How much farther do we have to go?" Maria asked.

"We're halfway there."

"Is a million bucks heavy?"

"Yeah, a little bit."

"I've never seen even $1,000 dollars. I can't imagine what a million looks like."

"It actually doesn't look like that much money."

"Did you count it?"

"Every dollar."

"I can't believe we're millionaires."

"We?"

"Well, you better share it, mister."

"Maybe."

"Hmm."

"Unfortunately, we have to be careful how we spend it," Fred noted. "Any unusual spending, and the Feds will be all over us."

"Are you sure they are not following us now?"

"Yes, I'm sure. There hasn't been anyone behind us for hours."

The waitress brought over their food, and they thanked

her and began eating. After twenty minutes, they were on the road again licking their ice cream cones.

About midnight they turned onto the dirt road that led to Devil's Canyon. It was a dark, overcast night, and it was difficult to see anything but the road immediately in front of them. Finally, at 12:41 a.m., their headlights flashed on the broken-down sign that once welcomed hundreds of daily visitors to Devil's Canyon Mining Camp.

"Here we are, babe."

"This is it?" Maria said, unimpressed.

"Yeah. We have to go through town up to the assayer's office. Isn't this place neat?"

"It looks just like the town in *The Good, the Bad and the Ugly.*"

"I thought you slept through that movie?"

"I did sleep through most of it, but I woke up a couple of times and remember seeing a town like this."

"Oh, I see. Okay, well, here we are. Are you ready?"

"Look around and make sure there aren't any snakes."

Fred laughed. "Snakes don't come out at night."

"Good. In that case, lead me to the money."

They got out and walked over to the door of the office. Fred gave it a stiff kick, and it swung open.

"Where did you hide it?"

"Under the floor. I marked the slat with three notches."

Maria carefully examined the wooden floor. "Here it is."

"Okay. I need the tire iron from the car. I'll be right back," Fred said as he went back outside.

"Hurry up!" Maria yelled.

"I'm hurrying. Keep your pants on!" he yelled from the car.

"Huh? That's a switch. Usually you want me to take them off," Maria replied playfully.

When he came back inside, Maria was standing there with a wry smile on her face. "Hurry up. I want to see the cash."

"So, if I share this million dollars with you, will you make love to me right now?" Fred asked hopefully.

She frowned. "Half a million dollars? Well, that's definitely tempting."

"Come here. Make love to me, and it's yours."

"Fred, don't do this. I want to be a virgin on our wedding night."

"We may never have a wedding night if I end up in jail. Wouldn't you feel bad if I went to prison and had never made love to you?"

"Oh, so we're going to make love for the first time on the floor of an old shack in the middle of the desert?"

"Yeah. Won't it be memorable?"

"I was thinking more of a suite at the Hotel Del Coronado." she said.

"Quit thinking and come here."

Maria walked over to Fred slowly, put her arms around his neck, and looked at him with her big brown eyes. "You shouldn't tempt a woman with so much money. It's not fair," she complained.

"All's fair in love and war."

"Do you really love me?" Maria asked.

"Yes. I love you with all my heart and all my soul, totally and completely," he replied.

"I want the money in small bills," she giggled.

"No problem!" Fred agreed.

Fred started to slide his hand gently down the back of Maria's pants, but she stopped him. "Wait a minute!" she protested as she pushed him away. "I want to see the cash before I give up my virginity."

Fred shrugged. "You're right. That's only fair. Hand me that crowbar." Fred took the crowbar and began prying up the slats. The rotted wood put up little resistance. When he had removed four or five slats, he looked up and smiled at Maria. "Okay. Hand me that flashlight." With the flashlight in hand, he peered into the crawl space, located the bag, and pulled it out. He brushed off the dust and cobwebs, cleared a spot on a big table with a swipe of his hand, and dumped the stacks of money out on the table.

"Wow! Look at that," Maria gasped. "That's a lot of cash."

"I know," Fred said, slipping his arms around her waist and pulling her off her feet. He swung her 'round and 'round and then set her on the table. "I've lived up to my part of the bargain," he said wryly. "Now it's your turn."

Maria smiled at him coyly. "Okay. If this is what you really want. A bargain's a bargain, I suppose."

Fred slid his hands slowly up her legs, all the way to her silk panties. He was planning to rip them off dramatically but a wave of guilt stopped him abruptly. "Oh, alright. I guess I can wait."

She lunged forward into his arms. "Oh, thank you, Fred. I'm so relieved. This isn't the way it's supposed to happen—not here, not now."

"Supposed to happen? You make it sound like our marriage is part of someone's grand plan."

"It is. Oh, Fred, I'm afraid I haven't been entirely honest with you."

"You haven't?"

"No. You're not the only one who's had visions. When I was very young, I was in a car wreck and suffered a concussion. I was in a coma for five days. During that time, I dreamt many times of my wedding day. You were in that dream, Fred. I've been waiting for you for a long time. When I told my mother after our first date that I was going to marry you, it was because I'd already seen our wedding day—and our wedding night as well. This isn't the place I'm supposed to lose my virginity."

Stunned, Fred set Maria down on the table and looked at her coldly. "Are you mocking me?" he asked warily. "I really did have the visions I told you about."

"I know you did. I believe you. That's why I couldn't let you go even after your indiscretion with Candy. We are meant to be together, and that's why I know somehow, we're going to get you out of this mess. We just have to figure out how to do it."

"Did your mother know about your dreams?" Fred asked.

"Yes. I told her, but she doesn't believe they were visions. She just thinks they were normal adolescent sex fantasies and my mind just conjured up my ideal man who happened to look like you. She made me promise if I ever thought I saw the man in my dreams not to do anything rash. That's why when you sat next to me at orientation, I didn't say anything, even though I was more excited than I'd ever been in my entire life!"

"Huh," Fred said, thinking back to the day they met. "You could have at least given me your telephone number. You don't know how hard it was to find you."

She slugged him in the shoulder. "Oh, I'm so sorry I inconvenienced you," she said sarcastically.

Fred laughed and took both of her hands in his.

"I knew you'd call me or we'd meet when school started."

"So, you saw us get married in your dreams, huh?"

"That's right. So, somehow this is all going to work out.

Obviously, it can't happen if you're in jail."

"Maybe your mother was right. When I think about it, in the dream after the snake bite I really couldn't make out the face of the naked woman in the pond. It could have been Marilyn Monroe for all I know. She was every boy's fantasy back then."

Maria laughed. "But you told Candy it was her, right?"

"Well, it seemed like the right thing to say at the time, but I'm not so sure now."

"What am I going to do with you, Fred?"

Fred shrugged. "Find another boyfriend would probably be your best move."

"Oh, come on. Don't start feeling sorry for yourself. You're going to get through this. You've got a million dollars for godsakes. How many guys your age can say that?"

"Somehow I just can't be as optimistic as you." Looking at his watch, he frowned. We better figure out what we're going to do with the money and get out of here."

Maria looked at the pile of loot and sighed. "I think $100,000 ought to be enough for now. We'll leave the rest here. This seems like a good place to hide it."

"Alright," Fred agreed, "a hundred grand it is."

They counted out $100,000 and stuffed it in a gym bag. The rest they put back into the bank bag and returned it to its hiding place. They kissed passionately one more time, and Fred silently wished he hadn't let Maria off the hook. He wanted her so badly.

Maria broke away. "Okay. We better get back to Santa Monica before the Feds figure out we're gone and throw us both in the slammer."

Fred groaned. "Alright, let's go. If we leave right now, we should make it back before dawn."

After nailing the slats back in place and straightening

up, Fred wiped the place clean so there wouldn't be any prints. Then he found a couple two-by-fours and tied them to the back of the car with a rope so they would drag behind them and erase their tire tracks.

When they were back on the main road heading home, they were filled with apprehension. Despite Maria's vision of their wedding day, they both knew the next year would be fraught with peril, and there was no guarantee her dream would actually come true. They knew their future depended on their actions and the grace of God.

Maybe we should turn around and head up to Canada like you and Candy planned to do," Maria suggested.

Fred turned and looked at her thoughtfully. "It would never work. Tomorrow morning, they'd figure out we'd run, and every law enforcement officer in the southwest would be looking for us. We might make it to Mexico before they discovered that we were gone, but I'm sure the Border Patrol has a list of everyone on trial and free on bond. Plus, we couldn't let your parents lose their house."

Maria sighed. "I know. It was just a thought."

"There is one pressing concern we need to address, though," Fred said.

"What's that?"

"This money. What are we going to do with it?"

Maria frowned. "Yeah, I was wondering about that."

"Well, I can't keep it, obviously, and I don't want you to get caught with it."

"Didn't you say you had a post office box?" Maria asked.

"Right. That will work for a $5,000 or $10,000, but that's about it."

"Okay. We'll use your private mail box to keep the money we need easy access to and hide the rest."

"Where will we hide it?"

"My dorm has a storage room. It's a mess, so it would be easy to hide something in there. Nobody will be going in there until the Christmas break starts in December."

"You sure it's safe?" Fred asked.

"Trust me. Nobody will find it in there. I'll find a better place later. It will do for now."

"What if someone sees you go in there to hide it?"

"I'll go in there tonight when everyone is in bed. There's no reason for anybody to be watching me yet, so we should be okay."

"Alright. How are we going to explain where we got the money to pay Roberts?" Fred asked.

"What about your inheritance? Do you still have that money?"

"No. That money is long gone. My parents needed it, so I let them have it."

"Is that common knowledge?"

"No. Just my parents and I know about it."

"Then that will work. If someone asks you how you're paying for your defense, just tell them you're using your inheritance."

"Good idea. I'll give my mother the cash, and she can give it to Roberts."

"Right. That should work."

They rode in silence for a while, feeling a little better but still apprehensive about how they were going to get through the next few months. When they got back to Santa Monica, Maria left Fred off a few blocks away from his apartment and then went back to the UCLA campus. Fearing the FBI was watching her dorm, she parked in a remote parking lot and walked up the hill to the rear of the dorm. She scanned the area for FBI agents before she came out in the open. She didn't see any, but as a precaution, she joined a group of swimmers coming back from early morning practice. They were all carrying gym bags similar to the one she had with the money in it, so she blended right in.

Back in her dorm room, she breathed a sigh of relief. She looked around and saw that all her roommates were fast asleep. Looking outside, she saw that it was starting to get light, so she quietly found the key to the storage room and left to hide the loot. A few minutes later, she returned, took off her clothes, and climbed into bed. She was so tired she fell right to sleep and began to dream.

She was in the back seat of a limousine. It was her wedding day, and she was seated between two of her bridesmaids. Three others were facing her, and they were all giggling and carrying on as girls usually did at weddings. The limo came to a halt in front of a big Catholic church. The driver got out and opened the door for the bridesmaids, who all piled out. The driver extended his hand and helped Maria to her feet. Her mother approached her and adjusted her veil as two of her bridesmaids straightened out her long train.

Maria carefully walked up the stairs to the church and went inside. Soon, she was at the end of the long center aisle, and "The Wedding March" began to play. Her father took her arm, and they walked slowly forward as family and friends looked on admiringly. As she walked ahead, she gazed at Fred lovingly, thanking God that they'd finally be joined as husband and wife, and then she felt the ground shake, causing her to fall to one knee. There were cries of anguish, and the lights flickered. Then there was nothing but darkness.

In her dorm room, Maria sat up and screamed.

Chapter 32

Willing Accomplice

The next morning, Fred had an appointment with Joel Roberts to begin preparation of his defense. Roberts' office was in Ventura, so he picked up Randy, who was home for Christmas break, on the way. As Fred drove in the driveway, he saw that Randy was in his garage talking to his father. He opened his window to say hello. Mr. Hanson wished him good luck, Randy got in the car, and they left.

"Hey! How are you holding up?"

"Okay, considering everything," Fred replied.

"How's Maria?"

"It's unbelievable, like she's a different woman."

"What do you mean?"

"Well, when I finally told her everything, she took it quite well. She's totally on my side and determined to get me out of this mess. Oh, she lectured me a little about Candy, but it was nothing I didn't deserve."

"That is strange. I would have thought she'd insist that you return the money, explain what happened, and throw yourself on the mercy of the Court."

"No, I really misjudged her. She's become quite the accomplice. In fact, she went to Devil's Canyon with me to get some of the money to use for my defense."

"Wow! That's great. It will be much easier on you with her at your side."

"You've got that right."

Fifteen minutes later, they had arrived at the small garden complex where Joel had his offices. They walked over to the elevator and pushed the up button. When the door opened, they entered and pushed the button for the fourth floor. As the door of the elevator opened, they heard a commotion.

"Oh shit. The damn reporters are back," Fred complained.

They pushed their way through the crowd. One of the reporters stuck a microphone in Fred's face and asked, "What's your reaction to the Judge canceling your bail?"

"Huh? What are you talking about?"

"You haven't heard? The Judge revoked your bail, and you're going to be taken back into custody." Fred's heart nearly stopped as he thought of having to go back to jail. This can't be happening. Why would the Judge change his mind?

As he stood in the hallway in shock with reporters barking questions at him, the door to Joel's office opened, and two FBI agents appeared. They muscled their way into the crowd and escorted Fred into Joel's office.

Joel was standing inside. "I guess you heard the news," Joel said.

"Yeah. What in the hell happened?" Fred asked angrily.

"It seems the Feds noticed something strange about your license plates."

"Huh? My license plates? Oh shit!"

"Your plates don't match the DMV records. They think you switched plates so the police wouldn't spot you during your escape. Frankly, it doesn't look too good, and judging from the look on your face, I think we may have a serious problem."

Fred had no response to Joel's comments. He just put

his hands over his eyes and tried to keep from bursting into tears.

Joel continued. "This is going to change our strategy quite a bit. If you were ready to flee the country, then you obviously can't testify. We'll have to just hope we can cast some reasonable doubt as to your guilt. Most of their evidence is circumstantial and inconclusive, so maybe we can muddy up the water enough to hang the jury."

"I don't want to go back to jail," Fred pleaded.

"You don't have any choice. Just as soon as we are done here, the FBI is taking you back into custody. I am sorry, Fred. There's nothing I can do."

"How long until the trial?"

"Probably about three to four months, I would guess. Whitehead is anxious to get it underway. He says he can smell victory. Oh, by the way, do you happen to have the $5,000 you mentioned?"

"Yeah." Fred reached into his pocket and pulled out ten $1,000 money orders and handed them to Joel. "I managed to raise ten grand. I took what's left from my inheritance money I was using for college, but I guess college will have to take a back seat for a while."

"Well, this is a good start, but you'll need to start talking to your friends and family about raising another $50,000."

Fred nodded. "Don't worry about money. Maria's already working on raising a defense fund, and when she sets her mind on something, watch out. "

Roberts laughed. "Well, that's good to hear. You're very lucky she's sticking by you. A lot of women wouldn't, you know."

"I know. She's got a big wedding planned, so don't spare any expense on my defense. I don't want her to be a jailhouse bride."

Chapter 33

FDF

Maria didn't lose any time setting up her Fuller Defense Fund, or 'FDF' as they liked to call it. The following week, she claimed one of the tables along the main Bruin walkway going to the Student Union. These tables were usually occupied by student organizations and political groups trying to influence student opinion and get media attention. A group of anti-Vietnam war protesters occupied the booth next to her.

She put up a modest sign that she had made by hand and set out a large pickle jar with a sign on it that read: 'PLEASE HELP!' She and Steve had agreed to take turns manning the booth for a couple hours each day. Each morning before she'd set up, she'd stick $500 or $600 into the jar from her stash in storage room, and then at the end of the day, she'd deposit the money in a bank account opened in the name of the FDF. Typically, they'd raise a couple hundred dollars, so, with her contribution, the fund was growing quickly.

The problem with the FDF was that it subjected her to a lot of scrutiny from students, teachers, and the media who liked to stop by and chat or interview her for a story. At first, Maria hated this, but after a while, she got used to it and actually enjoyed the outflow of sympathy and support from almost everyone.

As she was setting up one morning in late January, she was approached by a reporter. "Hi. I'm Alice Wolf from the LA

Times."

Maria extended her hand. "Nice to meet you."

"So, how's the defense fund coming?"

"Great. Everyone is so generous. It's very heartwarming."

"Well, there're a lot of people pulling for Fred. Do you mind if I interview you for a story? The trial is coming up in less than a month, and my boss wants me to do a feature on you and your efforts to help Fred Fuller."

Maria shrugged. "Sure. That would be great."

"Good," she said and dug into her purse for a notepad.

Maria smiled. "Come around and sit in this extra chair. It will be more comfortable."

"Oh, thank you," she said and walked around the table and took a seat.

"Would you like a cup of coffee? I can run into the Student Union really quick and grab you one."

"No, no, I'm fine, thanks. So, tell me how you and Fred met."

"We met at orientation. Fred sat down next to me, and we just started talking. We hit it off really well, and I knew right away we were eventually going to be together. In fact, Fred couldn't wait for school to start. He tracked me down at my home in Ojai and asked me out on a date."

"Oh, that's so romantic. So, I know Fred is a political science major, but what about you?"

"Me? I'm studying to be an RN."

"Really? Any particular area of nursing you're interested in?"

"Maternity or nursery. I love babies—watching them come into the world and taking care of them when they are so tiny."

"She laughed. "Yes, that would be a fun. What got you

interested in babies?"

"My sister is ten years younger than I am, and I just loved taking care of her when she was a baby."

"I bet your parents were surprised when she showed up," Alice said.

"Oh, yes," Maria agreed. "It was quite unexpected."

As they were talking, Steve walked up.

Maria stood up. "Oh, Steve, I'd like you to meet Alice Wolf of the LA Times. She's doing an interview about FDF."

Steve extended his hand. "Nice to meet you."

"Steve is one of Fred's best friends. He helps me man the booth during the day," Maria said.

"Yes, I've heard about you and Randy. Did I hear correctly that all of you are blood brothers?"

Steve laughed. "Yes, I guess we are."

"Okay, why don't you elaborate a bit? I'm sure my readers would be interested in hearing that story."

Steve shrugged and pulled up a stray chair. "Alright. Do you remember when President Kennedy took office and challenged everyone to get physically fit?"

"Right, I remember that," Alice said.

"Well, Randy, Fred, and I had decided we would accept the challenge and hike fifty miles through the Topatopa Mountains from the Ridge Route to California State Highway 33.

"We had never hiked that far before, but were confident that if we did it over a two or three-day period, it wouldn't be too bad. The weekend before our trip, we all gathered at Randy's house to plan our trip. Randy had just returned from a weekend excursion to Tijuana, Mexico with his parents and had brought home fireworks for us to shoot off and switchblades for personal protection."

"Oh, really," Alice said disapprovingly.

"Aren't switchblades illegal?"

"I guess," Steve replied. "But we were just going to use them for camping."

"Okay. Go on."

"Anyway, we planned our route, what we'd need to bring, and got our parents to agree to take us to the trailhead and pick us up at the end of the hike at Highway 33. The next week went very fast, and before we knew it, the day of our departure had arrived. Most of our camping experience had been in fair weather. California doesn't get that much rain, and the temperatures are pretty mild. We often slept under the stars and packed rather light. In fact, it was not uncommon for us to hike in tennis shoes rather than hiking boots."

Alice smiled and made some notes on a pad she was holding.

"Our mothers drove us to the Ridge Route and the trail head for the Topatopa Trail. I brought a small nylon, very light, pup tent just in case it rained. I had an old army hard hat, a canteen, and a backpack with assorted cooking utensils, light clothing, and food. Randy wore jeans, a t-shirt, and sneakers. Although I never searched through his backpack I would guess it had several issues of Mad Magazine, comic books, and lots of snacks. I, on the other hand, was a model Boy Scout who brought everything one could ever possibly need on a hike. Unfortunately, with all of these amenities, my pack was exceedingly heavy.

"Fred always brought fire starters on our camping trips. In an old issue of Boy's Life, it gave instructions on how to make fire starters out of rolled up newspapers and candle wax. Of course, we knew how to start a fire with a stick or flint and steel, but those methods were too difficult to be practical. Fire starters, however, were great because just one of them and a single match could start a fire under any condition. Earlier in the year, we'd made several hundred of them, so we always carried an ample supply.

"We were all in a good mood and eager to get started. We each kissed our mother goodbye and took off.

"The trail was not the greatest in the world. It obviously wasn't heavily traveled, and from time to time, it would seem to disappear. After a few miles, we came to a sign that read 'Lyon's Canyon 2, Topatopa Pass 7, Pyramid Lake 12 and Maricopa Highway 47'.

"By this time, I was beginning to pay the price for all the luxury items I'd packed. The weight was killing me, so I would frequently stop and shift my pack around to get comfortable. After a while, I began to lag behind a few paces. Fred and Randy kept asking me how I was doing, but I was too embarrassed to tell them how miserable I was. After another mile or so, we entered Lyon's Canyon. The trail was cut along the steep canyon walls above Piru Creek and was quite narrow. About midway through the canyon, Fred looked up and spotted a giant condor from the Sespe Condor Sanctuary north of Fillmore. He yelled in delight and pointed at the condor gliding through the canyon.

"When I looked up, I stumbled on a rock and fell off the narrow path. Before I knew it, I was rolling down the side of the hill. Of course, Randy and Fred dropped their packs and scrambled down the hillside to where I'd landed.

"Other than a few bruises to my pride, I was okay, and we hiked on until noon. Then we stopped on the top of the crest for lunch and to rest. We could see Topatopa Pass in the distance rising some 6,210 feet above sea level. We had started at about 4,500 feet and guessed we had climbed at least 1,000 feet already. After lunch, we continued on, figuring we would go another four or five miles and then camp for the night. Before long, thick, puffy clouds began to roll across the sky. We didn't think anything about it, as these types of cumulus clouds in the mountains are not unusual.

"As the day progressed, the clouds thickened up, and it began to get dark, even though it was only midafternoon. Before long, it began to rain. Luckily, we all had ponchos, which we immediately utilized. By this time, Randy was regretting wearing sneakers, as they began to get wet and his feet were getting cold with the rapidly falling temperature. Before long, we couldn't see Topatopa Pass anymore, as the clouds had totally concealed it."

"Oh, my God!" Alice said looking down while she took notes.

"At about four o'clock, the rain turned to snow. We couldn't believe it. Never in a million years would we have believed it would snow that time of year in those mountains. Although the Boy Scout motto was 'Be prepared,' we were totally unprepared for what lay ahead.

"Before long, the snow flurries turned into a blizzard. Randy kept complaining about his feet freezing, and Fred was too scared to talk. I suggested the wise thing to do would be to pitch our tent, all three of us get inside in our sleeping bags to preserve body warmth, and wait until the storm was over. Getting no opposition to my suggestions, we followed that course of action. It was actually pretty warm inside the tent in my sleeping bag. After a few minutes, I dug deep into my backpack, pulled out a transistor radio, and turned it on. We listened to reports about the freak weather and learned that a lot of hikers and campers had been stranded in the storm and that rescue parties had been dispatched to find some of them. We wondered if anybody was out looking for us.

"Fred was the first to awake the next morning. He quickly realized the tent had collapsed, and we were buried several feet in snow. It was warm in my sleeping bag, so I pondered whether I wanted to brave the bitter cold that I knew awaited me above. It occurred to us that our only hope of survival was to get a good fire going as soon as possible so we could keep warm while we ate breakfast and packed up.

"Fred unzipped the tent, and he and I struggled outside and climbed up on top of the snow. It was always impossible to get Randy up in the morning, so we didn't even try. As I gazed across the landscape, I was amazed at the incredibly beautiful transformation that had occurred during the night. It looked like about a foot of snow had fallen, and the temperature must have been about twenty degrees. We knew we needed to get a fire started so we could stay warm until the temperature started to rise. Since all of the dead wood lying around our tent was extremely wet, I knew it would not be easy to start a fire.

"We searched around to find the driest wood available. After we had a good supply rounded up, we got out our fire starters and some matches. Then we laid the wood tepee-style over half a dozen fire starters. I had never needed more than one before, but this was an extreme situation, and I didn't want to fail. I struck the match and lit one of the fire starters. They began to burn with a vengeance, and before long, we had a hot fire going and were eating a hot breakfast.

"After breakfast, we argued about which way to go, back the way we came or onward to our destination. Unfortunately, it didn't take long to realize the trail had been totally covered by the snow such that we couldn't even find it!

"Randy suggested we just go downhill until we got out of the snow. After a heated discussion, we all agreed to try the downhill strategy and get to a lower elevation where it wouldn't be so cold. After an hour or so of trekking through the snow, Randy began complaining about his feet, so Fred and I started another fire, and Randy took off his socks and shoes. After about thirty minutes, Randy was feeling a little better, so we started down the mountain again. Progress was very slow walking in the deep snow. I began to get panicky, as the depths of the snow didn't seem to be changing as we hiked down the mountain. After hiking all day, we stopped and set up camp before it got dark. Fred started another fire and began cooking our supper. After a minute, I began to smell the strong odor of the vegetable beef soup. I looked over and saw that it was boiling. Fred noticed it, too, and began dishing it out for everyone to eat. Before he had even filled one bowl, we heard the bushes rustle. We turned around but couldn't see anything in the darkness so I ran in and got a flashlight."

"Randy jumped up and ran to his pack, pulled out his flashlight, and flashed it into the bushes. Something moved again, and we all jumped to our feet. Whatever it was, it was keeping its distance.

"Just then, the bush moved yet again, and a curious raccoon came scampering across the snow, stopped a moment, looked us over, and then ran off. We all breathed a sigh of relief."

"I bet," Alice said chuckling. She turned the page in her notebook.

"Just then," Steve continued, "we heard rustling in the bushes again. This time, it wasn't isolated in one direction but was all around us. Randy flashed his light out toward the perimeter of camp. This time, the light fell on the cold green eyes of a pack of coyotes. My heart began to pound as I saw my life coming to a bloody end.

"Fred looked around the campsite frantically. He dashed over and grabbed a burning log. Reacting to his movement, the coyote bolted after him. Fred turned and waved the flames in the coyote's face. He growled as he backed off slowly. Unfortunately, the flame began to flicker out.

"Fred went for another log, but the coyote attacked and sunk his teeth into the left sleeve of Fred's jacket. Fortunately, the two sweatshirts and heavy coat he was wearing protected him from the coyote's sharp teeth. He fumbled for another flaming stick but couldn't reach it. I lunged for a log and waved it wildly in front of the coyote, but he wouldn't retreat. Fred reached into his pocket and pulled out his switchblade and flipped it open. The coyote let loose of his sleeve and lunged for his throat. Fred raised his left hand to blunt the attack and stuck the blade of his knife in the chest of the coyote.

"The other coyotes, reacting to the smell of blood, began to attack all of us. Suddenly, I heard gunshots. I wondered if a rescue party had arrived just in the nick of time. Then I saw Randy throwing cherry bombs into the fire. As the bombs exploded, the terrified and startled coyotes backed off and made a hasty retreat. Once they were gone, Randy and I ran over to where Fred was lying in the snow next to the dead coyote. He was okay, luckily."

"Wow!" Alice said. "What an adventure you guys had.

"For sure," Steve replied. "After the attack, we moved our camp a good distance away from the dead coyote. We didn't want to be anywhere near a dead animal with a forest full of hungry predators looking for food. We pitched our tent and settled in for another bitterly cold night. It snowed a little, but it was nothing like the previous night. The next day, we again began our journey down the mountain, hoping to get out of the snow and down to warmer weather.

"The going was slow, as the snow was deep and slippery. After hiking all morning, we stopped for lunch and then pressed on. Just as I was about to suggest it was time to stop again for the night, I heard Fred yell that there was a log cabin ahead.

"Randy and I rushed toward the cabin. We knocked

furiously on the door, but no one answered. When Fred caught up to us, we were peering in the front window.

"After brief discussion on the propriety of breaking into a cabin, Randy broke one of the windows and entered the cabin."

"How did that go?" Alice asked.

"Oh, Fred didn't want Randy to break in. He said it was illegal, but Randy said our dire circumstances trumped the law. I agreed, so Fred gave in under protest."

"Amazing," Alice said. "And Fred's a bank robber?"

"Right," Steve agreed. "Anyway, the cabin had a big fireplace and was well stocked with food. That night, we sat around the wooden table in front of a raging fire, pondering our adventure. We had stuck together, and we had survived. That's when we became blood brothers."

"So, you just decided you were now blood brothers?" Alice asked.

"No, Fred led us through a fancy ceremony and made us all pledge to be like brothers. We sealed the pledge by dripping coyote blood on our hands as we shook them.

"Fred then gave us our necklaces, and we put them on.

'Wear these necklaces as a symbol of our kinship and our strength as blood brothers,' he said.

"The next day, the Rangers found us."

Alice smiled broadly. "Wow. Everyone's going to love that story. . . . So, now you and Randy are going to make good on your pledge?"

"Absolutely," Steve said. "We're not going to let him go to jail for something he didn't do."

"That's right," Maria said. "And luckily a lot of people have stepped up and made contributions to Fred's defense fund."

Alice got up. "Well, this article should help in that

regard. "Thank you for talking with me."

They all shook hands and Alice left. Steve smiled at Maria and they got back to work as students began coming up out of curiosity or to listen to their pitch to get contributions for FDF.

Chapter 34

Damage Control

Alice Wolf's story came out in the LA Times the following week, causing quite a bit of media stir. Fred's heroic battle with a pack of coyotes and his reluctance to even break into a deserted cabin due to his respect for the law turned the tide of public opinion in his favor. More and more, people came to believe that Fred couldn't have been involved in the Bank USA robbery or the murder of Harvey Hamlin. Maria and Steve were soon overwhelmed at their booth each day with friends, well-wishers, and members of the media looking for new angles on the story.

This turn of events, just weeks before the trial was set to begin, stunned Whitehead, and he feared the tide of public opinion would prejudice the jury pool and make it more difficult for him to get a conviction. Reeling from this and fearing his run for Governor was in jeopardy, he called an urgent meeting with Special Agents Walters and Harper.

"This media frenzy over our little Boy Scout has got me worried. We've got to put a stop to it, or we won't be able to pick a fair jury," he told them.

"Well, it does appear this bank robbery is out of character for Mr. Fuller," Harper suggested.

"Bullshit!" Whitehead exclaimed. "This is just a carefully orchestrated PR campaign. Joel Roberts would do anything to keep me out of the Governor's mansion."

"I don't think it's Roberts," Harper replied. "It's Fuller's girlfriend Maria. She is obsessed with getting Fuller off and will do anything to make it happen."

"Yeah," Whitehead agreed. "That article in the Times made me sick. What I don't understand is why she's standing by Fuller when everybody knows he was cheating on her."

"Perhaps there's something other than love waiting for her if she manages to get him off," Walters suggested.

"I like your thinking," Whitehead said. "I bet she's been promised a nice chunk of change if Fuller goes free."

"That would explain a lot," Walters agreed. "Fred has hidden the money somewhere, and she needs to free him so he can lead her to it. Once they divide up the money, they'll probably split. Fred obviously doesn't love her, or he wouldn't have run off with that slut Candy."

"What about Stewart? He could be in on this too," Harper suggested.

"We don't' have time to worry about Stewart," Whitehead spat. "It could take months to find him, if we ever do. Let's concentrate on tainting Mr. Fuller's Boy Scout image. I want you to dig up all the dirt on him you can, particularly his sordid affair with Candy Clisby. Dig up everything you can. I want to bury him in filth in front of the jury so they'll realize his damned Eagle Scout façade is a bunch of crap!"

"Alright. I'll go see if I can locate any of Candy's friends," Walters said. "They'll probably have some details on the affair."

"Good," Whitehead agreed. "Harper, you concentrate on Maria and Fred's two buddies. There's bound to be some dirt on them. Everybody has skeletons in their closets, right?"

Harper nodded.

"Okay," Whitehead said as he stood up. "That's all for now."

The meeting ended, and everyone got up to go about their assignments. Walters started at the Palm Springs branch of Bank USA, and Harper arranged for a tail on Maria and Steve and ordered complete background checks on both of them. Walters first met with the cashier at the Palm Springs branch, and there he learned of Candy's friend, Jenny Madeira. He tracked her down at her job in Banning.

"So, I'm sorry to hear about the untimely death of your friend Candy."

"Yes, I can't believe she is gone."

"What do you know about the circumstances of her death?"

"Not much—just that she was camping with her boyfriend, Fred Fuller, when she was bitten by a snake."

"Yes, I've viewed her hospital records, but Fred won't talk about what happened. Did he tell you anything?"

"No, just that they'd gone, uh, swimming in a pond, and as they were getting out, the snake came up from behind her out of the bushes."

"They were lovers, right? They slept together?"

"Well, I don't know how much sleep they got. From what Candy said, they couldn't get enough of each other."

"So, they probably were skinny dipping then. That's why they went somewhere secluded, I suppose?"

"I don't know why they went there. It was a place Fred had discovered as a child. He loved it there and wanted to show it to Candy."

"Really? That's a long way to go just to go skinny dipping. Is there a lodge or something up there?"

"No. It's pretty deserted from what I was told."

"So, if they were planning to stay the night, they'd have to bring camping equipment, right?"

"I suppose."

"Did Candy have any camping equipment?"

"No, I don't think so."

"Where was their relationship going, do you think?"

"I don't know, but it was getting pretty serious. Fred gave Candy some money so she wouldn't have to work anymore."

"So, he was going to support her?"

"That's what I understood."

"How much money did he give her?"

"Two grand. He said he'd give her that much every month."

"Do you have any idea how he was going to manage that? I mean, his family isn't wealthy, are they?"

"She said something about an inheritance. It would be enough to keep them going until Fred graduated from law school."

"Do you know anything about them going to Canada?"

"No."

"When was the last time you saw Fred?"

"The night after Candy died. He called to tell me, and I invited him over so neither of us would be alone."

"Did you two have sex?"

"No!" Jenny exclaimed. "It wasn't like that. We were mourning the loss of someone we both loved."

"So, you're saying Fred loved Candy?"

"Yes. And she wouldn't admit it, but she loved him too. I could tell it by the way she was acting."

"Hmm. Do you have a key to Candy's apartment?"

"Yes."

"Can I go in and have a look around?"

"Sure, but I've already taken all her stuff out of there. She didn't have much, and there weren't any relatives."

"Can I look through the boxes?" Walters persisted.

Jenny shrugged. "Okay, whatever."

Jenny brought the boxes downstairs, and Walters went through them carefully but didn't find anything.

"Thank you for talking to me. We're going to need you to testify at Fred's trial, so don't leave town."

Jenny shrugged, and they both stood up.

"I'm going to go talk to a few of Candy's neighbors to see if any of them saw anything. Do you know their names?"

"Melba Brooks lives next door to Candy's apartment. She'd be the only one that might have seen something."

"Alright. I'll be in touch."

Walters left and went to Mrs. Brooks' apartment. She didn't know much, but she had seen them come and go a few times. Walters thanked her and left, and it was then that he decided to visit Devil's Canyon.

It occurred to him that Fred might have gone out there to bury the 6.7 million dollars. He didn't know exactly where the ghost town was, so he drove to Kelso, where Candy had been picked up by helicopter, but nobody there had ever heard of it. Frustrated, he returned to LA and reported what little he'd learned to Whitehead.

A few days later Harper gave his report which was even worse.

"They're both squeaky clean," Harper said. "Maria's never even been tardy to class, and Steve's some kind of Jesus freak who sings in the church choir."

"Well, keep a tail on them anyway," Whitehead scowled. " I know they're hiding something. I can just feel it. Maybe one of them will slip up."

Chapter 35

The Trial

When the trial finally began, it took three days to pick a jury. It seemed all of the pre-trial publicity had made it difficult to find jurors who hadn't been influenced by what they had been seeing and hearing in the media. On the fourth day, testimony was set to begin.

As the bailiff escorted Fred into the courtroom, he noticed Maria in the front row. He smiled, gazed at her, and wondered if he would ever walk down the aisle with her as she had so confidently predicted. Maria's parents were sitting next to her, and Fred's parents were in the row behind them. Fred sat at the counsel table and waited for the trial to begin. After a few moments, the bailiff commanded everyone to rise and announced, "The United States District Court for the Southern District of California is now in session, the Honorable Troy Sessions presiding."

Judge Sessions was an unpredictable commodity, according to Roberts. He was very loud and boisterous and frequently lost his temper. His tolerance level for courtroom improprieties was low, and he was not reluctant to throw an attorney or two in jail if they crossed him. Most of the defense bar hated him. Whitehead, on the other hand, loved Judge Sessions, as they were good friends, and it was well known that Judge Sessions loved to put criminals behind bars.

The first witness was the coroner, Dr. Paul Harlen.

Whitehead began, "Dr. Harlen, please state your name."

"Dr. Paul Q. Harlen."

"Now, Dr. Harlen, did you have occasion to be called to the San Bernardino Branch of Bank USA on October 20, 1967?"

"Yes, I did."

"And what was the purpose of that summons?"

"I was called to pick up the body of Harvey Hamlin, who had been found dead in the bank vault."

"What was his condition when you first saw him?"

"He was lying on the floor of the vault, bound and gagged with packing tape."

Whitehead walked over to the prosecution's table and picked up a paper bag. He reached inside and pulled out several strips of clear packing tape. "I am going to show you what has been marked as People's Exhibit 1 and ask you to identify it."

"Yes, this is the packing tape that was found around Mr. Hamlin's arms, ankles, and over his mouth."

"Your Honor, I request that Peoples Exhibit 1 be admitted into evidence."

"No objection," Joel said.

"Did Mr. Hamlin's body have any wounds or bruises?"

"No, sir."

"Did you perform an autopsy?"

"Yes, we did."

"What was the result of that autopsy?"

"We determined that he died of a massive coronary. We conjecture it was trauma induced."

"Objection, Your Honor—speculation."

"Objection sustained. Dr. Harlen, please just answer the question that was asked," the Judge said.

"In your opinion, Doctor, what caused this massive

coronary?"

"Mr. Hamlin had a history of heart disease, and any kind of intense emotional or physical stress could have triggered the attack."

"If Mr. Hamlin had been confronted by a bank robber and his life threatened during the robbery, could that have been what caused his heart attack?"

"Absolutely."

"Or, perhaps being bound and gagged and left in the vault for almost three days without food or water—could that have caused it?"

"That's consistent with his medical history. He might have been okay when they bound and gagged him, but he may have panicked later and had the attack while he was struggling to get free."

Whitehead continued to question Dr. Harlen meticulously for several hours before he turned him over to Joel. "Pass the witness," Whitehead finally said.

The Judge looked at Joel and stated, "Your witness, Mr. Roberts."

"Dr. Harlen, you previously testified that you determined the time of death to be when?"

"Between 5:00 and 11:00 p.m."

"You've indicated that the heart attack could have been trauma induced. Now, could that trauma have been something other than a bank robbery?"

"Yes, that's possible."

"Could it have been induced by an unpleasant phone conversation with a spouse?"

"It's possible, but I don't think just a phone call would do it."

"But it is possible?"

"Yes."

"How about a confrontation with a bank auditor?"

"I don't know. If it was an intense encounter, perhaps, but I'm just speculating. There is no way to know exactly what might have caused it."

"Suppose the evidence were to show Mr. Hamlin had instigated the bank robbery and his accomplice double-crossed him. Do you think that would be intense enough?"

"Certainly, but again, that would be pure speculation," he replied.

"Precisely. Your entire testimony about the cause of Mr. Hamlin's heart attack is purely speculation, isn't it?"

"Objection!" Whitehead spat. "Argumentative."

The coroner looked up at the Judge expectantly. "Overruled," the Judge said.

The doctor looked at Roberts. "No. My opinion is that he died of a heart attack that was trauma induced. Since he was found in the vault bound and gagged, it's pretty obvious what happened."

"Obvious to you, maybe, but you weren't there, were you?"

"No."

"So, you really don't know what exactly caused Mr. Hamlin's coronary, do you?"

"No. I can only give you my opinion from what I observed."

"And you don't know what time it happened precisely, do you?"

"Not precisely, but I think our estimate is pretty close."

"Thank you, Doctor," Joel concluded. "Pass the witness."

"No further questions, Your Honor," Whitehead said.

"Call your next witness," the Judge said.

"Yes, sir. The United States calls Cindy Brolin,"

Whitehead said.

Cindy Brolin was a thin woman of medium height. She wore her jet black hair tied up in a bun. Fred thought she must have been of Spanish or Portuguese descent. She stood up and made her way to the witness stand.

"Who is your employer?"

"Bank USA."

"At which branch do you work?"

"San Bernardino."

"What is your job there?"

"I am the assistant cashier."

"And who was the cashier at the bank on October 20, 1967?"

"Harvey Hamlin."

"Do you recall the events of October 20, 1967?"

"Yes. How could I forget them?"

"Did anything unusual happen that day?"

"Mr. Hamlin had Mr. Campbell, one of the bank auditors, in his office all day, and they had some words before Mr. Campbell left. Hamlin was pretty upset."

"What time of day was this?"

"It was nearly 5:00 p.m. when the bank auditor left. I had prepared the vault to be closed, but Mr. Hamlin had to put in his security codes before I could close it. When I went to him to tell him I was ready to close the vault, he couldn't be bothered with it just then. He told me he would do it later and insisted I leave."

"Did you see the defendant, Fred Fuller, at any time that day?"

"No, sir. He usually comes in later after everyone is gone."

"Did you see anything else out of the ordinary that day?"

"Well, when I went in to work on Monday morning, there was a towel on the floor near the vault."

Whitehead walked to the prosecution's table and picked up a paper bag. He stuck his hand inside and pulled out a towel. "Mrs. Brolin, I'm going to hand to you what has been marked as People's Exhibit 12 and ask if you can identify it."

"Yes, that's the towel."

"And you found it on the floor in front of the vault?"

"Yes."

"Your Honor, I would request that People's Exhibit 12 be admitted."

"No objection," Joel said.

"Admitted," the Judge said.

"This was before you knew Harvey Hamlin was lying dead inside the vault, is that correct?"

"Yes."

"Do you have any idea where the towel came from?"

"Yes, from the kitchen. Someone must have taken it from the kitchen and dropped it by the vault."

"Do you have any idea who might have done that?"

"No, sir."

"Do you suppose the robber used it to clean his fingerprints off the vault?"

"Objection! Calls for speculation," Joel said.

"Sustained," the Judge replied.

"Thank you, Mrs. Brolin. Pass the witness."

Joel jumped up and began questioning Mrs. Brolin eagerly. "Now, Mrs. Brolin, you testified that Mr. Hamlin was very upset that afternoon, didn't you?"

"Yes, he was."

"You said he had been in with the auditor, Mr. Campbell, all day and they had some words, right?"

"That's right. I was very worried about him. I knew he

had a heart condition and drinking problem, and—"

"Objection, Your Honor! Non-responsive."

"Objection sustained," the Judge replied.

"Isn't it true this was the fifth day the bank examiner had been at the bank?"

"Yes."

"And isn't it true Mr. Hamlin was already on suspension for leaving the vault open and drinking on the job?"

"For leaving the vault open, yes. I am not sure about whether his drinking problem had anything to do with his suspension."

"Had Mr. Hamlin been drinking the night of the robbery?"

"Yes. After Mr. Campbell left, I saw him take a few gulps from a metal flask he keeps in his desk."

"Do you think he was upset enough to consider robbing the bank?"

"Objection!" Whitehead said. "Prejudicial, lacks foundation."

"Sustained," the Judge ruled.

"Well, do you think having the bank examiner there could have contributed to his heart attack?"

"Well, that plus the fact he was worried about getting fired."

"Objection, Your Honor! Mrs. Hamlin is not a doctor; therefore, any answer would be pure speculation."

The crowd began to stir.

"Order! Objection sustained."

"No further questions," Joel concluded. "Pass the witness."

"No further questions," Whitehead echoed.

"Call your next witness," Judge Sessions said.

Whitehead called Dr. Dennis Winston from Barstow

Memorial Hospital. His testimony was essentially the same as at the bond hearing. Several police officers and detectives were called to testify about the crime scene, but late in the day when the Judge asked for Whitehead's next witness, Fred was shocked at who he called.

"The United States calls Jenny Madeira."

Joel looked over at Fred and whispered, "Who is that?"

"It's Candy's best friend," Fred whispered back.

"Objection, Your Honor! This witness was not on the witness list," Joel said.

"Your Honor," Whitehead quickly jumped in, "we only just located Miss Madeira a few hours ago, so we were unable to put her on the list."

"Very well. It's getting late, so we'll recess until ten on Monday morning. That should give you some time to prepare to cross-examine this witness, Mr. Roberts."

"Very well, Your Honor," Joel replied.

The courtroom cleared except for Joel, Fred, a couple of bailiffs, and Steve and Randy, who were hanging around in the visitors' gallery. Joel turned to Fred and said, "Why didn't you tell me about Jenny Madeira?"

Fred slumped back in his chair and stared down at the floor. "I don't know. I didn't think it was important."

"I'll decide what's important! If you will recall, I'm the attorney! I don't like getting ambushed in court. Now, what can I expect to hear from Ms. Madeira on Monday?"

"She's a friend of Candy's. I never even met her until after Candy died. She and I handled Candy's funeral together."

Fred's head started to throb, and his shoulder muscles tightened. He rubbed the back of his neck in a desperate attempt to relieve the pain and tension. Then he noticed the bailiff standing anxiously by the side door to take him back to the county jail.

"Why do you think Whitehead called her as a witness?"

"I don't know. I guess because Candy probably told her all about our relationship."

Joel stood up and began packing up his briefcase. "You may want to tell Maria to stay home Monday. It's not going to be too pleasant for her. Obviously, Whitehead's going to use Jenny to drag you through the mud."

"Maria is not stupid. If I told her to stay home, that would guarantee she'd be at the trial."

Joel looked up and smiled faintly. "Maybe it's a good thing you'll be spending the night at the county jail Monday."

Fred grimaced. His fling with Candy had been the subject of considerable media speculation, but nobody had discovered any hard facts. Fred and Candy had managed to keep it to themselves, for the most part, but on Monday, the entire affair would be revealed. It was going to be the most humiliating day of Fred's life. Maria, his family, and his closest friends were going to have to hear all the lurid details of his relationship with Candy. *Why did I get involved with Candy? It was such a stupid thing to do. If I'd have been stronger, she'd be alive today, and I wouldn't be facing such humiliation.* "Damn it!"

Roberts looked up. "What did you say?" he asked.

"Ah, nothing," Fred replied. "Nothing important."

As the courtroom was emptying, Steve and Randy came up to the railing to talk to Fred. Joel looked at them and then turned to Fred. "You can talk with Steve and Randy for a minute. I'll be right back."

Joel went and asked the bailiff to give them a minute and then went to catch Whitehead.

"What do you think Jenny's gonna say?" Steve asked.

"I don't think she could know much because I didn't tell

Candy anything about the money until after we left to go to Devil's Canyon." Suddenly, a cold chill came over him as he remembered Candy making a phone call. "Except. . . . oh God!"

"Except what?" Steve asked.

"She called Jenny from Palm Springs to ask her to feed her damn cat. She could have told Jenny something then, although it couldn't have been much because it was a very short conversation."

"Do you think Jenny knows you had a bag of money with you?" Randy asked.

"I don't think so," Fred replied. "Candy didn't know about it until after Palm Springs."

"Good," Steve said.

"What about Sam? Has the FBI found him yet?" Steve asked.

"I don't think so. I doubt they're even looking now."

Joel entered the courtroom, walked over to where they were talking, and joined the conversation.

"Maybe Steve and I can find him," Randy said.

"Find who?" Joel asked.

"Sam Stewart," Fred replied. "We think we need to find him. It might be my only hope."

"Yes, I would definitely like to talk to him, but if he took the money, you'll never find him. Our private investigator tried hard to find him but couldn't pick up a trail. He's probably out of the country by now."

"Would more money help?" Fred asked.

"No. You'd just be throwing your money away. Besides, the FBI has been looking for him, too, and they claim they can't find him either. Of course, they don't have much motivation to find him either, since all it could do is botch up their case against you."

"That's why we're going to find him if it's the last thing we do," Randy promised. "Fred is like a brother, and we will stop at nothing to save him."

"That's very admirable of both of you," Roberts replied.

The bailiff walked over and told Roberts he was needed in the clerk's office, and Roberts followed him out of the courtroom.

"Joel's right. They already have someone to pin the crime on. If they found Sam, there's no telling what impact that would have on their case," Steve said. "It's just too risky for them to find Sam.

"Particularly if he has the money," Fred said.

"Exactly. It would blow their case right out of the water!" Randy agreed.

"Maybe, maybe not," Fred reasoned. "If you find Sam, he'll just tell them I stole the money. If he does that, I'm still guilty and worse off because then they'll have the money and a witness against me."

"If Sam keeps his mouth shut, which he may well do, the jury may just be confused and unsure enough to acquit you."

"Why would he keep his mouth shut?" Fred asked. "If he's caught with the money, he's doomed. He'd have no motivation to protect me. In fact, misery loves company. He'll probably be dying to implicate me. Shit, he may try to bargain for a lighter sentence by agreeing to testify against me."

"Maybe not. Didn't you say he likes you?"

"Yeah. We always got along. I thought we were friends."

"Maybe he's feeling a little guilty about setting you up. If he gets caught, maybe he'll do the honorable thing and admit that he set you up."

"God, I hope so. It's probably my only chance. I have

a really bad feeling about how this case is going. If you guys don't find Sam, it may be all over for me."

"Don't worry, we'll find him somehow. I don't how, but we'll find him," Randy assured his troubled friend.

The door to the clerk's office swung open, and Roberts walked over to where they were talking.

"Well, I guess it's time to break up the party, guys," Roberts said.

"Joel," Fred said, "Steve and Randy are definitely going to try to find Sam Stewart."

Joel shrugged. "Well, I wish you guys luck. It will be a difficult task. Where do you propose to start your search anyway?"

"We don't know yet—maybe his home up at Big Bear," Randy replied.

"That makes sense," Joel said. "Keep me posted, okay?"

"Sure. We'll call you every day," Randy assured him.

"Well, I've got to get back to the office. See you guys later. Fred, I'll see you Monday."

"Right. Thanks Joel," Fred said.

He motioned to the bailiff and he came over to escort Fred out of the courtroom.

"Goodbye," Fred said. "I am counting on you guys."

"See ya, Fred. Hang in there," Steve said.

"We'll take care of everything," Randy added. "Don't worry."

Steve and Randy left the courtroom, and Joel turned to Fred and said, "You've got a couple of fine friends there, Fred. I can't believe they're going to just drop everything and go chasing after Sam."

"I know. I am very lucky."

"Get some rest over the weekend," Roberts said.

"You'll need your strength on Monday."

"Right," Fred agreed. "Thanks, Joel."

When Roberts got back to his office late Friday night he decided he better call Congressman Bartlett and give him an update. He particularly wanted to alert him to the fact that Steve and Randy were out trying to track down Sam Stewart.

"Do you think there is a chance in Hell, they'll find him," the Congressman asked.

"No. Not really, but they are pretty determined, so they might get lucky."

"Well, we can't let that happen. If Sam Stewart is arrested, he might confess and drag us all into it."

"He doesn't know you and I are involved."

"No, but he may know Sinclair is and Sinclair can be tied to me and you."

"True, but I'm not sure how we can stop it. I can't very well tell Steve and Randy to stand down. How would that look?"

"Well you better think of something. I don't want any surprises at trial."

"Aren't Lake Arrowhead and Big Bear located in San Bernardino County?"

"That sounds right."

"Well, that's where your old friend Deputy Sheriff Carl Johnson works, right?"

"I think so."

"You ought to give him a call," Roberts suggested.

"Yeah, good idea. He owes me a favor."

Joel hung up and headed for his car. It was almost a 45-minute drive home with traffic. As he was driving, he worried about Sam Stewart. If Randy and Steve were to find him, even if he didn't implicate Sinclair in the robbery, there still might be questions as to why Fred's defense counsel hadn't found him. Of course, the same could be said about Whitehead and the FBI. Why didn't they find Sam Stewart? It would be quite an embarrassment for all concerned and the media would have a field day.

Chapter 36

Amateur Sleuths

Fred was escorted down to the basement, where he was loaded on a shuttle to the jail. All he could think about was what Jenny Madeira would say when she took the stand on Monday. He knew his Boy Scout image would be greatly tarnished by her testimony if Candy had kept her fully abreast of their affair. Being she was like a sister to her, it was a safe bet she had.

Fortunately, on Sunday Maria came to see him. "Hi, babe. I've missed you."

"This is a creepy place. Joel's got to get you out of here."

"I'm sorry you had to come here. I'm starting to get used to it a little now, but the first day they brought me here, I was scared to death."

"Has anybody bothered you in here?"

"No. I've got a private cell."

"Is the food decent?"

"No. Actually, it's pretty bad, but I haven't had much of an appetite anyway. Have you heard anything from Steve and Randy?"

"No, nothing yet. Sorry."

Fred sighed as he looked into Maria's big brown eyes. *You are so beautiful. How will I bear to be without you?* She must have felt his anguish, as a tear rolled slowly down her cheek. "Listen, babe, I need you to do something for me."

"What?"

"I need you to snoop around and see if you can find out anything on Harvey Hamlin. If he was involved in the robbery, somebody must have known about it. Talk to Jim Wells. He can probably give you some suggestions on where to start."

"What about Joel's PI? Isn't he doing that?"

"He should be, but he hasn't come up with anything so far and Roberts isn't pushing him for some reason. Plus, a lot of people won't talk to a PI, whereas they might talk to you. You have a way with people, and you've been getting a lot of good press."

"Okay, but I don't know exactly what to do."

Fred smiled at Maria and replied, "Use your feminine ingenuity. I have great confidence in you."

The jailer walked over and tapped Maria on the shoulder, indicating her time was up. She got up, gave Fred a somber smile, and left. Although it was great seeing her, Fred felt worse than ever after she left. He wondered how many more times he'd be able to look upon that pretty face.

On Sunday, Father Bernard, Maria's parish priest from Ojai, came to see Fred. Fred contemplated confessing his sins and asking for God's forgiveness, but then he thought better of it. He wasn't so sure his cell was bug-free, so he'd just have to assume God would know that he was sorry for what he had done. After all, God was omniscient.

Fred thought about all that had happened to him. He wasn't an outwardly religious person, but he did believe in God. How could he not be a believer after so many people had come to his aid despite his unforgivable behavior; Maria bailing him out of jail and standing by him despite his betrayal; Steve and Randy dropping everything to chase after Sam; and Jim jeopardizing his job at Bank USA by snooping around and collecting valuable information for his defense.

Fred was profoundly grateful to have this cadre of amateur sleuths who had made it their mission to prove him innocent. Tears welled in his eyes just thinking about it. He knew he didn't deserve such good friends, but he was glad God had sent them to rescue him.

Chapter 37

The Search

After their discussion with Fred and Roberts in court on Friday, Steve and Randy left the courthouse to eat lunch and plan their strategy in searching for Sam. They quickly realized the job, for which they had so eagerly volunteered, wouldn't be all that easy.

"So, now what are we going to do?" Steve asked.

"I'm not sure," Randy replied. "We just have to think about it logically."

"Let's start at his home," Steve suggested. "Maybe he left a forwarding address or told someone where he was going."

"That's sounds good. Let's go home, pack a few things, and tell our parents what we're going to do."

"No, that might not be a good idea. You know how parents are. They might try to stop us."

"Hmm. I guess you're right, but what are we going to do about expense money?" Randy asked.

"Oh, Maria gave me $5,000 in cash from FDF."

"Oh, good. That ought to be enough for the weekend."

"I should hope so! You have some clothes over at your apartment, don't you?"

"Yeah, sure," Steve said, "and you can borrow some of Fred's."

"Okay, we're all set. Let's get going."

Steve and Randy went to the apartment in Santa

Monica. They packed everything they needed for their journey and then headed for Big Bear Lake in Randy's yellow '62 Volkswagen Beetle. Big Bear was a couple hours from LA, so it was early Friday evening when they arrived and pulled into a gas station to refuel. It was cool when they got out of the car, as Big Bear was over 5,000 feet in elevation, so they dug out a couple sweatshirts. While Randy filled the tank with gas, Steve checked the oil.

"Let's get a motel. We can snoop around town some tonight and in the morning, if necessary," Randy suggested.

"Okay. There is a Travel Lodge ahead. It looks pretty decent."

"Fine. Let's check it out."

A few minutes later, they checked into the motel and took their baggage to their room. Inside were two queen-sized beds, a night stand, a desk, and a TV.

Randy threw his luggage in a corner and collapsed on the bed.

"Oh, man, I'm tired. What a day."

Steve went straight to the desk and fumbled through its drawers. "Here's a telephone book. I'm going to look up Sam Stewart." He flipped through the pages until he found what he wanted. "Here it is! 2007 Crestline Drive, telephone number 555-4474."

"Give that number a call and see what happens," Randy said.

Steve dialed the number. After a few rings, a squeaky female voice came on the line. "This is a recording. The number you have reached has been disconnected."

"Damn. We'll have to go over there and check it out in person," Randy said.

"It's already dark."

"That's good, right? No one will see us that way."

"What do you mean? Why do you care if someone sees us? You're not thinking of—"

"Yes, I think we need to take a look inside Mr. Stewart's house."

"But that's breaking and entering," Steve noted.

"So what? You weren't worried about that when we were up in the Topatopa Mountains a few years back."

"That was different, and Fred certainly wouldn't approve."

"I don't think even Fred would mind if we took a look inside Sam's house tonight."

"Okay, okay. I can see you're not going to be dissuaded from this foolish escapade, so let's just get on with it."

Steve and Randy left their motel room and got into the VW. "Let's go to that Union 76 station down the street and ask for directions," Steve said.

"Good idea," Randy replied as he pulled the car out of the motel parking lot and headed toward the Union 76. They pulled into the station and rolled down their window. A tall, white-headed man walked up to them and asked, "Can I help you?"

"Sure hope so. Do you know where Crestline Drive is?"

"Sure. Who you looking for?" the attendant asked.

"Sam Stewart."

"Hmm. Haven't seen Sam around for a while, but you can go have a look if you want. Crestline Drive is up the road a half mile. Just take a left at the first stop sign and go about three miles. You can't miss it. It's an old log cabin on the right side of the road, kind of out by itself."

"Thanks. We really appreciate your help."

"You're welcome. Hope you find him."

They drove out to Crestline Drive and took a left as the

old man had directed them. They followed the narrow dirt road, weaving through a grove of tall pine trees for what seemed far more than three miles. It was a dark night and difficult to see much beyond the headlights. Finally, they approached a mailbox and what appeared to be a driveway going off to the right. The mailbox had the name 'STEWART' on its side in silver reflective decals. They rolled down their windows and peered down the driveway. It was as quiet as it was dark, not a light in sight.

"Okay, let's go check it out," Randy said.

"You're sure you want to do this?" Steve questioned.

"Yeah. Bring your flashlight."

"Okay, I'm coming."

They left their car by the mailbox and walked slowly toward the house. As they neared the log cabin, the bushes shook in front of them. Randy pointed his flashlight toward the noise. "Who's there?" he demanded nervously.

Steve looked toward the light and saw two eyes reflecting the light from the flashlight. "Shit! What is that?" Steve shrieked.

"Hang on! It's just some kind of animal."

Just then, the animal took off, almost knocking Steve and Randy over.

"What in hell was that?" Steve said.

"I think it was a big buck," Randy replied.

"The damn thing scared the shit out of me!"

"So I see. Come on. Let's see if the cabin is open."

They finally made it to the front porch. Randy knocked on the door to make sure no one was home. When they got no response, they tried the door. It was locked, of course.

"Now what?" Steve asked.

"Let's check the back."

Just as Steve and Randy were walking around to the

back of the cabin, the flash of headlights could be seen coming down Crestline Drive.

"Oh shit!" Steve said. "Someone's coming."

"Maybe they will just drive by," Randy said hopefully, though he didn't believe it himself.

The car kept coming and slowed down as it approached the driveway. It stopped momentarily, and someone shone a flashlight at Randy's car. After a moment, the car turned into the driveway and headed straight for them.

"Let's hide," Steve whispered.

"No, there's no use. Whoever it is already knows we're here anyway. We better just sit tight."

The car pulled up and shone a spotlight on Steve and Randy, blinding them. They both turned away and put their hands over their eyes.

A man got out and approached them. "What are you boys doing up here?" he asked.

"Uh, we're looking for Sam Stewart," Randy answered. "Who are you?"

"I'm Sheriff Johnson," the voice replied. "Paul at the gas station said someone was looking for Sam, so I came out to see what business you had with him."

"Uh, well, um . . . a friend of ours is a messenger for Bank USA, where Sam used to work, and he told us Sam was the best fishing guide around. He said Sam might take us out fishing if we came up here and asked him," Randy lied.

"You sure you weren't planning to rob the place since Sam is out of town."

"Oh, no!" Steve said. "We just wanted to go fishing."

"Sam's been gone for several weeks."

"I know. We called him, but since his phone was disconnected, we thought we'd come out to check."

"Well, I'm afraid you're out of luck. He went to Las

Vegas to do a little gambling, I guess."

"Bummer. That was kind of sudden, wasn't it?" Randy asked.

"Damn sure was! I've known Sam for ten years, and he was a creature of habit. He was up at six every day, had breakfast at the café in town every morning, did his morning route down to San Bernardino and came back for lunch. Then he'd play nine holes of golf in the afternoon or hang around the lodge shooting the breeze with some of his friends. At 4:00 p.m., almost like clockwork, Sam would have dinner at the café, and then he'd leave at four thirty-five and run his route down to San Bernardino again. You could set your clock by him."

"What happened to him?"

"Well, one day he came by my office and said he was tired of his miserable existence and was going to start doing a little living before he got too old to enjoy life. . . . said he was going to play around a little in Las Vegas and then maybe head out to the east coast."

"Oh, well. I guess we'll just fish by ourselves then," Steve said.

"Hey, I know another fishing guide I could hook you up with. It would only cost you twenty-five bucks."

"Really? That would be great. Why don't you just give us his name and number, and we'll call him in the morning."

"Okay. His name is Bart Small, and you can find him at the lodge after seven tomorrow morning."

"Did Sam leave a forwarding address or anything?"

"Nope. Far as I know, Sam never got any mail. He didn't have much of a family. They all deserted him when he was in the joint. His sister is the only one who stuck by him."

"In the joint?" Steve echoed.

"Yeah. Sam spent ten years in San Quentin for armed

robbery, but that was a long time ago."

"Well, thanks for your help, Sheriff," Randy said.

"No problem. You boys got a place to stay tonight? Don't even think about breaking in and crashing here."

"No. Never," Steve replied. "We're at the Travel Lodge in town."

"Good. Now you best be on your way. Folks around here don't much like teenagers loitering about."

"Okay. No problem."

The Sheriff drove off, and Steve and Randy breathed a sigh of relief.

"Well, I guess there is no need to go inside now," Steve said.

"I don't know. Do you think he really went to Las Vegas?"

"Now that you mention it, it doesn't seem logical to tell the Sheriff where you're going when you know good and well the FBI may be looking for you. That doesn't make sense at all. Surely Sam was smarter than that."

"We better take a look inside," Randy said. "You keep watch out here in case the Sheriff comes back, and I'll go in.

"No," Steve replied. "The Sheriff may be waiting down at the end of the road to see if leave. We'll have to leave and come back later."

Randy grunted in frustration. "But we're here now."

"I know, but we have to leave."

Randy thought a moment. "You leave. It's dark so the Sheriff won't know that I'm not in the car. Come back in a half hour and get me."

Steve took a deep breath. "Okay," he said reluctantly. "See you in a half hour."

Steve got in the car and drove off the way they had come. Randy watched him leave, then worked himself around the cabin perimeter, trying every window and door to see if there was any way he could get in. After circling the entire cabin, he considered breaking a window, but decided against it since the Sheriff knew they had been there and might put two and two together.

Figuring a key might be hidden somewhere he checked under the mat and over the front door. Finding nothing he checked under a flower pot, but there was no key. Frustrated, he went to the back door and started searching there. Sure enough, there was a key on the ledge above the door. Randy stuck the key in the lock and slowly opened the door.

Someone had obviously beat them to the punch he surmised looking around. The cabin had been ransacked. All of the drawers had been opened and searched with little delicacy. Papers and books were strewn all over the floor, Sam's bed had been overturned, and the dresser drawers were all pulled out, their contents scattered carelessly about. Randy quickly realized he was not going to find anything of significance. Any clues that might have been there, the FBI had clearly already taken with them. Just as he was thinking about what to do next, he noticed a broken picture frame with the photograph of Sam Stewart with another woman. He leaned over, picked it up, and then left the cabin. When Steve drove up ten minutes later he opened the door and got in.

"Find anything?" Steve asked.

"No. The FBI's already been here and taken anything that might have been useful. I did find a photograph of Sam Stewart, however, which might come in handy."

"Yeah, it might, but that's not a whole lot to go on."

"I know. Let's go back to the motel. It's getting late. We need to get an early start in the morning."

Randy turned the car around and drove back to the motel. Steve called the front desk and requested a wake-up call. Then they went to bed. They were both exhausted, yet neither of them could sleep. They had to find Sam, but how could they do it with so little to go on? The task suddenly seemed impossible.

Chapter 38

Hot on the Trail

The telephone rang in Randy and Steve's room at seven. They reluctantly dragged themselves out of bed and got dressed. They weren't sure where they were going to go, but they knew they had to keep looking for Sam. When they checked out, they asked the desk clerk where they could get a good breakfast. He pointed out a café down the street, so they walked over to it, went inside, and waited to be seated.

"Just have a seat anywhere, boys," the waitress said. "I'll be with you in a jiffy." After a couple minutes, the waitress came over and introduced herself properly. "Hi, guys. I'm Jesse, and I'll be your waitress today. What can I get ya?"

"Two eggs over easy, toast, and bacon for me," Steve replied.

"I'll take 3 pancakes, 3 scrambled eggs, hash browns, and a double order of bacon," Randy added.

"Jesus! How can you possibly eat that much?" Steve asked.

Randy shrugged. "Oh, and I'll take some coffee too."

The waitress finished writing, smiled, and then said to Steve, "What'll you have to drink, sir?"

"Give me a large orange juice," Steve replied.

"Okay. It'll just be a few minutes, boys."

Steve stretched and yawned. "I wonder if I can get a newspaper around here."

"I think I saw a rack outside."

Just as Steve was getting up, a tall, middle-aged man with a crew cut walked over to their table. "Are you guys the ones looking for fishing guide?"

"Well, yeah, we were thinking about it," Steve said.

"The Sheriff told me I should come introduce myself to you boys. I'm Bart Small. He said Sam Stewart was going to take you out."

"That's what we thought, but he didn't tell us he was leaving for Las Vegas."

"Las Vegas? Sam didn't go to Las Vegas."

"He didn't? How do you know that?" Steve asked.

"I saw his airline ticket. He was going to Toronto, Canada."

"Really? Are you sure?"

"Well, I do know how to read."

"I'm sure you do, but—"

"Sam and I are good friends. Before he left, he shot a game of pool with me. He laid down his jacket, and his airline tickets were sticking out of his inside pocket. While he was shooting, I couldn't help but see the schedule made up by the travel agency. It said his flight was to Toronto."

"Did you mention to him that you saw his ticket?"

"No. Why would I? It didn't really matter to me. I figured he'd be back eventually and then he would tell me what was going on."

"I suppose he will," Steve agreed.

"So, do you need a guide, or what?"

"Uh, actually, I think we'll take a rain check on fishing today. Something's come up. We appreciate the offer though, Mr. Small."

"Okay, but if you ever want to go fishing around here, just give me a call. I'm your man."

"We'll do that. Thanks," Steve said. They smiled as Bart found another table, sat down, and started looking at the menu.

"I guess, we better check the airlines for the next flight to

Toronto," Steve said.

"Do we need passports to get into Canada?" Randy asked.

"I don't think so—just a driver's license, I think."

"Good, because I don't have one."

"Neither do I."

After breakfast, they called Maria, gave her an update on their progress, and had her book them a flight to Toronto. Then they headed back to LA, and three hours later they arrived at LAX. Their flight to Toronto was supposed to leave LA at 3:10 p.m. and arrive at Toronto at 9:20 p.m. They arrived just as their plane was boarding and got right on, took their seats, and awaited takeoff.

"How do you suppose we're going to find Sam Stewart without an address or telephone number?" Steve asked.

"We'll have to do it like they do on TV. We'll go to every hotel and wave Sam's picture at all the staff. If he stayed in a hotel, we'll find him. If that doesn't work, we'll go to all the bars and nightclubs and do the same thing."

"There must be hundreds of hotels and bars in Toronto," Steve noted.

"No one said it would be easy," Randy replied. "I just hope we find him before it's too late for Fred."

"How much longer is the trial supposed to last?"

"Joel said another two or three days is all."

"We've got to find Stewart in the next two days. Otherwise, it will be too late."

The stewardess came over the intercom and greeted the passengers. "Welcome to Flight 267 to Toronto. We'll be taking off soon, so please be sure your seatbelts are fastened."

The plane began to taxi out to the runway, and they sunk back into their seats in anticipation of the takeoff. They knew they needed to get some sleep on the flight because for the next few days, it would be a luxury they couldn't afford. As they lay back in their seats, they were a little excited by the hunt they were about to begin, but their excitement was dampened by a gnawing fear that they might fail in their pursuit. The consequences of such a failure they could not bear. They had to be successful for the sake of their blood brother.

When they arrived in Toronto, they checked into the Cambridge Hotel and began a methodical search for Sam, utilizing the picture Randy had lifted from his cabin. As planned, they first tried all of the hotels. They presumed Sam would not use his real name, so the photograph had to be shown to each and every member of the hotel staff. After visiting the King Edward, the Hilton International, the Royal York, Essex Park, and fifteen other hotels that night, they ran out of gas and went back to their hotel to sleep. They vowed to get up early and continue in the morning.

By noon the next day, they'd already been to a third of the hotels in Toronto. They were tired and frustrated and stopped at a café for lunch.

"Do you think we're just wasting our time?" Steve asked.

"No way. This is just a long and tedious process. No one said it was going to be easy, and it's the least we can do for Fred. He'd do the same for us."

"Now I know why I didn't become a cop," Steve mused.

"You're right. I never realized how much work it was to be a detective," Randy agreed.

"We should be able to finish all of the hotels today, and tomorrow, we can start going to bars and restaurants."

Randy looked at Steve and yawned. "Boy, that sounds like fun."

"Well, we can just pack it up and go home if you want. If Fred is convicted, it will be on your conscience."

"Oh, come on. I'm just trying to keep my sense of humor."

The waiter walked over and asked them what they wanted for lunch. Steve pulled out his photograph of Sam and asked him if he had ever seen the man before. He responded by shaking his head no and asked again what they wanted to eat. After lunch, Steve and Randy continued their search, hotel after hotel, bellhop after bellhop, bartender after bartender, but nobody had seen Sam. At 2:00 a.m., exhausted and depressed, they finally went back to their hotel and went to bed, praying that their luck would improve the following day.

Chapter 39

Hamlin's Ex

Maria didn't relish the idea of talking to Harvey Hamlin's ex-wife. Even if they were divorced she still would have feelings for Hamlin and would be in mourning. Fred had known little about her, only that they'd been deeply in love until Hamlin's demons had made it impossible to be with him. She thanked God that her father had never become addicted to alcohol, drugs or gambling. He smoked a pipe and a cigar from time to time which she hated, but that was but a minor irritation that her mother and she could live with. It was the holiday season but there would be no mirth in the Hamlin household she knew, so when she stepped up to Marilyn Hamlin's door and rang the bell she forced herself not to smile.

A minute later the door opened and a short, middle-aged brunette with pale green eyes stood before her. She looked at Maria for a moment and then, without a word, stepped aside so Maria could come in.

Maria breached the silence. "Thank you so much for agreeing to meet with me. I won't take much of your time."

"I don't know if I'll be much help. I know very little of what Harvey was up to at the bank. We haven't communicated much since the divorce."

"You may know more than you think and you certainly know more than Fred or I do. We're just trying to learn more about Harvey and what was going on with him so we can figure out what happened the night he died."

"I'll tell you what I know."

"First, we want you to know we're very sorry for your loss. Fred only met Harvey one time, but he said he seemed like a nice guy. As for me, I have never lost anyone close, so I can't say I know what you're going through, but with Fred on trial the bank robbery and such, I'm beginning to get an idea."

"The agent from the FBI says that Fred closed the vault on Harvey causing him to have the heart attack. Is that true?"

"No. Fred told me he never saw Harvey that day. He has no idea what happened to him."

"But how do I know he's telling the truth?"

"You don't. But I know him well and I believe him. So, I hope you will believe me when I say he had nothing to do with your husband's death."

"Okay. So, what do you want to know?"

"Did Harvey have any good friends he hung out with?"

Marilyn thought about it a moment and then replied, "He used to have a lot of friends but the drinking drove many of them away. John Ford, one of the bank's loan officers used to play golf with him but John was transferred about a year ago. Ah, let me see, he was active in the Republican Party."

"Really? What did he do for them?"

"He was County Chairman for about five years until his drinking became a problem and his best friend ran against him and won the post. Harvey was very bitter about that."

"Who was this best friend?"

"Another Bank USA employee, Henry Sinclair. He works at the data processing center in downtown LA."

"Right. He was Fred's boss too."

"Was he?"

"Un huh. Was Harvey close to any of the other bank messengers?"

"Sure. Over the years he got to know many of them."

"How about Sam Stewart?"

"Sure, he used to hire Sam to take some of the bank's customers fishing. They were good friends."

"So, Sinclair was Sam's boss too."

Marilyn nodded. "I suppose he would have been."

"Who else?" Maria asked.

"Ah let me see. There were so many messengers over the years it is hard to remember them all."

"We are only interested in the more recent ones."

"Roger Wood, the messenger before Fred, Harvey knew pretty well. But he quit and went back to college."

"Okay. Did you have any conversations with Harvey after he left the vault open the first time?"

"Yes. Harvey called me that night very upset about the incident with the bank auditor and being reprimanded for leaving the vault open. He blamed it on me because we'd had an argument earlier in the day over past due child support. He said I distracted him from doing his job."

"So, he owes child support,"

"Yes. And my attorney has been leaning on him for a payment. In fact, he filed a motion to have Harvey held in contempt for not paying it in a timely manner. Harvey wanted more time to come up with the money and wanted me to agree to a continuance."

"And you said no?"

"No. I said talk to my attorney. That really pissed him off."

"Okay. Tell me about his health. He told Fred he had heart trouble."

"Yes. He's obese and has high blood pressure. He had a heart attack several years ago and is on a special diet and several medications. His doctor told him to avoid stress, of course, but that's impossible with his job and all the trouble he had gotten himself into."

"What about his gambling? Does he owe a lot of money?"

Marilyn shrugged. "I have no idea. He was very closed-mouthed about his gambling, but I have gotten phone calls from unidentified men asking if I know where they could find him."

"Well, he's not a hard man to find, I wouldn't imagine," Maria said. "They could always find him at the bank during the day."

"You would think, but I suppose they wanted to get him alone."

"Right," Maria said. "Well, you've been very helpful. Thanks again for talking to me. I hope we get to the bottom of what happened to your ex-husband. If you think of anything else Fred and I should know, please call me."

Marilyn nodded, stood up and showed Maria out. Maria forced a smile when she left and then walked deliberately back to her car. As she drove home she thought about what she had learned and wondered if any of it would help Fred's case. It seemed to her Hamlin had to be the mastermind behind the heist, or at least the one who executed the plan, if someone else was behind it. But Hamlin was dead so they had to figure out who was his accomplice and get him to talk. Sam Stewart seemed like the obvious choice, but he was long gone so they were screwed. A wave of fear and hopelessness washed over her as she wondered if they'd ever be able to discover the truth and prove that Fred was innocent.

Chapter 40

Nightlife

In spite of their yet-unfulfilled quest, Steve and Randy were dazzled by the Toronto night life. As they moved from one bar to another, they almost forgot their mission and began to enjoy the sights, sounds and beautiful women that frequented many of the night spots they were checking out. All day, they had searched for someone who had seen Sam Stewart, to no avail. Surely someone who resembled St. Nick so very much would catch the notice of many people, but so far, no one they had talked to had seen hide nor hair of the elusive Sam Stewart. By the time they entered the Morrissey Tavern on Yonge Street, they were in a somber mood.

"I don't know if can do this drill again," Steve moaned. "How did Fred get into this mess anyway? Mr. Honest Abe sure screwed up his life this time," Steve fumed.

"Well, what would you have done differently in his shoes?" Randy asked.

"I'd have put the money back in the bank and took off."

"Even with the cop lurking about?"

"Yeah, that's a load of crap! Fred wanted to keep the money, and that's that."

"Well, wouldn't you have?"

"No. Well, I might have wanted to keep it, but I wouldn't have actually done it."

"Even if you knew absolutely, positively that you wouldn't get caught?"

"Well, I guess if I were 100 percent guaranteed to get away

with it, I might have done it," Steve admitted.

"See. That's what I am saying. There are very few truly honest people in the world—just a lot of people who are afraid of getting caught," Randy said. "But personally, I think Fred would have put the money back had he had a way to do it."

"I don't know. You may be right," Steve conceded "Why don't we have a beer and rest a while?"

"Good idea."

They walked over to a small table near the bar and sat down. A tall redhead came over and took their order. In a few minutes, she brought them a pitcher of beer. Steve and Randy began to drink and loosen up. Before long, they noticed some of the female patrons sitting in the bar.

"Have you noticed there are a lot of hot-looking women in this bar?" Randy asked.

"Yeah, I was noticing that. Too bad they wouldn't give us the time of day."

"Speak for yourself. I could have one in bed within thirty minutes," Randy assured him. "I could probably even line one up for you."

Steve shook his head. "Fifty bucks says you can't."

"You're on."

Randy got up and walked over to a table at which two young dark-haired beauties were seated. Steve moved close enough to hear the conversation.

"Hi, girls. May I sit down for a minute and tell you a sad story?" Randy asked politely.

The girls looked at him, somewhat aloof, but nodded their consent.

"I'm Randy."

The blond girl smiled faintly. "I'm Susie, and this is Monica."

"Nice to meet you. My friend Steve over there and I just flew in a few days ago from LA. Our best friend, Fred Fuller, is on trial for murder, and we're here searching for a witness who could exonerate him," Randy said sorrowfully. "But so far, we haven't had any luck."

"I think I saw something about that on the news," Monica acknowledged.

"What does this witness look like?" Susie asked.

Randy showed them Sam's picture. "He looks a little bit like Santa Claus."

"I don't know him, sorry," Susie said. Monica nodded her agreement.

"Well, I didn't figure you would have. You're all a bit young for this guy. What we were wondering, though, is if you girls would like to party a while. We really need a break."

They laughed and then looked at each other. Finally, the blond said, "Sure. Come on over for a bit. You can buy us a drink."

Randy looked over at Steve and motioned for him to join them. Steve walked over and sat next to Susie. Randy introduced them to Steve and then ordered everyone a round of drinks. They talked for a while and found out the girls were college students at a local university. Randy told them all about Fred's trial and how the FBI had been following them. A half hour later, one of the girls suggested they move the party to Susie's flat. Randy looked at Steve and grinned broadly.

While the girls were powdering their respective noses, Randy tried to convince Steve that they should accept the invitation. "The last thing we need to be doing tonight is chasing pussy," Steve argued. "We need to concentrate on finding Sam."

Randy knew Steve had never been with a woman, and his strong religious beliefs would preclude him from engaging in casual sex, but he enjoyed pushing him to brink just to see him sweat. He decided he'd gone far enough. "You're right," Randy conceded, "but you owe me fifty bucks."

"Yeah, yeah. I'll pay you your fifty bucks. Don't worry."

Before the girls came back, Randy paid the bill, and they regretfully left the bar and hailed a cab to take them back to the hotel.

"Maybe we're looking at this from the wrong perspective," Randy suggested as they climbed into the cab. "We've got to put ourselves in Sam's place and figure out what he would do. What would a middle-aged ex-con with six million bucks do in Toronto?"

"It depends on whether he thought the FBI would be after him or not," Steve replied. "If he thought they were, he wouldn't be lounging around a hotel or hanging around a nightclub."

"You have a point. So where would he be?" Randy asked.

"He'd go someplace safe—a place where he wouldn't be conspicuous, at least for a few months until things cooled down."

"He's probably watching the TV news every day, hoping Fred will get convicted. Then he'll be able to come out of hiding and enjoy his money."

"Why would he come to Toronto?" Steve asked.

"Wait a minute! That's it! Toronto isn't a destination someone would ordinarily pick to hide from the law. You'd go to Argentina or one of the other safe havens of the world. The only reason he'd come to Toronto would be if he had a relative or acquaintance in Toronto, someone who'd be willing to hide him."

"I bet that's it, but how are we going to find his relatives?" Steve asked.

"Let's call Roberts. Maybe he can put his investigator on it."

"It's pretty late. Should we wait until morning?"

"No. Roberts won't mind. This is important. Let's find a phone booth."

"Okay. I'll call him when we get back to our hotel and see what he says," Steve agreed.

When they got back to their room, Steve took Joel's card out of his wallet and dialed the number on their room phone. "Operator, I want to make a collect call to Ventura, California, USA. This is

Steve Robins. . . . Okay, I'll wait." A minute later Joel Roberts was on the line."

"Mr. Roberts."

"Hi, Steve. How's the search going?"

"Well, it's been pretty slow but we just realized where Sam must be."

"Oh really? Where is that?"

"He must have a relative up here. Can you have Peter check and see?"

"Absolutely. I'll get him right on it."

"Good. I'm sure somebody's hiding him here."

"Where can I reach you with the information?"

"We're at the Cambridge Hotel on Dixon Road, Room 343."

"Okay. I'll call you tomorrow just as soon as I find something out."

"Oh, how's the trial going?" Steve asked hopefully.

"Ah. Nothing has changed. Sorry."

"Okay. Thanks."

Steve hung up the telephone and then joined Randy at the bar. "He's going to have his investigator check it out in the morning," Steve reported.

"Hmm. I wouldn't hold my breath."

"What do you mean?"

"Peter Stiller hasn't found shit so far," Randy complained. "We don't have time to be waiting around for him to get off his ass."

"So, what do you suggest?" Steve asked.

"We should call Fred's friend from the motor pool. What's his name?"

"Oh, you mean the Australian guy, Jim."

"Right," Randy said. "Fred gave me his number."

"Okay, it's too late to call him now. We'll call him first thing in the morning.

Randy looked at his watch. "Yeah. You're probably right.

He couldn't access company files this time of night anyway.

They were both tired so they watched the news and then went to bed. Neither of them slept very well, however, as they knew that finding Sam Stewart was still a longshot and time was running out.

Chapter 41

The Final Days

The next morning, Joel Roberts woke up exhausted. He hadn't slept well after Randy's call. All night, he contemplated what would happen if Steve and Randy found Sam Stewart. He'd never met Sam Stewart and didn't know if he could be trusted to keep his mouth shut. Hamlin apparently had hired Stewart to help him pull off the robbery. Roberts didn't know that for sure, but he thought it was a safe bet. Now it looked like Sam might have double-crossed him. He'd have to call Peter Shiller and pass along Randy's request for information on Sam's relatives, but he'd give him other things to do as well so it would be unlikely he'd find the information Randy needed quickly enough to do them any good.

Roberts thought about his closing argument. He had to be careful not to be perceived as providing anything less than a zealous defense. Any obvious errors on his part would be picked up by the judge and the press pretty quickly and raise questions. He wondered what he would do if Steve and Randy actually found Sam Stewart. That could be a disaster, but he had no way to plan for it since there was no way to anticipate what Sam would say or do. He was in an untenable situation and it had his stomach in knots.

As the morning sun began to flood into the bedroom, he wasn't anxious to get up and face the uncertainty that lay ahead. Finally, he worked his way out of bed and into the shower. He lingered under the soothing liquid massage much longer than usual. The hot water beating down on his back and his neck was very relaxing. Eventually, adrenalin began to pump into is system. He got dressed and made it to the breakfast table. His wife Jennifer had made him his favorite breakfast, French toast, bacon, and coffee, but he couldn't eat and risk losing it later.

"Well, just a couple more days, and this mess will be over." Jennifer said cheerily.

He forced a smile and took a few bites of food and then said, "I've got to go, honey. There's much to be done before the trial begins."

Jennifer frowned. "You better eat something. You'll need your strength."

"I'll eat when the trial is over."

When Roberts got to his office, he called his private investigator, Peter Stiller, and gave him several tasks to perform. The very last one was the need for information on Sam's relatives in Toronto, but he didn't indicate there was any urgency or give him any priority in completing the tasks assigned.

Next Roberts called Congressman Bartlett. He figured it must be lunch time in Washington and he'd be free. "Just wanted to let you know we may have a problem."

"What happened?" Bartlett asked warily.

"It's seems our amateur sleuths may find Sam Stewart."

"No. That can't happen."

"I don't think it will but they are very determined, so I've got to be prepared for the worst."

"Okay, do whatever takes to make sure they don't find him."

"I'll do what I can but they are thousands of miles away in Canada so my options are limited. Anyway, I'm about to head on over to court. I'm not expecting it to go well today for Fred. All of his sins are about to be revealed to the world."

"Good. I need to get this mess over with so I can concentrate on my reelection campaign."

"Right. It shouldn't be too much longer now."

Roberts hung up the phone and started gathering what he needed for court. He tried to focus on the day's proceedings but he kept thinking about Steve and Randy. There was no way they could find Sam Stewart, he kept telling himself. Still, they were just a bit too diligent for his liking and that made him nervous.

Chapter 42

Backup Plan

There was a four-hour time difference between Toronto and Los Angeles so Steve had to wait until 10:00 a.m. to call Jim. He dialed the number and waited. A female voice came on the line.

"Jim Wells, please," he said.

"Sure, one moment please," a female voice replied.

"Hello. Jim Wells here."

"Mr. Wells, thanks for taking my call. This is Steve, a friend of Fred Fuller."

"Right, lad. Fred has talked about you and your buddy, Randy, right?"

"Right. Randy's here with me too."

"So. How's the trial going?"

"Not so well. That's why I am calling. We need your help."

"Sure thing. I told Fuller I'd help him any way I could now. So, what can I do for you?"

"I need someone to look in Sam Stewart's personnel file."

"Oh. That would be bit tricky now. Those records are in Mr. Sinclair's office and I'm not authorized to look at them."

"It's very important. We need to know if Sam Stewart has any relatives in Toronto, Canada. Can you find a way to get into his office, take a peek at them and call me back?"

"I could probably manage that, but it could take some time. I'll have to wait for Sinclair to leave his office. Give me a few minutes."

"Thanks."

Steve took a deep breath and waited impatiently. A few minutes later Jim was back on the line. "Okay, I got lucky. Sinclair got called away for a meeting and he left his door open. You were right. Sam listed his sister, Regina Scott, as the person to contact in case of an emergency. She lives at 88 Cokesbury Lane, Toronto, Canada."

"Oh, thank you so much, Jim. You're not going to get into trouble giving me this information, are you?"

"How they gonna find out I gave it to you? You're not going to tell them, are you?"

"No. No way."

"Okay. Then there's not a bloody thing to worry about."

"Thanks, Jim. You may have just saved Fred's ass."

"I bloody hope so," Jim replied.

Steve hung up the phone and gave Randy a thumbs up. Now he just hoped Sam would be there when they showed up at his doorstep. If he wasn't, all their efforts would have been for naught.

Chapter 43

Silver Stallion Saloon

The next person on Maria's interview list was Jim Wells, who Fred said would have a wealth of information about Bank USA and its employees. Fred had told her how helpful he'd been, so she called him at home on Saturday.

"Hi. Jim Wells?"

"That would be me, miss."

"This is Maria Shepard, Fred Fuller's girlfriend."

"Ah, yes, the dark-haired beauty with the dazzling brown eyes. Fred has told me all about you, m 'dear. I just hung up with Fred's friend Steve. It seems they are closing in on Sam Stewart."

"Wow. That's excellent news," Maria said appreciatively. "I'll try not to take much of your time. I know you have a busy job. Fred really likes you. He talks all the time about you. You're his hero, I think."

"That's good to hear. What can I do you for?"

"Fred says you've been very helpful to him since the bank robbery."

"I hope so. He's a good lad, and I'm happy to help."

"Well, Fred can't do very much from his jail cell, so he asked me to talk to you about Harvey Hamlin. It seems to Fred that Harvey Hamlin must have been in on the robbery but his heart attack messed up the robbers' plans. The bottom line is that Fred thinks Harvey had an accomplice, and he thought you might have some ideas about who it might be."

"Ah, yes. I'd look into Jake Johnson and, of course, Sam Stewart you already know about."

"Jake Johnson, is he the driver that trained Fred that first day?"

"Yes. I'm sure Fred told you about Jake and his demotion."

"Right. He mentioned it. What makes you think Jake Johnson might be involved?"

"Jake had that route a few years back, so he got to know Hamlin pretty well. In fact, Sam took Jake and Harvey fishing a few times. I know that for sure 'cause Jake was bragging about all the big catfish he caught. That's why I've been trying to help Fred out. I think those three robbed the bank and tried to make it look like Fred did it. It wouldn't surprise me if they didn't plant a bit of evidence inside the vault incriminating poor Fred even more."

"Did you tell this to the FBI?"

"Of course, but it fell on deaf ears, if you know what I mean."

"Yes, I'm afraid I do. So, how do you think I should go about checking on Jake Johnson?"

"Well, actually, I've already been doing a little checking on him myself. I looked in his personnel file, but there wasn't much there. He's from Portland, Oregon, and he grew up with his mother and three sisters. His father deserted the family when he was seven. He did list a reference though—a Lieutenant Buster James from Oxnard, California. You could start there, I suppose."

Maria took down the information on Lt. James. "Okay. I'll do that. Anything else you can think of?"

"No. That's all I have. If I think of anything else, I'll let you know."

Maria took Jim's advice later that afternoon and called Lt. James. She couldn't tell him who she was, so she made up a phony name. "This is Maria Maldano from Bank USA," she said.

"Oh, okay."

"We're just doing a routine employment application verification on Jake Johnson. He listed you as a reference."

"Oh, yes, Jake and I go way back. What would you like to know?"

"Oh, nothing really, we just wanted to be sure you were a real person and you knew Jake. You know, there are so many people out there who give fake references."

"Yes, I've heard about that," Lt. James said.

"So, how long have you known him?"

"Over ten years. We actually met in high school up in Portland."

"Portland, Oregon?"

"Yes. We were both anxious to leave home, and the Navy was a quick ticket out of town after graduation from high school."

"I see. You were good friends then?"

"Oh yes. The best of friends. Neither one of us had a really happy childhood, I'm afraid. Jake's dad was a drunk and beat him all the time. My dad was a total loser—couldn't keep a job for more than a week."

"Where in Portland did you live?"

"Jake and I lived across the street from each other in Felony Flats."

"Felony Flats?"

"Yeah. That's what they called our neighborhood."

"Well, it's good that you had each other. Do you see much of Jake these days?"

"No. We've lost touch these last few years. If you see him, tell him to give me a call, would ya?"

"Sure. I'll do that."

Maria had a lot more questions, but she was afraid to ask any more for fear of making Lt. James suspicious. She wondered why Jake left the Navy and what he had been doing since then other than driving for the bank. The only way Maria could think of getting that kind of information would be to follow him for a while. If she was lucky his daily routine might provide her some answers.

That night, she parked across the street from the motor pool in a spot where she could see everyone coming and going. When Jake walked out, he went straight to his car, got in, and drove off. She quickly accelerated and cautiously took up a position several cars behind him. She had no training in surveillance but it seemed fairly straight forward—don't get so close that they will spot you, but don't lose them either.

Jake drove straight to the Harbor Freeway, got on and went south. He was driving fast and Maria had to speed to keep up with him. She prayed a Highway Patrol officer wouldn't spot her and pull her over. Just before the Harbor Freeway ended, he got off and drove several miles north. She stayed several cars behind him until he reached a bar called the Silver Stallion Saloon, where he parked and went inside. She followed him in the parking lot and parked a few rows behind him.

Maria got out of her car and started to walk slowly toward the entrance. She watched Jake disappear into the club. Suddenly, a young lady came running out the same door in tears. Maria stopped her to see if she needed any help. "What's the matter?" she asked.

"Oh, nothing. I just got roughed up a bit by an old boyfriend who can't get it through his thick skull that it's over."

"Did he hurt you?"

"No. I got away from him before he did any damage."

"Can I take you somewhere?" Maria asked and then regretted it immediately. She knew she shouldn't let herself be distracted right then. Finding out what Jake was up to was too important to let herself be sidetracked.

"No, but would you go inside with me so I can get my purse? I am afraid he might hassle me again if he sees me alone."

"Sure, if you'll do me a favor."

"Huh?"

"Will you sit with me a minute so I can check out the customers in the bar. I don't usually go into places like this, and I'll be less conspicuous if I'm with someone," Maria reasoned.

"Sure. I'll buy you a beer," the lady replied. "What's your name?"

"Maria."

"Hi, I'm Tammy. Come on."

Maria followed closely behind Tammy as she entered the saloon. The thick smell of smoke made her cough, and her eyes began to water. As they walked through the crowd, she looked around for Jake.

Tammy stopped in front of an empty seat at the bar. "I was sitting right here," Tammy said. "Bartender, what happened to my purse?"

The bartender gave her a glance and then walked over, bent down behind the bar, and came up with a lime green purse.

"Thanks for keeping it for me," she said. "Give us a couple of beers."

"Just a Coke for me," Maria said.

"Coming right up," the bartender replied.

Tammy looked at Maria and smiled. "So, who you looking for?"

"A guy named Jake."

"Hmm. I don't know any Jake."

Maria began to carefully scan the room. "I know he's in here somewhere. He's short and stocky . . . wait, there he is," she said.

Jake was sitting at a table in the corner of the bar with another man. They were engaged in what appeared to be an intense discussion. Maria wished she was a fly on the table so she could listen to the conversation. She pointed across the room. "He's over there in the corner sitting with the guy in the dark blue shirt."

"Why are you looking for him?"

"It's a long story. Let's just say I'm investigating him as a possible robbery suspect."

Tammy stiffened up and said, "You a cop or something?"

"No, no, nothing like that. My boyfriend is on trial for a bank robbery he didn't do, and we think Jake might be the real thief."

"Oh. Is there anything I can do to help? I love cop shows."

Maria smiled. She liked Tammy's enthusiasm. "I wonder who the man with him is," she asked. "I need to find out his name."

"You want me to go find out?"

"Would you?" Maria laughed.

Tammy jumped out of her chair and said, "Sure, leave it to me."

Before Maria could reply, Tammy was halfway across the room. She walked up behind Jake's table and then stumbled and fell to the floor. Jake's companion got up to see if she was hurt. Tammy got up and dusted herself off. Then she sat down with the two men at their table. The man hailed the waitress and ordered a round of drinks. Tammy drank and talked with the two men a few minutes and then returned.

"Nice performance," Maria said appreciatively.

"Thanks."

"So, did you find out who the mystery man is?"

"Yep. His name is Harold Clifford."

"Oh my God!" Maria exclaimed.

"What's wrong?"

Maria smiled broadly. "Nothing. This is great news! Harold Clifford is a suspect in another robbery case. He and Jake Johnson being together could mean he had something to do with the robbery my boyfriend is charged with. Thank you so much for your help, Tammy. This could be just the breakthrough we've been looking for."

"Well, good. I'm glad somebody had a good night."

Maria laughed. "I'd like to stay and chat, but I've got to go and report this information to Fred's lawyer."

"Sure, get out of here. Nice meeting you."

"Likewise."

"Oh," Tammy said, "before you go why don't you write down your phone number in case I learn anything else about Jake."

Maria nodded. "Sure, good idea," she said and the dug into her purse for a pen and a piece of paper. When she found them, she wrote down the number and handed the paper to Tammy. "Thanks again."

When Maria got back to her dorm, she called Joel Roberts to tell him what she'd found out. He listened to her but cautioned her on getting her hopes up. "I'll tell Whitehead about this, but I doubt he'll do anything. It's going to be up to us to connect Johnson, Clifford, and Sam together and put them at the scene of the crime. I'll get Peter on it. Maybe he can find someone who saw Clifford at or around the bank the day it was robbed. But honestly, we have so little time, I'm not optimistic he'll be able to get that kind of evidence."

"Okay," Maria said dejectedly. Is there anything else I can do?"

"No. Just visit Fred as often as you can. He seems pretty depressed. We need to keep his spirits up. If the jury thinks he's given up they may think he's guilty."

"I'll do that," Maria assured him. "See you in court on Monday."

"Alright. Thanks for the info."

Maria hung up the phone feeling drained and deflated. She didn't think Roberts had been the least bit impressed with the information she had obtained. She knew it was late in the game to be coming up with new evidence and theories about who did it, but Jake Johnson and Harold Clifford were damn good suspects who couldn't be ignored. She took a deep breath and tried to relax but her neck and shoulders just got stiffer and tighter and she could feel a headache coming on with a vengeance.

Chapter 44

The Connection

The next day before the trial began, Roberts spoke to Whitehead and told him about the connection between Jake Johnson, Harold Clifford and Sam Stewart. Harper listened to Roberts silently for a moment and then shrugged. "So what?"

"Well, I'm putting you on notice that I may call Harold Clifford, Jake Johnson and Sam Stewart as witnesses."

"Good luck with Sam Stewart," Whitehead chuckled.

"Well, we actually have a lead as to his whereabouts."

"And where is that?"

"Toronto Canada."

"Do you have an address?"

"No, not yet but we are working on it."

"Alright, let me know the minute you have one." Whitehead said evenly. "Thanks for the update."

As he returned to his seat, Roberts heard the Judge bang his gavel and ask Whitehead to call his next witness.

Whitehead called Jenny Madeira. She took the stand and the Judge administered the oath.

"Miss Madeira, do you know the defendant, Fred Fuller?" Whitehead asked.

"Yes, I do. He was Candy's friend," Jenny replied.

"And who is Candy?"

"Candy Clisby. She was my best friend. We lived in the same apartment complex."

"She and Fred were more than just friends, weren't they, Miss Madeira?"

"Well, yes, I suppose so."

"In fact, they were lovers, weren't they?"

"Yes."

The crowd stirred. Fred looked over at Maria apologetically, but Maria appeared unruffled by the comment.

"Did you ever see them together?"

"No, but Candy always filled me in on what happened between them."

"Did you ever meet Fred Fuller?"

"Yes."

"How did you meet him?"

"I met him the night of Candy's death."

"How did he contact you?"

"He called me and told me Candy had died."

"Did he tell you how she died?"

"Yes. He said she had died of a snakebite."

"Did you see him that night?"

"Yes. He came over to my place."

"What did you and he do?"

"We talked about Candy and cried a lot."

"When was the last time you spoke to Candy?"

"That Saturday morning, she called me from Palm Springs."

"What did she tell you?"

"Objection, Your Honor. Calls for hearsay," Joel said.

"Your Honor, Miss Clisby is dead and obviously can't be called as a witness. Although we concede Miss Madeira's testimony as to what Candy Clisby said would be hearsay, it's admissible if it can be corroborated."

"I'll allow it if you can corroborate it," the Judge ruled.

"We can, Your Honor."

"Exception, Your Honor."

"Noted," the Judge said. "You may answer, Miss Madeira."

"She asked me to feed her cat while she was gone."

"Anything else?"

"She said Fred had agreed to support her so she could quit her job. She wanted to be an actress and wanted to devote all her time to that pursuit."

"And what would Fred get out of this?"

"She'd be his lover then and his mistress later, after he got married."

The gallery erupted in conversation, prompting the Judge to bang his gavel and say, "Order! Order in the court! Any more outbursts like that, and I'll clear the courtroom."

"How long did she tell you she was planning to be gone?"

"She didn't know. Fred hadn't told her where they were going yet."

"Didn't you think this whole thing a little odd?"

"Yes, I thought it was completely mad, but there was no dissuading her."

"Did she say anything about going to Canada?"

"No. She just wanted to be sure I took care of her cat. I assumed it would just be for the weekend."

"Later on, when Fred came by your apartment, did he mention a trip to Canada?"

"No, he did not, although he did say the FBI was following him."

"Thank you, Miss Madeira. Pass the witness."

"Yes, Miss Madeira, Fred didn't go to Canada, did he?" Joel asked.

"Obviously not."

"You testified he came to visit you after Candy's death but never mentioned going to Canada, isn't that right?"

"Right."

"Now, you testified Fred and Candy were lovers?" Roberts

said.

"Yes."

"I can understand that, but this mistress thing makes no sense. Would she really stand by and let Maria marry Fred?"

"That was her plan."

"Candy had a good sense of humor, didn't she?"

"Yes, she did."

"Didn't she take great pleasure in shocking people, telling them strange things just to watch their reaction?"

"Yes, she was kind of playful—sort of a jokester."

"Could it be that she was joking about being Fred's mistress, just trying to shock you?"

"Well, it's possible, but—"

"Isn't it true that Candy told Fred she wanted to be his mistress just to lure him away from Maria; make him think he could have both of them."

"Not exactly."

"What exactly was the plan then?"

"At first, that was the plan, but later I think she fell in love with Fred."

"So, this was a simple case of seduction? Candy wanted Fred and would say or do anything to get him. Is that what you're saying?"

Jenny shrugged. "Yes, you may be right," Jenny said softly.

"That's all, Miss Madeira. Thank you."

"Redirect, Mr. Whitehead?" the Judge asked.

"Yes, Your Honor. Miss Madeira, do have any personal knowledge of Candy Clisby's financial condition?"

"Yes."

"Was she a wealthy woman?"

"Are you kidding? She worked part-time for the bank, and as far as I know, her income from that job was all the money she had in the world."

"Did Fred Fuller ever give Candy money?"

"Yes. He gave her $2,000 one night."

"Was Candy a prostitute?"

"No! Absolutely not. Like I said, Fred was going to support Candy so she could study acting."

At this point, Maria got up and left the courtroom. Her mother followed her, as well as several reporters.

"Do you have any idea where Fred got the $2,000?" Roberts continued.

"Supposedly from an inheritance."

"Did he write her a check for this $2,000, or was it cash?"

"Money orders."

"Money orders. I see. Huh, so, this wasn't all about love, was it? It was about money, and Candy must have known Fred was about to come into a lot of it."

"Objection!" Roberts yelled. "Counsel is leading the witness and testifying."

"Objection sustained," the Judge ruled.

"No further questions."

"Mr. Roberts?" the Judge said.

"No further questions, Your Honor."

"It's getting late. We'll adjourn until tomorrow morning at ten," Judge Sessions announced.

The courtroom cleared. Roberts began to pack up his briefcase and then he turned to Fred and said, "This hurts us, Fred. I wish you would have told me about Jenny earlier. This doesn't help us at all. Is there anything else you haven't told me?"

There's a lot I haven't told you. How about that I have a million dollars stashed away in the desert? What would you do if I dumped that on you? "No, I don't think so," Fred said evenly.

Joel closed his briefcase and looked Fred in the eyes. "Well, if we get any more surprises like this one, I may not be able to keep you out of prison. I'll see you in the morning."

Fred swallowed hard. "Okay," he said dejectedly. "I'm sorry."

The bailiff took Fred back upstairs to the Federal Marshal's office. Just a few minutes after he'd arrived, the Deputy Marshal brought him a TV dinner. He set the dinner on the food door and then began chatting. "Here's your dinner, Fred."

"Thank you."

"So, where did you stash the money?"

"What money?"

"Come on. You don't expect anyone to believe that you don't have the money, do you?"

"I don't have any money," Fred lied.

"Yeah, right. Too bad you'll never be able to spend it."

"What makes you think the jury isn't going to let me off?"

"You're a dreamer, Fuller. After today's testimony, you might as well give it up. You're just another greedy little bastard. They've already got a cell waiting for you at Lompoc."

Fred just stared at the Marshal in horror. *Is he right? Is it all over for me? Has the jury already made up their minds? No! They won't convict an innocent man. It can't happen, can it?* Anger began to well in him. He took a deep breath, trying to control himself.

"So, you're the Judge and jury now? I didn't rob the bank, okay. I may have screwed up my love life, but I'm not a thief or a murderer. So, take this damn food and shove it up your ass!" he said as he kicked the TV dinner, spilling it all over the Marshal's pants.

Chapter 45

Cross Examination

After Fred's outburst in his holding cell, depression overcame him, and he was despondent the next morning when he was brought back to the courthouse. It seemed to him that Jenny's testimony may have done him in, as Roberts seemed to be losing his confident, cocky attitude that had prevailed during the first week of the trial. For the first time, Fred could see the worry and fear in Roberts' eyes.

They brought him into the courtroom right at nine, but the Judge was running late. Fred hated just waiting around with everyone staring at him, so he closed his eyes and tried to think of something pleasant. The first thing that popped into his head was an image of Maria and him on the library lawn at UCLA. They had just eaten lunch together, as they often did. His head was in her lap, and she was stroking his hair gently. It was a warm day, and he could smell the sweet, erotic aroma of her body. It embarrassed her, but he loved to bury his head in her lap and take a deep breath. It was so intoxicating.

Unfortunately, his daydream was interrupted when the Judge finally made his appearance twenty minutes late. He asked Whitehead to call his next witness.

"The United States calls Joe Harper."

"Agent Harper, do you swear to tell the truth, the whole truth, and nothing but the truth, so help you God?" the Judge asked.

"I do."

"Please state your name for the Court," Whitehead said.

"Joseph P. Harper."

"What is your occupation?"

"I am a special agent for the Federal Bureau of Investigation."

"Do you know the defendant, Fred Fuller?"

"Yes, I do."

"Can you identify him for the Court?"

"Yes. That's him next to Mr. Roberts."

"How did you come to know the defendant?"

"I questioned him first in regard to an embezzlement at the Hermosa Beach Bank USA in September."

"Was he a suspect?"

"No. He was a potential witness."

"And since that time, have you had any other contact with the defendant?"

"Yes. He was the messenger that picked up at Bank USA, San Bernardino branch."

"Is that the same branch that was robbed on October 20, 1967?"

"Yes."

"Have you been assigned to investigate this robbery?"

"Yes, that and the death of Harvey Hamlin."

"What does the job of a messenger entail?"

"The messenger picks up the bank's work for the day and takes it to the data processing center. Mr. Fuller's route started at the Palm Springs branch, then he picked up Banning, Beaumont, Redlands, and San Bernardino."

"Would a messenger have a key to the bank?"

"Yes."

"Did Mr. Fuller have a key to the San Bernardino branch of Bank USA?"

"Yes. At the time of the robbery and murder, he did have a

key."

"How did you learn about the robbery?"

"I got a call from Bank USA headquarters about 8:30 a.m. on the Monday following the robbery, which apparently occurred on Friday, reporting that they had found a body in their vault and some money missing."

"Did you take any action as a result of that report?"

"Yes. Agent Walters and I immediately went to San Bernardino to investigate."

"What did you find?"

"It was just as it had been reported. Harvey Hamlin was lying face down in the vault with his hands tied with duct tape behind his back and his mouth taped so he couldn't speak."

"Was there any sign of struggle?"

"No."

"Why did it take three days to discover the body?"

"Once the vault is closed on Friday night, it isn't opened again until Monday morning at 8:00 a.m."

"Would you surmise from your observations that Harvey Hamlin was alive when the vault—"

"Objection, Your Honor! Counsel is leading the witness and asking for speculation," Roberts said.

"Objection sustained."

"Did you do any testing for fingerprints?"

"Yes, we did."

"And what were your findings?"

"We found the defendant's prints on the counter in front of the tellers' windows, a couple on the coffee table, one thumb print in the President's office, on the packing tape that bound Harvey's hands and one index finger on the teller's cart, which had been locked up in the vault."

The courtroom erupted in conversation, and the Judge frowned, banged his gavel, and said, "I'll have order please!"

"So, you found a fingerprint of the defendant, Fred Fuller, inside the vault?"

"That's correct. Oh, yes, and on the wheel on the front of the vault."

"By the wheel, do you mean the locking mechanism that is turned to open or close the vault?"

"Yes. It's like a steering wheel on a car, except it's made of steel, and when you close the vault, you turn it until it locks into place."

"I see. How did you know these were Mr. Fuller's prints?"

"Mr. Fuller provided the bank his prints when he was first hired and we got them again during our investigation. We compared the prints we found around the bank to his and came up with these matches."

"In the course of your investigation, did you have occasion to examine Mr. Fuller's automobile?"

"Yes. He has a 1959 blue Ford Falcon which we thoroughly inspected after obtaining a search warrant."

"And did you find anything unusual about this vehicle?"

"Yes. The license plates didn't match California DMV records."

Whitehead went over to the prosecution's table and picked up a license plate. "Agent Harper, I'm going to show you what's been marked as People's Exhibit 17 and ask you if you can identify it."

"This is the license plate that was taken off the defendant's car."

"What's wrong with this license plate?"

"It's not the license plate that should have been on that car. Apparently, someone switched license plates so that if a license check were done, incorrect information would be pulled up."

"Why would someone do that?"

"Objection! Calls for speculation," Roberts said.

"I think Agent Harper is qualified to give an opinion on that.

I'll allow it," the Judge ruled.

"One reason someone would switch plates would be if they knew they had a hot car and didn't want it to be discovered."

"Did Mr. Fuller in fact elude the FBI due to this license plate switch?"

"Yes, Mr. Fuller drove by one of our agents on a stakeout in front of Candy Clisby's apartment. The agent called in the license plate and didn't get a match, so he ignored the vehicle. Mr. Fuller was able to enter the apartment, pick up Miss Clisby, and leave without detection because of this deception."

"Your Honor, the prosecution requests People's Exhibit 17 be admitted."

"No objection," Roberts said.

"Peoples Exhibit 17 is admitted," the Judge said.

"Did Mr. Fuller do anything else to evade the pursuit of the FBI?"

"Yes. He painted his car blue. It used to be maroon."

"Based on your investigation, was Mr. Fuller preparing to flee from this jurisdiction and perhaps leave the country?"

"Without a doubt."

"Now, Agent Harper, has any of the 6.7 million dollars been recovered?"

"No."

"What has been done to find it?"

"Well, all the obvious places were searched. . . . Mr. Fuller's apartment, his home in Ventura, Candy Clisby's apartment, among other places. We've also got all the banks in southern California looking for the money."

"What about Devil's Canyon, the place where Ms. Clisby was bitten by a snake and later died?"

"No, we haven't searched Devil's Canyon because nobody knows where it is exactly. There is no such place on any of the maps of that region, and no one we've talked to has ever heard of it."

"I see. Pass the witness."

"Agent Harper, isn't it true Mr. Fuller had been in an accident which required him to have a new car door installed?"

"I wouldn't know that."

"Well, in your surveillance, did you notice his driver's side door didn't match the rest of his car?"

"Yes."

"In fact, it was blue, and the rest of the car was maroon, isn't that right?"

"Yes."

"So he probably had good reason to get his car painted then?"

"I suppose so."

"Agent Harper, isn't it true that Mr. Fuller went back to work after he painted his car and allegedly switched his license plates?"

"That's correct."

"Now, would that make any sense to go to all the trouble of painting your car and switching license plates and then going back to work?"

"No, except his plans were upset by Miss Clisby's untimely death."

"Perhaps, but if he were a desperate bank robber and murderer, don't you think he would have just kept on going rather than go back to work on Monday?"

"You would think so, unless he was very clever or very stupid."

"Now, Agent Harper, you testified you found Mr. Fuller's fingerprints inside the vault on a teller's cart, correct?"

"Yes."

"Isn't it true the tellers' carts are usually kept outside the vault?"

"Yes, during the day, but they are brought inside the vault at night when the bank is closed."

"So, isn't it possible that Fred Fuller may have touched the teller's cart while it was outside the vault in the course of picking up the bank data processing for the day?"

"Anything's possible, but he would have no reason to go behind the tellers' windows.

"Objection, Your Honor! Non-responsive after 'possible'."

"Sustained. Just answer the questions, Agent Harper," the Judge said.

"Now. You testified that Mr. Fuller's fingerprints were found on the packing tape that bound Mr. Hamlin."

"Yes."

"Where was the packing tape stored?"

"Ah. In a drawer in the kitchen, I believe."

"Isn't it true that Mr. Fuller often went into the kitchen to wait if the bags weren't ready?"

"I wouldn't know that, but he did tell me he had been in the kitchen on the day of the robbery."

"So, isn't it possible he saw the packing tape and touched it or picked it up to look at it?"

Agent Harper shrugged. "Anything is possible, I suppose."

"Agent Harper, isn't it true that Mr. Fuller on a previous occasion found that same bank vault open and called and reported it to his supervisor?"

"Yes."

"So, isn't it possible he touched the wheel on that occasion, perhaps helping the bank cashier close the vault?"

"That was weeks earlier. I couldn't imagine his prints still being on the vault."

"But you don't know that they weren't, do you?"

"I guess not."

"Isn't it true that the FBI has another suspect in this case who has not been apprehended?"

"Well, there was another suspect—Sam Stewart. However,

he had an airtight alibi."

"Who is Sam Stewart?"

"A messenger who met Fred Fuller every night and gave him the work from the Big Bear and Lake Arrowhead branches."

"Where did they meet?"

"At San Bernardino."

"What is the alibi you mentioned?"

"Mr. Fuller advised us that Sam Stewart showed up after him on the night of the robbery. It just so happens that Mr. Stewart was late because he stopped at an army surplus store to buy fishing gear. The proprietor of the store talked to him for over fifteen minutes, and he remembers it vividly."

"What exactly did Sam tell him?"

"Objection, hearsay," Joel said.

"Sustained," the Judge replied.

"Aren't you making an assumption for that alibi to be valid?"

"What do you mean?"

"You're assuming that when Sam met Fred, it was the first time he had been to the San Bernardino Branch that night. What if he had been there earlier, before Fred got there and before he went to the army surplus store? Isn't that possible?"

"I don't see how he could have managed that and picked up Arrowhead and Big Bear."

"Isn't it possible that Sam Stewart knocked on the door after everyone had left except Harvey Hamlin? Since Harvey knew Sam Stewart, he wouldn't have thought anything about letting him in. The vault was still open, so Sam could have bound and gagged Harvey, put him in the vault, and then cleaned out the money. During the night, Harvey might have had a coronary from the stress of being tied up and left in the vault. Isn't that possible?"

"It's possible, but not likely."

"Isn't it just as likely as your case against Fred Fuller?"

"I don't think so."

"Do you know where Sam Stewart is right now?"

"No."

"Isn't it true Sam Stewart quit his job the day after the robbery and left town?"

"Yes," Harper said, "but that wasn't unexpected. He'd given two weeks' notice."

"In the course of your investigation, did you happen to check on the criminal history of Sam Stewart?"

"Yes."

"What can you tell us about Mr. Stewart's criminal history?"

"Objection, Your Honor. Mr. Stewart is not on trial here." Whitehead said.

"Your Honor, we have a right to explore evidence of other culpable parties to this crime."

"Objection overruled."

"What about Mr. Stewart's criminal history?"

"He served ten years for armed robbery at San Quentin."

"Thank you. Pass the witness."

A commotion broke out again in the gallery. The Judge whacked his gavel one more time and then announced a recess for lunch. As soon as the Judge left the bench, the reporters swarmed around Maria and her family. The bailiffs had to come over to rescue them and chase the reporters out of the courtroom.

Fred looked at Roberts, smiled, and said, "That was a good cross-examination."

"Thanks, but the jury will never remember it."

"What do you mean?"

"All they're going to remember about Agent Harper's testimony is that the FBI found your fingerprints inside the vault."

Fred just stared at Roberts for a moment and then turned toward Maria, who was still sitting a few rows back in the gallery. He motioned to her, and she came up to the rail. He grabbed her hand and squeezed it gently. "How you making out, babe?" he asked, trying to seem cheerful.

"I'm so worried," she replied. "There's been so much damaging testimony that I am afraid the jury might convict you."

"Roberts hasn't put our case on yet. I am sure things will change a lot."

"I hope so."

"Any word on Steve and Randy?" Fred asked.

"Yeah. They got a lead on Sam. They think he's in Canada."

"God, I hope they find him."

"What will happen if they do?"

"Well, if he has the money, it will look pretty clear to everyone that he did it. If he doesn't have the money, finding him probably won't make much difference."

"God, I hope they find him with the money then," Maria said hopefully.

"Me, too, and it better be pretty soon, or it will be too late."

The bailiff motioned that it was time for Fred to leave.

"I've got to go, sweetheart. I love you."

Maria leaned over the railing and gave Fred a gentle kiss. Her soft, sweet lips quickly revitalized his spirits, and for the first time in days, he mustered a smile.

"I love you too," Maria said. "Don't give up. I know you're going to get through all of this."

Tears welled in Fred's eyes and for the first time in his life, Fred began to appreciate the power of love, and in the midst of all the adversity that had befallen him, he enjoyed a brief moment of peace.

After lunch, Sam Whitehead finished putting on his case, and now it was Joel's turn to present his defense. Joel, however, had no intention of putting on a real defense. His strategy was simply to tear down the State's case and make it look like he was trying to create reasonable doubt. His case, in chief would be short—a few character witnesses and bank employees who hadn't seen anything. Joel's first witness was Jim Wells from the motor pool.

"The defense calls Jim Wells."

Jim walked up to the witness chair and sat down. After taking the oath, Joel began to ask him questions.

"Do you recall October 20, 1967?"

"Right, quite clearly."

"Did you see the defendant, Fred Fuller, that day?"

"Yes, sir, I did. He came in right on time and checked out his car to go to Palm Springs."

"Did you notice anything unusual about him that day?"

"No."

"When did he come back?"

"It was pretty late. He had a flat tire on the way back, which delayed him over an hour."

"How did he appear when he came in that night?"

"He seemed alright. I didn't notice anything strange."

"Did you inspect the flat tire?"

"Yes. It appeared to be a nail. I took it over to the garage and patched it."

"Did you see Fred carrying anything when he came in after doing his route?"

"No. He was empty handed."

"Did Fred look like he had just robbed a bank and murdered someone?"

"No, not at all. He just looked a little tired."

"He looked tired?"

"Yeah. The lad was burning the candle at both ends. School started at nine each morning, I think, and he didn't get back from his route until eight thirty at night. He was running nearly a twelve-hour day, not including his homework and social life."

"Did you talk to him at all when he came in?"

"No. It was late, and I had a young lass waiting for me. It was no time for idle chatter."

There was laughter in the gallery.

"Are you familiar with the decedent, Harvey Hamlin?"

"Yes. I knew him quite well."

"Were Mr. Hamlin and Sam Stewart good friends?"

"Yes, they were. Sam often took Hamlin fishing on Lake Arrowhead."

"Objection! Non-responsive."

"Sustained," the Judge said. "Just answer the question asked, Mr. Wells."

"Yes, sir," Jim replied.

"Do you know a driver named Jake Johnson?"

"Yes."

"Did he at one time have the San Bernardino route?"

"Yes, he did."

"Were he and Hamlin good friends?"

"Yes."

"How do you know?"

"Jake used to tell me about his fishing trips and other things he did with Sam and Harvey. They were all three good friends and spent a lot of time together."

"Objection!" Whitehead yelled. "This is all irrelevant."

"It's very relevant, Your Honor," Roberts retorted. "We're entitled to bring evidence of other parties who may have equal opportunity and motive to commit the crime."

"Overruled," the Judge said.

"You may answer."

"Where was Jake on the night of the robbery?"

"He was on a parallel route?"

"What do you mean by parallel?"

"Well, it's a route that runs north and south but about twenty miles farther inland."

"And does this route ever get close to San Bernardino?"

"Yes. At one spot, it comes within five miles of the San Bernardino branch."

"The same branch that was robbed?"

"Yes."

"Did Jake get in on time the night of the robbery?"

"No. He was almost an hour late too."

"Did he give you any explanation for why he was late?"

"He said his branches were late, but I smelled liquor on his breath, so I asked him if he had stopped at a bar."

"What did he say?"

"He denied it, but I could tell by his reaction that he was lying."

"Objection! Speculation."

"Sustained," the Judge ruled.

"So, in your opinion, isn't it possible that Jake, Sam, and Hamlin were the perpetrators of this crime?"

"Objection!" Whitehead screamed.

"Withdraw the question. Thank you, Mr. Wells. Pass the witness."

Whitehead began, "Didn't you think it was strange that Fred Fuller just happened to have a flat tire on the night the bank was robbed?"

"Never thought much about it really."

"You testified Fred didn't have any extra baggage when he came in."

"Yes. I believe that is right."

"Couldn't he have dumped the money somewhere—like the trunk of his car—before he came into the motor pool?"

"I suppose anything is possible."

"So, you really have no idea who robbed the bank, do you?"

"No. I wasn't there, so I can't say I know what happened."

"That's what I thought. No further questions, Your Honor."

A man came through the double doors that led into the courtroom and rushed up to Joel Roberts. He whispered something to him, and then Roberts turned to the Judge.

"Your Honor," Roberts said, "I have just been informed that one of the witnesses I subpoenaed for this afternoon has just shown up at LAX and is trying to get on a flight to Mexico City."

The Judge frowned. "Well, we can't have that. What's his name?"

"Harold Clifford."

"What airline?"

"American."

The Judge turned to his bailiff. "Contact airport security and have them detain Mr. Clifford. Then contact the U.S. Marshal's office and get someone to pick up Mr. Clifford and bring him here."

"Yes, Your Honor," the bailiff said and then scampered off.

"We'll go ahead and take a break. Maybe when we return, Mr. Clifford will be here to explain why he's so anxious to leave the country. Let's reconvene in one hour." The Judge got up and hastily left the bench.

Fred looked out in the gallery but didn't see Maria. Her parents were there, so he called them over. "Where's Maria?"

"She said she had something she needed to do," her mother said.

"Like what?"

"I don't know. She said she'd be back in a few hours."

Fred frowned. He wondered what she was doing, and he hoped it wasn't anything dangerous. The deputy tapped him on the shoulder, indicating it was time to leave. Reluctantly, he followed the deputy back up to his holding cell.

When the court reconvened, Harold Clifford was sitting on a bench with a U.S. Marshal seated next to him. The Judge glared at Clifford and then said, "Mr. Roberts, call your next witness."

"The defense calls Mr. Harold Clifford."

Clifford got up warily and walked to the witness stand. The judge swore him in.

"Mr. Clifford," Roberts began, "did you receive a subpoena

to testify in this court today?"

"I don't know. Somebody shoved something in my face, but I didn't look at it."

"Did this person tell you that you'd been served?"

Clifford shrugged. "He may have said something like that."

"Just so there's no misunderstanding, do you realize you're under oath and you must truthfully answer any questions that are asked of you?"

Clifford took a deep breath. "Well, that could be a problem."

"A problem? Why is that?"

"I don't think I want to answer any questions without my counsel present."

"Objection!" Whitehead said. "Your Honor, can we sort this out outside the presence of the jury? I fear this could all be inflammatory and prejudicial."

The judge nodded. "Alright. Bailiff, take the jury back to the jury room until we figure this out."

The bailiff stood and escorted the jury out of the courtroom. The Judge then continued, "Mr. Clifford, are you invoking your right to remain silent under the Fifth Amendment, or do you just want to have a lawyer at your side to confer with?"

"Both. I'm not going to sit here and let a couple lawyers rip me to shreds."

"Well, the Fifth Amendment can only be invoked if the answers that you give might incriminate you. Since your testimony here today will be concerning the Bank USA robbery and anything you might know about it, you can only invoke the Fifth Amendment if you fear your truthful testimony might tend to incriminate you in that particular bank robbery. Do you understand?"

"Yes."

"So, do you still want to invoke the Fifth Amendment?"

"Yes," Clifford said. "I'm not going to say a damn thing."

"Very well," the Judge said. "Bailiff, take Mr. Clifford into custody for contempt of court for failing to honor a subpoena and attempting to flee the jurisdiction of the court."

The bailiff grabbed Clifford, swung him around, and cuffed him. Then he led him out of the courtroom. Fred watched him leave, upset that he had refused to testify. He wondered what he was hiding. Then he noticed Mrs. Hamlin standing up and making a quick exit. He wondered what was up with her.

The Judge looked at Roberts expectantly. "Do you have another witness?"

Roberts frowned. "Uh, well, in light of Mr. Clifford's refusal to testify, I'd like to re-call Special Agent James Walters."

"Your Honor," Whitehead interjected, "if Mr. Roberts is planning to question Agent Walters about the investigation of the Venice Beach robbery, I'm going to have to object on the grounds that it would be irrelevant and highly prejudicial."

"Your Honor, by invoking the Fifth Amendment in this case, Mr. Clifford has made any information the FBI has on him highly relevant to this case, whether it might be prejudicial or not."

"Objection overruled," the Judge said. "Bailiff, bring in the jury, and then get Agent Walters back in here."

The bailiff left and came back with the jury, who took their seats. A minute later, Agent Walters took the stand, and Roberts began questioning him.

"Mr. Walters, have you been involved in an investigation of a theft of funds from the Venice Beach branch of Bank USA?"

"Yes."

"How does Harold Clifford fit into that investigation?"

"Well, he is the cashier of the Venice Beach Branch."

"How much money is missing from that branch?"

"Shortly after Mr. Clifford took over the job of cashier there, it was discovered one morning that $178,000 was missing."

"Was Mr. Clifford a suspect?"

"Of course, along with the assistant cashier and a couple of tellers, all of whom had vault access."

"Who was the messenger handling the Venice Beach branch when the loss took place?"

"Jake Johnson."

"Are Jake Johnson, Harvey Hamlin, and Harold Clifford friends?"

"I wouldn't know."

"They knew each other, didn't they?"

"Yes."

"Did you know they often went fishing together with Sam Stewart, the messenger from Big Bear?"

"I've heard that, but I have no personal knowledge of it."

"How is the search for Sam Stewart coming?"

"He's disappeared. We haven't been able to find him."

"Don't you think it's rather curious that two of the suspects in the Venice Beach robbery were friends with Mr. Hamlin and Sam Stewart?"

"Not particularly."

"Isn't it possible that Clifford, Johnson, and Hamlin were in on the San Bernardino robbery, and they enlisted Sam Stewart to take the money out of the country to be split up later on?"

"Objection!" Whitehead said. "Calls for speculation."

"Sustained," the Judge said. "Careful, counselor," he cautioned Roberts.

"Pass the witness," Roberts said.

"No questions," Whitehead said.

"Thank you. You may stand down," the Judge said.

Joel swallowed hard. He was out of witnesses and wanted to rest, particularly if there was a chance Sam Stewart would be found. But he knew he'd likely be criticized if he rested before making a more diligent effort to prove this new theory that Hamlin, Clifford and Jake Johnson were in on the heist together. Then he got an idea. He'd noticed that Mrs. Hamlin had been in the courtroom. He didn't know where she'd gone or if she was still in the building, but if they could find her he could put her on the stand and ask her about the relationship between her husband, Clifford and Jake Johnson. That, at least, would be another witness he'd put on to bolster his alternative theory. He knew it wouldn't be enough, but it might make him look a little better.

"Your honor, due to Mr. Clifford's failure to testify here today we have decided to call Marilyn Hamlin, since she might be able to shed some light on the relationship between Mr. Clifford, Jake Johnson and her husband. I believe I saw her in the courtroom earlier."

"Very well. Bailiff, see if you can find Mrs. Hamlin in the hall."

Joel didn't think there was a chance in hell Mrs. Clifford would say anything earth shaking when she got on the stand. That was one reason they hadn't had her there ready to testify. The other reason was if she did testify there was a danger she might say something damaging about her husband that might lead the jury to think he was involved in the heist rather than just a victim. Joel knew it was never a good idea to call a witness when you had no idea what they might say, but he felt he had no choice in this instance.

Five minutes later the bailiff came back with Marilyn Hamlin following close behind him. "Your honor, I found Mrs. Hamlin in the cafeteria. She's ready to testify."

"Thank you," the Judge said looking at Marilyn Hamlin. "Mrs. Hamlin. You've been called to testify. Please take the stand."

"Yes, sir," she replied walking into the witness box and sitting down."

The bailiff gave the oath and Joel began to question her. After she'd identified herself and stated her relationship to Harvey Hamlin Joe asked, "Mrs. Hamlin, do you know a man named Jake Johnson?"

"Sure. He's a messenger at Bank USA. My husband knew

him because used to pick up the bank's data processing each day."

"Did they ever socialize?"

"Sure, they'd go fishing together and they were on a bowling team together."

"I see. Where did they go fishing?"

"Up at Big Bear Lake. Sam Stewart, another messenger, had a guiding service there and he'd take them out a couple times per year."

"Do you know a man named Harold Clifford."

Marilyn shook her head. "I have heard the name. I think he was a cashier at another branch. I'm not sure which one. Didn't he get into trouble?"

"You tell me. I can't testify. What do you know about him, if anything?"

"Nothing. I didn't know him. I just remember Harvey mentioning that he was under investigation or something."

"So, to your knowledge your husband and Harold Clifford did not socialize or have any business dealings together?"

"Not to my knowledge."

"Were you ever present when your husband and Sam Stewart were socializing?"

"No, I don't go fishing or bowling."

"So you've never overheard any conversations between them, in person or telephone conversations?"

"No. Not that I recall."

"Did Harvey ever talk about Sam Stewart at all."

"Yeah. He'd talk about the fish they caught and how the trip went."

"Did you ever hear them talk about the bank?"

Whitehead stood up. "Objection, your honor. "Relevance."

The judge took a deep breath. "Mr. Roberts. Where are you going with this? Does Mrs. Hamlin have any relevant information regarding Mr. Fuller's guilt or innocence."

Roberts nodded. "Yes, your honor. She does. Just a few more questions and I'll be done."

"Very well. Overruled. You many continue."

Roberts turned to the witness. "Does your husband owe you alimony and child support?"

"Yes, almost $30,000."

"Did he have any other personal debt?"

"Yes, he had over a hundred grand in credit card debt and I have no idea how much he owed his bookies."

There was a stir in the courtroom. The judge gave the gallery a hard look.

"So he was a gambler?"

"Yes, and a drinker. His drinking is what drove us apart."

"So, your ex-husband was desperate for money?"

"Objection, calls for speculation," Whitehead said.

"Your honor," Whitehead replied. "She can state her opinion based on her knowledge of her ex-husband and his financial situation."

"Overruled," the Judge said.

"Yes, he complained about his dire financial situation every time I brought up past due alimony or child support. He was forever complaining about being broke."

"Do you think your husband would have been capable of stealing money from Bank USA."

"Objection!" Whitehead screamed. "Calls for speculation, inflammatory and prejudicial."

"Withdrawn," Roberts said. "Pass the witness."

The judge looked at the clock on the wall and said, "This would be a good time to take a break. Court will reconvene in 30 minutes.

Joel sat down wondering if he'd gone too far. His instinct as a defense counsel was to go for the jugular when he had a witness on the ropes. He had been scoring some points with Mrs. Hamlin, but he hoped he hadn't introduced reasonable doubt. The last thing he wanted was for Fred to get acquitted. That would leave the robbery and murder unsolved and lead to further investigation. He was glad the Congressman hadn't been attending the trial.

Chapter 46

Running Out of Time

The door to the Judge's chamber opened, and the bailiff stood up and asked everyone to rise. Harper quickly left the courtroom. The Judge sat down and peered at Whitehead, "Do you want to cross examine Marilyn Hamlin?"

Whitehead nodded.

"Bailiff. Would you bring Mrs. Hamlin in please?"

Marilyn Hamlin went back to the witness box and took a seat. Whitehead took a step toward her and began. "Did you talk to your ex-husband during the one-week period before the robbery?"

Mrs. Hamlin thought for a moment. "Yes, I'm sure I did but everything is fuzzy back then."

"Did you talk to your husband after he went to work on the day of his death?"

"Yes. I remember that day very well. He called to say he was going to be late picking up our daughter, Melody. It was his weekend to have her."

"What time was that?"

"Mid-afternoon, 2 or 2:30."

"What was his mood?"

"Angry . . . depressed . . . worried."

"Did he elaborate at all on what was going on?"

"He thought the bank examiners were being unreasonable and trying to find a reason to get him fired."

"Did he have a strategy for dealing with them?"

"He may have, but he didn't share it with me."

"What do you mean?"

"Well, when I asked him about the bank examiners his usual response was for me not to worry about it. He'd deal with them."

"So, he wasn't very communicative."

"No."

"Did your ex-husband say anything or do anything that would lead you to believe he was planning to rob Bank USA, either alone or with Sam Stewart or Harold Clifford."

"No. Absolutely not."

"Did you hear or see anything that might shed some light on who was involved in the robbery of Bank USA and the death of your husband?"

"Well, only one thing?"

"What was that?" Whitehead asked.

"When Mr. Fuller found the vault open the first time and my husband was called to go close it—"

"Yes," Whitehead said.

"Well, my husband said when he told Fred that there was over six million dollars in the vault and he could have walked right in and taken it, his eyes got as wide as the Mississippi."

"Objection! Your Honor," Joel exclaimed. "Hearsay and pure speculation."

"Withdrawn," Whitehead said with a smirk. "No further questions."

"Mr. Roberts. Any further witnesses?"

"Your Honor," Joel replied, "I move for a continuance due to the recent location of an important witness."

"And who might that be?" the Judge asked in an irritated tone.

"Sam Stewart, Your Honor. If you will recall, Mr. Stewart was a messenger that met the defendant at the San Bernardino branch every day. He quit his job and disappeared two days after the robbery. He could well exonerate my client."

"Is he in custody?"

"No, sir. Two of Mr. Fuller's friends are in Toronto, and they are pretty sure he is staying with his sister there."

"Pretty sure? You mean they don't know for sure."

"Well, they haven't actually seen him yet, but they are pretty sure he's there."

"Pretty sure isn't good enough to stop a murder trial, Mr. Roberts. When you find out he is actually there in Toronto, I'll consider your motion, but as for right now, let's get on with the trial. Call your next witness."

"None other than Sam Stewart, Your Honor."

The judge looked at his watch and said, "Due to the late hour we will recess until tomorrow morning at 9:00 a.m. at which time we will hear closing arguments, unless by some miracle Sam Stewart is here to testify."

Roberts smiled. "Thank you, your honor."

The judge left the bench and Roberts turned to Fred. "Well, now it's up to Steve and Randy. You better hope they find Sam."

Fred nodded. "God. I hope they do. . . . How do you think it looks right now?"

Roberts shrugged. "Honestly, not so good."

Fred slumped in his chair, closed his eyes and prayed for a miracle.

Chapter 47

Stakeout

Once Steve and Randy were provided with Sam Stewart's sister's address at 88 Cokesbury Lane, they began a stakeout, hoping to see Sam coming or going. With no action for the first two hours, they were both getting very anxious.

"We just can't sit here all day," Randy complained.

"Maybe we should just go up to the door, knock, and ask if Sam is there," Steve replied.

"We may spook him if we do something so blatant."

"Yeah, but we've got to flush him out somehow."

"But how?"

"We could set his house on fire, and then he would have to come out," Steve noted.

Randy laughed. "Yeah, right, but neither of us is an arsonist, and it does Fred no good if we end up sitting in the cell next door."

Steve surveyed the neighborhood for an idea. He observed a gas utility truck parked up the street. The workmen were nowhere in sight. He remembered one time in his youth having to evacuate his neighborhood due to a gas leak. "You're right. I've got a better idea," Steve said. "See that truck up there? Let's get a couple of hard hats and force Sam out in the open."

Steve got out of the car, grabbed a couple of hard hats from the utility truck, gave one to Randy, and then started walking up and down the street, knocking at each door, telling the occupants there was a natural gas leak in the neighborhood and they needed to evacuate the area for the next hour or so until they got the leak fixed. By the time he got to 88 Cokesbury, the streets were full of nervous residents. He knocked on the door and waited.

The door opened, and an elderly lady appeared. "Sorry to bother you, ma'am, but there's been a gas leak up the street, and we need everyone to evacuate the area until the gas dissipates," Steve said.

"I don't smell anything," she protested.

"You can't smell natural gas or see it for that matter. Please, ma'am, for your own safety, we must insist that you and anyone inside the residence evacuate the neighborhood."

"Okay. I'll need to go get my brother out too."

Steve's pulse quickened with her words. After a few minutes, Sam Stewart appeared at the front door, in the flesh. Steve smiled and then continued, "Okay, just walk up the street about two or three blocks just until the gas dissipates. We'll come and get you when it's safe."

The crowd moved reluctantly up the street. About this time, Randy entered on the scene and whispered into Steve's ears. Steve then yelled to the crowd, "Ladies and gentlemen, I've just been informed the leak has been fixed and the danger is over. You may return to your homes. Sorry for the inconvenience. Thank you."

At that moment, there was a screeching of tires. From around the corner, a half dozen police cars suddenly descended on 88 Cokesbury Lane. Sam Stewart was startled by the sudden onslaught of police. He tried to run into his sister's house but was cut off by two Canadian Mounties. He ran down an alley with two officers hot on his trail. As he approached the side street, a squad car squealed to a stop in front of him. He jumped a small fence and cut across a yard.

One of the officers yelled, "Halt, or I'll shoot!"

Sam ignored the warning and headed into a vacant field. The officer fired a warning shot over his head. Sam veered to the left into a wooded area. He approached a small cottage, where a gardener was working next to his pickup truck. He jumped into the truck, cranked the engine, and screeched down the driveway toward the street. He made a hard right and accelerated away from his pursuers. Suddenly, from a side street, came a squad car with its sirens blaring. Sam disappeared over a hill with the squad car on his tail.

As Randy looked back at all the activity around Sam's house, he recognized Agent Harper getting out of one of the squad cars. He waved and walked over to them.

"Mr. Hanson, I heard you were up here in Canada searching for Sam Stewart. We thought we would give you a little assistance."

"Well, it looks all you've managed to do so far is let him escape."

"Don't worry. They'll catch him."

"I know you're not here to help Fred, so what made you suddenly decide to get serious about finding Sam?"

"My real purpose for being here is to tie up a loose end. We know your friend is guilty, but until Sam Stewart was apprehended, there could be some doubt. Now, with Mr. Stewart in custody, we can verify his alibi and prove he was not involved in the robbery."

"Agent Harper, you need to come inside!" an officer yelled.

"Excuse me, boys. Let me see what this is all about."

Harper walked into the house, where a search was underway. Steve and Randy followed behind him closely.

"Look over here, sir. There's a gray bag."

"What's in it?" Harper asked.

"Money, sir . . . lots of it!"

Harper looked at Steve and Randy and then scurried over to the bag. He looked inside and began rummaging through the stacks and stacks of cash. After a moment, he looked up, rather embarrassed and said, "Well, I guess I owe Mr. Fuller an apology."

Steve and Randy smiled at Harper's words. A great sense of

relief engulfed them. They looked at each other, fighting off tears of happiness and relief. They shook hands at first but soon embraced. Steve went over to Harper and gave him a hug too. Harper laughed and shook his head.

Randy suddenly remembered Sam's sister and started looking around for her. He was worried about what Sam might have told her and what she might tell the police. He finally spotted her standing near one of the patrol cars, weeping softly. He walked up to her and said, "Sorry we had to track down Sam. You just have to understand that Fred is like a brother to Steve and me. He even saved our lives once. Fred's only nineteen years old, you know. He has his whole life ahead of him."

She looked at him but didn't speak. Steve handed her a handkerchief, and she wiped the tears from her eyes. "I hope they don't hurt him," she said.

"I'm sure they won't," Steve replied and then looked down the road where Sam had disappeared, wondering if he had gotten away. "Fred always said he really liked Sam and couldn't believe he had taken the money. Did he tell you about the bank robbery?"

"What bank robbery? He didn't tell me anything about a bank robbery."

In a few moments, Agent Harper appeared from out of the house. "Well, there's only a little over $250,000 in there so Fred's not off the hook. They could have been in it together and this was Sam's cut," Harper suggested.

"That's bullshit?" Randy spat. "Fred had nothing to do with the robbery. There may be somebody else involved but it wasn't Fred."

"Tell that to the jury."

As Harper was enjoying Randy's discomfort, a voice came over the radio. "Unit Forty-Four, come in"

One of the officers picked up the microphone and responded. "This is Unit Forty-four."

"Sir, we were pursuing the suspect east on Southwell Road, where he collided with a freight train at the Hanover Crossing," the radio crackled.

"What is the suspect's status?" the officer asked.

"You won't need an ambulance. The suspect has been incinerated."

Steve and Randy looked at each other in shock. Mrs. Stewart let out a scream and nearly collapsed. One of Harper's men grabbed her and took her back into the house. Steve and Randy looked at each other in shock and confusion. They didn't know whether this turn of events was good or bad for Fred but they knew Joel needed to know about it immediately.

"Agent Harper, we need to contact Joel right away before the jury renders its verdict!" Steve said.

Agent Harper stared at Steve for a moment and then replied, "Okay. Follow me over to police headquarters, and we'll phone LA."

Harper got into a squad car, and Steve and Randy followed him to the station. They went inside, and Walters got on the phone and called FBI headquarters in LA, where Agent Walters had been waiting for a report. Walters promised to go tell Joel and advise the court of this most recent development.

Steve and Randy went to their hotel, gathered together their luggage, and headed for the airport. They were anxious to see what would happen when the court found out about the recovery of a portion of the bank's money and Sam's death. They arrived and got in line to go through customs. Not having passports or birth certificates, the custom's officers refused at first to let them through. Finally, when they produced drivers' licenses and draft cards, the officer gave in and let them onto the plane. A bit shaken, Steve and Randy sat down at the gate to wait for their flight.

"What do you think will happen now?" Steve asked.

"If the jury hears that Sam got caught with some of the money, they will have to assume he was in on the robbery," Randy said, "but that doesn't help Fred."

"Right. Fred could still be an accomplice?"

"But they don't have any evidence of Sam and Fred working together. There's a chance the jury will give Fred the benefit of the doubt."

The airport announcer came on and advised them that the flight to LA was now boarding. Steve and Randy got on the plane, feeling pretty proud of their accomplishment but worried it wouldn't be enough to save their blood brother.

Chapter 48

The Revelation

Maria was standing in the back of the courtroom when the Judge recessed for the day. As soon as he'd left the bench, Special Agent Walters went over to Joel and Fred and conferred with them for a moment. Maria could tell by Fred's body language that something significant had happened. She rushed up to him to find out what was it was. As soon as he saw her, he embraced her and gave her an excited hug.

"We have good news!" Fred said.

"What?" Maria asked.

"They found Sam Stewart in Toronto."

"What?"

"They found Sam," Roberts confirmed.

"Oh my God!" Maria said. "Did he—"

"Yes, they found part of the stolen money in his sister's house, where he was staying."

"Oh, thank God!" Maria's mother exclaimed. "How much."

"Almost \$250,000."

Maria frowned. "That's all? What happened to the rest of it?"

Fred shrugged.

"We don't know. Sam was killed in a chase trying to evade the police," Roberts said. "He collided with a freight train, I'm afraid."

"So, what does that mean?" Maria asked worriedly.

"It means I haven't been exonerated. I could still be an

accomplice, so nothing has really changed."

"Oh, no!" Maria exclaimed. "I thought if we found Sam this nightmare would be over."

"That's what we all hoped, Maria," Roberts said. "But this is still helpful. It complicates matters and will confuse the jury. They may be more likely now to find reasonable doubt."

Maria wasn't appeased by Roberts reasoning. Her stomach was in knots, she hadn't been able to sleep at night and was becoming more and more depressed each day trial dragged on. She didn't how much longer she could bear it.

Chapter 49

Unwanted Witness

After Walters had given the news to Fred and Joel he told Whitehead and they walked across the street to Whitehead's office to discuss the ramifications of what had happened in Canada. It had been a cold rainy day in LA and the streets were still wet. Neither of the men seemed to notice the cold as their minds were still trying to get around the bizarre events of the day. Before they went into the Federal Building they stopped and got a cup of coffee from a street vendor.

"A cold front must have come through. It wasn't this cold this morning when I came to work," Whitehead remarked.

"It arrived right after noon," Walters said. "It was starting to get when cold when I went to lunch."

"Lunch? You got lunch? You're a lucky guy."

Walters shrugged. "Well. It was a working lunch. I ate but I did a lot of work too."

After they had their coffee they went inside and got into an elevator. Whitehead pushed the button for the 9th floor. Several other people got in and each pushed the button they wanted. The door closed.

"Killed by a freight train. Can you believe it?" Whitehead said, shaking his head."

"Yeah. Go figure," Walters replied.

The door opened onto the 9th floor, they stepped out and began walking slowly down the hall.

"You said he had $228,000 with him?

"That and some change, according to Harper. It was stashed in a duffle bag they found in the coat closet of his sister's house."

"And you sure it's from the bank heist?"

"Yes, we read off some of the serial numbers on the new bills to the new cashier at the San Bernardino branch and they were a match."

"So, where's the other $6.5 million?" Whitehead asked.

"He must have stashed it somewhere between here and Canada. He just kept out some spending money."

They made it to the U.S. Attorney's office and went inside. The receptionist nodded and smiled when she noticed them walk through the front door. Whitehead ignored her and went straight for a big oak door with his name on it. He opened the door to the spacious office, walked over to his desk and picked up a stack of phone messages. He went through them, pulled out one and threw the rest back on his desk.

"What about his sister? Does she know anything?" Whitehead asked.

"She claims she had no idea her brother had been involved in a bank robbery and didn't know the money was in her closet."

"Does Harper believe her?"

"He thinks she probably knows more than she's admitting, but apparently Sam showed up unexpectedly, so she probably had no part in it."

"He might have told her where he hid the rest of it," Whitehead said. "Or maybe he wrote it down somewhere. Did you find anything in his personal things?"

"No," Walters said. "He didn't have much. A toothbrush, underwear and couple T-shirts is all."

"Guess he figured he had plenty of money to go shopping."

"Right."

"Well, this isn't good but it could be worse. I think it should be fairly obvious to the jury that there had to be at least two or three accomplices. It is clear that Sam Stewart was one of them and Fred Fuller another. I doubt either of them was the mastermind, though."

"No," Walters agreed. It had to be orchestrated by someone inside who was more knowledgeable about the bank's operations, but who that would be, I don't know."

"If he hadn't been bound and gagged and left in the vault I would have picked Harvey. He certainly had a motive."

"Yes, but he couldn't have tied himself up. So, Fred or Sam must have done it."

"Well, without evidence to the contrary that's what we are going to have to argue to the jury tomorrow," Whitehead concluded. "But I'm sure Roberts will have a long list of other potential accomplices and some of them will even have motive and opportunity."

"Like Marilyn Hamlin or one of the bank officers," Walters suggested.

"Exactly. . . . Okay, if you learn anything helpful between now and tomorrow morning call me. I've got to tweak my closing arguments a bit since we have this new evidence. I'll see you tomorrow."

Walters left and Whitehead opened his briefcase and pulled out a file that contained a draft of his closing argument. He opened it up and started reading the pages making changes as he went along. When he was done he looked at his watch and saw it was after 11:00p.m. Then he remembered the telephone message he'd looked at earlier and stuffed in his shirt pocket. After retrieving it he dialed the number and after a minute a woman's voice came on the line.

"Hello?"

"This is Sam Whitehead. I'm sorry I'm calling so late, but your message said it was urgent."

"It's okay. I was reading. I hadn't gone to bed yet."

"Let's see. According to this message you are Paula Dupree?"

"That's right."

"How can I help you, Paula?"

"I just got back in town and I have been catching up on the Fred Fuller case. I understand you are getting close to the end."

"We are, yes. We're down to our last few witnesses and then we'll have closing arguments."

"Well, I just wanted to tell you that there was somebody at the bank that day that nobody has mentioned, so I wanted to be sure you knew about it."

"Really?"

"Yes."

"Go on, I'm listening."

"I work at Savon drug store next to the bank and I was there on the day of the robbery."

"You were? I don't recall your name on the list of potential witnesses?"

"I went on vacation the next day, so nobody interviewed me."

"I see, continue."

"I also do my banking there and know the tellers and Mr. Hamlin, so I pay some attention to what's going on there."

"Understood."

"Well, after the bank closed on the day of the robbery and everyone had left except Harvey, who is always the last to leave, well another car pulled up. It was a bank messenger car, a white Impala, and a short young man with a crew cut and wearing jeans and a white T-shirt got out and went into the bank."

"Was it Fred Fuller?"

"No, and it wasn't Santa Claus either."

Whitehead laughed.

"Okay, so what did you observe this messenger do?"

"He was in the bank for quite a long time and when he came out he loaded a lot of messenger bags into the trunk of his car."

"How many?"

"At least two or three and they were bulkier than the ones they usually take in and out of there."

"I see. So what else happened?"

"Nothing. He left and I went home and packed for my vacation. I didn't hear about the robbery until I got home yesterday."

"Okay. I'm going to have an officer come by and take your statement tomorrow. He might bring a sketch artist."

"All right."

"Thanks for calling me. . . . Have you mentioned this to anyone else?"

He wanted to tell her not to mention this new information to anyone, but restrained himself. If she did tell her story to anybody it would probably be too late to help Fred Fuller.

"No, I just realized you didn't know about this a few hours ago."

"You did the right thing calling me. Thanks again."

Whitehead took down Paula's name and address and then hung up the phone. After staring at the piece of paper for a long moment he opened a drawer and tossed it inside angrily. Would anyone believe he forgot about this 11th hour witness? No, they wouldn't. He couldn't believe his luck. Now he'd have to hand Joel Roberts evidence, on a silver platter, that might tip the balance enough so that Fred Fuller might walk.

He took a deep breath trying to calm himself. He had to think of a way to keep this witness off of Joel's radar until it was too late for him to call her. But he had to be very careful or he might have trouble if the case were appealed. He dialed information and got Joel Roberts' office number. The operator connected him but it was after hours so nobody picked up. He left a message that he had called but didn't say why, knowing that he wouldn't be going into his office before the trial resumed in the morning. When Joel returned the call, Whitehead wouldn't be there and nobody in his office would know where he was or why he had called.

Chapter 50

Fred's Last Hope

Maria went by Joel Roberts office early the next morning hoping to talk to him about Sam Stewart and how he thought his involvement in the robbery and subsequent death would affect the outcome of the trial. But that was only what she was going to tell him. The real purpose of the visit was to make sure he hadn't given up. She'd gotten the feeling that he was only going through the motions now and didn't believe Fred could win. That concerned her and she wanted to give him a pep talk because from her viewpoint it shouldn't be that hard to sell reasonable doubt to the jury. She breathed a sigh of relief when she saw his car in the parking lot.

As she stepped off the elevator Joel was just coming out of his suite. "Mr. Roberts. Hi."

"Maria. Hi. What are you doing here?"

"I just wanted to talk with you a minute before the trial begun."

"Well, I don't have much time. You can talk while we walk to my car."

"Okay," she said as he locked the door. "So, finding Sam with some of the money should really bolster our case, right?"

"Maybe, but the amount of money is the problem. There is still so much of it missing," he said as he started to walk toward the elevator.

"Well, Sam probably stashed it somewhere, don't you think?"

"Sure, but I have no proof of that. It is pure speculation."

The elevator door opened and they stepped in.

"But we know for sure now that at least two other people were involved in the robbery. Somebody at the bank must have been involved, an insider, right?"

"Again, that's just speculation."

"But it brings up reasonable doubt, doesn't it?" she asked.

The elevator door opened and they stepped out onto the first floor.

"That's what I will argue to the jury, but I don't know if they will buy it."

"Have you talked to Whitehead about it yet? What does he think?"

"I don't know. He called me last night but there is no way I will be able to talk to him before the trial resumes at 10:00 a.m."

"Really? Did the message say what he wanted to talk about?"

"No. It didn't, which is annoying as hell. He called me after midnight."

"Do you know where he hangs out in the morning?" Maria asked very curious and worried about the reason for Whitehead's call.

"He's usually in his office, but he may be avoiding me."

"Hmm," Maria mused. "We need to find him."

Joel smiled. "What do you expect me to do?"

"Nothing. I'll find him and let you know why he called."

Joel shook his head. "Okay. Be my guest. Good luck."

Maria rushed to her car wondering how she would find a U.S. Attorney in Los Angeles who didn't want to be found. She thought about it and realized he could be anywhere. If he was killing time what would he do? It's morning so he'd probably be having breakfast or a cup of coffee somewhere, but where? There were hundreds of coffee shops, restaurants and diners in downtown LA. She could start going by them one by one, but that would take too much time. Then she got an idea. She started the car and drove back toward the courthouse and stopped at the first convenience store she saw. She went inside and used the payphone to call Whitehead's office number."

"U.S. Attorney's office," a pleasant female voice advised.

"Yes. Mr. Whitehead's secretary please."

"One moment."

Several moments later another female voice came on the line. "Yes, this is Ruth."

"Ruth, I'm sorry to bother you. Oh, I'm so embarrassed."

"What's wrong?" Ruth said.

"Oh. Mr. Whitehead called last night late but didn't say where to meet him this morning."

"Who are you?"

"It's me, Maria. It must have been important if he called just before midnight. Do you know where he usually goes for breakfast?"

"Ah. You might catch him at Brighton Coffee Shop in Beverly Hills."

"Oh, great. Thanks," Maria said and hung up quickly. She remembered seeing the Brighton Coffee Shop while cruising around with Fred in Beverly Hills. Now she just hoped she could find it and Whitehead would be there.

Twenty minutes later she pulled into a parking space just down the street from the popular restaurant. Fortunately, Whitehead was a big, noisy man who wouldn't be hard to pick out if he was there. She held her breath as she opened the door and walked in then exhaled happily when she saw him sitting across from another man in a booth. She'd seen the other man at trial but couldn't remember who he was. She strolled right over and stood over them. Startled, Whitehead looked up at her and frowned.

"Mr. Whitehead. Sorry for the intrusion, but Joel Roberts said you called him at midnight last night. He wants to know what you wanted. He figured it had to be important."

"Maria? You shouldn't be here. I can't talk to you."

"Sure you can. Just tell me why you called Joel last night. He asked me to find out. He won't see you until the trial resumes and then there won't be time to talk."

Special Agent Harper started to slide out of the booth. "Do want me to take care of this, Sam?"

Whitehead sighed deeply. "No. I got it. Thanks," he said and then fished a piece of paper out of his pocket and handed it to Maria. "This is a new witness who came forward last night. I don't plan to call her but I was obligated to tell Joel about her. There is her address and telephone number."

Maria took the note and smiled broadly. Must be a good witness if you were trying to hide her from us, she thought. "Thanks. I'll get this right to Joel."

She turned and walked out of the restaurant. When she looked back Whitehead was pulling out his wallet and summoning the waitress. When she got back to car she wondered what she should do. If she took the note to Joel, he wouldn't have time to do anything. Her only hope would be if she could find this witness and bring her to the courthouse. Unfortunately, the address was in San Bernardino, at least an hour away, so she decided to call and see if she could get the woman to get in her car and drive to the courthouse.

She stopped at the first gas station she came across and used a payphone to call the witness. A boy answered the phone. "Hello."

"Hi. Is Mrs. Dupree there?"

"No. She's at work."

Maria's heart sank. "Really? Do you have her work number?"

"No."

"Where does she work?"

"Savon."

"Savon Drugs?"

"Yes. That's it."

"Which one?"

"By the bank."

"By the bank. Ah. . . . oh . . . the Bank USA in San Bernardino?"

"Un huh."

"Okay, thank you," she said and hung up to call information. When she got the number the operator connected her and the employee who answered the phone said she'd find her and to wait. A few minutes later Paula answered the phone.

"Hello."

"Mrs. Dupree?"

"Yes."

"This is Maria Shepard, Fred Fuller's girlfriend."

"Are you kidding me?" she said excitedly. "Is it really you?"

"Yes," Maria laughed. "It's me."

"You are one hell of a woman. I have been reading about you in the newspapers. I don't know if I would have forgiven Fred, but you know him much better than I do, so I guess he must be worth it."

"Yeah, he's like most men, a little weak when it comes to a pretty face."

"Ain't that the truth. So, why are you calling?"

"I heard you had some information that might be important."

"Yes, I called Mr. Whitehead just as soon as I got back in town and started reading about the trial."

She told Maria what she had seen.

"Listen, Paula. This information could be enough to create reasonable doubt in the minds of the jurors. We need you at the courthouse at 10:00 a.m. The judge will only let us put on one more witness and it needs to be you. Can you get in your car right now and come to the courthouse? You'll just have time to get here."

"But I'm at work, hon. I just can't up and leave work."

"Sure you can. If you are summoned to the court, employers

can't do anything about it. They have to let you go."

"Really. They can't dock my pay or anything?"

"If they dock your pay, we'll reimburse you for whatever you lose. Don't worry."

"Okay, then. I'm on my way."

Maria hung up the phone as tears began streaming down her face. She cried hard for several minutes as all the fear and anguish that had been building up in her for the past few months came pouring out. When she regained her composure, she got in her car and raced to the courthouse to tell Fred and Joel the good news.

Chapter 51

Final Witness

The courtroom was packed with spectators and the press when Roberts walked in and put his briefcase on the defense table. He looked over at Whitehead who was studying his closing argument. He wondered if Maria had found him and asked about the witness.

"You called me last night?" Roberts asked.

Whitehead turned and grimaced. "Yeah. Haven't you talked to Maria?"

"No. I haven't seen her since early this morning."

"Well, I gave her the name and address of the witness who came forward last night."

"A witness. A witness to what?"

"Talk to Maria. You sent her to get the message, right?"

"Yeah."

"Well. I gave it to her the information. So, it's not my fault if she didn't give it to you."

"Okay, fine. I'm sure she'll be here soon."

A side door opened and a marshal escorted Fred to the defense table. Roberts and Fred shook hands.

"Good morning," Roberts said. "Your girlfriend has some information about a last-minute witness. I hope she gets here soon."

"What kind of witness?"

Roberts shrugged. "I don't know exactly, but a woman contacted Whitehead with some new information. Whatever it is it better be good because as things stand right now the odds of an acquittal are not good."

Fred closed his eyes. "Oh God. Let it be good."

The door opened behind the bench and the bailiff came out and said, "All rise!"

The judge came walking briskly through the door and took his seat at the bench. After shuffling through some papers on his desk he looked up and said, "So, do we have another witness or are going straight to closing arguments?"

Roberts stood up. "Your honor. It turns out the witness we were hoping to have has been tragically killed."

He explained briefly to the Court what had happened in Canada.

"Well, that's unfortunate? So, you don't have any more witnesses?"

"No. We would like to recall Special Agent Harper to the stand to explain to the jury what happened to Sam Stewart and testify as to other relevant events that transpired in the last 48 hours."

"Mr. Whitehead. Any objection."

Whitehead shook his head. "No, your honor. I think it is a waste of time, but I can't deny that it may be relevant to the issues before the court."

"Very well. Bailiff, bring in Special Agent Harper."

Harper walked in through the back doors and proceeded to the witness stand. The judge reminded him he was still under oath.

Roberts smiled and began. "Agent Harper. You're just back from Toronto, Canada, is that right?"

"Yes."

"What were you doing up there."

"We got a tip that a suspected accomplice in the Bank USA robbery had been spotted in Toronto, so I went up there to check it out."

"Did you find Sam Stewart?"

"Yes, he was living with his sister and when we confronted

him he ran. So, the local police pursued him.”

“Did they catch him?”

“No. Unfortunately he tried to beat a freight train through a crossing and didn’t make it.”

“So, he is dead?”

“Yes.”

“Did you find anything relevant to the Bank USA robbery in his possession?”

“Yes. We found nearly $250,000 of money that was stolen in that robbery.”

“Thank you, Agent Harper. Pass the witness.”

Whitehead took the witness on cross and pointed out that the $250,000 was only a small portion of the $6.8 million that had been stolen, but when he tried to get Harper to speculate on what that meant, Roberts repeatedly objected and Whitehead finally gave up and the witness was excused.

“Okay, Mr. Roberts. Do you have any more witnesses or do you rest?”

“Yes, we are expecting a witness momentarily.”

“Who is the witness?”

“I don’t know her name, but Mr. Whitehead does. He’s talked to her.”

“Your honor. The witness is Paula Dupree, but I didn’t tell her to come down and testify, so I don’t know why Mr. Roberts thinks she will be here.”

The judge stiffened. “Mr. Roberts. Is this witness or her way or not?”

Roberts looked toward the rear of the courtroom anxiously. “Well, I—” Suddenly the door opened and Maria rushed in, but she was alone.”

“Your honor, if I can confer with Maria Shepard a minute I’ll get a status on our witness.”

“Very well,” the judge growled. “We’ll take a ten-minute

recess and when it's over we will either hear from Mrs. Dupree or start closing arguments."

The judge stood up and hastily exited the courtroom. Maria rushed to Roberts and Fred and said, "She is coming. She should be here but she's coming from San Bernardino so I can't say how soon."

"Well, if she doesn't make it in the next ten minutes I'm screwed," Fred moaned.

"I'm sorry, Fred," Maria replied. "I was lucky to find her. Hell, I was lucky to find Whitehead this morning. She explained to them all she had been through.

"Oh, my God," Fred said. "What did I do to deserve you?"

"Yeah, well you better be worth it," Maria replied with only a glimmer of a smile.

The back door opened and the bailiff came out again and said, "All rise!" Fred looked anxiously at the doors in the back of the courtroom. Roberts took a deep breath and grimaced. Maria looked at the judge worriedly.

At that same moment the doors at the back of the courtroom swung open and a tall brunette strolled in wearing a Savon Drug Store uniform. Everyone in the courtroom turned to see her. Maria rushed over to greet her.

"Paula. You made it. Just in the nick of time."

The judge took the bench and said, "Mr. Roberts. It looks like you have a witness."

"Yes, your honor. The defense calls Paula Dupree."

Mrs. Dupree smiled as the bailiff escorted her to the witness stand. After she was administered the oath she testified to everything she'd told Whitehead the night before and Maria over the phone. Neither Roberts nor Whitehead knew for sure what impact the testimony would have on the trial but one thing was clear, the jury found the testimony very interesting.

"Alright. Mr. Roberts. Are we done?"

"Yes, your honor the defense rests."

"Mr. Whitehead?"

"Yes, your honor. Nothing further, we close."

"Alright then, Mr. Whitehead," the judge said. "You may give your closing argument."

Whitehead nodded, stood up and approached the jury box. "Your Honor, ladies and gentlemen of the jury, for the past week and one half, you've heard the story of Fred Fuller, an excellent student, Eagle Scout, Congressional Intern, honest, dependable, and loved by all. That may all be true. We don't dispute Mr. Fuller's past. But a strange thing happened to Mr. Fuller. He was tempted by fate, not just once but twice tempted. The first time, he resisted the temptation. You remember the testimony of Mr. Sinclair where he told you Fred called him when he found the vault open and stood there guarding the bank's money until someone could arrive to secure it?

"But I ask you, ladies and gentlemen, was Fred Fuller really such an honest person, or was he just unprepared to take advantage of the opportunity to steal the bank's money the first time around? You see, the first time, Fred was caught off guard. He had no plan, and he hadn't considered the fact that someone would be so dumb as to leave the vault open. So, he had no choice but to report the vault open because it would be too dangerous to concoct a plan in the five or ten minutes that a decision had to be made.

"But don't you think those wheels began to turn in Fred's head after he watched them close the vault on over six million dollars? Don't you think he was kicking himself for not being prepared to grab that money and run? Don't you think he went through the mental exercise of planning what he should have done? I bet it was the subject of conversation with his friends and relatives. Obviously, he didn't know if he would ever get a second shot at the money, and frankly, it's amazing that the vault could have been left open a second time. But it happened . . . and this time, Fred was ready for it.

"You remember the testimony of Cindy Brolin, the assistant cashier. She testified when she left the bank just before 5:00 p.m. that the vault was still open. Now, the defense has tried to suggest a lot of different theories of things that could have happened, but you must remember speculation is not evidence. You can only consider the evidence that has been presented. There has been no evidence that anyone was in the San Bernardino branch of Bank USA after 5:00 p.m. on the day of the robbery other than Fred Fuller.

"Now you heard from a last minute witness that another messenger showed up before Fred Fuller and went in the bank and came out with some bags. But that doesn't prove anything. We don't have any evidence as to what was in the bags nor of the identity of this mystery messenger.

"We know Fred picked up a number of bags after 5:00 p.m. on the day of the robbery. We know his fingerprints were found inside the vault and on the tape that was used to bind and gag Harvey Hamlin. We know he was familiar with the vault having a previous encounter with an open vault at this same branch. Now we don't know if Harvey was in the heist and Fuller double-crossed him so he could have all the money for himself, but either way Fred Fuller is culpable for this crime. Ladies and gentlemen, there has been no other explanation presented of what happened at the bank on that fateful day that has been supported by one shred of credible evidence during the course of this trial. I submit to you that our version of the facts is the truth.

"Ladies and gentlemen, at the beginning of this trial, we discussed the burden the government has to prove its case. That burden is to prove its case beyond any reasonable doubt. We believe we have met our burden. It is quite obvious that Fred Fuller found the vault open a second time or conspired with Harvey Hamlin to rob the bank and made a decision to steal the over six million dollars he knew was in the vault. Now what exactly happened to Harvey Hamlin, we'll never know. No one will ever know. The medical examiner testified that Harvey Hamlin died of a heart attack. Maybe Fred Fuller didn't intend to kill Harvey. Maybe Harvey Hamlin was alive when he was bound and gagged and left in the vault. It doesn't matter. The fact is, he died during the commission of a bank robbery. Under California law, that constitutes murder, and Fred Fuller must be held accountable.

"Ladies and gentlemen of the jury, it's time now for you to perform your duty. It's time for you to find Fred Fuller guilty of the murder of Harvey Hamlin and guilty of the robbery of Bank USA. Thank you for your attention, and may God be with you in your deliberations."

"Thank you, Mr. Whitehead," said Judge Sessions. "Now. Mr. Roberts, please give us your closing argument."

"Yes, Your Honor. Ladies and gentlemen of the jury, if there is anything we know after a week and a half of trial, it is that no one knows what happened on October 20, 1967. You have heard a lot of circumstantial evidence that Fred Fuller was at the bank or near it during the time of the robbery, and because of that, it is assumed he committed the crime. Ladies and gentlemen, you are all aware of the great American tradition that a man is presumed innocent until proven guilty. That's where we started in this trial. Fred Fuller was innocent the day we started this trial, and, guess what. . . . he's still innocent today, because the United States has been unable to prove its case beyond a reasonable doubt.

"Through the course of this trial, several witnesses have discussed different scenarios of what might have happened on October 20, 1967. Each one of those possible explanations is just as plausible as what the United States would have you believe about Fred Fuller.

"We have produced witness after witness who all testified that murder and robbery was totally out of character for Fred Fuller. You have seen Fred is a model student, a leader, an Eagle Scout, a deeply religious person who has ambitions to be a lawyer and politician. It doesn't make any sense that Fred Fuller could have committed these crimes.

"Not only is there some reasonable doubt of Fred Fuller's guilt, but there is substantial doubt as to his guilt. The only serious piece of evidence the United States has is one lone fingerprint on a teller's cart inside the vault, prints on the packing tape and fingerprints on the locking mechanism on the door of the vault. But you heard the witnesses testify that the fingerprints could have been placed on that teller's tray before it was wheeled into the vault. In fact, it could have been placed there several days before the robbery ever took place. We know that Fred Fuller helped Harvey Hamlin close the vault the first time he left it open. And, the packing tape was kept in the kitchen where Fred could have easily picked it up prior to the robbery since he went into that kitchen on a daily basis.

"Ladies and gentlemen, the government desperately wants to solve this bank robbery and the murder of Harvey Hamlin. They want to solve it so badly that they picked the first person that fit their profile for a suspect. As you will recall, just two days after the robbery, another messenger, Sam Stewart, quit his job and disappeared. Isn't this quite a coincidence? Isn't it rather strange that the government is not pursuing Harold Clifford, who refused to testify in front of this court on grounds he might incriminate himself? Doesn't that tell you he was somehow involved?

What about Jake Johnson, who came in late to the motor pool? He could have easily taken a detour to the San Bernardino branch to participate in some manner in the robber. It's very likely he is the mystery messenger that Paula Dupree testified about. It's curious that he was also the messenger when the Venice Beach branch was robbed. Doesn't all this leave a reasonable doubt in your mind about Fred Fuller's guilt?

"Ladies and gentlemen, look at Fred Fuller. Does he look like a murderer? In a week and a half, have you heard one thing negative about him other than his short fling with a pretty bank teller? What red-blooded young man hasn't been lured away at one time or another by a pretty woman? That doesn't make him a thief or a murderer.

"The time has now come for you, as jurors, to decide Fred Fuller's fate. We are confident you will make the right decision and give Fred Fuller back his life. Make the government go out and find the real perpetrators of these heinous crimes. If you have any reasonable doubt as to Fred Fuller's guilt, set him free. Don't take a chance on putting an innocent man in jail for the rest of his life. Thank you, ladies and gentleman, for the patience and consideration you have shown throughout this trial. Good luck, and may justice be served."

"Thank you, Mr. Roberts," said Judge Sessions. "I believe it's about time to send the case to the jury. We'll adjourn for thirty minutes and resume at 3:30 p.m. I'll take any motions before sending the jury into deliberations. Court adjourned until three 3:30 p.m."

During the break, the deputy on duty allowed Fred to watch television. The afternoon news was on.

"Good afternoon, ladies and gentlemen. This is George Putnam with the Channel 4 afternoon news update. Well, in federal court in LA, it was the final day of the Fred Fuller murder trial. In testimony today, the defense put on its final witnesses, a woman who claims to have seen another messenger enter the bank and leave with several bags full of something. Could it have part of the $6.7 million that was stolen from the bank? Earlier in the trial another witness, Harold Clifford, invoked the Fifth Amendment and refused to talk. This led to speculation that Mr. Clifford may be somehow involved in the robbery. Legal experts observing the trial indicate that while the testimony was favorable to Mr. Fuller, it was far from conclusive, and it's anyone's guess what the jury verdict will be. After both sides give their closing arguments today, Judge Sessions is expected to send the case to the jury with deliberations beginning tomorrow."

At one thirty, the Judge entered the courtroom. He asked the bailiff to bring in the jury. There was great anticipation of the panel's imminent deliberations. Fear paralyzed Fred. Twelve strangers would soon be determining his fate as a human being. He knew he was innocent, but would the jury come to the same conclusion? He prayed to God they would.

The jury finally was seated, and the Judge instructed them on how they were to conduct their deliberations. He explained the law and how they should not come back until they were ready to render a verdict. He thanked them and asked the bailiff to escort them to the jury room.

"Alright. This court will be adjourned pending the jury's deliberations," the Judge ordered.

Chapter 52

Verdict

It was still dark outside Maria's dorm at 7:00 a.m. as a cold front had come through during the night bringing thick clouds and drenching rain. She'd gotten word from Roberts late the previous afternoon that a verdict was in and that it would be read at 10:00 a.m. the next day. Maria hadn't been able to sleep knowing that Fred's fate would be decided in the coming few hours. On the one hand she felt encouraged by Paula Dupree's unexpected appearance and stunning testimony. But while her testimony showed the possibility that another player was in the game, it did nothing to diminish the evidence against Fred.

Maria pulled herself out of bed, dreading the day ahead. She wanted to get it over and get on with her life, but the thought of Fred not being a part of it was incomprehensible. He was part of her now, part of her very being and his demise would be her demise. She got in the shower and felt the hot pulsating flow melting away the stiffness and tension that had built up during a sleepless night. She was to meet Steve and Randy downstairs for breakfast at 7:45 so she got dressed quickly and rushed out the door only to be confronted by Jessica Jamison, a quiet girl that she barely knew, holding the bag that had once contained the $100,000 that she and Fred had taken from Devil's Canyon.

"Is this yours," Jessica asked irritably.

"Ah. . . . Yeah. I have been looking for that. Where did you find it?"

"Somebody put it in my cubicle. I had to go through it to

figure out who it belonged to."

Maria's heart sank. That cubicle had been overflowing and looked like it hadn't been touched for several semesters, so Maria had picked it as good hiding spot. She wondered if she'd taken all the money out of the gym bag the last time she accessed it. She thought she had deposited all the cash into the FDF bank account along with the cash donations that had come in, but she might have left one or two bundles of hundred-dollar bills for expenses. She swallowed hard.

"Thank you for returning it," She said shakily.

"Don't you believe in banks?" Jessica asked curiously. "There were stacks of cash in there."

"Oh, that. My uncle gave those to me from my college fund. I meant to go to the bank and make a deposit last week, but I forgot. I believe in banks, but he doesn't. He says there's going to be a major financial crisis in the next few years and a lot of banks will fail."

"Really?" Jessica said seeming alarmed. "Should I tell my parents?"

Maria had done a paper on the perilous condition of our national banks for her economics class, so she started recalling some of her research.

"If you want. My uncle isn't the only one who believes this. Many believe the real estate that secures billions of dollars of bank loans has been overvalued and that soon the bank examiners or creditors will demand fair valuations. If that happens banks will be forced to demand more collateral and call in notes if additional collateral is not forthcoming. When notes are called, businesses are forced into bankruptcy and when loans are not paid banks fail."

"Holy shit! Why isn't somebody doing something about it?"

"Because nothing can be done. It's too late. Greedy bankers and gutless regulators have let this happen and now the people will suffer when there is a collapse."

"What about Congress? Can't it do something?"

Maria laughed. "Seriously? No, there is no legislative fix for this. They will be spending their time pointing the finger at whoever they think is to blame."

"Wow! That's depressing."

"If you want to talk about this some more, we can get together later, but I'm having breakfast with some friends and I'm late."

"Oh, no problem. See you later," Jennifer said thoughtfully. "Oh, and good luck in court."

Maria gave Jennifer a hard look. She wondered if she bought her story or not. It was hard to tell. A vision of her and Fred in adjoining jail cells flashed in her mind. She shook it off knowing that co-ed jails didn't exist except in dreams. When she stepped into the cafeteria she saw Steve and Randy sitting somberly at a table. She joined them.

"Sorry I'm late," she said. "Had a brush fire I had to put out."

Steve frowned. "Oh God, what?"

She described her encounter with Jennifer.

"Wow, that was quick thinking," Steve said. "Is that the bag you have with you?"

"Yes. I couldn't put in my room. My suite mates are nosy and they are smarter than Jennifer. They would put two and two together."

"Shit," Randy said. "What are you going to do with the bag, you can't bring it to court?"

"We'll just leave it in Steve's trunk, nobody will know we have it."

"In my trunk," Steve protested. "What if they search my car?"

Maria laughed. "Nobody's going to search your car, you dummy, relax."

After a few silent moments, they got up and got in line to get their breakfast. When they had filled their trays, they reconvened back at their table.

"I'm not hungry," Maria said after staring at her food for a moment.

"I'll eat anything you don't want," Randy announced.

"Help yourself," Maria replied dejectedly.

"Cheer up," Steve said. "I think the jury is going to acquit Fred, don't you, Randy?"

Randy shrugged. "I hope so, but there was some pretty damning evidence. The whole thing with Candy makes Fred look like a womanizer."

"Oh, and if a beautiful, sexy woman tried to seduce you, you wouldn't melt like a slice of cheese on a griddle?" Maria asked.

Randy smiled. "Well, if you throw in the $6 million it could happen, I guess."

"Yeah, that's what I thought. Men are all weak kneed around a pretty face."

"No, not me," Steve protested. "I always think things through before I act."

"Yeah. When's the last time a woman has tried to seduce you."

"Ah, well—"

"Yeah," that's what I thought. "Talk to me when you've lost your virginity."

"I'm saving myself for my wedding night."

"That's good. I wish Fred had done that."

After breakfast, they got into Steve's car and drove to the courthouse. The courthouse lobby was crowded and they were mobbed by reporters as they entered and made their way to the elevators.

"Ms. Shepard, do you think your boyfriend will be acquitted?"

"We'll see," she replied.

"Ms. Shepard, will you stay with Fred if he is acquitted after he betrayed you?"

Maria looked briefly at the reporter. "I think so. He's probably suffered enough for his mistake."

The elevator door opened and they went in with the crowd that was waiting. When the elevator opened in the hallway outside the courtroom, they faced another onslaught of reporters and spectators.

"Ms. Shepard, what will you do if your boyfriend is found guilty? Will you stick with him or get on with your life?"

Maria ignored the question as Steve and Randy escorted her into the courtroom. Maria's parents had saved seats for them, so they joined them. When Maria looked up, she saw Fred looking back at her hopefully. Then the judges' door opened and the bailiff cried out, "Please rise for the Honorable Troy Sessions."

The judge whispered something to the bailiff and then took the bench and looked out over the courtroom. "Bailiff, bring in the jury, please."

The bailiff nodded and went through the door to the jury room. A moment later the jurors came filing out and one by one and took their seats. Maria watched each one carefully to see if their expressions might indicate which way the verdict would go, but it was impossible to tell. She sighed heavily in anticipation.

"Madam foreperson, has the jury reached a verdict?"

Maria was surprised a woman had been elected foreperson. She didn't know if that was good or bad. Would a woman be harder on Fred than a man? Then fear washed over her. Of course, a woman would be harder on Fred. They'd be angry over his betrayal. *Oh, my God. They're going to convict him!*

The foreperson stood, "Yes, your honor, we have."

"Alright then, please read the verdict."

The foreperson stiffened and replied, "On the count of felony murder we find the defendant, not guilty."

There was a stir in the courtroom. The judge glared at the gallery and said, "There will be order!"

Maria breathed a sigh of relief. Did that mean Fred was off the hook. Could he not be guilty of murder but still guilty of robbery? She looked at Roberts but his face was expressionless.

"Continue," the judge commanded.

The foreperson looked back at the written verdict. "Yes, your honor, "and on the count of bank robbery we find the defendant, not guilty."

The courtroom erupted in bedlam and Maria jumped to her feet. She looked toward Fred but couldn't get a look at him. Randy suddenly grabbed her and swung her around. Then Steve put his arms around her and hugged her so hard she thought her ribs would burst. Suddenly she felt a hand on her shoulder. She turned and saw Fred smiling with tears running down his face. She grabbed him gratefully and held him for a long time, not wanting to let him go.

Chapter 53

Dilemma

After the jury acquitted Fred, Maria insisted they get married immediately. She said she didn't want to take a chance on Fred doing something stupid and ruining their marriage plans. It was a bright, sunny Saturday in May when the limousine pulled up in front of Our Lady of the Assumption Catholic Church in Ventura, California. The driver got out and opened the back passenger-door and offered his hand to Maria. She got out, dressed in her long white silk wedding dress. The crowd of late-arriving guests and press covering the event admired her as she walked up the steps to the church. Cameras flashed all around her like she was a royal princess.

Fred was waiting patiently at the altar with Steve and Randy at his sides. It was a day he didn't think he would ever see, and he was overwhelmed with joy. Randy smiled at him as the organist began to play the traditional "Wedding March." The crowd rose to their feet as Maria slowly made her way down the aisle on her father's arm. When she reached the altar, Fred thanked God for granting him this moment. From the balcony came the sweet melody of the soloist singing "Ave Maria."

After the wedding, Maria's parents had a big reception, which lasted into the night. Maria and Fred ran off on their honeymoon to the Hotel Del Coronado in San Diego. It was a wonderful week, followed by a weekend at Cabo San Lucas in Mexico.

They had promised Maria's mother that immediately upon their return, they would come by and retrieve all of their gifts and mail, which were piling up in her dining room. Maria also wanted to send out thank-you notes right away, as everyone had been so generous. Maria was sitting at the dining room table as Fred was going through cards and admiring all of their gifts.

"I can't believe we got all of this loot," he commented.

"I know. There are a lot of gifts from people I don't even know," Maria noted.

"We won't be able to fit all of this stuff in our new apartment."

"Maybe my dad will let us borrow part of his attic for a while."

"That would help," he agreed.

Fred began opening mail. "Here's a card from Sam Whitehead Can you believe that? Hey, a gift certificate for fifty bucks!"

"You've got to be kidding," Maria responded. "Send it back!"

"No way. Fifty bucks is fifty bucks. Look, here's a card from Congressman Bartlett. Let's see what it says. . .

"Dear Fred,

It was with greatest relief that I learned of your acquittal. You have always been a favorite of mine, and I knew you couldn't have done the terrible things with which you were charged. Congratulations on your marriage. I know Maria's parents well, and they have often bragged about their wonderful daughter. So, if what they tell me is true, you are a lucky man.

After your life gets back to normal, give me a call. I think we could probably find a job for you while you finish up at UCLA. You've become quite a celebrity, and your employment on my staff could probably benefit both of us.

With deepest regards,
Congressman Charles Bartlett

"That was sure nice," Maria said.

"Yeah. I didn't think the Congressman would touch me with a ten-foot pole after the mess I got myself in."

"And he's offering a new job which you sorely need since you lost your job with Bank USA."

"Right. I hope working for the Congressman will pay as well as the bank," Fred said as he rummaged through more mail. "Let me see what else we have here."

As Fred shuffled through the mail, he picked out a plain, letter-sized manila envelope with a postmark from Toronto, Canada. "Look at this," he said as he held it up for Maria to see.

"What is it?" Maria asked.

"I don't know, but it's from Toronto," Fred replied.

"Open it up. I wonder what it is."

"Okay."

He took the crystal-handled letter opener that someone had given them as a gift and slit open the top of the envelope. Inside was a smaller envelope containing a wedding card and a note on a plain piece of white paper. Fred looked at Maria and then began reading the note.

Dear Mr. Fuller,

Even though we have never met, I just wanted to tell you how sorry I am that my brother caused you and Maria so much trouble. Sam has been a big disappointment to the family and caused us much grief and agony over the years. Although we still loved him and never wished him ill, now the family will finally have some peace.

Congratulations on your wedding and best wishes to you both.

Yours truly,
Molly Stewart Miller

P.S. Now that Harvey is dead, nobody knows about the million dollars, except me, so don't worry about it. Consider it a wedding present from Sam.

"Oh my God!" Maria gasped. "She knew about it. Sam must have told her all about the heist."

Fred swallowed hard. "So, he did put it in my trunk while I was in the bank."

"Don't you lock your car?" Maria asked.

"Not necessarily. I'm only inside a couple of minutes, and canceled checks aren't worth anything. The trunk is locked, but you can pop it open from inside the car."

"That's how he did it then. He left and then came back and planted the bag of money in your car."

Fred nodded. "Yeah, I think you're right."

On the drive back to LA, they discussed the topic of the money buried at Devils Canyon, now that they knew the truth. They both had carefully avoided the topic during their honeymoon, as it was a very delicate issue, and they didn't want anything to spoil their romantic trip. But Fred knew sooner or later they'd have to deal with it.

At first, they let their imaginations go wild. They both agreed it would be nice to spend the rest of the summer taking a Mediterranean cruise and then come home and buy a beautiful house with a swimming pool. Then Maria suggested they both get new cars—a Lincoln for her and a Porsche for Fred. They, of course, would have to give Sam's sister some of the money to ease the guilt they'd be feeling spending all that free money, but there was plenty to go around.

By the time they got to Palm Springs, however, their excitement had subsided, and the harsh reality of their situation reared its ugly head.

"You know, we can't really buy anything with the money," Fred said, "at least not for a while. Even then we'll have to be really careful not to attract attention."

"I know, but it's fun to think about spending it. At least we'll have some security, and if we really need money, we'll be able to get it," Maria replied.

"I don't know. I am scared to death having it. I am not going to be able to sleep at night. What if we get caught with it? How will we explain where we got it?"

"What about double jeopardy? They can't try you again since you were found innocent, can they?"

"Technically, that's right, but the bank could sue me for conversion and, if they won the lawsuit, I'd have to give it back plus be liable for punitive damages and their attorney's fees."

Maria snuggled up next to Fred in the car and put her head on his shoulder. "Oh, Fred, you're right. The money's not important as long as we're together."

"That's right. I'll make plenty of money as a lawyer."

When they got home there was a message on the recorder for Maria. It was from Tammy, the girl she had met at the Silver Stallion Saloon. Maria called her back while Fred unloaded the car. When she hung up the phone, she was as pale as a ghost.

"What's wrong?" Fred asked, fearing the worst.

She told him.

The following Saturday night, they had gone to the movies and returned home close to 11:00 p.m. Fred flipped on the TV to catch the news before they went to bed. Being newlyweds, they were still making love at least once a day, so they had just ripped off each other's clothes and jumped under the covers when George Putnam and the eleven o'clock news came on. They surfaced momentarily to listen to the familiar newscaster when they realized they were the topic of the story.

"Well, tonight we have a follow-up to our story on the sensational Fred Fuller murder trial that ended just weeks ago with the jury's acquittal of Fuller on charges of bank robbery and murder.

Today, Agent Jim Walters of the Federal Bureau of Investigation announced that another one million of the 6.7 million that was stolen from Bank USA had been recovered. The money was found near Big Bear, California, buried behind the cabin of former bank messenger Sam Stewart. Stewart recently died in a fiery collision with a Canadian Midwest freight train in a suburb of Toronto, Canada. With this discovery, $1.25 million the bank's money has been recovered. That leaves over $5 million dollars still missing.

"In a footnote, Fred Fuller and his new bride, the former Maria Shepard, just returned from their honeymoon amidst continued speculation by some that, notwithstanding the jury's verdict, Fred had the missing money and had stashed it somewhere in the Mojave Desert.

"In a related note, Bank USA messenger Jake Johnson was arrested today in conjunction with his alleged involvement in the Bank USA robbery and the death of Harvey Hamlin. Reportedly, over $200,000 cash from the robbery was found in his possession. Informed sources have told this reporter that Johnson and the late Sam Stewart conspired together to rob the bank. So, perhaps with Johnson in custody the missing $5.2 million will finally be found."

"So, did that tip come from your friend, Tammy?"

"I think so. She said Jake found her after I left that day, bought her a drink and they started dating."

"Big mistake," Fred chuckled.

Maria nodded. "Yeah. Tammy's a nice girl as long as you don't piss her off."

"I wonder what Jake did?"

"He was going to leave the country without her?"

Fred raised his eyebrows. "Well, I'm glad that's over."

Maria shook her head. "Thank God."

"Now that we've given all the bank's money back. How will we live?"

"Oh, if we're careful with our money, we'll be okay," Maria

assured him.

Fred frowned. "What money?"

"FDF, of course. There at the end, the money was flowing in like lava out of a volcano. Even after replacing the $100,000 that belonged to the bank and ended up paying Roberts, there's still over $200,000 left."

"Holy shit!" Fred gasped. "But don't we have to give it all back since we don't need it?"

Maria shrugged. "I don't know how. I don't have any record of who gave it to us. Besides, I don't think a single person will ask for a refund, do you? We provided a lot of entertainment for a lot of folks, and people expect to pay for their entertainment these days, don't you agree?"

Fred thought about that for a moment and couldn't think of a thing wrong with Maria's reasoning, so they both laughed as they ducked back under the covers to finish what they'd been doing before George Putnam had so rudely interrupted them.

Epilogue

Eight Years Later

It was early evening on election day and a large crowd of supporters had gathered at the Pierpont Inn in Ventura for what they hoped would be a victory celebration for Fred Fuller, their candidate for the California State Assembly. After being acquitted of charges of bank robbery and murder while in his sophomore year at UCLA, Fred continued his education and was awarded his bachelor of arts degree in 1969. Without taking a break, he started law school and obtained his law degree three years later.

Due to all of the publicity he had received during his trial, Fred Fuller was a household name in Ventura County and, not surprisingly, was recruited by the party to replace the retiring assemblyman from the district, Paul Bryan.

Fresh out of law school Fred jumped at the opportunity to get into politics because he knew the power and notoriety that came with the office would jump-start his new law practice. Maria was not thrilled with Fred's candidacy because she knew, if elected, he would have to spend several months each year in Sacramento and now that Fred was finally out of law school, she wanted to start a family. But Maria knew Fred really wanted to run and an opportunity like this didn't come along every day, so she reluctantly put her family plans on hold for a few years and threw herself into the campaign.

There were three candidates in the race, the mayor of Fillmore, Fred Garcia; a real estate developer, Paul Grimes; and Fred. With Paul Bryan's endorsement and the support of Congressman Bartlett, Fred was expected to win handily and all recent polls supported that expectation, but Fred was still worried.

Nothing he'd wanted to achieve in life had come easily, let alone handed to him on a silver platter. And this election night celebration didn't feel right.

Fred and Maria arrived by limousine to the Pierpont Inn at 8:00 p.m. A small crowd of well-wishers braved a cold ocean fog to welcome them and congratulate Fred on, what all expected would be, a victorious night. Fred stepped out of the limousine and then turned and helped Maria out. She looked stunning in her black velvet evening gown and pearl necklace. Several reporters yelled questions to Fred as their photographers took pictures of the couple.

Fred took Maria's hand and escorted her inside. Joel Roberts was the first person they saw as they entered the exclusive venue. He immediately came over and shook Fred's hand. "Fred! Congratulations. Several precincts are already in and you have a double-digit lead."

"That's great," Fred said evenly. "Hopefully that trend will continue."

"It will. Don't worry."

Other supporters and well-wishers began to crowd around and Fred and Maria did their best to be polite and show their appreciation for their support. Joel excused himself to thank some contributors, leaving them stranded. Fortunately, Fred's publicity chairman showed up to rescue them.

"There you are," Shirley said. "I've been looking for you two. We have some special guests who want to meet you. Come on."

Fred smiled at the people around him and excused himself. "Nice meeting all of you."

Shirley escorted them to a private suite where a dozen well-dressed men and women were drinking champagne, talking, laughing and eating hors d oeuvres. When Fred was spotted, several of them came over to greet them. Maria recognized one of them as Margaret Thompson, Congressman Bartlett's administrative assistant.

"Mrs. Thompson," Maria said. "So nice to see you."

Maria and Margaret had met at the trial when Margaret testified. She liked her very much and was very appreciative of her testimony at Fred's bond hearing and her support of Fred throughout the trial.

"Yes, this going to be an exciting night!" she exclaimed. "Your life is really going to change. Are you ready?"

"I guess I have no choice," Maria replied warily.

"So, Fred. I want you to meet Priscilla Prescott. She has been my assistant for the last year and she's been dying to meet her new boss?"

Fred looked at the petite middle-aged brunette and said, "New boss?"

"Oh, you haven't talked to the Congressman yet. Oh no, am I bad? I just spoiled his surprise."

"Surprise," Fred said, confused.

"He's been having me train Priscilla to manage your local office. Isn't that wonderful? We've found a great location for you too, huh, Priscilla."

"Oh, yes," Priscilla beamed. "Up on the hill near the Courthouse. You'll have a great view of the ocean."

Maria looked at Fred and he shrugged.

"I am so excited to finally meet you two," Priscilla went on. "You've been through so much and now you've been elected to public office. Wow! Who would have believed it?"

"Not many, I'm sure," Fred replied curtly taking Maria's hand. "Excuse us. I think I need another drink."

When they were alone Maria asked, "Why is the Congressman making staff appointments for you?"

"Yeah. That's what I'd like to know."

"I guess he thought he was doing you a favor."

"Yeah, maybe, but I have a bad feeling about this."

"Why? What do you think is going on?"

Fred took a deep breath and let it out slowly. "I don't know but I'm going to find out."

They walked around until they spotted Joel Roberts. When he finished his conversation with an elderly couple, they approached.

"Joel. Can we have a word?"

"Sure, sorry I deserted you two but I have to pat everybody on the back and thank them for their support, so we can count on it at the next election."

"Of course," Fred said. "Listen, Margaret just said the Congressman has already found me an office and a manager to staff it."

"Yes, Priscilla. You'll love her. She's very efficient."

"I am sure she is but it's not the Congressman's place to be hiring my staff and making decisions that I should be making."

Joel gave Fred a hard look and then shook his head. "Fred, you are so naive. Did you think they'd just give you this job without expecting something in return?"

"What are you talking about?" Fred protested. "I won this election fair and square. The voters elected me. I'm not beholden to anybody!"

Maria glared at Joel then looked at Fred worriedly.

Joel chuckled. "Don't worry. We just need to have a few key personnel in place to keep you honest. It won't be so bad and you'll be well compensated. You can vote your conscience on most issues, but once in a while you'll have vote how we tell you. Sometimes we have to deliver a vote and we have to be sure we can do it."

"I won't. I never agreed to this?"

"Yes, you will, Fred," Roberts said with a confident smile. "We know about the million dollars?"

"What million dollars? We don't have any of the bank's money."

Roberts nodded. "Okay. But even if you were foolish enough to bury it in Sam's backyard to ease your guilty conscience, there is still over five million missing."

Fred's eyes widened.

"Ah!" Maria gasped.

Fred just stared at Joel in disbelief. Then he said softly, "I've already been tried and acquitted of the bank robbery. I can't be tried again for that— double jeopardy, remember? You don't have a damn thing on me."

"Ah. So true," Joel agreed, "but you can be recalled by the voters, and what about Maria?"

"Maria has nothing to do with this!" Fred spat.

"Oh, but she does. She's an accessory, Fred. You're a lawyer now, you know I am right. So, step out of line and you'll be kicked out of office and visiting your wife in prison."

Fred and Maria looked at each worriedly but said nothing. Fred wondered if Roberts was bluffing or if he had the proof to back up his threats. He pondered his response for a moment, then replied, "Well, Joel. We know about the $4.8 million embezzlement from the Congressman's campaign fund and how you covered it up by orchestrating the Bank USA robbery."

The grin on Joel's face fell away and he swallowed hard. "What? That's ridiculous."

"Is it? You know, at the time I just thought your PI was incompetent and you were, well, just a lousy lawyer, but now I know you were doing your best to get me convicted. You and the Congressman were going to make sure I took the fall for your crime."

"No. No. You've got it all wrong," Joel pleaded.

Fred took a menacing step toward Joel, looked him in the eyes, and cautioned, "So, if you want to go the FBI and tell them how you tried to set me up, be my guest. I gave back the money you had planted in my car, so I'm sure they'll forgive me for my transgressions, especially if I agree to testify against you, Sinclair and the Congressman. What do you think?"

Joel forced a smile and started backing off slowly. "Listen, you're right, Fred. What were we thinking? You should pick your own staff. The Congressman was just trying to help out, but I can see now you don't need our help."

"Of course, I'll have to file a complaint with the State Bar too," Fred continued. "How many canons of legal ethics did you break? I lost count at about twelve."

"Okay. Okay," Joel agreed. "You made your point. This won't come up again."

"I'm glad to hear it. Now get the hell out of my sight, and take Priscilla with you!"

Joel turned and made a hasty retreat.

Maria took a deep breath and let it out slowly. Then she smiled wryly. "We're gonna owe Tammy a drink."

Fred nodded." Yeah. You better make it a bottle."

About the Author

William Manchee is originally from California. He earned his B.A. degree from UCLA in 1969 and a J.D. degree from SMU Law School in 1976. Now a resident of Plano, Texas, Manchee has practiced law in Texas for over 40 years. He is the author of the Stan Turner Mystery Series, the Rich Coleman Novels and the Tarizon Saga.

THE STAN TURNER MYSTERIES
by William Manchee

Undaunted
Disillusioned
Brash Endeavor
Second Chair
Cash Call
Deadly Distractions
Black Monday
Cactus Island
Act Normal
Deadly Defiance
Deadly Dining

"...appealing characters and lively dialogue, especially in the courtroom . . . " (*Publisher's Weekly*)

"...plenty of action and adventure . . . " (*Library Journal*)

"...each plot line, in and of itself, can be riveting . . . " (*Foreword Magazine*)

"...a courtroom climax that would make the venerable Perry Mason stand and applaud . . . "
(*Crescent Blue*)

"...Richly textured with wonderful atmosphere, the novel shows Manchee as a smooth, polished master of the mystery form . . . " (*The Book Reader*)

"...Manchee's stories are suspenseful and most involve lawyers. And he's as proficient as Grisham . . . (*Dallas Observer*)

"...fabulous-a real page turner-I didn't want it to end!" (Allison Robson, CBS Affiliate, *KLBK TV, Ch 13*)